Praise for The Sly Company of People Who Care

'What a voice, what a startling, funny, charming, provocative voice! Rahul Bhattacharya's narrator is a true wanderer and a gifted poet of description. The journey he takes us on, through Guyana, through histories and selves, is a wonder.'   Sam Lipsyte, author of *The Ask*

'It's the style that seizes you by the throat—alternately lyrical, abrupt, whimsical, sexy, informative, seductive and always full of surprises, most of them couched in "creolese". The language works a hypnotic magic and you soon feel you're in Guyana yourself.'
      Amitav Ghosh, author of *Sea of Poppies* and *River of Smoke*

'Quick, cool, astonishingly assured, it awakens with its landscapes and characters a Conradian sense of wonder.'   Pankaj Mishra

'This ferociously gifted writer has already been hailed as the natural successor to the great Naipaul – and yes, he is that good. His narrator has a charming, confident voice that engages instantly, and his descriptions of landscapes and people are ravishing . . . He's escaping from his own dissatisfaction, yet he describes his surroundings in rich, loving detail. We look forward to seeing this on (at least) the Booker longlist.'   *The Times*

'He is clever, insightful and funny. With a style resonant of some of the best Asian writing by giants such as Naipaul and Rushdie, this restless first novel is packed full of oddball characters and atmospheric description . . . The writing is sometimes melancholic and often unusually paced – more in tune with the way a mind and a life really chop and change, rather than following a more traditional plot and narrative form.'   *Daily Mail*

D0817136

'The consequences of colonialism are subtly explored . . . a deft synthesis of travelogue and Bildungsroman, by turns antic and introspective . . . so satisfying' *Wall Street Journal*

'From the novel's very first line, we know we're in the care of a narrator unmatched in his lyricism and sensitivity . . . Bhattacharya has established himself as a generous voice in fiction, one who knows how to thrill but never at the expense of his readers' stamina' *Boston Globe*

'Bhattacharya's voice is thick with bizarre humor, poetic pidgin and images lush with faraway magic' *Washington Post*

'Naipaul, if he had been a young man exploring an unknown world today, could have written it. But Bhattacharya's understanding of displacement and drifting comes from a completely original place, and he has all of the humour and the sharpness of the young Naipaul, with none of the spleen. This book, and this writer, are here to last.'
India Today

'Among the many accomplishments of this exceptional book is Bhattacharya's ability to portray sex with an unabashed, edgy abandon . . . It is certainly the best first novel by an Indian I have read in a long time.' *Outlook*

'Bhattacharya's writing has incredible depth and artistry, a kind of achieved poise that sets it apart from anything else, even when he's only talking about the experience of being violently drunk or describing house-fronts in Georgetown.' *Indian Express*

'As the lone narrator wanders through this wonderland, he builds a sense of adventure, surrealism, love, empathy and passion. The book is a sum of the adventure of being in a place where everything is turned upside down and one has to navigate by improvising' *Asian Age*

THE SLY COMPANY OF PEOPLE WHO CARE

Rahul Bhattacharya is the author of the cricket tour book *Pundits from Pakistan*, fourth in *The Wisden Cricketer*'s list of best cricket books of all time, and winner of the Crossword Award for most popular book, 2005. *The Sly Company of People Who Care* is his first novel. It won the *Hindu* Literary Prize 2011 and is shortlisted for the Man Asian Literary Prize 2011. He was born in Bombay in 1979, and now lives in Delhi.

By the same author

Pundits from Pakistan: On Tour with India 2003–04

RAHUL BHATTACHARYA

THE SLY COMPANY OF PEOPLE WHO CARE

PICADOR

First published 2011 in paperback by Picador

This edition first published 2012 by Picador
an imprint of Pan Macmillan, a division of Macmillan Publishers Limited
Pan Macmillan, 20 New Wharf Road, London N1 9RR
Basingstoke and Oxford
Associated companies throughout the world
www.panmacmillan.com

ISBN 978-0-330-53474-1

1 3 5 7 9 8 6 4 2

A CIP catalogue record for this book is available from
the British Library.

Typeset by InoSoft Systems

Printed and bound by CPI Group (UK) Ltd, Croydon, CR0 4YY

Visit **www.picador.com** to read more about all our books
and to buy them. You will also find features, author interviews and
news of any author events, and you can sign up for e-newsletters
so that you're always first to hear about our new releases.

All this was Dutch. Then, like so much else, it was English.

—James Salter, *Light Years*

A NOTE

The term Indian in Guyana and this book refers to East Indians. They are the descendants of the coolies, indentured labourers from India. The last census shows them as 43.5 per cent of the population, comfortably higher than the Africans (30.2 per cent), Mixed Race (16.7), Portuguese (0.20), Chinese (0.19) and Whites (0.06). The indigenous people (9.2 per cent) are called Amerindians. Indians from India are referred to as Indian nationals – condemned to squareness by the nomenclature itself. Keep in mind that the Guyanese are also West Indians.

Like Sam Selvon said, 'Christopher Columbus must be killing himself with laugh.'

THE SLY COMPANY OF PEOPLE WHO CARE

PART ONE

I

LIFE, as we know, is a living, shrinking affair, and somewhere down the line I became taken with the idea that man and his world should be renewed on a daily basis. Those days I liked thinking in absolutes – life, man, the world – but people like to be specific about things. Hence, my actions were a little difficult to explain. To be a slow ramblin' stranger! It made perfect sense to me.

I still had to make friends, and my first one was Mr Bhombal, a waterworks technician. Mr Bhombal was, like me, an Indian national. Bhombal was his first name, yet I took to calling him Mr Bhombal. He just had that vibration. He wore polyester trousers. His steel watch faced up palm side. To read the time he would raise his forearm to his eyeline.

Ordinarily I would deflect the question of why I was in Guyana: 'Nice girls, eh' or 'The people here are all leaving' – wholly correct – 'so somebody had to come'. But as Mr Bhombal was so sincere in his effort to play elder brother, I told him the truth. I told him I came here once and afterwards had dreams. The low sky, red earth and brown water made me feel humble and ecstatic. The drenched wooden houses on stilts wrenched my soul. I told him I'd be here for a year.

Mr Bhombal had a way of conveying that one was on the precipice of a dreadful mistake; however, not to worry, with practical thinking one could make something of the situation. He had gloomy eyes, a fat, melancholy face, framed precisely by drooping eyebrows and defeated lips. He was not bald or even balding, but his hair was extravagantly spaced. He would consider the facts sociologically (was his word), then logistically (at this stage he asked detailed questions and closed his eyes as the replies came). My needless arrival here, he contended, could be swiftly rectified by application to another country: each time he called up a different one. Ultimately, after much deliberation, he would conclude – indeed, it was Mr Bhombal's conclusion for any issue – that the secret of the resolution lay in discerning 'how much goodness there is in the good, how much badness in the bad'. His facility to believe this was a fresh insight each time amounted to genius. I would insult Mr Bhombal and he would take it well, in fact with glee. He felt he had provoked thought.

Such triumphs were fleeting. Soon Mr Bhombal would return to his cocooned misery. 'Up-down,' he said wearily of his days, from the engineering office below to the shared living quarters above. He made the journey in green gumboots – longboots they were called in Guyana. When he did venture out, it was before dark, to the seawall or to the young Sindhi assistants of the variety stores on Regent Street who deflated him with their sad ambitions of owning shops here. Being an Indian-national sort of Indian national, Mr Bhombal struggled in this kind of place. He was scandalised easily. He was aghast when I told him that many reggae songs were a bhajan for an Ethiopian king. The Africans were one thing, but what of the East Indians? At least Trinidad had malls and cinemas. 'Is this life?' he despaired, donned in longboots hours after he had traversed the single flight of stairs. 'Is this country?'

Guyana had the feel of an accidental place. Partly it was the epic indolence. Partly it was the ethnic composition. In the slang of the street there were chinee, putagee, buck, coolie, blackman,

4

and the combinations emanating from these, a separate and larger lexicon. On the ramble in such a land you could encounter a story every day.

Take the one recounted to me at the bar in the cricket club by the lawyer. The case was of a lady he'd once badgered so hard in the witness box that she fainted. A year after the event she knocked on his door. 'Thick Indian girl, country manners, powder on chest.' He was not good with faces, but he remembered her on account of the fainting. She wanted to retain him. She had been accused of killing her own baby. Everybody suspected that the child was by a black man. Certainly her behaviour was odd. She would shave the child's head every week, so nobody got to see its hair. And when the child died she didn't report it, she buried it. She claimed he choked on his vomit. They proved the presence of vomit. He won her the case. But he had no doubt whatever she killed the baby. No, why the arse should it bother him? It was not his to decide guilt and innocence. He was a professional. Anybody could kill their baby.

The lawyer was putagee – of Portuguese extraction. The Portuguese had come to Guyana as indentured labourers even before the Indians and the Chinese. They were light-skinned and independent-minded. They rose up the ranks, and now, small in number and of high position, they could look at race as something they were not a part of.

I walked plenty in the early days. There were no shadows in Georgetown. A young town, poetic and wasted, its exquisite woodenness going to rot or concreted over, it was cleaved and connected by trenches which fumed, blossomed and stank. There were no tall buildings. Under the high equatorial sun, shade trees, some so large and spreading as the saman, rarely crept beyond their own peripheries. When 'sun hot', as them boys said, it had no place to hide.

One day, idling in town – Sunday, quiet – I sat to rest on Carmichael, one of the streets that spoke out from the big church, when a man with a rice sack over his shoulder approached me. 'Gimme a lil t'ing nuh, soldier,' he said.

His hair was browned with dirt, a face like shattered dreams, idealistic and corroded equally. He made one want to say, 'No man, don't worry, it's not you, it's the world.' He had come out of jail, done time for murder. He was a pork-knocker. He went into the interior and hunted for diamond. One night, sleeping with his kiddy at his crotch, he found his own pardner trying to get into it. He always slept with a cutlass under his head. He grabbed it and chopped the man's face nine times, till the man dead.

I bought him a juice and gave him the fare to his home in the Cuyuni, three rivers west. In return he handed me a hideous plastic pebble. He had made it by melting toothbrushes in the big prison on the Mazaruni.

'You could keep that,' he said, as I studied the grotesque glory of the object.

'Thanks.'

He offered his fist for a bump. 'Baby's the name,' he said and slid away.

In less than a fortnight after my arrival, Mr Bhombal was gone. He told me only hours before. A matrimonial match had been found for him in Bhubaneshwar. The matter needed to be settled at once. I saw him off at his house. He departed with hasty clumping movements, leaving behind nothing, only the prints of his green longboots on the wooden stairs.

It was a lovely raining day, the kind of Georgetown January day that would singe me forever. Clothes flew on the line against a palm. Wooden houses cried on corners. A frangipani dripped over a crook paling. A goat bleated through thick slanting drops. The trenches were aglimmer darkly. Guyana was elemental, water and earth, mud and fruit, race and crime, innocent and full of scoundrels.

2

THE house was a peculiar creation, neither one thing nor the other, in half measures concrete and wood, of an old style and new. One could discern the reputed Guyanese elegance in the slenderness of the banisters, the decayed fretwork under the roof, and it had been built in the Guyanese way, upon high stilts. You could tell at one time, before the bottom was walled up, before the back extended and part of the yard shedded – you could tell it had been a house of proportion. But now it was a mass, the thin man inside the fat man forever obscured.

By these disfigurations, Action Jackson, the gold-wearing, gum-chewing husband of my landlady, could juice rent from six tenements. It was an act of ambition that drew both respect and resentment. 'You see how the gold around he neck get poundish? I know the man when he was just a limer.'

The house was hidden behind Latchman's Hardware ('We there in hard time and soft'). You entered through a long passageway made by the shop and a wall of rusted tin. That corridor tapered into a makeshift entrance where Rabindranauth Latchman and Action Jackson had been waging a cold war over a small patch of land, leading to sudden and always temporary captures of territory with barrels or scraps of tin. Beyond these battles was the staircase.

In the tropical way the house was built for ventilation: walls of wood which stopped short of the ceiling, doors whose top halves could be latched open for breeze, louvred windows which let in air but not rain.

The place was in considerable disrepair. The wooden floor had rotted in parts. The stays on the windows had rusted to amorphousness and to attempt a change in angle was to shatter a slat of glass. Elsewhere cobwebs joined broken glass doors to shelves littered with sad pellets of lizard droppings. The toilet bowl, once a baby pink but now its own singular shade, had deep stains in the porcelain imparting the water at the bottom a yellow-brown colouration so that it always looked freshly soiled. There was a crack in the porcelain too, just below the seat, so one always tried to not sit too hard, taxing for a reader and idler. These features subsidised the rent.

I was one of two flats on the upper storey; there were three below, another in the yard, holding a total of anywhere between eight and fourteen tenants. These included Hassa the dead-eyed minibus driver; a pair of busty Indian-Chinese cashiers who people called Curry-Chowmein and who shared my floor; Kwesi the youthman who did electrical odd jobs and often came upstairs to make pining phone calls that contained the words 'I got true feelin for you baby, I ain't lie'; his mother, a hard-working churchwoman who worried for Kwesi and passed around magnificent trails of black pudding on Sundays; and a secret couple whose secret fights had everybody's attention in quiet times.

The first door as you entered the gate was enlivened by the graffiti, 'Let them talk, talk don't bother me'. But in fact it was its occupant, Lancelot Banarsee, who people called a talkman or a gyaffman.

'Indiaman,' Uncle Lance had said to me on the first day. 'Nobody could imitate like Guyanese, you know . . .'

8

For a moment I suspected he was making a stinging criticism.

'. . . Tha'is why Guyanese could succeed anywhere. We go New York, Canada, Flarida, we could become jus like them. But they can't become like we! I know you mussee hear all kind of t'ing about here. But we's good people, eh. Good people. I ah tell you the problem. Too much politricks. Poli*tricks*, you hear. Ha! G'lang bai, but you must come down fuh gyaff.'

As Uncle Lance was always on the bench by the staircase, this was unavoidable.

'So, how's India?' he would ask. I was still not versed in gyaffin – the key was to make a joke, preferably obscene, denounce something strongly, share a rumour or at the very least discuss somebody's plight – so I would earnestly reply, 'What do you mean, Uncle Lance? Like politically, economically?'

'Economically. Growth, bai, is ten per cent they be aimin for.'

'That's right—'

'How about Bombay? Flimstars! They callin it Mombay now.'

'Yes.'

'How about Delhi? Is a rape there every one minute, rass. Rape capital of the world.'

It was true that Uncle Lance could make talk out of anything. He was armed with nuff nuff conspiracy theories, many of them involving Americans. Like he knew that Hurricane Katrina was put out to disperse Haitian immigrants. To express his true contempt he would go Latin American. Seeing the red swarms of mosquito bites on my forearms he might remark, 'Gringo would be proud to go back so. They could go back and say: watch, we been South America. Blasted fools.'

Uncle Lance knew everybody in the neighbourhood. He had a thin frame and thin limbs that curved like flower stalks into child-bearing hips. He wore boxers and a vest which clung steadfast to his little dhal-belly. It was the vest, and the way he breathed in the neighbourhood, which made one feel that he should have had a top flat: Guyana was full of men in vests who leaned casually in

9

their balconies and watched street-life below. It seemed an injustice that Uncle Lance hadn't that vantage.

Though I myself didn't have much of a view of the street because of the hardware shop, there were sceneries to the side, across the tin partition, where a bruck-up house thrived with many beings. It had fowl-cock and chicken who called each other at shameless hours of the night, two dogs, a dozen or more pups and a wire cage twittering with birds. Children ran about the place with tremendous hollering energy. They got hard licks and thereafter bawled with terrible passion, which, in the rare instances when the mammy felt in the mood, was followed by such prolonged soothing and cooing it brought to mind Nabokov's words that there is nothing so atrociously cruel as an adored child.

Kitty was the name of the ward. Kitty! Its soft ts fluttered like eyelashes. For a long time I didn't know why it was called so. Afterwards a learned man told me it was named for the daughter of the Dutch planter, Mr Bourda. By then I had come to associate it with the sexual innuendo of the soca Kitty Cat. Kitty had that kind of mood. Boys stood on corners, under the crisscrossing wires, sooring every girl who passed. The sound of a soor, a puckered kiss. 'How you mean, bro!' they said when asked if it caused trouble. 'They get vex if you *don't* show em. Is only the ugly ones who make style.'

Till not very long ago Kitty was its own village. It still retained some of its pastoral disposition. Several people minded animals. Goat, chicken, bird; and in the news was the story of the Kitty cowherd who had been battered to death at dawn after grazing his cows in the national park where Georgetown bourgeoisie took their constitutionals. There was among Kitty's residents an old village pride. Even those who despised Forbes Burnham, the late dictator, cited with satisfaction that he had sprung from Kitty. They were proud of its size and scope. 'It have everything in Kitty,' Uncle Lance said. 'It have Hindu chu'ch, Muslim chu'ch, chu'ch of Christ. We got embassy, orphanage, vulcanisin, pawnshop, cookshop, rumshop, short-time' – the by-the-hour humping rooms. 'You want teacher, we got teacher. We got pastor, we got businessman. You want bandit, we got bandit. We got blackman, redman, buck, chinee, coolie, dougla all lashin each other.'

In the context of small Georgetown, Kitty was a sprawl, running down from the seawall on the Atlantic in a dozen or so parallel streets. At an intersection in the southern end, not many doors from my house, stood the long, rusted roof of Kitty Market, and atop it a tiny clock tower. The tower gave it the feel of a toy market, and Kitty a toy community. The market itself was dank and dark. Many of its businesses opened for but a few hours a day or a few days of the week. The zinc leaked in parts, and since it was election year, members of both the Indian and the African party had come by to promise repairs.

Late in the mornings, when the air hung around the neck like a wet towel, I would go to the market for cold coconut water.

The coconut lady stood at the front gate with her son, a boy of maybe ten, who wore a cap and had an air of experienced proficiency that kept me in awe of him. She had a round fat face with dimples like plums. She was Bibi Rashida Rawlins. Annie was her call name, which, along with Shelly and Sherry, was the most common call name in Guyana, as receptive to a Roopmattie or Gwendolyn as to a Bibi Rashida.

Bibi Rashida was terribly nice. Because I was from India she refused to accept payment at first, and invited me to her house on the coast. At the year's end they would do a Qurbani, a bull would be sacrificed and cooked, and I must come for that because I was like family. She used to mind chicken but four hundred of them died in the big flood, and it was a real bad experience, dead chicken floating about her yard and she couldn do nothing bout it. The government gave her back two hundred and fifty chicken and twenty-five bags of feed, but she was stayin away from chicken for a while.

She was dougla, mixed African and East Indian, Afro-Guyanese and Indo-Guyanese, black and coolie: the term, I realised, from the Hindi word for bastard, *dogala*. Neither family truly accepted her. It didn't help that she was fulaman, Muslim, this from the Fulani tribe of Africa. Growing up she always heard people say, 'look foolerman deh, don't trust them'.

'I like Sharook Khan bad,' she said whenever wanting to change the conversation to more pleasant matters. 'I would like to meet he sometime.'

Bibi Rashida's circumstances touched me, caught in the middle of so many things, the dead chicken floating in her yard.

But when I brought up her suffering with Lancy in order to gyaff – 'the coconut lady does have it hard': I was pleased with the approach – he grunted dismissively.

'Is only elections time we fight so. Just see how much dougla born after election. How come so much dougla born after election? You know what is the problem?'

'Too much politricks.'

'Damn true, bai. You bright.'

Uncle Lance was a reader and could often be found perusing obscure pamphlets on the bench. He was a newspaper junkie, as I too was becoming.

In the afternoons a cross-section of Kitty folk would assemble on the stairs of the house around a newspaper-wielding Uncle Lance whose undertaking it was, in the words of one participant, to instigate n agitate the population. He ran the sessions democratically, throwing up an item in the air and letting whoever wanted run with it.

CARIBBEAN MEN IN HIV NIGHTMARE

Was Mr C. a Bajan who loved both soca music and a white woman in England?

Was Mr B. a Jamaican with reggae music running through his entertainment veins but whose complaint started a police investigation and ended up blowing the whistle on what the authorities are calling a terrible crime?

Finally did Emma Baxter, a white English receptionist in London set out to have unprotected sex with a host of black men who trace their roots to Barbados, Guyana, St Vincent, Antigua or Dominica, to name a few island-nations in order to infect them with HIV/AIDS, apparently in revenge?

The point of instigate n agitate here was not the conduct of Ms Baxter, though one man did present the Guyanese truism, 'Pussy make man skunt.' No, the issue was that Guyana was referred to as an island. The report had been reprinted from the *Nation* of Barbados. 'The problem with island is they from I-land,' a man with hair buns remarked. 'Is only *I* they unstan, not you or we.' Trinidad came in for licks too, 'is sheer oil they got, too much aisle in they brains'.

AFRO DHULAHA AND DHULAHINE

Dear Editor,

I wonder how many of your readers have taken note of that rice advertisement on television, in which an obviously Afro person is featured as the Dhulahine, and an equally Afro individual acts as the Dhulaha.

Of course, I did read an article recently which tells about an Afro gentleman of the incumbent regime who, sometime back, saw fit to convert to Hinduism. But that's his affair, and such cases must be rather rare here in Guyana.

These are clearly not Afro roles however, and the landscape teems, surely, with actors and actresses eminently skilled and appropriate to the parts. What is also notable is that no attempt is made to disguise the ethnicity of either that purported Dhulaha or the Dhulahine.

So I ask once more; 'What is afoot here?' Or will I be dubbed a racist for even noticing this not very amusing attempt at comedy.

Yours faithfully

'Prapa talk, bai! Dah prapa talk!'

'Don't make stupid, banna. You know how that man go make racial out of anything. Besides, is not blackman who getting insult, is Hindu.'

'Hold on, hold on. You even wonder *why* it have blackman with the rice? Is because till now coolie don't accept that it was African who bring rice to Guyana.'

'Don't speed me head in morning time, banna. Blackman *think* he can plant rice. Give he one square yard and is ganja you going to find there.'

'Hold on, hold on. Who bring the ganja here? Is them coolieman sadhoo who bring it.'

'All two ya'al wrong. It's chinee who bring it.'

Uncle Lance took the stage now.

'Hear nah, ya'al hear about Robert Waldron? It had one Robert Waldron in Wakenaam, good. From when he a boy Robert would wake up every morning before sunrise, good. Walk from house to house, fetch the milk, walk to the stellin, ketch boat to Parika, ketch bus to GT, sell the milk in GT. Wakenaam see him back not till nightfall. Robbie wukkin hard. Next thing he get a cycle, good. Robbie prospering, going by more house, makin more collection, sellin more milk. Bam, next thing Robbie buy a vehicle. Bam, next thing he get a man to work fuh he in town. Robbie doin real good. And then he decide fuh mind cow *heself*. Everyone in Wakenaam big up they eye. You ever hear of blackman or fulaman minding cow? Is only Hindu who can mind cow. Bam, inside two months they all dead out. One cow ketch disease, next one get mash down by van, next one die at chilebirth, next one feel lonely and take he leave for heavenly abode. And Robbie back to where he start.'

'So what that have to do with rice?'

And so it went, restless early days in Kitty, ripe with heat and rain and Guyanese sound and Guyanese light in which the world seemed saturated or bleached, either way exposed.

3

I WAS frankly unimpressed when I saw that blasted scamp again.
I should say I was not wholly unprepared for it. I had described
our meeting to Uncle Lance and friends, attaching to it a strange
spiritual dimension. Now Guyanese are born sceptics. Their
foreparents were either forced or tricked into coming here, and
thereafter white man, black man and brown man had each scamped
the hell out of them. To take things at face value was considered
the most basic weakness.

So they laughed when I told them about the suffering murderer
and the terrible burden he carried in the vagrant streets. More so
when I showed them the plastic pebble.

'Man who could scamp with melted toothbrush, bai, that man
gafo be professional.'

'True professional.'

One or two people gave me a hard scolding. These were people
who left their wallets home and walked with exact change to the
market. To the bank they went in pairs. If they saw a pretty girl
thumbing down a car they stepped on the gas.

Yet there was some delight taken in my man, since scampery was
so rampant that the ones who shone amid the competition were

reverenced. Of course I had been a packoo – packoo, the monkfish, superbly ugly, so ugly that it must also be stupid though it was very sweet to eat – I had been a packoo but I was also privileged to have been had by a scampion.

I was about the city trying to extend my stay in Guyana. When I had come to Guyana first there had been a good basis. I was a cricket reporter. The first Test against West Indies was in Georgetown. I was twenty-two, and naive beyond my years. The visit had been for a week, a week of bewilderment and curiosity, moods and images, names and rhythms, contours of a mystery world one could perceive but not grasp.

Now I'd come on the longest return-ticket available, of a year, and without valid reason. At the airport the suspicious Sherry had stamped me in for a month, leaving me a ladder of paperwork to climb. I didn't mind it. To reinvent one's living, to escape the deadness of the life one was accustomed to, was to be hungry for the world one saw. Every face, every bureaucrat, every office held in it a code to be cracked.

I followed due process. I wrote to the Ministry of Home Affairs expressing cultural and topographical interest which would take a year to satiate. They asked me to prove my medical credentials. I went to the hospital, supplied stool, underwent a chest examination, took the doctor's certificate to the Port Health Office.

This vividly colonial-sounding entity stood bang on the Demerara, by Stabroek Market, or big market as it was known. Big church and big market: in a short town of white and rust, big church and big market were supreme, the cathedral looming white, wooden and airy as a large dollhouse, and big market, a heat-shimmered expanse of red and silver-grey, built half on land, half on river. Its four steel gables were like industrial tents, crowned by a clock tower that made a mockery of my little Kitty's. Guyana converged and diverged from here via bombish minibuses. The streets sold everything. The sense of movement, the mood of hot shifting trades, the hustle in the air, Rick Ross declaring it from the music carts: it was the closest GT came to the ambition-cloud that is a city.

One could give up on the world with ease at the Port Health Office. The brown river drifted by your feet like molasses, the air thick with river. The wooden torpor, it seeped through every sweating plank. The ceiling was high and beamed. On the first floor there was construction on – not true, it was not active in any way, but something had been taken apart with a view to perhaps one day rebuild. I walked through the wooden skeletal frames of the thing being contemplated. In a room a man sat with his legs up on a chair, one Mr Rose. In one corner an ancient knobby boombox, a machine from its original days. In another corner a flat groaning freezer of similar vintage the size of a single bed.

Across the port health officer I took a seat without being asked and pondered things with indecent laze. There was a blackout. The table fan clunked to a halt. Mr Rose spread a kerchief on his dome, undid two buttons of his shirt jac. We sweated gently in the warm river breeze, doing nothing with the air of people who had congregated there for that precise purpose. At last, when I was least expecting it, Mr Rose said he was tripping. What was he tripping on, I asked. He said he was dripping. He added that if he was tripping he wouldn't know if he was dripping, and thereafter leapt forward to render signatures with a burst of vigour that one sensed would require hours of recovery.

I went back down and had beef stew and rice in a cinnamon-coloured shop. It was the Ocean View Snackette, wrong on every count. It didn't view the ocean and it was actually a roaring cookshop. It had pink walls, burgundy panelling and mesh windows. People were dripping here too. They were slaying Ivanoff vodka with coconut water and telling jokes. A man burst into the room with an awfully promising line – 'Seven men get a divorce last night' – but was drowned out by a commotion surrounding a knocked-over bottle. A row broke out. Somebody threatened to send somebody to hospital, 'but me ain't sure if they would accept an ugliness like you.' There was supreme disinterest from the ladies running the shop. Every now and then they sent out large chunks of ice in a sad pink plastic bowl. Flies settled on their dresses, their cheeks.

It was another hot wasting day downtown for the wasted. And coming out of the snackette after the inadequate stew, turning a corner, I saw Baby. We both realised this was a moment. His mouth gleamed with a gold tooth-cap and he was wearing a red beret, striking for how new it was in contrast to the rest of him.

'What you doing here?' I asked. 'I not give you fare to go back?'

I gone and I come back too, soldier, he said. There was more hardtime waiting for him. His ole man had been shot by the Venezuelan coastguard on the Orinoco. He was only smuggling in three-four case of Polar beer. Venezuelans real wicked that way. Till now they want half of Guyana, did I know that? So now he came back to ketch a lil wuk to send the family.

With every passing moment I was more distracted by the tooth. It was an inverted heart.

'You put a heart on your tooth?' I asked at last.

'That ain't heart. That a batty.'

'It's an upside down heart.'

'Is a big, round beattie. She sitting pon the iron. Heh heh. Watch close, soldier.'

There were more pressing matters at hand. I told him he had taken advantage of me. I said I took pity on him because of his filthy crime which it seems he did not in fact commit. I thought of recovering my money from him, but he looked so smug I left and walked away.

To my surprise he followed me, trying to correct the misunderstanding. He followed me to Raff's on King's Street where I was to buy the racquet which electrocuted mosquitoes, a useful tool to stun humans with as well. All the while he kept telling me that he had murdered his pardner in the Cuyuni and I must not doubt it. He chopped him nine times, went to prison. He was relentless.

As it was mildly entertaining I let him carry on. He suggested we go down to the court to meet Magistrate Van Cooten. Magistrate Van Cooten would tell me the truth. Fine, I said.

We set off towards the court, as though Magistrate Van Cooten was waiting there just for us, poised with gavel in an empty courtroom to redeliver the judgement whereupon I may hug Baby for truly being a killer.

Naturally, Magistrate Van Cooten was not there. Surprisingly, I was offended.

I walked off in a funk into Regent Street. Amid honking minibuses and the commerce Regent Street had its own order. At the bottom the two photo shops and the two gas stations, followed by a row of Indian-national variety shops, all really the same shop run by different Sindhis, a single room which sold toilet seats, vases, prams, music systems, gotten on ships from some staggeringly large warehouse in Panama. In between the site of a new mall, which was to feature Guyana's first ever escalator, and further up Bourda Market, first the unappetising covered market, hung with caps and long T-shirts and meat, and outside it, bursting with divine freshness, crinkled passionfruit, orange pumpkin, bold green pakchoi and tremendous herb, the scents of lovely life. Past it, in the Brazilian salao Brazzo strippers got their nails done or hair reblonded. Atop them in a hotel two red Brazilian men under an umbrella drank coffee, one sensed, with a touch of regret. The men were always there, sometimes different ones. They were an installation. Then the automobile spare-parts shops, and the street getting quieter past them, the two old trenches appearing, and the spacious wooden ministries, and opposite them Bourda cricket ground where they played terrifically ambient run-down flooded matches which could last a fortnight, a month, half a year, and nobody would be able to tell the time.

By the time we reached the cricket ground, or maybe because of it, my mood was restored.

There was a coconut vendor on the bend. I stopped to drink a cold one. Baby was still with me. The thing about Baby was that he never looked happy or vexed or sorry or anything like that. He appeared complacent and a tad downpress.

As though there had been no gap between our first encounter and now, he started telling me about the conditions in the prisons. He spent seventy-one months in the Mazaruni, which was much nicer than Georgetown prison. In Mazaruni they could breathe some natural air, grow a little bhaji, pull some cassava, do a little good wuk. He did see some bad months. He got into a fight over a cigarette – a single cigarette – with a policer and was put in solitary confinement for a month. But even so it was alright, he learnt a lot about he ownself.

Camp Street prison was hard. Nasty conditions, rough people, long-water stew. It was the long-water stew which caused trouble once. Convicts flung their watery bowls of salt and potato against the wall and bust a hole in the roof in protest.

'You know, a hungry mob is an angry mob.'

Roots! Of course I recognised it. I said, 'Them Belly Full (But We Hungry).'

For the first time in our dealings I noted a flicker of surprise in Baby.

He gave me a touch and we spoke about roots reggae with exploding excitement. He sang a couple of tunes with a cracked voice and enormous meaning. Take any tune, I began saying, delving into thoughts since I couldn't much sing, take a big tune – take the big man and the biggest tune. Like how he said let them pass their dirty remarks. Dirty remarks! Regular wise ones would not have put it so. What a simple and great writer. Roots was full of simple and great writers. Check Pete Tosh, check a line like I hear your words, but I don't see no works. Music of truth, bai, Baby said, music of truth. Ska is the root, the rest is all roots, I proposed, modifying from the great Willie Dixon of Mississippi, who correctly laid down that the blues is the roots and the rest is the fruits. Yeah, yeah, soldier, he said, music of truth, adding incongruously, check me out anytime.

Before parting I asked him if he regretted his actions. He said, 'No, brother, if you can't face what you done, you can't a better man make.'

It was a day or two later, drifting along Camp Street, that I came upon the high tin and barb of Georgetown prison.

Across it was an officers' club. There I fell into a conversation with a man by the gate. I mentioned a recently paroled life-sentence convict. No such person, he insisted. I provided details of the murder in the Cuyuni.

'I would know, man,' he said impatiently. 'I run the place.'

'Where will I find Magistrate Van Cooten? He's supposed to have handled the case.'

'Magistrate Van Cooten? He bin dead twenty years.'

The next time I saw Baby skunt, we decided to go pork-knocking.

4

THE OPERATORS of no. 72 Sita Sita had recklessly inverted minibus protocol. The driver was scrawny; the conductor was meaty. Possibly it was a father grooming his boy. That was very well for the family, but not a single passenger was about to be foregone to adjust for the excess volume in the back. A big lady with an accusing voice was not pleased with the strategy. The scrawny driver, who had foolishly given away the game by sitting at the wheel before time, escaped again to the pavement.

Everything moved slow in these dripping Georgetown mornings, and a Mahdia bus took long to fill up. It occurred to Baby that I had no hammock, and we ran down to the road by the library where a man sold them. Then it was another hour of waiting.

One watched things through sweat in the eyes: blots of loose checked shirts, fades of slanted caps, dark lipstick in soft focus. Small-time hustlers hustled, *huss-lin huss-lin* in the air, a soundtrack to the trade of aphrodisiacs, sex oils.

'It must have nuff birds in India,' a youthman said to me.

Before I could respond another youthman intervened.

'Puerto Rico, bai, dah is where I would like to go.'

The first youth sucked his teeth. 'Wa'm to you, buddeh? It have a ratio of *nine* bird to one banna in certain district of Venezuela.'

Thus, without my participation, the topic was closed.

Gradually the van was populated. A dreadlocks came with empty cages to bring back birds from the interior. For bird-racing.

'They don't fly away?' I asked.

'Nah, man, they in they cage.'

'How do they race in a cage?'

He emitted a series of high-pitched cheeps.

'Is a race of whistles.'

A presidential candidate arrived. Nobody gave an ass. In India garlands would have beheaded the man. As it was he had an eminently garlandable face, a bald, round head with successful, bespectacled eyes. He wore a waist pouch and a knapsack like a happy scout. He was a serious leader, defecting from an established party to begin a mixed-race one. Though elections were not expected till the second half of the year, he was going to the interior to spread the word. He settled easily into the cramped bus with the electorate. A sidekick, a jolly walrusy man, made running streams of rude jokes about the incumbent president.

Final hustles took place. 'Gal, put the child pon you leg nuh?' 'How much child I could put pon me leg, I ga one ahready.' 'You gon pay for the second child?' 'Like you ain't ever was a child' – till a crisp old black man with a startling British accent elocutioned, 'Are you waiting for two hundred more people?' It was the accent which did it; and with hoarse cries of 'leh we go, leh we go, leh we go' from the meaty conductor, Sita Sita burst out of the blocks.

Dancehall on the stereo, no sweetness, empty hard riddims thudding in the bones, sleaze, mood of the streets, fake rudeness, men talking their vulgar minds. But now came a lady, Macka Diamond in a champion collaboration with Blacker. It was splendid comic deejaying, a mock squeal, a serious lament, sex and gender. She made complaints and Blacker counselled her. *Bun him!* Bun him: cheat back on him. Baby decoded the stuff for me. My affection for new dancehall was limited, but the good 'uns were the good 'uns.

We pounded out of the decaying perimeter of GT and past the clustering villages whose sequence of names from Agricola to Land of Canaan would come to trip off my tongue. We made a great number of stops. At any point someone was liable to yell, 'Mash the brake!' or 'Jam it to the side!' Someone wanted to pick up a roti and fishpie from M&M's by the harbour bridge, someone to drop off a PVC pipe by his aunty in Friendship, and at Garden of Eden people chipped in to buy a case of grenades – the small XM five-year rums.

The grenades began to detonate quick. Already vistas were opening up. The Demerara peeped in, peeped out. By the road women in floppy hats sold pine and pawpaw. Grandfathers cycled in the sun. And look how those fascinating houses went by, high and stilted and tearing, with their bruck-up families inside the yard, the childfather made off somewhere and the young mammy with her belly big again. We passed mandirs tiered like pagodas, and the sickly new cricket stadium the government of Indian nationals was constructing. Car shells grew out of the mud, shot through with razorgrass. We whizzed by a dozen dead kokers – sluice gates, fallen sentries. Run-over dogs were ground into the asphalt. We turned perpendicular at Soesdyke where the sign said 'Brazil': infinite promise.

Mounting exhilaration on the highway, thin, miraged, built on white sand – the illusion that it might begin to wobble (we were also on grenades). Enormous sandpits appeared by the sides, big enough to swallow whole villages, and then it was low and rising bush, saturated by creeks of cool black water veining off the Demerara. The driver lit a ciggy, took calls on his phone, shifted gears and manipulated the wheel all at once, invincibility writ large upon his face, drawing appreciation. 'Skills, bai, skills, dah is skills!' His possible father beamed. 'Full de clock, bai, full de clock.' Upon

24

Baby's encouragement, the candidate's sidekick cussed out batty-boy politicians and delighted the bus.

The town of Linden arrived, its air sprinkled fine with bauxite dust. But bauxite was in shambles, and Linden a sullen reflection. Baby sympathised with the situation. 'Guyana having hardtime. Worlprice of bauxite low, worlprice of sugar low, worlprice of timber low. Is only diamond and gold which could do the job.'

A short way beyond Linden, after the asphalt turned briefly to loose gravel, then to stark red laterite, we were in the interior – that moody Guyanese abstraction. The interior is not fixed by topography. It could be savannah, swamp, jungle, plateau. It could begin anywhere. You just know, just as we knew now by the freshening scent of forest that rose in great walls around us.

There were deep, wide pools of water in the mud, and Sita Sita coursed through or swerved past them, cutting wicked shapes in the trail. 'Skills, bai, skills!' Things glistened outside. The clouds came out. The wind smelled of herb, of growth.

At 58 Miles we stopped for a very late lunch at a sudden shack with an extensive menu, deer curry included. The late start, the stops on the way, and now the slackness over lunch raised the vital Guyanese fear among some passengers that 'darkness gon ketch we'. The candidate and his sidekick went to the latrine to 'shed a tear', that is, urinate, but it was suspected that they had gone to 'post a letter', that is, defecate. The large accusing lady, sombre in between, bellowed, 'How them going to stop racial when they cyan stop theyself?'

And so when the vehicle was stopped again for inspection at Mabura, it did not go down well at all.

Something about Sita Sita did not appear entirely innocent. The soldiers declared that every man and his bag would be searched. The van was emptied. The candidate went into the checkpost to have a word with the seniors.

It began raining energetically, the kind of afternoon rainforest shower one read about in school. People ran to a shelter. The soldiers waited for the cloud to spend itself – but with every passing minute they felt the pressure of darkness ketching we. Somewhere deep down they knew that with their guns and their boots they were no match for the lady now heckling them with 'yuh got goadie', that is, swollen testes. Eventually two young ranks fled into the rain and clambered on to the roof to rifle through the bags.

An older soldier eyed the passengers, considering me suspiciously.

'He speak English?' he asked, not addressing me, curiously, but Baby.

'Reasonayble. Not good-good.'

'What age he got?'

'The man say he be twenty-six. Me not sure he meet that much though.'

'What he does do?'

'The man from India. Govamen send the man to study botanical specimen, y'know, butterfly and thing.'

'Hm.'

'The man say they en got butterfly an crappo an thing in India nice like heye.'

Crapaud: the French too had been here.

The ranks climbed down from the roof.

The cloudburst finished.

We were off again. We turned sharp west, no longer on the trail to Brazil – another dream, another time. We climbed, and curved along drenched curves, and on one particular curve the conductor let me know that this here was the longest curve in the country, just as he had told me of the longest pontoon bridge in the world on the Demerara.

We were down to the last of the grenades.

People took hungry gulps and, led by Baby, made raucous claims that bounced in the bus and the forest beyond.

'. . . Nah talk skunt, bai. If Da Vinci code true for true, how come other religion en take advantage of the findings to increase they following? . . .'

'. . . Don't tell *me* about Selassie I, bigbai, you wan know about Selassie I, *me* tell *you* bout Selassie I . . .'

'. . . I tell you, banna, the more you make woman work for they rights, the more vicious they going to become . . .'

The forest deepened and lengthened. There were beautiful flooded scenes at Mango Landing, river and bush and forest tugging at each other. The top of a shack poked out of the water like a dead hand. And here our run was finished. Sita Sita ejected us peremptorily, turned, and squelched away whence she had come.

Passengers took off their shoes and waded through the weeds and bush in the opaque brown water to the motorboat and made the crossing in batches.

Two jeeps waited on the other side. We took the one which bore the sticker: 'The Lord sends no bird without a branch.' Amsterdam was its proprietor. He had got the sticker custom-made in Florida. He was a tough man who believed in sacrifice, prayer and the holy purity of the bush. There was a hole through the consciousness of the nation today. He took the wheel and sped off as if to rectify the situation.

It was after-rain cool and faintly misty. Somewhere beyond the trees and the faint mist the sun fell towards horizontal. The air tingled with wet scents. We were moving closer to the essence of things. Places were called Tiger Creek and Eagle Hill.

A man tapped me.

'Guyana the most beautiful country in the world.'

I nodded in agreement.

'The interior, it got a lot of history behine it. For example, it have a place called monkey mountain in the Pakaraimas. It got a lot of rocks, plenty plenty small rocks, shape like monkey. They claim it was a mountain with a lot of monkey. And the monkey turn to rock. So it got a lot of history behine it.

'You cyan see Guyana in one life, you know,' he continued. 'You *could* see all of it – but not in one life. Too beautiful and too big fuh see in one life.'

As one feared, there was an interjection.

'How much country you seen, buddeh?'

'Don't tell me stupidness, bai. You jus *know*, right. Some islands and islets in Essequibo, right, they as big as England.'

'Guyana as big as England.'

'Well, as big as UK, you ever hear of UK?'

'I hear they as big like Barbados.'

'Bai, me batty bigger than Barbados.'

'And you fine.'

When they said fine in Guyana, they meant thin.

'Gimme a touch, banna. Bajan does be driving BMW an thing but they stupid bad. You hear the one about Everard an Everton?

'So Everard tell Everton about Neil Armstrong. Everton ask, Who, the same Armstrongs from St. Andrew's parish? No, boy, say Everard, the Armstrong fella who climb the moon. So next time they go climb the sun, Everton ask. Boy, Everton, is too hot up there. Hear what Everton say: so why they cyan go at night?'

'That's Bajan.'

At Mahdia an old black man with black hair and a grey moustache approached the jeep – it was the grey moustache rather than the black hair that looked artificial. 'Ya'al must know me.' No, everyone said, with unexpected enthusiasm. 'But ya'al must seen me pon the TV!' No, everyone repeated, emphatically again. 'Ya'al suppose to recognise me from the TV. Me daughter qualify for Miss Guyana last year.' He gyaffed with Amsterdam for a while. But his hurt was palpable. He did not so much as look at us again.

Mahdia had the feel of the cusp of things, frontier to the interiormost interior. Girls wore Brazilian yellow and some had copper hair and copper skin. Some were Brazilian by nationality, some by aspiration, some daughters of miners, some their mistresses, which term included mistresses, wives and reputed wives. The main street was pure red mud, and from it rose a cenotaph, short, white and pointed, as if it had perforated its way out of the earth rather than been stuck into it. Baby said it was the centre point of Guyana.

'And when the Lord make the world and he take out all he gift and shower them down, the gift of mineral fall down heye, right pon that spot. All round you got El Dorado.'

He went off somewhere and returned with a branch of genip and two mangoes, and he showed me how to squeeze and suck out the mango from a single slit in the skin.

We watched the sun go down on Mahdia. Everybody had dispersed, the large lady, the bird man, the presidential candidate and the sidekick, from whom Baby had acquired a set of party bandannas and flyers to distribute in the forest, and of the Sita Sita travellers only Baby, I and a small, nondescript man, practically faceless, continued with Amsterdam.

Darkness caught we well and proper on the nine miles of twisting, turning mud till Pamela Landing.

We rushed to the riverbank to check for the boat. It had long since left.

Amsterdam had a little shop here, supplying the dredges in the area, run by a girl people seemed to be calling Fatgirl. A thing was what it was in Guyana. As a coolieman was a coolieman, as a man with one arm was Onehand, as the elephantiasis-afflicted was Bigfoot, so a thin man was Fineman and a fat girl was Fatgirl.

Fatgirl had shining eyes and a fabulous swaying backside. She wore short red hair and a sleeveless red tee and when we caught sight of her, she was hammering a nail into a chipped board on her counter. Baby, jumping exuberant by now, broke into a grinning song.

'Hammerin a wah de young girl want . . .'

She looked at him with a half smile. She resumed the hammering and jumped songs.

'Empty barrel mek the most noise.'

'You ent seen me barrel yet,' Baby protested.

Fatgirl finished hammering and went inside. Baby called out behind her for some water.

'First time I hear man ask woman for water,' she called back.

Amsterdam came to the counter, cutting short the conversation. He offered us the night in the shed. We accepted.

The shed was a wooden frame covered with blue tarpaulin. Beneath the polin we slung up our hammocks. They were thin rollable camouflage hammocks, pierced with ease by wind and mosquito. We finished the rest of the mango and genip and ate some vanilla biscuits we'd brought from town.

At the shop, in community spirit, Fatgirl showed a movie for whoever gathered. 'Some movie got nice slogan,' Baby declared, and thereafter for the benefit of Fatgirl did repeated impressions of an alleged Denzel dialogue: 'Forgiveness is between them and God – I'm here to arrange the meeting.'

I fell asleep, on the bench, then in the hammock.

I remember next when at a late and raining hour of the night Baby got up to check if our bags were getting wet. He flashed a light in my face.

'Alright?'

'Cold.'

'But you pullin punts, soldier. Serious punts.'

I went back to sleep.

THERE WAS evangelical fervour at dayclean, to use the beautiful Guyanese for dawn. The first stirrings of morning were in the air when the sound system, a six-pack of speakers, each the size of a child, erupted with praise. Amsterdam was well into his day. He had risen at 3.30 to put diesel into the generator – we were interior enough that there was no electricity anymore. Bathed, breakfasted, in very dark glasses looking somewhat like Ray Charles he prepared for his first pick-ups. 'You need sacrifice,' he boomed, revved his jeep for a few minutes, and made off into the forest. Guyana need more patriot like that, Baby muttered.

We lay in our hammocks. The music ran out shortly after Amsterdam's departure. Baby filled the silence humming a Beenie Man gospel. A wisp of a cloud floated by. To lie beside the cloud in the perfect dewy dayclean was something like bliss.

I cannot say if anything had occurred between Baby and Fatgirl at night, but she was exceptionally sweet on him. Our breakfast was complimentary, saltfish fried up with onion and garlic and tomato, along with tumblers of coffee. Guyana used to grow its own coffee – indeed, the first plantations were coffee, and in parts you could still find the bush – but the fashion now was global instant taken with powdered milk, the final concoction white and brown clumps in warm water. He also charmed a bottle of cola from her. No small deal: things were already twice the price of town.

We walked down the slope to the bank. No boat. The morning water was cool and muddy. We waited in a wooden riverside booth. We leant back and said nothing.

A wee naked lad came by. He was Fatgirl's son. He gifted me a cherry. I ate it. It was a wiri pepper. I ran ablaze to the river. He ran off deliriously to tell his ma.

We idled. We walked into the forest, towards the sound of a dredge. Studying three or four men hosing down enormous slopes of red mud, Baby hissed without provocation, 'fockin slaves'.

Back by the Potaro a few others were now waiting as well. It was killingly idyllic: slow white foam adrift on drowsy water, the suggestion of the river opening out beyond, the wood booth on the slope of the bank. Every now and then the calm was broken by a miner hollering a desperate roger on Fatgirl's radiophone.

At last a small wooden motorboat by the name of Edwin arrived.

WE went west on the South American river, a little north and a little south, but due west. On either side vegetation exploded up in all shades of green, trees at all kinds of heights, leaves in all manner of shapes, and sometimes we saw a flashing toucan or a macaw or a floating blue butterfly. We passed pontoon water dredges, tinny industrial works I could not fathom. Our halts were at places such as Two Mouth.

Throughout I maintained awed silences, beginning to attract attention.

'He does talk English?' a man asked Baby.

'Reasonayble. Not good-good.'

'What he does do?'

'The man from India. He learn them girls kamasutra. Sexual posture-making, you hear about the thing?'

'Dah wuh you call job, bai! What he doing here?'

'He sent fuh learn it to gals in the bush.'

'Wuh he name?'

'We's just call him Gooroo.'

As I stared at the terrain, so the man stared at me.

Two hours on we came upon an unsurpassable bit of rapids, glinting like rippled sheets of steel in the sun. We got off.

In a forest clearing, upon the counter of a marvellous Rasta bar an Amerindian lady lay on her belly, short, plump, aggressive. She wagged her legs over her bum as she spoke, and emitted constant cusses which accumulated over her head like a squall.

We settled at a table. Baby went into the bush and brought back a blob of sticky sap on a leaf. From his bag he pulled out the candidate's flyers. He spread sap on two of them, tenderly working it with his pinky towards the edges. He pasted them together with the printed sides facing each other, and carefully ironed it with his hands. He lifted it in the air and considered his work from several angles.

I assumed he was entertaining himself while we waited for our next boat, whenever that was. It was hence a surprise when he handed me the glued sheaf.

'Make the application here.'

'What application?'

'Make it like from the govament of India. Like you got to come to Kaieteur National Park for doing the study of certain specimen like plant and crappo and them kinda thing.'

'But why!'

'They start a rule that you need a permit if you going by overland route. Not by plane, if you take a plane you don't need no permit. Only overland. You see how stupid the govament?'

'But nobody asking us for a permit.'

He sucked his teeth. 'Jus do it nah, man.' He added proudly, 'Look, I make it a nice thick paper so it carry the govament style. You unstan what we doing, right, pardner?'

'Of course, man, I come from India.'

'Good. Make it in a nice handwriting. Cas it's a nice thick paper you got there. The handwriting got to match it.'

I formulated the thing in my head. Baby tapped his fingers with impatience. I wrote.

Your Excellency,

As per our understanding with the government of Guyana, the Flora and Fauna Department of the Government of India has deputed a scientific observer to study the botanical and zoological specimen in the Kaieteur National Park. Kindly extend him the necessary access for fieldwork so that our nations may learn from each other and raise their positions in the world of science.

Thanking you,
Purana Purush
Director, F&F Dept.
Govt. of India

I handed it to Baby. He glanced at it dismissively.

'Well, it could be a lil more fancy. You cyan add a lil cyurls or something? Put a signature too.'

I felt like an underappreciated secretary.

'What about the letter, you like that?'

'Read it nuh, man.'

I read it aloud.

'Well, is alright.'

I added curls. I signed it.

I handed back the paper for approval. Without further comment he reached into his bag and bunged a rubber stamp on it.

It was a seal. Office of the President.

'But it says Guyana.'

'Rest yourself, brother. Watch.'

He took a little sweat off his brow and sprinkled it on the paper. He lightly touched his finger on the stamp.

'You cyan see now what it say. We tell the man the thing get wet up in the boat.'

Rummaging through his bag once more he produced another item from the Office of the President, this one an overly folded letterhead.

'Put a permission pon it from de big man. For all two o we.'

I wrote.

> To Whom It May Concern,
>
> Kindly permit the bearer of this application and his guide entry to the Kaieteur National Park for purposes of scientific observation. There is to be no removing of any specimen.
>
> That is an order,
> President of Guyana

Armed with these documents Baby rose with the menace of a diplomat to locate a man named Travis. I followed him.

Travis, an Amerindian, was our next boatman, and his reaction to Baby's documents was a perfectly angelic rejection. Them thing don't matter, he said, without the receipt from Carl Balgobin. Travis worked for Carl Balgobin; and Carl Balgobin, somehow, had the monopoly on this particular boat-leg. We got an order from the president, Baby argued in pally tones, erroneously referring to Carl Balgobin as Bal Carlgobin. Don't matter, said Travis, who had the advantage of being completely devoid of expression. The boat belonged to Carl Balgobin. Carl Balgobin paid his salary. Only Carl Balgobin could authorise it; rather could have authorised it. It was surprising the Office of the President did not tell us this. This line of conversation continued for a few minutes till, somewhat abruptly, the elaborate scheme seemed to degenerate into straightforward bribery.

Travis quoted an official price of 12,000 Guyanese dollars per person: he would make a receipt and give it to Carl Balgobin later. Even at two hundred Guyanese to a US dollar, this felt stiff. Baby made no effort to negotiate. Travis added two gallons of fuel to be purchased at an outrageous price, because the boat burned eight times more fuel going upstream. Here Baby took him away to the side to talk. Passive in the heat, I returned to the bar, where the lady was still lying on the counter, but now on her back. She began to cuss down Carl Balgobin. Thereafter she cussed down the government. Transport was the job of the government, but the government had made Carl Balgobin the blasted government. She called Carl Balgobin an antiman; in fact she referred to him as she. 'I know she skunt good-good, fockin badmind skunt. I stop wuk for she mudderskunt, an she cry now "do me this nuh, do me dah nuh."'

Energised by the broadside I awaited the pair neath the ripening noon. They arrived soon with a deal in which the only certain result was that I did not gain in any manner. The lady cussed out the lot of us, and with the cusses still afloat in the clearing, we beat out.

Baby boasted that without the first show of letters we would have paid twice the amount. He put out his fist for a bump.

We trekked twenty minutes through middling forest to the other side of the rapids. With Travis was his wife, and a small child attached to her breast. Travis himself carried a loaded warishi, a backpack made from vines and worn around the forehead with a band. He cut such a Gurkha figure it was disorienting.

AT the monitoring station it became obvious why we needed all that fuel. Travis fetched his extended family and put them on the boat: his brother, the brother's wife, two little girls, an infant, a dog who was slapped repeatedly and flung in like a sack of coal, and a grandfather, or possibly great-grandfather, a superb ancient man with a sagging chest behind an open shirt. He was so very old and gorgeous. He hadn't a single tooth. He polished fishing arrows while the younger generations filled the boat. He spoke only Patamona – the Patamonas one of the nine tribes of Guyana, carrying the sinister reputation of being 'full of kaneima', the spirit of death. Travis and his brother spoke almost no Patamona, wore a cross, and in every outward way had been proselytised.

We chugged up the Potaro, up and up. The river bubbled and rushed as we went higher, and the boat trod a fine line. Navigation is the artful handling of channels: too much water and the vessel might be thrown off balance, too little and it might crunch against rock. Tall, straight delineations of plateaux came into view, draped in relentless green, broken only rarely by a deviant rock face plummeting into the water. There was the quality of a carpet to the green cover, something to be touched and caressed, but closer to the eye, on the immediate banks, it was an intricate, untameable denseness. Travis's brother attempted to guide me through it. Up high was the canopy of the great timber trees, the famous darkwoods of greenheart and purpleheart, the red-maroon bulletwood, the mora and the wallaba, so slender for their towering lengths, and so daintily tentacled at the top. Lower came the austere spears of various palm with their various fronds; lower still, though sometimes higher, fruit trees, bright-leaved and manic, wild mango, wild sapodilla. Beneath this was the absolute deranged mess of undergrowth, buttresses, roots and vine, a wildness so thick that if a man were tossed in chances are he would not hit ground.

Miles away in a cleavage we saw a brilliant white sliver cracking open a mountain. One sensed it would come closer to sight but the river turned corners and it disappeared altogether.

It was early afternoon when we reached Tukeit Landing. The boat was moored and hidden behind trees in the bank. Wordlessly everybody disembarked and began to walk up the rainforest. As we started to climb I felt the frisson of that great white sliver, the suddenness with which it had come and gone.

It was dark and cool and wet, though not raining, and only occasional pinpricks of sunlight made it through. The path was strewn with sodden leaves and wild squelched fruit and branches slippery with moss and lichen and sometimes entire trunks sprinkled with blue flowers and wild orchid. The ladies scampered up in slippers with babies in their arms; the older children, also in slippers, followed them with elastic grace. From the earliest they were used to this. Travis and his brother powered up with their warishis. The ancient man slouched some, but generated slow, steady and ever-churning momentum, the dog by his side. Baby walked with casual ease. I hadn't climbed for a few years, had forgotten its sweet pain. We climbed for three hours, perhaps more, soaked in the enclosed humidity of the forest, before the gradient began flattening. Travis and his family went off into another path; I never ever saw them again.

It was evening by the time we mounted the tabletop, there more or less since the world began. Here was a bare beauty. It had appeared to have rained recently. On a drenched wood post perched a wet eagle, shrugging shards of water off its feathers. The hidden sky was now revealed in a frightening expanse, a deep bright indigo, with the suggestion of a creeping, fluorescent dusk underneath. The steaming undergrowth was gone, yielding to white, sandy soil and smoothened round stones as from a prehistoric riverbed. The forest was no more, except at the edge of the plateau. We walked towards it, and as one approached it one could already feel rather than hear the sound: a frozen roar. Treading through the trees once more past little caverns in dark rock and over a small ravine we came to the brink. Across was the most hypnotic thing I ever laid my eyes on, and probably the most authoritative. Water fell,

I suppose that was all there was to it. The top was a foam of thunder, the bottom a pandemonia of reactionary spray shooting up like geysers, and in between, the utter, cathartic wall of . . . something like an emotion, a large feeling, both stoic and ecstatic, a triumph and, to the eyes of mortals, a humiliation, a momentary reconsideration of the world.

I sat and watched in silence. Low in the gorge lingered remnants of a dissolved rainbow. Up in the setting sky a million specks circled towards a convergence like bees to a giant hive. Thereafter they began to dive down in swoops, the dots getting quicker, shapelier as they freefell. 'Watch,' said Baby. They were swifts. They made for the falls, a mass deathwish, so rapturous and so graphic that one couldn't stop looking and one couldn't bear to look, and at the final moment of execution they slipped miraculously behind that fantastic curtain and into unfathomable space. The symphony ran for long minutes, maybe ten or fifteen.

We went around to the head of the falls and bathed like lunatics, tempting starbai deaths ourselves.

THE SETTLEMENT of Menzies Landing was a mile or two away. The white sand and smoothened old stones gave way to coarser soil and shinny tufts of grass as we walked towards it. We saw a dead labaria in the grass. Baby claimed a labaria could sting dead a horse in full gallop on all four legs. Look who dead now, I countered. He sucked his teeth.

Closer to the settlement there was straggling bush and patches of pineapple, the young rough fruit emerging unexpectedly in the amphitheatre of leaves; and classic Caribbean debris, rusted tin, shanks of wood, stray fronds of palm.

The settlement had instant Rasta vibes, for the first shack one saw was painted in primary red, yellow and green; a 'no drugs' sign hung on the tree outside. A short way beyond was the main cluster of houses, a scattering of withered, patched-up shacks. Some were raised, and then only a couple of feet; many were not. Most were a single room, rectangular, but some seemed to be partitioned in the centre. Most used wood-boards, but there were one or two of shingles. All except the Rasta bombshell were grey-black.

The settlement was arranged around a mango tree in a central clearing that fell on a wide path to the river. Beneath the tree a few people sat and talked. On the path itself there was a game of cricket on.

People came and went all the time from the settlement, lives temporary as the whistling wind, so nobody reacted much to an appearance unless it was a complete stranger. The folk seemed to know Baby. Some gave him a hug or a fist-touch, some simply muttered 'alright?', and some did not care. They called him a manner of names, Cookup, Chase, Aubrey, and one man greeted him with 'Baby Saw you raw you raw you raw.' He was Labba.

'And wah bout you friend here?'

'The man from India.'

'He walk a long way.'

'Eh he. He come fuh teach Indian sexual posture to gals in the bush.'

'Man be a Gooroo!'

'Yeah, yeah, Labba, you know the thing.'

'We got to carry the man to Chenapau. Gooroo, you seen buckgal pattacake? High and pink, like so' – he cupped his hands together – 'like a mound. Jus like a mound.'

It was the final minutes of cricket. The stumps were a rusted round barrel cover propped up by a stick. A man with green eyes bowled quick with a round-arm action. Batting was a man named Nasty (because, I was told, of his face: not that it was nasty, but nasty that he showed it to others). He wore knee-length socks on hairy red legs, and a white floppy hat with a string around the chin. His sweating eyebrows were like wet charcoal smudges. He held the bat like a walking stick. In comical, traumatically un-West Indian fashion he held back the lashes, moving to the ball and pulling out at the last instant. Maybe not altogether un-West Indian: Courtney Walsh did it so. In between deliveries he patted down stones with his bat and marked his guard with a twig.

A Rasta lay in a hammock wearing dark shades and called the play. He was Roots. Nasty evaded every last effort at his wicket almost exclusively with his stomach. 'A whole heap of disparate disparity from Nasty there,' Roots toasted.

I met a few more people. The green-eyed fast bowler was Siddique, proprietor of one of the two shops, the one with the yard enclosed fastidiously with corrugated tin and barbwire. Big Leaf ran a second shop. There was the mystic Dr Red. The village elder was Mr Johnson, a compact man with Gandhi spectacles and the neatest room, his sense of order extending to the scrupulously lettered warning on the door of his pit latrine: 'Watch for fine ants.'

We stayed by Labba in his little partitioned sodden shack. There was a tiny front room, where we slung our hammocks, an equally small back room with a table and a wooden platform for a bed, and a shed for cooking, avoided by Labba for bees.

At night I took a last dip in the Potaro, cool and brown in the morning at Pamela Landing, hot and foaming at the head of the falls in the evening, now red and viscous in twilight.

I returned to the settlement. And here we stopped awhile, Baby and I, among the shops of the Siddiques and Big Leaf, among Nasty, Dacta Red, Roots and Labba and other creatures like us, alone, amiss and awander.

5

IT WAS much later, when these days peeped and flashed like hidden stars of my life, that I could summon any focus on the folk of Menzies Landing. I had little back-knowledge and naturally no foreknowledge.

It was a coastlander's settlement. Any Amerindians, the people of the interior, were women by marriage or passing through. The Siddiques were the only East Indians. Mr Siddique himself with his green eyes seemed to be of mixed blood, and his son had taken an Amerindian wife from Chenapau. She was a beautiful short girl with long black hair and sad eyes. She sat in doorways breastfeeding and seldom spoke. She looked twenty-four but was sixteen. Labba said it was because she was unhappy, having left the tribal village, and feeling here an outsider. If she chose to go back it would be hard. She would be made to do the dirty work. Labba had been in the bush for thirty years, and at this spot for eighteen, so I took his word for it at the time. But after a while I was sceptical of anything he said about Amerindians. He was contemptuous of how they ate big-belly animal, drank river water without letting the sediment settle, used poison-plants for fishing though it was banned. When he castigated Brazilians, in taut statements that rang like headlines – 'Brazilian miners invadin Guyana', 'Brazilian pirates lickin out Guyanese mineral' – then too it was the Amerindians who were disdained. 'Brazilian come and fuck buckman wife, and buckman just skin he teeth.' Afterwards I thought to connect this with a historical animosity – Amerindians had been used to hunt down runaway African slaves. Eventually I came around to thinking that the contempt was perhaps not so particular after all. It was the uniform, universal contempt for indigenous peoples everywhere.

The folk at Menzies Landing were black, or more often red, like the mystic Dr Red, whom no less an authority than Mr Johnson considered an intellectual. In the direct Guyanese way a red person was a direct visual thing. It implied mixed blood and, obviously, a certain redness of skin. Black and Portuguese could be red. Black and Amerindian could be red. East Indian and Portuguese could be red. If the outcome was red then a 'clear skin' dougla might come to be called red.

Dr Red was a red man with a red beard. It crept wispily down his chin till the wisps gathered into an unexpected plait far superior to the sum of its strands. He had a good amount of putagee and plenty buck, he said. Yet his true last name, Wong, was Chinese, and he claimed ancestorship from a rich and famous European prospector. He liked to play up the European blood, yet when he told his stories, in slow hypnotic baritones that could stretch to half an hour clean, it was clear he carried the Amerindian flag.

Consider the story he told about Bones.

'He was my friend, Bones. A blackman. One time me and Bones limin, drinking Heineken. Bones point to a buck gal and say he wan to fuck she. Now Amerindian girls, you don't court them. You don't hold they hands and tell them they got eyes like moon and lips like rose and them kind of thing. You take their hand and go away and fuck them. It's a rape in a kind of way. Bones raped a lot of buck girls. When he want to rape this girl, as a buckman I tell he to fuck off. He throw me some punches. I bang my head on the table and I pass out for the night. The next mornin I find a trouble. Bones gone at night to the girl's home and try to rape her. He knock aside the child. The child get hurt. The girl husband Victor, he try to stop him. Bones chop him. Victor go to get some people, he come back with six people. They come with cutlass, 22-inch. They chop Bones thirty-two times. Bones get put in the hospital. I hear all this in the morning. I hear it quietly. I gather me thought. I say nothing. I say, Okay. I take my axe. I take off the blade, conceal it within my clothing. I go to the hospital. Is just like one room. I tell the nurse, Nurse, please leave us alone as he is my pardner and we have a private matter to discuss. I take out me blade and attach it and I begin to chop and thrash Bones. I lash him in all respects. I almost kill him. I go to the police and ask them to escort me. They charge me for aggravated assault with intention to injure. I get let off – cause I represent myself. I's always be able to represent myself, never get convicted. That is because, you see, I have a spiritual belief within myself. I make remedies. My bones be hard and clean. My inner might is very clear.'

The mutilation had occurred at Kamarang, near where Guyana met Brazil and Venezuela. The western regions, Mazaruni and Cuyuni, there was more action there. More diamond and much more gold. The dredges were bigger, the settlements were bigger. There were prostitutes, murders, robberies. 'Up here nice, up here quiet,' Menzies folk liked to say.

It had been years since the last killings. They talked about notorious Linden 'Blackie' London. He was a former army man who turned into a bandit of preposterous daring and became a national figure. He came up to Kaieteur to reform. Here he killed again, plunged into the river to escape, returning thereafter to his life of banditry. A few years on Blackie died. His denouement was spectacular. It came shortly after a massive heist in Georgetown. They cornered him in a hotel room. Blackie fought on, keeping police and army at bay for, depending on who told you, anywhere between twelve and thirty hours. When the building went up in flames he agreed to surrender. He promised to talk about a lot of things, expose the government. He emerged unarmed only to be riddled with bullets. Half of Georgetown and the coast, they said, turned up for his public funeral. His coffin was draped in the national flag.

The very last killing at the settlement was Watusi's. For that man there was no sympathy. Dr Red described him as a serial killer. Some pork-knockers had owed him money. When they returned from the backdam they didn't tell Watusi they'd come back. He went into their room with two guns and opened fire. One man survived, as he held up a plate against the bullet and fainted. Afterwards Watusi tried to kill another man, whose brother then killed Watusi. Nobody wanted to touch him. He was left under a tree. The ants ate him.

IN FULL bloom there could be as many as fifty people in the settlement, babies included, but at most times there were unlikely to be more than twenty. When it began the settlement was a base for balata bleeders, of whom Mr Menzies was a pioneer. But too many of those bulletwoods were felled rather than tapped; the supply dwindled; the bleeders left, and only pork-knockers remained. They pork-knocked in the forest around Kaieteur – illegally, as it happened, rebelling against the government order that prohibited all mining in the national park. It was impossible to monitor pork-knockers. And they carried on pork-knocking.

There was the simplest economy of barter and credit. Pork-knockers would spend weeks or months in the forest hunting for 'mineral' before returning to the settlement. Here they would contemplate a trip to the coast to sell the bounty and drink of wine and women, but they rarely did go. After repaying the shop-keepers with diamond and gold against which they'd taken supplies, there wouldn't be much left. They limed in the settlement till mood or necessity took them back into the forest. Despite the idea and vices that they talked up all the time, I sensed many of them didn't actually like town. They were institutionalised by the bush, its freedoms and compulsions, the smallness of the community, the eternity of its surrounds. It was the shopkeepers who routinely went to the coast to trade.

At times I could scarcely believe a settlement like this, so little and rudimentary, existed beside the wonder that was Kaieteur. Anywhere else Kaieteur would have been a hive of tourists, the largest single-drop falls in the world, five times the height of Niagara, and so much greater than the statistic. But this was Guyana. Nobody touch she. There might be one plane a day, sometimes two, sometimes none – and a plane carried nine passengers. It would come in at about noon. A small guest-house had been built by the airstrip, but the tourists rarely stayed. They would take a guided walk for an hour or two, then fly right back.

The days started early and the time was all ours. It rained often, in thrilling bursts, rain running down shingles in ecstatic bumps, the entire settlement, the shacks, the mango tree, pixelating in sheets of water. We went walking on the plateau, usually in threes or fours, most often it was Baby and me with Labba or Roots or both. We collected smooth stones from the creek and stroked them and placed them on our foreheads while lying on the airstrip. We laughed at the little scuttling planes when they couldn't land in the clouds.

There was a brilliant strangeness to the tepui, the word for plateaux like this with their own ecosytems nourished by the constant fine spray of the Kaieteur. The phenomenon of the tank bromeliad, for instance – the marvel was that it had every appearance of a potted plant, except that it was so garrulously outsize. The largest ones were two or three times as tall as I. The miniscule golden frog that lived within its leaves I could never spot. But I often saw the orange cock-of-the-rock. Such a funny bird! He was a startling orange neckless mohawk. He sat in the trees hamming it up to attract mates and nested in sheer rock face. The golden frog, the cock-of-the-rock, they were endemic species, special to the small area around the falls.

It was the ranger's son who let me in on these secrets, allowing me a look at a photocopied set of notes for a bounce of rum. He was a young, handsome lad, keen on dancing. He was planning to write and direct a movie in which he would star as Kaie who had plunged down the cliff to save his tribe, the Patamona, from the Caribs, and left the waterfall in his wake.

Everybody in the bush was a hero in a small way, and they thought of themselves as heroes in much bigger ways. They walked golden on the tabletop. They thought they could do anything, turn flimstar, fly fighter jet, fuck the greatest women, open casino in Brazil. They boasted without irony, in amusing, endearing ways. They spoke about real aspirations in humble tones. Labba said he could catch butterflies and sell them in town. He could chop the tree that obstructed a view of the falls for two grand. He could make warishis and sell them for eight grand. He could dig up a lil pond for tourist and dam it with rocks, start a pool parlour too, and then there might be a long, detailed debate on whether a pool table could be folded so as to fit in the tiny Islander planes.

We slow-watched Kaieteur for hours from various points. The mist was horizontal in the morning and vertical at night and in between times was the revelation. The shorter rainy season, anyway strong only on the coast, was meant to have finished. But this year was different, Labba said, because the white man and his policies and his gluttonies were mashing up worldclimate. Earlier you didn't need the calendar because you had the weather. This year the light rainy season had been so long and hard that it had rained more than in even the heavy months. We were in the first days of February and it still continued. The water in the river was the highest he had seen in his eighteen years, and the falls had never been thicker than now. You felt it could wrap the globe in its immense flowing tendrils.

The swifts that lived in the mysterious place behind the falls were reputed to come out at dawn, but I also saw them come out an hour before noon, swooping up in unison and exploding and scattering high in the bright blue sky like pinpricked tinsel. If you lay on your stomach and crept to the edge of the overhang by the head of the falls, it was the closest you could come to feeling like the swifts. Below was the gorge, a surreal lushness. Sound rose up it like steam. The rainbow was a halo around the violence of impact. The river gathered itself after the spill, sidewound away through the forest, forever changed.

We would lime on the mad overhang beside the sign that warned of the 741 ft drop. We'd gyaff, smoke herb, though I had nothing like their capacity. It was breathing to them. They took entire little branches, didn't bother with cleaning, housed them loosely in paper and lit up.

We talked about music. I felt indebted to Roots. I'd liked him very much ever since he was calling the cricket from his hammock in his dark glasses, but I felt indebted to him. It was he who let me know that it was not Abul Bakr the big man sang about in Duppy Conqueror, but *a bull bucker*, and it was he who explained to me 'sipple' from the terrific cosmic opening wail of War Ina Babylon: sipple, Jamaican for slippery, like watch your step. We agreed it was a fine name for Baby and added it to his list of names. We were on the overhang and Roots sat shirtless – they all were usually shirtless or in fishnet vests, with thin muscular bodies hard as, scarred as old school desks – Roots sat shirtless, legs crossed and shoulder-length dreads blown back and ganja emerging softly from his nostrils.

He had spent some time in Jamaica and spoke highly of the vibe up there. He was down with dreadtalk. He used overstand for understand and shitstem for system. To signal agreement he said 'ites' and 'seen'. He sometimes did the whole 'I and I' thing but more, I suspected, as performance. He considered himself a conscientious Rasta. He showed me a terrible festering gash on his finger, which, like Marley's toe that killed him, he refused to amputate. He ate ital. He was drawn to the idea of Repatriation. 'Yeahman, some day. Not right away but some day, some day when the vibe is right. I going fly ome . . . Yeahman . . . fly ome.'

And high above the swifts flew. And in the benab, Dacta Red and the ranger's son perused the Bible in order to 'locate the solution for certain spiritual problem we run into'. Over at the settlement, Mrs Siddique, who liked it here – 'homeside got too much them-say me-say', a phrase that felt to me directly translated from the Hindi *tu-tu main-main* – Mrs Siddique stirred her pot of curry. And you could pick up all these vibrations. I cannot explain it. It was heightened vibing. I'm not even certain I realised at the time.

ON OUR fourth day a group of pork-knockers returned to the settlement. They were seven in all, rougher than rough, steppin like razor, they could chew bullets, kick down trees. They came with great big cheer and a supply of wild meat, eager to sport like sport going out of style.

All afternoon they curried labba, a kind of large rodent, its meat close to pig. And as white and then red rums were killed alongside the rodents, by the time the evening officially began, with people congregating beneath the mango tree, there was already a kind of latent madness in everybody's eyes.

We played a session of semi-drunken cricket. End of play was signalled by a firesnake, darkly orange, slithering across the pitch. Men went for it with a stick and a prong. The Siddique ladies squealed. The reptile was beaten with the stick and hoisted on the prong, a bulge pressed against the stretched skin of its stomach. Somebody tore it with a knife: a frog fell out with a bloody splatter, fully made but for severed limbs. The snake was sacked for its skin. The crappo was dispatched with a kick under the shop. It was the rudest dinner interruption I ever saw.

People drifted into one of the two shops. The generators were switched on. An action movie was on at Big Leaf's. I settled in Siddique's.

It had the special feel of a small inexplicable place in South America. Rice and flour sacks were heaped in the corners. Everything was wooden, the walls, the tables, the benches, the floor, the beams, the counter, the shelves, the windows. A Hindu Dharmic Sabha calendar was nailed on the wall, beside it an Islamic calendar of the Peter's Hall Sunnahtul Jama Masjid, and beside that charts of snakes and frogs in the region. There was a living powis in the room as well. This is an exceptionally silly kind of turkey, jet black with a white belly. She was disconcertingly large and underbalanced. She pottered about on the beams above us. She made me terribly insecure, for she discharged droppings in unreasonable quantities and moreover was liable to sudden flapping flights, often landing on someone's foot or thigh and nobody noticed but me.

The Siddique daughter was minding the counter. Baby frequently expressed his admiration for her, 'Wouldn't mind some of that coolie hair pon my face,' 'the gal real come of age'. The music ran loud – soca, chutney, chutney-soca. The games began. Dominoes, but to accommodate me one of the tables moved to Rap, which was the card game I knew from my childhood as Knock Knock. A returned pork-knocker sponsored a bottle of five-year, and I sponsored one too. Somebody also came along with high wine. This was a cheap colourless spirit of sixty-nine per cent alcohol. If you peered into the bottle the vapour singed your eye. Spilled drops burnt holes in the wood like acid. We drank the five-year, but along with that, the loser in each game of Rap was to down a capful of high wine, two capfuls for a particular kind of loss. Also, there were these very fat joints floating about. The whole thing was doomed from the start.

The games proceeded apace, with people gaily threatening each other, 'I gon drunk you skunt tonight mudderskunt'. Soon the high wine capfuls were making dents in everybody. I felt the bones in my head softening. I could not escape the feeling that strangers were lifting me by the hair and dropping me for laughs. In a faraway corner bench Dr Red leant back against the wall and stared at the powis on the beams and said, 'I would feed you, powis, I would feed you in a natural manner.'

The wooden room grew in din. Baby began making forays to the counter to talk to the Siddique daughter, routinely breaking into his slow gold-gleaming laugh and saying, 'Eh heh heh, that is a very am*biguous* statement gal, eh heh heh. Very am*biguous.*' He said this no matter what the poor girl said or didn't say. The elder Siddiques soon caught on, and the girl was dispatched inside. If she emerged later, it was only in the company of Mrs Siddique, putting an end to Baby's ambiguity.

Things within and without were aclatter. I thought racoons were chewing up the shack and began giggling. I exited Rap in order to exit high wine. I compensated with an extremely large five-year. I took a seat beside Dr Red. He showed me a British halfpenny from 1938. He stared at it a very long time. Thereafter he broke into an uncalculated monologue, looking mainly at the powis.

'Right now I been celibate for about four years. When I spent two years up on the mountain top in Kurupung, when I come to the landing I kinda see that this whole . . . I see this Aids, I see this different diseases, I see this people dyin, I see beautiful girls, they got the virus and I's not a man to be so protective to be using condoms and I just say to myself this is stop for me. If I don't get to know a girl properly inside out when I could afford not to use a condom then that's gonna be it. I just knocked it out. Before that I's speculate birds you know. In Kamarang I get six wives one night, and the remarkable thing is that none of them is meet eighteen. Like fourteen-eighteen. Akawaio girls. All the wannabe girls say, You give me a chile, man, Uncle Red, you my chilefadder but still you don't love me. I say, I love you with all my heart, I love you, but I lie. So she say, You have to ask me for my fadder. So I say, No, I got to correct you because of this language barrier. She's supposed to be saying I got to ask her father for her. So it's more or less like a nice teaching. You got them young girls now

50

more or less look to you like a father figure. They come an say, Uncle Red, I would like to have panty.'

About then Labba arrived in a heavy smokeshroud of Haile. And behind him, tottering, Nasty, in long white socks! I was delighted to see him and behaved, much to his surprise, in the manner of a host. We engaged in rapturous praise of the premier batsman of the West Indies and the cosmos, Sir Prince Brian Charles Lara. He recalled an innings, I recalled another, he struck one pose, I struck another, each one shamelessly demolishing the coiling-uncoiling slithering grandeur of the great man. Nasty had the voice of a man with something like sand in his throat. When he spoke excitedly you feared for him. He told of the time he was at Bourda when India toured in '89. 'J. Aroon Lal and Navjoe Sidoo Sing! Oh boy. Sreekant hand bust in the previous match. It was down to J. Aroon Lal and Navjoe Sidoo Sing! Walsh flick Navjoe Sidoo Sing edge and the bossman' – he meant Sir Emperor Vivian Richards – 'the bossman flick up he hand and pouch the catch, just like so.' Nasty stretched high to his right with arms thrown up. 'I was deh, right deh behind him.' I applauded the effort, and we downed a quick one, both believing that indeed it was Nasty's presence right behind Sir Emperor Vivi which caused the catch. We gave praise (as well as thanks) to Sir Shree Carl Hooper, a beautiful Guyanese who moved at the crease with the softest sweetest paws and the slowest sleeping winks. Perhaps we also moaned to Sir Shree Carl, long fluttering moans drowned by the music, audible to only us. Last but not the least, we struck deep respectful impenetrable Shiv Da Chandapaul eyes-on stances with twitching brows and itchy hands and flickering tongues and bottoms upped to Unity village.

The sound mixes in the room began to make me mad. The same tired sexual soca jokes, the same badman dancehall soundclashes. Two youthman were taking it serious. They brought out their finger guns and went poom-poom and bullet-bullet to all corners. Repeatedly they strode across the room, raising hell with their digits.

I felt for escape. I began to crave musicality of the musical kind. Was deep urges. Horns! Keys! Upstrokes! A-ha! I left with Baby and we went to Roots, who was at Big Leaf's, where the night was mellow and intoxicated but untouched. The movie had finished; Mr Johnson had gone home; the revellers had moved to the Siddiques. We cooked up a session. I brought my iPod. Roots had old tapes – how beautiful those tapes! – that he played on his small old portable. We took the stuff to Big Leaf's sound system where by the grace of Jah there was a lead that could hook these to the amp.

We gave immediate thanks via the Maytals and their great gospel-soaked romps, Toots and his mighty fraying voice rising from deep, deep within and around him other voices peeping out, hitting different planes, different meanings. With Toots it was never what he said but how he said it, hence the plainest euphoria. We surrendered to the Skatalites on Flowers for Albert, and David Murray himself appeared, and the new trombone man was no Don D, what do you expect, but he was pretty damn sweet, and McCook's sax sang, and the trumpet sang, like ecstasy distilled from old desire as Langston Hughes said, solo segueing into solo, layered over all that upstroke, all that keeping of time, all that *discipline*, tremendous tight construction, enough to support an island and coming together so correctly and precisely that Baby kept calling, 'is cooking, is cooking, let she cook, let she cook' and then it was cooked. We inhaled and slow-nodded to Burning Spear's heavy cutting militant incantations, the refrain springing forth from beneath that colossal opening cascade of horns and above the oldest school reverb. Roots was hard into militant reggae and he skanked in the moonshine, and we stayed in the mood a while, went to Tosh and crucial Mutabaruka, but when he started sinking into Buju I switched back to jumping fat choons.

We gave shoutouts to the great departed and those still living. We went to Dekker's intensified falsetto – *rum-babaloo-bam-bam-bam-balooey!* – and bigged up Guyana in the person of Eddy Grant.

That little genius Scratch Perry, not at all a little genius, a very monstrous genius, but a little man, Scratch Perry arrived tumbling down with straightforward botheration. Prince Buster came in shakin long, shakin strong. U-Roy toasted, Big Youth boasted. We made a foray into vital dancehall when dancehall was dancehall, sizer than sizeway days. Dekker and his falsetto kept returning every now and then, and so did Toots, over many forms, over many years, with many different people, including Shaggy on Bam Bam!, he came over ska, over rocksteady, over reggae, but with the same fraying imperishable voice.

After two hours I was spent. Huge heights had been scaled. Babylon had kind of fallen. And now we began to cool off to Family Man's bass licks, the vibratory truths of those timbres, to dreams of sweet rubadub inspired by Bunny in Ballroom Floor – which, when you trace it back to the mouth, to the earliest '66 or thereabouts ska, was cut to a version of Rolling Stone – but the lonesomeness of these dreams was killing and so we stopped. We stopped right there and left.

I realised I was no longer drunk. But I was stoned crazy. I sought to revert to drunkenness. Guyanese rum was round and ribald, ached with the pure sweat of slavery.

We returned to the Siddique shop – bacchanal and how. People were wrestling arms. The two youths were gunning down different parts of the wall. The music had grown louder. Bounty Killa and Baby Cham and friends were putting out some homo-hating lady-disrespectin shit. The powis was fluttering about, terrified by the commotion and not knowing where to go. Nasty was slumped upon a sack of flour, his chin resting on his Adam's apple, his eyes three-quarters closed, a gently spilt drink cupped in his hands.

'Wounded soldier,' pronounced Baby, 'grievously wounded.'

I myself felt wounded. I took a seat again beside Dacta Red, who remained oblivious of the surrounding anarchy, though the plait in his beard was undone. He reached into various pockets of his soul and painted, over another terrific baritone monologue, a picture of his life's thoughts and lessons, sailing through time and space, from big to small, from abstract to specific.

'As I grew older I knew that material wealth is nothing. I like it more or less spiritual. At one time when my girl was suppose to get her first child I had actually become a pimp, like going to those discotheques and looking after girls in terms of protection and fencin whatever booty they may be able to get their hands on so I could earn an extra dollar. That was my personality in those days in the 70s. Being a buck in Georgetown more or less pass off like a low caste, like you don't have anywhere to face, you're stupid. Maybe you would not be able to represent yourself or your family. Street hustle, you don't find a buckman streethusslin. Mostly they were the blacks, the negroes, they wouldn't like a buckman being a leader for a gang or whatever. I's always a leader when I grow up. When we have streetfight and gangfight I's always be at the head. Represent myself and represent others. The thing of it is that you have to know to fight well, y'know, the way it take itself, material things, you got a lot of gold chain, you got a motorbike, and these kind of things. I never liked stealing an the guys go stealing an if I don't take part the guys go against me. Ambush me or try to set me up with the law. We have only one gang per street. We normally do streetfightin and then you have gang, I would call it pilfering, we had motorbike gangs, gangs would steal motorbike, housebreakers. I's not someone who steal. I be someone who represent.'

As Dr Red imbibed high wine and spoke, and we both stared spent at the powis, Nasty expertly maintained his position on the flour sack. At some point, however, Labba and Baby provocatively began to call Prince BC a battyman, 'not a batsman, he a damn battyman'. At this Nasty leapt off the flour sack. Buoyed by his resurrection, I too joined him in the defence. Labba and Baby kept attacking, Nasty and I defended steadfastly, letting nothing through. It soon emerged that Nasty and I were defending different things, Nasty from the very possibility of the prince being a battyman, I of its relevance. Never mind. The thing gathered storm and people arrived from various corners of the room to contribute.

'They find he antiman skunt in bed one day with the bowler, wuh he name, Cummins.'

'You only saying that cause of the name!'

'You ever seen how he hug up them other player?'

'Who got de record? Who got de record?'

'Antiman.'

'Shut up your stupidy mouth, banna, shut up you jokey skunt.'

'Antiman must dead.'

'What if I'm antiman? You'd kill me?'

This was me. The man looked me square in the eyes.

'Yeah.'

'Alright, I'm an antiman, kill me.'

'You en't. You jus saying so.'

'How do you know?'

'I could tell, banna. You wouldn be standing here before me otherwise.'

'I'm an antiman, kill me.'

'Turn round and show me.'

'What?'

'You batty.'

'Why!'

'I could tell if you a battyman or not.'

'Alright, but not here. Come outside.'

I went outside with a person whose name I did not know. He had shining teeth. We walked a short distance from the shop.

I turned around and showed him.

He crept closer.

'What you doing?'

'Shh. Bend over.'

I bent over.

He went on his haunches, studying my anus quietly, intently, and then leapt to life.

'You got a pleat! You cyan be battyman! I tell you so! You en't no antiman!'

He ran back triumphantly towards the shop.

'The man have a pleat! The man got a pleat!'

His victorious march had little impact. For a much greater fight had broken out. It was the two youths. The fight had just finished as a matter of fact. I could not tell the damage. But by the tin wall of the yard I saw Labba lecturing the defeated youthman.

'A little provocation is a dangerous, dangerous thing, bai. *Learn* that. *Learn* that. Learn it *over*. You ain't hear Sparrow sing provocation is against the law? You a yootman. Vibert's cousin, Odetta, you hear she story? She just a harmless chile but always like to be *seen* as a badgirl, always carryin a knife pon she. One time she uncle tell she she dance like a goat. She flick out she knife for joke, but it ketch the man straight in the jugular. *Kachack.* The man dead. And I blame him. Yes! I blame that man for he own death. Because why? Because he make the provocation. The same thing going to happen to you one day, y'unstand? *Kachack.*'

'What happen to Odetta?' I asked inquisitively.

'She done come out of jail, buddeh, she come out quick. She have a baby and the court go easy on she. But the man – he dead dead dead.'

Labba glared at the youthman.

The youthman looked chastened.

And I was flushed with gratitude that my pleat had been located.

I went back in, to such a terribly poignant event, I almost wept. As humans and the powis around him rose and fell, the dacta had stayed fixed at his spot on the bench, eyes set like quartz stones.

'I'm veveveve very rich spiritually. I do say my prayers because I do recognise there is a Supreme, and I get answers, I get clairvoyance, I could actually do telepathy, I actually recognise that you could talk to the supreme source, you could get answers. I personally come from a family which know a lot of herbal remedies and cures so as I was in desolate situation and places. I's be in the mountain there's be no hospitals. After some time I start seeing this is good thing and I start doin my own research. I write potion within my head that I could just lay my hands on, the type of illness the patient may have and get em going. Sometimes for weeks you don't see another person, just there by yourself. No, no, no, you don't. I enjoy that, we live in close contact with animals and birds, know the time when they would come and know the time when they would go, the time when they would feed cause normally I would feed them. Just like I would feed this powis. Know when the rain would be there, when the storm would be there. Know when a person coming. As bad as it may sound on them, I don't like really hypocrites. To be hypocritical I feel is a terrible sin. Know wha I mean?'

And upon that the Siddique man came and uprooted Dr Red and plonked him outside the shop. It was startling, so unjust. He tried to come back inside, bumping up the three steps like his knees were giving way. The Siddique man held his palms out again and administered a simple, firm push that toppled Dr Red to the ground. His cap fell off, exposing a patch of bald, which, in the circumstances, carried an unbearable pathos. I gathered that Dr Red had as usual imbibed and not paid. Even so. I had assumed that he commanded respect in his surroundings; that he had insight, gravitas, and mere merchants at the very least would look up to him.

He petered out into the dark.

Below the mango tree Nasty and a short dreads in denim hotpants had drawn long knives and were holding them at each other like fencers. They had clothing wrapped around their free hands and made to use it like a shield. The moon was a ghostly galleon, as we learnt in school, and underneath such a moon they went at each other in grasshopping jabs. I could not tell if it was a serious affair or not. Where Labba and Baby were cracking up watching them, slapping their thighs and the tree trunk in laughter, Nasty seemed to have some blood on him. Neither of the combatants looked amused. It was actually a little distressing.

Things, one sensed, were getting out of hand. Morning was not far. I felt multiple organ failure coming on. I went to the nearest shack and lay down on the floorboards and rolled into a ball. I was struggling. It was the shack of December, a returned pork-knocker. As I lay there like a wretch he kept saying he cyan sleep on any surface but a hammock because for the last twenty years he'd slept in a hammock so a flat surface don't make sense no more. He lit the small gas stove in the corner and said he would cook an overland omelette. He could cook any damn thing at any damn time and this damn thing was an overland omelette. And that was the last thing I remember before somebody shook me awake and poured cold water down my throat with the words, 'Drink it up, Gooroo, drink it,' and then I balled up again, with groans that I could hear in echo but not repress. In the morning December said, 'The man chant in Indian all night.' He made a sound of tumbling marbles. 'I try talk to the man, right, but the man dreaming in Indian. All night he go on in Indian.'

6

THE river was red as blood underneath. I held myself down as long as I could, coming up with a gasp for life, trying to clutch at the new day. Baby was at work already, on his haunches, sawing a piece of wood. Apparently we were to leave soon. We were to borrow Labba's boat. Labba himself was not coming. The last time out he'd been bitten by a snake. He was carrying no antivenom and his foot had swollen up like a pumpkin. He spent a month laid up alone, pacing his supplies before gathering the strength to return to the settlement. He still hadn't the vigour to go backdam. But Foulis would be there most probably.

We had a boat but no paddles. This is what Baby was working on. He had collected discards, a broken plastic barrel cover, a torn mosquito net, planks of wood, a tattered foam suit somebody had retained from their time as a water-dredge diver.

He whittled the planks of wood to thin shafts with a saw. With a knife he cut two large almond shapes out of the barrel cover. He nailed an almond to the end of the shafts. The opposite ends he nestled in pieces of the diving suit and fastened them with shreds of the mosquito net. This was the grip for the top hand. He fished out the multiracial candidate's bandannas and tied them a quarter of the way down the shaft. This was the grip for the lower hand, for the wood was abrasive and cuboidal.

Labba's was a weathered blue and red boat and too big for two. We loaded the supplies on the polin in the centre. Roots brought us cane, lemon, plantain and ganja from his patch of farm across the river, and we picked half a dozen pineapples from the bush behind Labba's shack.

Baby had a final chat with Labba about location. We fist-bumped goodbye to all. 'Time slip away, brotherman,' said Roots; and with that we left.

Baby took the bow, striding it with a crazed Ahabian glint in the eye and burning bush at the mouth, and I, lily-limbed coolie I, the stern. The early thrill! To think we were hitting this fantastic reptile, to think that we'd be making that bend in the river there, confronting the epic scopes beyond.

It was gruelling work. It was not ten minutes in and I felt the first surges of lactic acid. Baby repeated what Labba had told us, that the water was the highest in eighteen years, and we got to pull. I took a while to start paddling smoothly, to work out the angle at which the almond best entered the water, the balance between pushing down and pushing back. It was so easy to be overcome by the river. The current, so placid from afar, felt colossal. Our movement, if the word applied, was laboured and defeated. To look up was a chilling exercise in futility. The river and its immemorial force furrowing a continent – against that two pointless paddlers. Mistake to stop a moment and marvel at the scale of this helplessness. A flicker of doubt could stall progress; if recovery was not immediate, the work of five minutes could be undone in thirty seconds. The only strategy was to stare into the tugging brown water with a dumb, blind competitiveness.

I suspect I contributed appallingly little to our propulsion. Baby stood most of the time, making powerful muscular incisions into the current, sometimes on one side and sometimes another. We crissed and crossed the river. I could not tell if it was deliberate.

Sometimes we got enmeshed in the vegetation at the edge of the water and pulled ourselves forward using vines and branches. Baby called this monkeyjumping and said it was necessary to monkeyjump across certain parts. He looked like a real pioneer, bare-chested, ganja still in his mouth, cutlassing the creepers and hauling us forward, asking me to mind the whiplash of the branches. I received the vines he left behind and pulled us on. Sometimes the bottom of the boat would scrape against the roots and you had to push out again. We took several breaks, in which we turned to the only snap of rum we had, chasing it down with river water. Though Baby warned against stopping too often, I needed the breaks. He talked incessantly through them. One time, monkeyjumping just like this, he saw a camoudi looking at him. He stretched out the paddle to frighten him away, but the camoudi leapt on the paddle and landed in the boat. He said it was twenty feet. He stamped on its neck and flipped it over with the paddle. He added wistfully that he would like to be a male camoudi cause the ooman be four times more heavy and that is a nice thing to have pon you.

We paddled on, looking for turbulence, crissing, crossing, monkeyjumping, the efforts diminishing me towards a standstill. Even the breeze was against us. The trees were thin and tall and the water so high that it felt like they were floating. Two or three hours into the ride a hard rain began to fall. It was so fucking beautiful. The tall dark forest shook and swayed, hundred-foot timber trees flailing about like dandelions. Winds of forest fragrance whooshed out in wet gusts. Brown ripples swept across the river and stung the skin. We rowed hard and sometimes shouted and rowed. We stopped occasionally to bail out water and tighten the polin over the supplies, and thereafter shouted and laughed and rowed. 'If you en pulling hard you en pulling at all,' hollered Baby. 'Pull, bai, pull. You cyan be saaf, bai, you cyan be fockin saaf. Pull it now, Gooroo, pull yuh fockin skunthole.'

We had entered a fifth hour when Baby began to make halts to check. Several false stops later he was convinced he'd found the spot. We took a minute. We'd done seven miles, he said. Alone in a smaller boat with a good paddle he could lick it down inside two hours.

He went out to find the trail. I waited in the boat.

I couldn't feel my shoulders and arms. I chewed on a piece of cane and watched and smelt and got pinged by the rain. I thought of how it might be to surrender to the torrent and let it take you all the way like old Kaie of legend.

Baby was soon back. He tethered the boat and concealed it behind bushes. The paddles and the polin he hid inside the hollow of a trunk. We put on shoes and gathered our things and began walking. The trail was fresh squelch and the trees were still swaying apocalyptically though the rain was now beating slower. The immense wetness of the rainforest made one feel submerged, but for the smells. The smells were many, mud and leaves, heart of trunk and rotten fruit; the rustle of small animals, the slither of lizards, they all came scented. It was soggy underfoot, thick squelch or big drenched leaves, brown, red and green, twenty or thirty deep. It was walking on marshmallow. My shoes were heavy with water and mud and the backpack was eating into my shoulders. I had two stalks of cane in one hand with my slippers looped through them, and a cutlass in the other. I was tripping over roots and branches.

After thirty minutes we reached a clearing which looked like it had been hit by a great storm. There were ditches and deep furrows and enormous fallen trees. We walked along a palm trunk that ran over ditches and pools of slush, and then through a tunnel of head-high bush we walked into another little clearing. Here a creek gathered briefly into a small pond, and beyond it a thin path led to two raised shacks.

The shack we took had a blissful front veranda. In one corner a tilting table was carefully placed an inch away from the wall with its legs in plastic bowls of water, measures to keep out the white ants that had eaten much of the country. In another corner stood an iron barrel with its top taken off and a slot bust open in its side, the fireplace. On the front door was visible the faintest chalk writing: 'labba you boat under water'.

Inside, the space was divided by a partition as in the shack at Menzies, making two rooms of identical size and symmetry, with a door and two wood windows that had swollen beyond their frames. We sat down for a few minutes on a low wooden platform in the back room, constructed, I think, as a bed. The Bible lay on it. The window framed a solitary Congo pump, long, lofty and lonesome. The rain had stopped.

Presently we heard a man call out, 'Yes, Labba, yes.'

Naturally he was surprised when two gents who were not Labba emerged from the shack.

From what I gathered Baby and the man, Foulis, did not know each other much, but were both pardners of Labba. And it was Labba they talked of for a while, about how he was getting on after his snake bite. Foulis warned us about the evening vipers around the shack – he'd killed six in the last fortnight. He was a quiet welcoming man with an understated air. He had large brown eyes, lovely against the rest of his body which was close to pitch black. He kept himself to himself.

Only a few pieces of coal we'd brought with us had remained dry. Baby used them to get a fire going in the barrel. He went out to fetch some bush for bush tea, leaving me to hot up the pot. I filled water from the vat which caught the rain and placed the pot on the barrel top. The surface was kinky; the pot toppled over and put out the fire.

Baby returned to damp fumes. For the first time he lost his patience with me. He muttered about where the skunt we gon get wood now, all the wood outside wet. More embarrassing still, he cussed himself for letting a man who knew nothin bout fire mind the fire.

Eventually, with hard-won scraps of dry wood, he got a flame going again.

Dinner was rice and a spicy blackeye stew, consumed in silence.

Darkness came suddenly and absolutely, and with it exhaustion. Baby lit a ghostly bottle flambeau in the shack. We slung up hammocks on each side of the partition. I fell asleep for a few hours and woke because I was full of piss. Heeding the viper warnings, I did not go out till Baby, who had the torch, got up to go as well. *Genetha, Genetha* he hummed plaintively as we pissed into the bushes. He said it was a long-time song, the tale of a woman who had fallen from a high position.

It rained hard again at night, and everything had to be rearranged to fit the holes in the roof, and the tin din, loud, vibratory, uncompromising, was both pleasure and noise – not, I suppose, unlike steelpan.

WORK began the next morning pretty much. As it was going to be for a short time, Baby talked to Foulis about the prospect of joining him. 'Yes, man, yes,' Foulis responded. 'Nah take worries.' He offered Baby a quarter of the takings. It didn't sound like much, but it wasn't a bad deal. At the dredges the owner kept seventy per cent, and the remaining thirty was shared by the workers – the people at whom Baby had hissed 'fockin slaves' at Pamela Landing. But the dredge owner didn't contribute his own labour, as Foulis would, and Foulis had already done the ground work. The offer was really because Baby was Labba's pardner, and as Foulis said more than once, Labba had taught him all he knew about pork-knocking and life in the bush.

Water is the essential truth of Guyana. One's encounters with it were so frequent that one felt a little amphibious. Water everywhere, beneath the house, at the gate, at the margins of a road, falling from the roof into the yard, on leaves, grass and on sodden wooden posts, in canals and trenches and 'blackas', in the dark rivers and the ocean – too much of it, in too many forms, you sensed, for it to be of any account. Yet the most innocuous drop carried a stealthy force. Leave a cutlass in a shallow of the creek where the water barely trickled. Nothing in it, you might think. In a few hours water and sand will have filed the blade so that you could 'slice clean through caiman'.

And if water was Guyana's essential truth, then pork-knocking was its most essential endeavour. It felt to me a miracle. There is a man in the forest; it rains; from this he makes diamond. The water cuts the land, washes away the filth and the soil and the sand down to the gravel, and there buried in the mounds of worthless pebbles lie the shimmers of desperate human coveting.

A pork-knocker carried little equipment. He might work as part of a gang; equally he might be alone. In the old days he knocked about with rations of salted pork. Saltpork had given way to saltfish and saltbeef. But fishknocker sounded like a coital position and beefknocker like bootlegged gin. Whereas pork-knocker got the glory, got the rawness, got the adventure, got even the lone sorrow.

Foulis, like Labba, mined diamond. It was easier to do by oneself than gold, free of the processes of gold. And the idea of the diamond, the elusive single piece that could change one's life forever, was the more alluring.

Our days passed slow and voluptuous. Although its volume dwindled with every shower, the rain still fell every day and night. We woke usually to the wet tingly aftermath of the night rain. There would be a heavy shower in the late morning and another one in the late afternoon. At dusk there was sometimes a spell of thunder, often without rain, the accompanying lightning was not in streaks but shapes, along the outline of large clouds, and not white but a fluorescent violet. Sometimes without thunder or lightning there could be a great rustling through the trees that bode a biblical downpour. But not a drop would fall. The trees would continue to shake violently for an hour, followed by a period of utter still, the kind of still that can make a man go mad, and Baby told of a Berbician unaccustomed to the forest who wandered off for a few minutes into the bush, and began to scream, just so. Afterwards, in the heart of the night, came again the melodramatic tin-roof orchestra. Here, waking up to see that nothing was getting wet, Baby would give praise to the rain. It meant the gutters kept denuding, the gravel kept collecting.

I would rise at six without prompting. Though you couldn't see the sun rise because of the forest cover, the morning light beamed in strong and direct through the eastern window, its frame laced with heavy clinging drops that made a man pine for a sweetheart. Baby would have already brought some fresh bush to brew, and its tea tasted not unlike peppermint, softer, more medicinal. Over in the other shack, Foulis, an earlier riser still, would have got his pot going. His shack was of a unique floor plan, with a small room in the front and a large veranda behind, three times as long as the room: or perhaps someone had simply taken down the walls. As the pot cooked he would sit on a flat stone in the absolute centre of the space and read and reread a thriller (he'd read the current one, *Never Bitten, Never Shy* five times). Sometimes he would stop reading and stare into the bush for ten minutes at a time, getting up only to check his pot. Nobody said anything to each other in the mornings, save for maybe 'maanin' and often not even that but just a nod.

We'd make breakfast and lunch at one go. They could be the same thing, or else lunch and dinner could be the same thing, it depended, but the idea was to cook no more than twice. Breakfasts could be of budder, a pot bread: three cups of flour to a cup of water, three spoons sugar, two spoons oil, a spoon of yeast, a pinch of salt, knead it 'till time reach', let it sit and rise, knead it back again, grease the pot and let the dough brown a half hour, flip the side and brown it again, then let it sleep through the night. In the morning the entire round loaf was gorgeously formed. We'd cut conical slices from these and hot it up pon the fire again and eat it with nut butter and coffee.

The finest breakfasts were the bylanfry – boil-and-fry. Afterwards I would have the full-glory bylanfry, with egg, bacon and sweet potato in addition to the basic forest mix, but under the circumstances ours was perfectly glorious. Boil the salt off the saltfish, boil the plantain and peel and slice it, fry them up with onion and garlic and red peppers and bottled seasonings. This was pretty much how we cooked everything – with onion and garlic and red pepper and bottled seasonings, of which we had two, a blended green seasoning of eschalot, thyme, celery and married-man pork, which was a kind of basil, and a dark Miracle seasoning, the charm of which I was reluctant to kill by looking at the ingredients. We had tomato paste and coconut milk and curry powder, and these would distinguish one creation from the other. Saltfish, saltbeef, and potato, red beans, blackeye peas, and sometimes fresh heart of palm, from manicole: we ate everything with rice.

The activity happened early, so it was still a good hour of the morning when we put on longboots and made for the backdam. Literally this word meant back of the dam, aback the rear mud dam of plantations, where labourers had been allowed to grow their own crop. Now, like interior, it had become an abstraction, easily understood.

The backdam here was the area which last evening had looked storm-hit. The upturned roots were big as bare rooms, the mud on them caking in the sharp sun. Around the felled trees was a strange maze of pits and channels. Fragrant transparent water ran in them with silent noise. This was the most elemental kind of diamond works, and to work this miracle you needed to know how to work the water.

The pork-knocker prospected a site. He might find two carats at one spot, eleven a few miles on. He cleared the treasure patch of its vegetation, felled the big trees, stripped away the bush. He dug the gutters in which water ran with its constant pressure, washing, denuding. It may not be enough to rely on the rain; and so he dug reservoirs at the head of the gutters. The clearing would be worked down in this manner, and then he moved on. In six months the clearing will be bush again, perhaps more a pork-knocker's boast than fact, and in a few years there will be no trace of anybody ever having been here. 'Me no leave no oil spill or nothin like the dredge. Me leave nature as me find it.'

Foulis and Baby did the work proper. I 'assisted'. It was out of kindness that they allowed me to assist. Their work constituted digging new gutters, re-damming gutters which had gone out of shape, digging new reservoirs. My work, on the other hand, due to a shortage of shovels, consisted of hoeing patches of short bush or clearing the grates of twigs and leaves. I would do this in fair conscience for a while, and then accept that I was not actually needed. I would return to perform 'bitch duties' as Baby called them: washing wares, filling buckets of water, collecting firewood, chopping onion and garlic, making bowls of lemon juice. I would wash my clothes in the creek and bathe where it stilled briefly into a round pool the colour of lava. I would read in the hammock. I would watch dragger-ants carry off whole lemon rinds upon their backs like a trail of palanquin bearers. It would occur to me that I ought to be doing something more responsible with myself and my time, but I couldn't see what. We weren't like the ants. They had collective insight and collective force. Man was doomed to be subservient to his personality.

One day I thought to fish. I caught worms and, ignoring the advice that it was spawning season, stood at various parts of the creek with a stick and a line. Naturally I caught nothing. I did bring back in a bucket half a dozen tiny things with striped sides – yarrau I was told. I kept them in the veranda to watch them grow. We threw them bits of things to eat. But they cannibalised each other instead. After a day three of the six remained; and some hours later just the lone supremo. There were traces of blood in the water, and little stray rotting fragments of fish. It was sick. I released the supremo back into a pond, wondering if he had felt triumph or shame at swimming over those corpses, if we'd made this of him, or he had himself.

By early afternoon the backdam labour was done. Working in the water you needed to know when to stop, for you could catch chills and ruin your joints. On the way back Baby and Foulis would stop at the creek and after the afternoon rain had intervened in the drying of washed clothes we would walk about the freshened earth for a while. Sometimes we would shoot arrows at tins with a bow Foulis had made or kick about a deflated football. We'd find a spot and gyaff. The talk was scattered. Short musings might fill easy silences. 'When I meet the big man I got plenty question for he.' 'The Bible say nothin about marriage, it only say go forth and multiply.' Baby might tell of sexual exploits, claim to have a dozen childmothers – 'an dah is only the ones I know of'. They might list for me the synonyms for genitals. The feminine tended to be from the animal kingdom – cat, fish, pork – and the masculine from the elements – wood, iron, steel – though in the Caribbean any noun with the correct inflection could do the job. I might do my India routine, its numbers, its languages and so on, to reactions of 'Tha'is one mix-up place, bai.' They had heard, but did not believe that Indian nationals used their fingers to clean their battyhole. I assured them it was true. 'You too?' 'Yes.' 'O skunt, Gooroo, me nah shake you hand ever again.'

While they remarked often about freedom from the seven-to-four work routine of townpeople, I could not help but think how much more discipline this life needed. You had to be on top of all things at all times. Every task had to be done oneself, every fire, every meal to be made. You could lie dying as Labba had and have nowhere to go and nobody to call. You needed to know every trick, lime for malaria, mustard for cramps, this leaf for arthritis, that bark for fever. You needed to remember to upturn hammocks for snakes and longboots for scorpions.

Diamond stories were popular. Foulis told of the largest stone he'd found. When he went to the settlement, there was a Brazilian about to whom he sold it for 600,000 Guyanese. Afterwards he learnt that the man, after polishing and cutting, had sold it for 2.5 million. It vexed him bad. He'd never felt like such a fool in his life. He done all the work and somebody else take the benefit.

Of Foulis more than anyone else I'd encountered in the bush, I felt he was here because it was the only place he could be. He did not go to Menzies Landing unless he had to. He'd taken a Patamona wife at Chenapau, further upriver, and that is where he would normally return. He was a tranquil man, and in some way unmovable. The only times I saw him animated was when he spoke of diamond. His eyes would gleam, and he might say, with a coyness betrayed by his thick voice, 'Yes, man, I like diamond bad, yes.'

As usual, Baby would take over. 'The way a diamond wink at you, no gal could wink at you like so.' He felt less than warmly towards gold. 'It have 338 documented ways of pilferin gold, but there is always more ways. Not even obeah could explain how gold disappear. I know two bannas disputin over twelve ounce of gold. They take the t'ing to the police to split it in two. The policer do the division in front of them face. When they gone back home, them two part only adding to eleven ounce. Gold wicked prapa, bai.'

In the bush everything could be wicked, everything left to chance. Foulis showed us a pile of gravel in a dry creek he'd worked earlier. He was still to sieve it for diamond. Pork-knockers sometimes left it like this. It was an act of unfathomable faith, or perhaps the exact opposite, of extreme philosophy, that the rain which brings can take. Foulis had already suffered once for this, gravel washed away in a late-night torrent. It hadn't upset him so much, not like the Brazilian who bought his diamond. No, that was different, that man made a fool of him. He pointed with the pork-knocker's twinkle to the gravel. 'Yes, me sure there's a nice surprise in there, yes.'

ONE morning, maybe ten days in, it emerged that our supplies were all but finished. At once there was an anticipation, for it meant it was collection time.

In the backdam Baby and Foulis sifted through the gravel they had accumulated. For hours they jigged through the mound expertly, sieves half submerged in water. Diamond being heaviest gravitated to the centre of the concave as they made frisky rotations. They say the glitter of a diamond in water is unmistakable, that you can take something for a diamond but never ever a diamond for something else. I found that I could and with ease. I did not exactly expect the Kohinoor, but these nondescript flakes were a puzzling anticlimax.

In the afternoon we returned with the haul.

Foulis brought over his equipment, an old-fashioned pair of magnifying spectacles that strapped around the head and a miniature set of scales with pellets for weights.

We sat on the rickety wooden platform in the back room. The stones were laid out on a piece of paper. They were sad and crusty, like fragments of broken glass, some mildly white like chipped plaster. If I found them in my house I'd throw them away. But it was my eye which was untrained: when a good one was held up against the light it sparkled with that particular fragile hardness. Symmetry was elusive in all but a few pieces, and symmetry was the thing, not only because symmetry in itself is beautiful, but because of how it played with the light.

They began to grade the stones, the glasses and baby scales giving an air of mock gravity to proceedings. They organised them first by weight, then shape and clarity. The majority of the stones were ten points or less – a point is a hundredth of a carat. The heaviest was forty points, less than quarter of a fingernail but a boulder in that pile of splinter. It was long, hexagonal, mildly yellowing. It might require cleaning with acid. It might fetch up to twenty grand at the Siddique shop, twice that in town.

There were seventy-four stones in all, amounting to about six hundred points. They did the division, with a proportional mix of stones, though, of course, Foulis retained the forty-pointer.

On the coast Baby estimated his share might fetch fifty or sixty grand, that is 250 to 300 American dollars. Up to a third could go into travelling back. And then, it depended. A careful man might make it last a month or more. Another might splurge it in an afternoon of high gamble or an evening of Brazzo strippers.

'You make what you make so when you dead you can tell the big man you enjai you life,' Baby said with abandon.

'Yes . . . yes,' Foulis responded, tentatively agreeing.

There was a brief, hectic discussion about jewellers in Georgetown, on the East Coast, on East Bank, which man t'ief, which man skunt, which man tight-fist, which man stupid, most names put forward by Baby and then, with fist bumps all round, the session ended.

We sat in a cloud of satisfaction.

Baby lit herb and leaned back against the wall by the window with a loose smile. It was a still, thick day.

Foulis tipped his stones off the paper into a hard plastic case, the kiddy.

'Don't leff me own on the paper, she gon blow off,' Baby said. 'Leff it on the scales.'

'No, man, she nah blow. Fold up the paper pon she.'

Baby took a deep drag and looked out the window, towards the lovely top of the Congo pump. He passed me the joint.

Foulis collapsed the scales, picked up his magnifier and his kiddy, and got up to leave. And at that moment, as he stood up, I could not tell if it was the disturbance caused by his movement or a puff of wind that blew, but the sheet on which lay Baby's tinsely stones fluttered off the platform and flew to the floor. It ran away, tumbling, to the far wall. The specks of diamond scattered on the floor, now rolling to a standstill, now urged on again, and as they encountered the thick gaps between the floorboards they fell in, casual as dandruff.

All of us leapt down towards the fallen crumbs. It took less than a moment to tell that, basically, they were gone.

Thereafter it was a series of heartbreaks.

Baby turned, first, violent, with an angry cry of 'fockin pusshole' running out to the front veranda and returning with a cutlass, then chasing Foulis, who, having spotted the madness which had claimed his eyes, had bolted out the back door into the bush. Baby gave chase after Foulis and I gave chase after Baby. It was primal sprinting. They ran hot, jumping over bushes and ditches. They veered off the clearing and into the low bush. The gap between us increased, till I could see only quivering leaves and trampled grass and disturbed soil in their wake.

When I caught up with them, Baby was towered over Foulis with the cutlass, poised for the kill. And then he flung it down, somewhat dramatically, so that it stuck into the mud maybe five or six inches from Foulis's head. He muttered something, I cannot be sure what.

Foulis was breathing hard. He lay on his side. His eyes were shut. His legs were curled foetally. One hand covered the top of his head. The other hand clutched a tuft of weed, which he had already uprooted. His nostrils dilated and contracted rapidly, then slower and slower. At last he opened his eyes with a suddenness that suggested that he had willed himself to the task.

Nobody said anything.

Baby turned away.

Foulis straightened himself.

I pulled the cutlass out of the earth and held it feebly by my side.

After a minute or so Baby turned to face Foulis.

'We gah find what we could find.'

We returned to the shack in a silence that for the first time in the forest felt like an absence rather than a presence.

WE COMBED the floor carefully. Two of Baby's stones were recovered; two of the smallest. The rest were beneath the shack.

It was getting to evening, and though bright at the moment, darkness would arrive swiftly. There was perhaps an hour of good light left.

They tried to bash out the floorboards to climb down. The beams below creaked and sagged so precariously that it was feared the entire construction might collapse. That would not only destroy the shack, but also ruin any chances of recovering the stones. The idea was abandoned. Instead they decided to work the filth below like gravel sometimes is in mines.

They sliced off the tops of plastic bottles to give them wide mouths. They crawled below the house. It wasn't easy to get under: it was raised off the earth by a foot and a half, if that. Beneath was pure squelch: rot, clumps of weed, bits of wood, nails, tadpoles, kakabelly fish. There were spiders and scorpions. They hoped there would be no vipers and took the meagre precaution of flashing a torch.

They crept in flat on their stomachs, barely squeezing through, trying to keep their mouth and nose and eyes out of the sick filth. I received the plastic bottles from them, emptied them into a bucket, wet muck with soil and pebbles, vegetation and darting living things, and passed the bottles back to them. The relay continued till the bucket was filled.

They crawled out. The bucket was emptied out on a sieve in batches, and Baby jigged it in the vat of rain water. Momentarily the filth would be awash with hope, which flushed out as the water drained away. There was simply too much of all kinds of filth. It is futilities that most obsess man. The entire process was repeated again: the crawl, the filling of the bottles, the relay, the sieving. At the third bucket, with the light dying, Foulis spotted a viper at the edge of the shack.

It was finished.

The exercise was exhausting for its uselessness; but exhaustion did not bring its exhausted relief. Quite the opposite. The tension had been mounting rather than dissipating. Everybody wanted to be away, by themselves, or with different people. I felt my presence was resented; from Baby there was a distance that verged on hostility. And I myself saw him in a very different light.

Brusquely, briefly, they discussed the possibility of starting over in the morning. It was a stupid idea. The likelihood of retrieving a dozen pinheads from the debris was negligible. Our supplies were finished. Forget any of that. A man had almost murdered another. No, this was done.

A resolution was needed. Without looking him in the eye, Foulis handed Baby five or six stones from his box, saying, firmly, cautiously, 'Leff here tomorrow.' I thought it was a well-judged gesture, I could not tell whether from guilt, magnanimity, pity, fear, or all. It was sheer dignity. Baby accepted the stones with the air of a man who believed he was being scamped.

And with that Foulis, he was a slender man, he retreated slenderly to his shack.

THERE was a light drizzle as twilight fell. The wonder of the water felt a nuisance. Mud got on to one's ankles and toes, dried there slowly, attracting insects. On the line the clothes were damp again. The sandflies, which came out for a hungry hour at dusk, had an aggressive session. Despite my faithful applications of Shoo, there were clayey mounds on my arms and legs.

We had our first meal since breakfast, and at different times. The rice was lumpy and had to be treated like balls, rolled in a long-water potato curry.

I got into the hammock earlier than usual. I could not fall asleep; and afterwards when Baby climbed into his on the other side of the partition I sensed he couldn't either. When a man shifted in the hammock the beams creaked – when a man shifts rather than sways in a hammock he cannot really be asleep. That night was long and creaky.

It occurred to me that I did not actually know him – not in the ordinary way. I played events over and over in my head. With a little distance now, things seemed obvious. Foulis had done nothing wrong. He'd asked Baby to be careful with his stones – he hadn't touched them. Even the spillage could not properly be seen to be his error. It had simply happened. Baby had come here a near stranger, a pardner of a pardner, and Foulis had allowed him to work on his site. For this he almost had his head split open by a cutlass.

Yet when I considered things from Baby's point of view, it seemed surprisingly compelling. He'd worked hard. Foulis might indeed have placed the stones on the scales as Baby had requested. Of course, his stones were his responsibility. At that moment he was swimming in common complacency. Perhaps the confrontation was really his confrontation with the complacency. I tried to give him benefit of the doubt. It had simply been a lapse of sense. And yet – the terror of a man quivering for his life.

It was a rainless night, cool and welcoming. I felt to go for a walk. Baby did, too, for I heard him get up and leave through the back door. I thought of joining him, but I let it drop. I lay in the hammock, creaked myself to sleep.

THE MORNING broke orange and fresh. Every day with my first step into the veranda I would be struck by how busy the vegetation was around the shacks. One went to bed thinking it was a clearing, and woke to lush bush, patches of Spanish nettles, a noni tree renowned for its medicinal properties and used by Labba during his convalescence, a few ité palm, the most distinctive of all palms, with its lovely round fronds, though I was told this was not supposed to be ité territory.

For breakfast we ate the cane and pineapple that remained.

Foulis cooked his pot in his back veranda. We nodded at each other but said nothing. Afterwards, when I went over to say goodbye and thank you, he wasn't there.

It was a pleasant, peaceable day of lengthy bird tweets, gently humid, a day for picnic, playing, snoozing. We set out on the half-hour walk to the boat. The trail was much drier now; my shoe did not once sink.

The paddles and the polin were intact in the tree trunk, but there was no sign of the boat. Eventually it was located. It had foundered in the dropping water. Baby threw a rope over a branch to fashion a pulley. We spent half an hour tugging it out.

We spent another forty-five minutes bailing out water. We were drenched.

As Baby was about to push off he stopped. He jumped off the boat with a hasty 'Jus now', the Guyanese for any length of time. I waited in the boat. I thought he'd gone off to shed a tear before the journey. Persuaded by the good sense of this measure, I too decided to piss.

I climbed out and I saw him through vines and tendrils – I saw him pull out a little knot of cloth from his crotch and untie it. He heard me coming and whirled around. I had alarmed him. As I approached him he maintained his poise, emptying the contents of the open cloth into a small plastic cylinder without accident. Diamond! Many more than the six or seven stones he had. He placed the cylinder in his bag and walked back towards the boat.

I pissed. My instinctive reaction had been of excitement, as if a cruel twist of fate had been ironed out. But now I felt involuntarily disturbed; then confused.

We got into the boat. We sailed downstream like driftwood. It was the greatest luxury. The river had fallen drastically. The trees now visibly rooted in earth were robbed of their earlier mystique. You could see water marks on the trunks.

I sifted through my confusion. The slow rush of thoughts and images ended each time with Baby leaving the back door at night. Did he take them off Foulis? But how? Foulis would have guarded them on his body, surely. Perhaps Foulis had given him some more in the morning, before I'd risen. But why? At any rate, it did not square with Baby's reaction when I stumbled on him.

There was only one other possibility. It seemed too far-fetched. Yet the more I thought of it, the more it made sense.

Our journey breezed by. What had taken us four hours against the current with supplies was done in an hour. And I was shocked when, after the last big bend before the settlement, we pulled into a stelling. I had no idea there had been one: it had been wholly submerged. It was one of those little mind-images that had been misshapen without reason. There used to be a slide in the playground of my childhood school; when I visited years later, it had moved to a different position. It had upset me for days.

Baby tethered the boat.

As we were about to get off, I asked: 'You worked his old pile of gravel?'

'Leff it, bai.'

'O fuck, man. You did.'

'Rest yourself, bai,' he said, assertively now.

He added sharply, making eye contact, 'Sorry fuh maga dog, maga dog turn around bite you.'

I knew the saying, because I knew the song good and I knew Tosh good. Maga dog. Maga: thin. Sorry for maga dog, maga dog turn around bite you. Bite the hand that feeds you. I hadn't expected the stinging self-assessment.

The settlement was quiet. Nasty wasn't around. Neither was Dr Red. Roots and his wife had gone across the river for a few days to tend their farm. There were a couple of people liming beneath the mango tree.

I slept through the afternoon.

In the evening I took a last walk on the plateau, a last sit-down before Kaieteur, thinned, snipped from the sides.

At night I heard all the versions of Maga Dog I had on the pod, the first playful ska which bounced to the Skatalite harmonies of Simmer Down to the later biting reggaes, each more biting. I heard its offspring, Skanky Dog, Maingy Dog, Fat Dog, Boney Dog; their cousins, Dog Teeth, Once Bitten. Perversely I felt a thrill in mining the meaning first hand, a true rising thrill. I felt so thrilled that I felt debased. And it occurred to me that Baby had not made a self-assessment at all. He believed that Foulis and not he was the maga dog.

THE FOLLOWING morning, waiting in the benab for the plane, I felt terribly removed from everything. There were four of us. Baby was bringing down the roof with his tales. Labba and the ranger's son were doubling up, slamming the benches with their palms. The current one was about a thick red t'ing he ketch.

I don't know, I watched him with idle curiosity, like he was television.

Soon light-eyed Siddique arrived with a bag on his back. He was looking for a passage to town to sell diamond, among them perhaps Foulis's. There was no guarantee of either of us getting a flight. A plane may not come at all. If there was one, there may or may not be a free seat to cut a deal with the pilot.

We waited. Baby talked of a gal who could take a whole fist inside she. Labba fixed the handle of a cutlass. The ranger's son pulled dance moves. Siddique drank cola.

Eventually one heard the distant mechanical whirring of an Islander. We watched it make a slow landing. White folk stepped out of the craft, each carrying a bottle of water and a camera. They were followed by the guide. We counted them: there was place for one. This worried me. Though I had been waiting before him, Siddique was sure to hustle me if we both got to the pilot. I did not want to stay another day. Before either of us could move I proposed we toss a coin. The suggestion was cheered on. Bemused, Siddique agreed. I won; I knew I would. It led to much merriment. Labba said 'man bright' over and over. They gave me high fives, laughed at Siddique. He concealed his resentment by sipping cola.

The tourists came into the benab. They were Americans, spoke loudly. They set off for their guided walk, leaving behind a young, desperately ill blonde. He lay sideways on a bench and groaned profusely. Sometimes his head fell over the side as if severed.

'They come out here but they en't able,' Labba pointed to him with derision. 'En't able at aal.'

For the benefit of the ill blonde the walk was wrapped up fast. Time to leave.

Baby came out to the cratered airstrip to see me off.

'So you enjai youself, soldier?'

'Yeah.'

He said he'd beat about here and there for a while. We talked of perhaps catching up in town, though we both knew. We parted with a fist touch.

'Walk good, Gooroo.'

'Walk good. And thanks, right.'

The Islander worked itself into a toy fury. We bumped along the tarmac and made a strenuous ascent. I looked down at the airstrip, the benab on the tepui, diagonal Baby, with an arm raised.

The pilot regaled everyone by circling the fall. It was the most spectacular view yet. The river was a simple stroke of brown, so that one could be deceived into thinking it was stationary, and as we rose higher, so too the great white spill. We left it all behind. And now there was only forest. The extensive carpet was like so much pubic hair, mile upon mile of it, and from up here and now in my current state of mind, too monotonous. The sun hit me straight in the temple. Maga Dog played in my head – riddim. The sick American groaned loud. He could be heard over the engine. Other Americans pointed and clicked. 'I'm *so* gonna upload these.'

I was sat at the back with Tony the guide. Basdeo Kumar was his right name. He loved India, would like to walk there sometime, check out the mothership. His grandfather was a pandit, he had repatriated to India. But the village hadn't accepted him. He had returned to Guyana. All that journey just to come back. I felt he looked it and asked him if he was mixed: it was polite conversation in Guyana. I hurt him. 'Pure, man,' he said defensively. 'Pure all the way.' He took off his cap, ran his hand over his very short hair, buzzed down to the scalp. He pulled the strands up to their exerted millimetres, inviting me to touch. 'Watch man, straight. It straight.'

7

BABY was a black man, black going to red – not red enough for red, but red enough for his childhood call name Cookup: a bit of this and a bit of that. He had shed the name quick. As he grew older his skin, his whole face, turned more like a blackman, no longer showing a strain of 'every blasted thing that ever step into Guyana'. This was the power of black, he said in a way that was half pride, half boast. In America pardners with much lighter skin than his, and even clear skin like mine, they could get called blackman. 'Drop a lil single drop of black in any colour, see how much the colour turn black. Anytime you got a little black in you, you is a blackman. Eh he. That is the power of black.'

He had short hair, browning and greying in parts, in which he made a clean two-inch slit for a parting. On his face he kept an impeccably slim French beard – he could use any kind of knife to maintain it, did not even need a mirror. It was a chubby, button-eyed face: a baby face, though not by any means a young face. I took it to be the genesis of Baby. It seemed so obvious that I never asked. And anyhow they called him by so many names, I thought anything goes.

Of his childhood it was a different story each time. Once he told me he 'never had an ole bai, neither an ole lady'. He was left at the hospital gate a few weeks old. A nurse took him in, left him to her sister who worked at Parika stelling. He grew up hustling with her on the stelling, selling any little thing that might be sold, a training for life. 'I learn fuh *unstand* people, y'unstan?' One day he got a gig going up the Essequibo with a dredge party.

Another time he told me that he grew up in Albouystown in something like a range yard, with eight siblings, and he was the smartest of them all, and they all dead out because they were not so smart. One of them had taken him into the interior and trained him as a pork-knocker.

Ask him which of these was true and he'd reply, 'How you mean, Gooroo, all two is true.'

I knew this much about Baby. Also that he was a 'Nonpractising Fundamentalist Eighth Day Adventurist'.

Of me he knew less.

Our entire knockabout adventure was born of a kind of bravado. Perhaps we saw something in each other that we recognised; but it was bravado that propelled us. After being twice scamped I went looking for him in that same street by the big market. I found him sitting by a barrow of cherries, pretending to sell. 'Come nuh, sweetheart, lemme be the godfather,' he called out to a pregnant girl as she walked by. 'I only givin out stepfather,' she winked back. He dragged you involuntarily into that sort of play. I told him that I'd caught up with Magistrate Van Cooten after all. He remembered the case: he thought the crime vicious but had good words for the conduct of the criminal. Baby kept responding with 'eh he', looking interested and downpressed, staring into the cherries. Finally, he asked, 'So the magistrate tell yuh this at Le Repentir cemetery or Bourda cemetery?'

We talked old reggae again. Reggae was the key for reggae is a brotherhood. Once you've imbibed the upstroke of ska, the zen of bass, the roots of reggae, repetitions like body pulse, words like fire, like ice, it becomes a kind of possession – music like a gravity, as Burning Spear said. For a while you turn tone-deaf to everything else. The symmetries and the concerns of other music, they feel unenlightened to the genius of this simplicity. So our understanding was at this crucial level.

I asked him about pork-knocking and the interior, and he told me stories. I said he should let me know when he's going in next. Sure, he said. Let's go soon, I said. Alright pardner, why not catch me back here two days, he said by way of putting it off. My paperwork was finished, I had itchy feet. I proposed we buy supplies the next morning and leave. This was bravado. He didn't expect it would happen. It did.

My only condition was that we go overland – it was cheaper to fly. I would pick up the fare and the supplies. In this, of course, he had a subsidised trip and I have no doubt he scamped me a little here, a little there. Yet, if anything, I was the more dependent. The expertise was all his. On the river I had been an encumbrance, and perhaps elsewhere too. He'd taken me deep into the heart of something. In sum, I felt, I probably owed him. Under the umbrella of bravado it was difficult to see the truth of things.

I reflected on the Foulis affair in many ways. It occurred to me that had there been no near-murder I would have looked at things differently. A plain theft – it was possible to bathe the incident in a scampish light.

'. . . So Baby vex now after the man hand he a couple of piece of fine-fine stone like sand. So he gone now in the middle of the night to the man gravel, flick on he tarch, jam up the tarch by he neck, howler monkey making noise, all kind of jumbie floating about but Baby focus! Is diamond he t'iefin in moonlight! . . .'

It didn't feel that way, though. The raised cutlass, the trembling man beneath, it had heightened one's sense of judgement. Yet the first was an act of instant madness, the second a calculated deceit and perhaps the more depraved.

When I played him back in my mind, which was often and in a variety of moods, the reel finished at the finish, with him waving diagonally on the tepui, distorted and shameless, and over the end credits Tony the guide demonstrating his hair over the maga dog riddim in the laser blaze of the parallel sun.

I RETURNED to Kitty exhausted. I could not shake off the pall of lingering inspection, introspection that had enveloped me. My motion had ceased. To stop is to sink. Yet I did not feel sunk so much as afloat, which with its attendant lack of drama was the more frustrating.

Physically I felt drained. Cooking and washing and all the things of everyday living felt like too much to do. Rather than recovering vigour I felt more depleted with the passing days. Effort made me vomit.

It took me a week to find out that I had a low-grade dengue fever. Its chief effect was listlessness. The temperature subsided in some days, but the passivity remained. I felt bloodless. There was nothing to do, I was told, but rest, hydrate, pop pills and wait for my mosquito-ravaged platelets to regenerate.

The illness brought on a period of emptiness I hadn't felt since ma and papa died. They were good, decent people, rooted in their efforts, never taking the car when a bus could do, never a bus when they could walk. Ma had died from infirmity, and papa afterwards from sadness really. My childhood memories of sickness were glorious – skipped school, whiled-away pampered days. Ever since ma I associated sickness with the weight of a sad house, a strange, unregistering kind of grief lost in the suffocation of relatives.

It is not nice to be sick alone. I wished I could sleep through the period. I didn't call home. I dropped a short jaunty email to my three older siblings telling them of the wonderful trip into the rainforest and a plan to approach *National Geographic* with a feature. 'Hopefully they will say yes and you can show it to the relatives when they come home! Love.' I didn't want to worry them with the illness. And to speak it would have been admission of a misjudgement. I didn't want to give them that.

For a fortnight I lived on Gatorade, coconut water, pineapple, French cashew, sapodilla – *chikoo* – and tinned Van Camp's Pork and Beans, bought from the appropriately named Survival supermarket. The beans I ate with sweet tennis rolls, which with butter could be a little like Bombay's bun maska. There was one especially trying aspect to this period. Little crappos would find their way into the house. I was tormented by them. When in panic I feared they, like fluttering pigeons, were liable to do anything. I had seen Guyanese swoop them up like a fallen peanut and fling them out the window. I couldn't bring myself to it. If they were on the floor, I had a technique worked out for them. I covered them with a bucket and dragged them across to the door. But more often they were wont to get into the sink. I spent hours in distress, staring at them, cursing them. Tapping around them with a stick would worsen the situation: they would hop about among the washed utensils.

One day I willed myself to grab the thing. It took a great deal of psyching myself, and then with my hand encased in a polythene bag. *He's small*, I told myself, *he's small*. After pulling out a dozen times, I snatched it. I felt it pulse in my hand as I ran towards the back door and let go of it. It caught the grille on the way out, fizzed across the air, rotating like a wild Ferris, and crashed into the water tank below the whitey tree. It stayed still a few seconds, and then I saw it hop away. I knew I had damaged it. I felt a dishonour I cannot explain.

In a few weeks my energies began to restore. I became acquainted with the new developments in the building. Kwesi Braithwaite, fake diamond on his ear, Kangol on his head, had recently taken to booming loud RnB (Beyonce, Ne-Yo, T-Pain, I'm 'n Luv (Wit a Stripper)). The nuisance was one thing. The practical implication was for the power bill that was on a single meter shared by the six tenements using a formula. The formula was a mathematical miracle. I understood it had led to uprisings in the past, and though nobody understood how it worked, they always returned to it. The formula could not be changed to accommodate the 'laalessness of one body or two body'. And some days later, Rabindranauth Latchman from Latchman's Hardware came to bust Kwesi tail for t'iefin a lead from his shop.

Otherwise it seemed like life, old life. And two months of life had never felt older to me. On the weekend Hassa still brought home a set of black whiskery hassar in a bucket from a trench by the national park, cheerily thumped them dead on their heads with the back of his knife and curried them, dousing the building in flavour. The cashiers were still busty. Uncle Lance could still be spotted on the bench studying, say, a booklet on Duncan's Signals, or a Jehovah's Witness report on world population.

I didn't lime much with Lancy and friends. I spent time in the sweet breeze discovered at the back of the house, at the top of the back stairs, reading, snoozing, watching the yard over the tin. It was a spare lot with high grass at the edges and a small neat house on stilts in a corner. The yard held just the single tree, a great breadfruit tree with luminous leaves which pointed and curled. In a shed, bigger than the house, a braided welder worked. He worked alone to the radio, at whichever hour of the morning or night he liked, and from afar it felt that he was at one with his work. Beside the simplicity of his self-made shack, under the ornamental majesty of the breadfruit tree, to watch him spend his days, building, mending, was a solace.

The exact moment of recovery was when I inexpertly pierced the top of a coconut. I had found the tenderest spot. The knife went straight through. It had been in the fridge. The chilled water gushed into my face, my eyes, like fizz from a soda bottle. I was stunned. Then I laughed. I hadn't felt that alive in a long time.

Outside, Georgetown shimmered in the heat in between the rains. In the months which followed I began to tramp about again, in town, and up and down the coast. Often I found myself in the stray countryside, hosted by generous acquaintances, some freshly made, some from the cricket tour, and some entire strangers, for I had walked all the way from India.

The mood was very different now. One escapes one's life, for however long, seeking adventure – I think of the Hindi word *dheel*. This is what kite-flyers in Bombay shouted when they wanted the spooler to let loose the thread. I could not fly a kite, as unnavigable to me as chopsticks, but I liked giving dheel, and I liked very much the thought of dheel. So one escapes one's life seeking adventure, and with enough dheel and some luck, that happens. But the thread is anchored. You can only go so far. The impulse must change. Instead of adventure one seeks understanding. It comes with a heaviness. The only way to be exempt is to resolutely not ponder, but I was given to pondering.

It struck me forcefully there wasn't much to do. The loneliness of acknowledging this can be difficult. I began to walk less, take the bus more. In sun or rain it was the more practical thing to do, but I know I did it to counter loneliness. I liked the minibuses. I liked how there were no stops. You could flag one down where you wanted and you got off where you wanted, bellowing a specific instruction above the roar of music: 'over the bridge' or 'when you turn' or 'corner', or with absolute precision, 'by the blue rubbish bin'. There was a packed, peopled sexuality to the bus. They played the vulgarest soca and duttiest dancehall. Nasty stuff. Sweat, smells, sounds, hair, skirts, fingernails, tapping feet, there was a hot tropical charge to it.

But where to go? A stop here, a stop there, a meal here, a conversation there, humid lethargy, slow ruin. And I was liable to absorb the slow ruin. For instance, at that hallmark of the tropical colony, the botanical gardens. The famed old collection had dwindled and now there were mainly unlabelled palm. No brass band played on Sundays anymore, the old timers rued. In the abutting zoo, the lioness appeared eager to be put out of her misery. The birds were gorgeous, fluorescent toucans and macaws, the absurdly large harpy eagles who clawed at chunks of meat the size of a human face, but hardly anybody came to look at them.

Loneliness it was that led me to two or three little affairs so full of tacky fraudulence that I escaped them before they could develop. Never mind.

I found nourishment in the shaded cool of the national library. Georgetown was where a bookshop was a stationery shop, and of the three actual bookshops, one was about to shut down. The library too was in decline, you could tell by the paucity of new books. People tended to use it for siestas. Sun-sapped souls would come in at lunch hour, put down a stack of magazines by the foot of the chair and sleep. I myself fell into a few good ones there. It was the most peaceful spot in town, a small table with four low, steeply reclined chairs set around it. Beside this was a beautiful big jalousie door and beyond that a lush yard in which the serrated shadows of plantain and banana leaves swayed like passing thoughts, and sometimes if it rained the drops pinged in through the slats. One remembers little things about places. And of the library I remember the hand-me-down colonial bureaucratic militancy with which a membership query could be entertained only on a Tuesday or a Thursday morning – people were not exactly ramming down the door to get in – though a question on any other matter was permitted; I remember how immaculately one of the ladies at the counter balanced her pregnancy against her stilettos; I remember the disgruntled vibe of the ageing security guard at the gate with the baton at her waist, how, though she made as if to be further disgruntled, only the clamour of schoolchildren at 3.30 could ever revive her.

I remember, gratefully, the reading. In particular from the too-small *Caribbeana* section which wrenched me outwards to a necessary distance from the world I had flung myself into headlong with no preparation. Here came comprehension.

You could encounter entertaining comments in the books. Naipaul was a favourite target. His *Finding the Centre* bore the pencil dismissal on the title page: 'This man has a Psychosis. Its name is Self loathing.' Puzzlement at one of the denser Wilson Harrises was expressed with a succinct, 'What the man write?' The single Roy Heath was untouched.

Once I found a curious paean to the Dutch civilising mission. It was a four-page fine-print pamphlet, organised in sections, composed by an apparent descendant. It extolled the courage of the pioneers – 'who risked life and limb for the sake of the generations to come'. It lamented the passing of the Dutch Reformed Church – 'which had given the people moral organisation for prosperity'. It praised the Dutch efforts in building Georgetown which, though established by the French in their brief period of ascendancy as Longchamps, went for a while by the name of Stabroek, for the Lord of Stabroek, chief of the Dutch West India Company. The enterprise of the Dutch West India Company itself was honoured with its own sub-section. Here the first three words had been struck out by a blotted, once garish, purple nib. They had been replaced by a single word. SLY. In the margin a sentence had been started, *they think like they care* – and abandoned there due to excessive blotting.

Coming out from the shade and knowledge of the library back into the sensory streets, or vice versa, was a source of anxiety for me, reconciling the two. To pass time I sometimes slipped into the perspiring Magistrate's Court where Baby had once fooled me. In the papers one read about murders between brothers, between couples, over a game of dominoes, a stray glance. There were all manner of sensational cases, gruesome ones, murders by hot oil or broken bottles. The matters I walked in on were usually trivial, somebody not paying their childmother for upkeep, a catfight between ladies resulting in a burnt forearm for one, fowl stolen from a neighbour's yard. Surreal was the juxtaposition of these Guyanese transgressions and the Guyanese talk of the transgressors ('she ah lie like a dog, is *she* who jook me fust': the forearm-burner) against the taught British manner of the court. The lawyers, some thin and greasy, some with large ears who spoke beautifully, all of them in Guyana carrying the reputation of failed doctors, they said things like 'of course, your worship, of course'. And your worship herself used phrases such as 'very well, then', and might call upon somebody with the words, 'Mr Nazeer Abeed Ally, on the night of January 21, 2006, at the southern end of East Street, Alberttown, a muskmelon projected by you damaged the windshield of a white-colour Nissan, vehicle licence plate PJJ 2121, belonging to one Mr Vincent Totaram. How do you plead?' It was a play, a movie set.

Now and then I stopped at a rumshop and scrap metal shop on Robb Street. Joshua's it was called, though Joshua Rahamatullah himself was dead. I would be spoilt with sweets by the ladies who ran it. Mittai and parsad, generic terms in India which here referred to specific items, and gulgulas, which in India I knew as gulab jamun, and stupendously fatty Fat Tops, which I didn't know from anywhere – cornmeal and coconut milk and raisin, vanilla-sweetened and baked. It was uncertain times at Joshua's. The government was talking of banning scrap metal exports. People were thieving metal all over the place, from cables in the power company yard, from iron punts in the sugar estates. Citizens were getting electrocuted because the earthing systems from electricity poles had been stolen. Outlawing the business was no solution, felt the Joshua's folk. It was like banning jewellery cause people t'iefin gold. All the government had to do was monitor the utilities because the trafficking was done from within. We would drink to scrap metal. And then I would be off, alone again.

I watched the amazing houses of Georgetown, and sometimes their mere memories, burnt-down patches, a shock of grass overcoming cinder and charred beams. Since I'd come here last I could tell how many more concrete homes had been built, with a peculiar front of painted convex cement brick like a cheap weave. The wooden houses were each an individual creation, some as grand and white and tiered as a wedding cake, some rotten and ruminating. The living ones, their white old timbers gleamed and their forest green zincs glinted. They had unexpected gables and sometimes little towers, they had series of Demerara shutters that could be propped up, intricate latticework on bargeboards, papery walls which transmitted every whispering breath. It's the dead ones I was drawn to most. The ones which leaned and sagged, whose wood had lost every colour, where vines crept round pipes and spurted out of windows, whose doors had long lost the strength to open let alone guard. Whole states of being were in their single image. In this they were like the finest reggae, which could lay proverb upon bass upon melody and catch the mood, the meaning of so much in a single music frame.

Sometimes in the evenings I went running on the seawall, not unlike Bombay's Marine Drive, and one always could find Indian nationals on their Indian-national walks. This tended to depress me. I caught snatches of their conversations as I went by, beset with the superior sorrow of being here.

I did briefly get friendly with a Sindhi shopowner, a dandyish, articulate supremacist by the name of Mr Mansukhani. He had begun his career by going to Ethiopia and starting a successful variety shop there. Then in a stroke of bad luck the famines had come. He sought opportunity in other parts of the world. He arrived in Guyana in the late eighties when the time was right. The dictator had died. Imports were allowed again. Anything you put up in a shop people were desperate to buy. And so he had stayed. He preferred Ethiopia. 'They are not like other Africans. The people are not bad-looking, you'll be surprised, fine noses, good complexion. The blacks in the Americas, they've become really lazy. At least in Africa they're getting fucked over.' And the East Indians? 'Mutated Biharis, imagine that.' He doubted if Guyana ought to be a country. 'Coolies and slaves celebrating getting buggered.' Whenever possible, he'd head out to the islands, for, from Montego Bay to Martinique, the community of Sindhi traders was everywhere, and between his travels and my gallivants in the country, we later never met. We'd run out of things to say anyhow.

Inescapable sadness befell Georgetown at night. There were hardly any streetlights. Crime, the fear of crime, the population in steady exodus, conspired to make a ghost after sundown. It brought with it brittleness, lonesomeness.

One evening I went to the passa-passa, a Jamaican street lime of famed vulgarity raging like fire through the Caribbean. Roused by condemnatory letters from the church, unmindful of the warning that 'it rough out there, real rough', alone in the lonely hot night, I headed down to watch the duttiest dances ever born by the prison which once allegedly held Baby. Werk-en-Rust the ward was called: work and rest, Dutch: another old plantation. Such brutality, such gingerbread names! But I reached too early, woefully early. I was the only person on the block not black. I walked to a melancholy corner bar, with dim fairy lights, where everybody wore a sad gold tooth and everybody well knew there's nothing going down in this town and I scribbled things on a paper napkin with such a rising sadness that the matron at the counter tenderly asked, 'Why you look so, babylove?' An hour later I returned to the vulgar intersection, but it was still too early. Till I departed at half past midnight – after Warren, a one-eyed moocher had mooched off me, I fully aware of the mooching but tolerant of it – there had not been, aside from a drunk moonwalking to inevitable collapse, a single wine-down, a single batty shaken.

Narrate this to a Guyanese and you will be told, 'Of course, they was waiting for you to leave!'

It was on another evening of nothingness, dark and streetlight-free, the dance of fireflies on patches of grass everywhere, that I went to Castellani House, a mansion turned gallery of magnificent white-wooden airiness. I had seen a notice in the paper of their monthly world-classics screening. It was Ray's *Pather Panchali*.

There was a gathering of thirty or forty, almost exclusively expat and white, grabbing at any morsel of culture on offer. I had read the book as part of the school course. I remember having been moved by it, but I had forgotten it. In a beautiful scene of departure a mean-spirited lady reflects, 'If you stay too long in a place you become petty. It has happened to me.' It is a key realisation. It stayed with me. Perhaps that is the easy answer to why anyone leaves; it was maybe why I had left.

But more, the peasant life, the winds and the fields, the palm and fruit trees, the poverty, the slowness of the country, the buffalo ponds and water lilies, the lanterns and wicks, rain and storm, innocence found and lost, it resonated with something I'd been reading. It was Edgar Mittelholzer's *Corentyne Thunder*, scored not from the library, where they didn't stock it, but from da Silva the cobbler's cartful of non-selling second-hands in Kitty Market. The Corentyne was a stretch on the eastern coast of Guyana, between the rivers Berbice and Corentyne; and the peasant life of the film was set in rural Bengal, not far from where had sailed the ships bringing impoverished Indian peasants to the Corentyne – people whose lives were shot with defeat, who knew that the only way was to leave, not to defeat pettiness, but to defeat defeat.

PART TWO

I

YOU leave: what wound do you leave behind?

At this moment in, say, Barabanki, Basti, Buxar, in little villages of dust that dot the vast plains of north India, cyclostyled sheets are arranged in heaps at a roadside stall. A hot dry afternoon, the edges of the sheets occasionally upturned by the hot dry breeze. A tentative young idler appears at the stall. He has come with adventure on his mind, or perhaps out of compulsion, perhaps out of the slow torment of his life. He browses the yellow and white notices, not quite sure how to react to them. One is read out to him. He could become a class IV worker in the big city, a watchman, a peon. He thinks about it, eventually buys a form for five rupees.

He makes the big journey to the city to try his luck. Having reached, and applied, he fails. But the distance travelled has been great, the effort too much, the expense too high. He falls in with a community of migrants from his state, a gang of daily-wage labourers. He works in the sun, sleeps in the cold, fortifies himself for each day's backbreaking miseries with cheap liquor. A few years on he has saved enough to visit the village. The next visit comes after a longer gap, and the one after that longer still. In time he is forgotten. His body unable to combat everyday damage, he dies young. In the village, other youngsters have left or have died, the elders in the family have passed on, and the village is slowly remade. Does anybody remember?

In the Guyanese country – a coastal frill on either side of Georgetown – in the Guyanese country the East Indian and the Indian national look at each other. It seems an innocuous enough exchange. In fact, it is loaded. It is only here, away from town and the interior, and amid the fields of the country that the absurd foreignness and familiarity of the interaction registers.

To the Indian national the image across him is vaguely recognisable: the dark, slightly flat, small-featured face and small-made body of the 'purabi'. The skin is smooth, shining, the mouth mildly open, a visage on the whole enduring, durable.

Then the minor surprises start to accumulate. The East Indian has worn a cap (a fringe peeping out the front), a checked shirt from which the sleeves are ripped, and long grey shorts which were once trousers. The hairstyle, the outfit, it seems incongruous in these surroundings so evocative of peasant India – the smell of Indian food emerging from houses, more men and women just like the purabi, even the cattle herded along with the ancient *hurr, hurr.*

Surprise turns to disorientation when the East Indian peasant speaks up, in English, and disorientation to bewilderment as the dialect kicks in, the accent of the Guyanese country so raw and rasping that comprehension arrives minutes, sometimes months later, with a retrospective piecing of the puzzle.

Equal shock to the East Indian when the Indian national speaks, not in the language of the Indian flims he sees, but an odd, lumbering English. Further, the Indian national does not have a name like a name in these villages. What strange mannerisms he has! What a strange India does the Indian national come from!

The mind goes back to the wound. To the East Indian the wound has been profound, in ways he knows and does not. But in the geographical India, that pitiless, unceasing land which bothers

98

not for whom it crushes or expels, there has not been the slightest cut. The numbers have been undramatic, the impact negligible. The people have been of the unimportant kind: nobodies whom nobody remembers, nobody knows of and nobody can be asked to care.

Perhaps the exchange between the East Indian and the Indian national is a flickering recognition of this poignancy.

IT WAS a Cuban lady and her husband who made me think of the wound in a more tangible way. She was a psychiatrist, one of only three in the country she said, and the only one in that county. She claimed to have dealt with 7,000 patients the previous year. I didn't believe it. Well, check the records, she said. Country Guyanese had among the highest suicide rates in the world. Every now and then a news report alerted you to this fact. Most of them were male Indians; and many hung themselves from the ceiling. (I was once asked casually by a mixed-race youth from town, 'They love suicide in India, right?') All manner of depressives arrived at the doctor's door: women beaten by men, alcoholics, madmen. She offered sound socioeconomic reasons for the phenomenon. Guyana was the poorest state on the continent. It was hard to make a living. Out in the country there was little recreation besides drinking.

But afterwards, the husband, a Guyanese, told me, 'You asked why there are so many depressed people. My wife, due respect to her, she cannot be able to see like we. I tell you why we are sad. We are sad because ever since we left India we have a hole in our hearts. Nothing can fill that hole.' He thumped his palm on his chest – he was a big man, which made the gesture somehow more affecting. It was one of those wide open sentimental Guyanese country evenings: fry fish and rum and Lata across a night-time canefield on the Corentyne.

'And yet, brother,' he added, 'we find that Indians do not consider us to be Indians.'

It was an accurate observation. But I thought it might be patronising to tell him what I felt, which was two, perhaps conflicting, things. That, you know, you are out here where the Caribbean meets South America under these brilliant stars and you should be fucking delighted. The other was that you, brother, are more Indian than I.

The latter point revealed more about me than them. But that is how it felt. Their Indianness felt more intimate than mine. They longed for it; I had no such longing. I was wearied by it, and in fact in flight from it. They had the power to imagine their India, never having to grapple with it.

The idea extended itself from India of the mind to India of the soil. Their forebears had worked the land in India, and they came here across the oceans and worked the land. I saw a romantic continuity in this. The idea of the land suggested to me a special intimacy. You worked the land; you understood seasons, seed and grain, the wind and the rain, birds and animals and insects. And with that you had an intuitive and precise understanding of the people and society which evolved around the land. I felt they carried this intimacy with them in their blood and their veins from the soil of India to the soil of Guyana.

And their land here was so very beautiful. Much of this was not because of the land but the sky. In the forest, beneath the immenseness of the dripping vegetation, one did not register the incredible low lie of the Guyanese sky. But on the coast the sky felt as close as the ground and as flat. The horizons were immaculate and distant. You felt bare on the face of the world. The scale was such that the blind starkness of noon rather than dawn or dusk did it best justice.

The fields in the eastern country were mainly sugarcane. They had a blessed symmetry, canals and paths at right angles to one another and the fields engraved in perfect strips. Men in longboots bent at the waist, cut the crop; others gathered and loaded it into iron punts. Oxen sometimes pulled these iron punts on the canal, towards an industrial-age factory that loomed in the distance, still looking like a thing of wonder as it must have done a hundred years ago, then so futuristic, now so anachronistic.

The western country was more rice paddy. The crop was short and you could see across sweeping expanses of field broken only by lines of palm. Depending on the time of the year the fields could be dry or lush or submerged in brown water that mirrored the fallen sky, and depending on the time of the day the sun painted them in very different hues. Sometimes you could drive past fields with different varieties of seeds shied at slightly different times so that they covered the entire gradient from straw yellow to fresh green. A donkey might be loitering by the edge of the field, a bright blue saki pecking with obsessive jerks at a stray fruit. A woman might be cleaning fish by the trench, and further up the trench, a boy having his hair cut in the Indian way, sitting on his haunches, and in the backyard of the house a man might be boiling coconut shavings to make oil, and these transplanted Indian scenes stirred in me always a sense of broken wonder.

The country was dotted with the moody houses of Guyana. These houses were not as dramatic as those of Georgetown. Except for the old plantation houses, the grand ones were rarely so grand, whereas the bruck-up ones appeared merely poor or abandoned rather than disfigured by slow tragedy, though they could appear in the most surprising states of disrepair, the more elaborate or absurd the construction, it seemed, the more ruined its fate. The new concrete houses were painted pink or blue or green – neither pastel nor primary, but kind of failed bright colours. Inside, the Indian aesthetic was intact in its predilection for dark tapestries and too many cabinets. The balconies were often balustraded, and there hung in them lovely hammocks, an assimilation from Amerindians. I had read that the front balcony was more an Indian preference, but passing through a village I could never tell if it was an African village or an Indian village from the architecture alone.

Most of the living got done in the unwalled space below the house, the bottomhouse. Here were more hammocks, tables and benches for evening limes, children's toys and cycles. The front yard would be aspill with flowering plants, hibiscus and frangipani and marigold and little jump-up-and-kiss, and maybe the odd low fruit bush, cherry, lime. Many Hindu households mounted *jhandis*, flags, on bamboo sticks, red, yellow, white – you would not find such a thick concentration of jhandis in any part of India – and sometimes the richer houses could have a short concrete mandir by the entrance.

What riches in the backyard! Everything grew in those little lots: shrubby pigeonpeas, low, leafy bhaji, purple boulanger, rows of squash on trellis, yam and sweet potato, aloe for skin and tulsi for prayer, and mango and coconut for the soul, and maybe a fowl coop too and fluorescent Polly squawking in her cage. The more enterprising working class families could live almost entirely off their backyard, off the magic of the land.

EVERYTHING starts with the land, and for so long I did not pay attention to this. This land of agricultural wonder, where you could spit into the earth and sprout a stalk, a grove, was once worthless swamp. Nothing grew on it but mangrove and mosquito. For centuries the Amerindian tribes had settled inland, and with good reason. The water was fresh. Fruit, palm and animals were aplenty. When the European invaders arrived, their first trading posts too were upriver, and there too were their first efforts at making plantations.

The danger of the coast was that it lay below sea level so the threat of flood was constant. In the enthusiastic conquests of rival invaders it was historical happenstance that the Dutch consolidated their hold over this particular malarial piece of New World coast. But not happenstance that they made a success of it. The mother country was like this; they knew how to master it.

The Dutch technique was to dig polders: to enclose swamp land, drain it, and reclaim it. It was a complex system, requiring a precise regulation of sea water in the front and swamp water at the back. It needed an extensive network of dams, canals and kokers – the sluice gates which, conveying the ideas of the elemental challenge of a low-lying land and a community meeting point, came to be an enduring Guyanese symbol, celebrated in paintings and poems.

The kokers, the canals – the charm of this unusual national architecture, pleasant and only casually intriguing at first – were the first clues to understanding the land and the settlement of the land; to understanding, for instance, that all the earth required for this colossal project would not move by itself.

It was a terrible amount of earth to move, estimated afterwards to be about one hundred million tonnes. It wasn't about to be moved by the invaders. The upriver Amerindians proved too slippery and combative to be enslaved and anyhow were not available in sufficient numbers. As with elsewhere in the New World, slaves were imported from Africa for the task. There were no machines, of course. The slaves used bare hands and shovel, excavating the enormous polders, building thousands of miles of mud dams, digging the vast grids of trenches and canals – in short, creating the plantations on which they would then lead the life of slavery.

The brutality of this life was so total that it defies comprehension. Slaves were shipped across sometime in the middle of the seventeenth century – nobody knows exactly when and where from, but at any rate, as Booker T. Washington observed of his birth, it must have happened at some point and some place. We know who brought them, the Dutch West India Company, to whom Africans sold Africans for cloth and weapons and utensils, and we know how. They came dying, festering like slabs of meat, so much so that sharks began to follow the trail of blood from slaveships, changing their ocean migratory routes of centuries old. Upon arrival the slaves were stripped naked for examination and sold to planters. Care was taken to separate family, friends, tribes, anything that might provide a community. Thereafter they were worked worse, it is said, than beasts of burden: animals were scarcer. For this they received no wages and paltry rations. They were tortured at the merest excuse. They were whipped to tens, hundreds, and up to a thousand lashes though few bodies still remained alive. The whips were pickled in brine or chilli. Their body parts could be mutilated. They had no rights of any kind: not to family, to language, to names, to faith, to social order. *Obliteration*. When horror is of such a scale, it begins to feel like fantasy, and fantasy is the easier to digest.

European powers played out their games and their wars; slavery continued. The colonies of Essequibo, Demerara and Berbice came to be united under the British; slavery continued. And when at last it was abolished it 1834, it was not really abolished.

There were to be four years of 'apprenticeship'. This cute term meant more slavery, but now limited to seven-and-a-half hours a day. It was only after these hours of slavery that apprentices were entitled to wages. Apprenticeship was not instituted for the slaves; it was for the planters. Abolition was inconvenient business. The planters needed time to make new arrangements. The slaves were never paid reparations: the planters were! Millions of pounds to the planters, not a cent to the slaves!

At the end of apprenticeship the emancipated slaves began to leave the plantations. Full of hope, they set about trying to settle the land, an aspiration not as simple as it sounds. They owned no property and had no right to any. The land belonged to the crown or to the planters. To keep the freedmen on the plantations they made it impossible, at first, for the Africans to buy land. Yet with the sugar industry in recession, with slave-produced American cotton more viable in the international market, and now a shortage in labour, many plantations had sunk or were sinking.

Some planters sold small parcels of land to freedmen, and a cluster of these became a proprietary village. Other freedmen conceived the idea, the old African idea, of the village as a collective, of and by the people. They would pool their resources together to establish cooperative villages. Each person would be entitled to an equal share of arable land, and involved in the running of the village.

With virtually no money for their lifetime of labour, with no money in reparations, they had little purchasing power. But by selling crops during slavery, earning a coin here and a coin there during the years of apprenticeship, they had made some savings. Eighty-three freedpersons pooled these together and raised enough to buy the former cotton plantation of Northbrook (and renamed it, with the imagination of the colonised, Victoria). The money, the saved coins, still muddy after being unearthed from their hiding spots, they took across in clanging wheelbarrows to cheering in the streets.

Buoyed by this success, the collectivist movement caught on. More struggling estates were purchased by emancipated slaves, more villages formed. The residents ran their own affairs, often with a degree of enlightenment: for instance, women had the right to stand for and vote in committee elections. In this manner was born the first civil organisation in the land, a stark contrast to the bloody plantation society. It was too improbable to last.

With each successive purchase the planters began to raise their price; each successive village became harder to form. After the effort required to purchase land and establish villages, the Africans were on the brink of penury. Above this they were taxed. And these taxes, latterly, were channelled largely towards bringing in indentured labour – the next step in the evolution from slavery – from Portuguese Madeira, from China, from other West Indian colonies, even from Africa, but primarily from India. This too was a blow. It was felt that the supply of cheap overseas labour depressed wages for the freelance Africans. The antagonism was instant.

There were other troubles too. The government did not provide for nor assist in drainage and dykes, the critical necessities of Guyanese coastal life. Quite the opposite. To keep the freedmen bound to the estate, planters were known to release water to flood village farmlands.

The dream was untenable. Not long after it had begun the village movement stuttered, struggled, and finally died. African settlement of the coastal country had been partial. Some went off into the interior on gold or balata missions, and later to the bauxite works up the Demerara. Many went into Georgetown and New Amsterdam to seek town employment: they became porters, carpenters, welders, hucksters. Most of them had already become Christians. They slowly integrated with the urban white and mixed populations, took to education, and over time there emerged among them a professional class: low-level civil servants, policemen, nurses, teachers – Western, respectable, but largely a serving class.

MEANWHILE ship upon ship of coolies from India kept coming – and kept coming steadily for almost another eighty years, by which time they outnumbered the Africans in Guyana. It is a forgotten journey; few, even in India, are now aware of it. The history was too minor compared to slavery and the Middle Passage, its damage not so epic.

The ships sailed from Calcutta, and a few from Madras. The immigrants were drawn mainly from the peasant population in the Gangetic plains of the United Provinces – modern-day Uttar Pradesh and Bihar – and a minority from the presidencies of Bengal and Madras. They were mostly young and middle-aged, mostly male (which led to the sensation of 'wife murders' arising from jealousy), mostly Hindu, and mostly taken from the agricultural castes, lower castes and outcastes. The largest caste groups were the chamars, the lowly leather workers, and the ahirs, the cowherds. What was common to them was the fate they were escaping: the famines and revolts, the poverty and destitution of British India. Making their way, that is, from the mess of one end of Empire to another.

Lured by local recruiting agents and their tales about the land of gold, they set out to cross the seas. Crossing the sea: *kalapani*: this was the great Hindu taboo. It came with a loss of caste, of one's place in the social order – but also, for the wretched, a liberation. When victuals among the castes spilled and mixed on the stormy waters, when each person was treated by the white man with equal indignity, the curse of being judged by birth was lifted. From here on they could be anything.

But arriving on the plantations in Guyana, the coolies found themselves living a kind of captive life. They were not mere coolies but 'bound' coolies – physically bound to the estate. Leaving the premises was not allowed unless by special permission. There were improvements, of course, from the days of slavery. But work, especially in crop season, was gruelling; wages were low; health and sanitation poor. There was a contract, yes. But the predominantly illiterate coolies knew little of its scope and its loopholes. Besides, it was the contracts themselves that were exploitative. Apathy at work would result in criminal prosecution. You could be jailed for reporting late.

The coolies were housed in the barracks in which slaves had lived – the niggeryards. In due course fresh 'logies' were built, and there was relative prestige in occupying the boundyard over the niggeryard. In construction these were not very different: long narrow mud-floored barracks with partitions at every ten feet, in which space the entire family would dwell. Every tenement in the logie had a bed, beneath which the labourers assiduously collected their savings in a canister, as did Mittelholzer's cowherd in *Corentyne Thunder*.

The canister contained the dream. One day they would return to India wealthy and happy. This was the fundamental right of indenture: to be returned home at the end of five or ten years, whatever the period of contract.

And it is this which was hurting the masters most. The expense involved in continuously repatriating ships of coolies was too high. Further, each new lot of coolies had to be trained over again. Each person who returned took his savings, and so canister by canister drained the wealth in the colony.

Something had to be done. As ever, the first attempt was devious. To make return harder, the rules of the game were changed so that the cost of the journey would be borne in part by the coolies themselves. This was deterrent, but not enough deterrent. Coolies kept repatriating. The crown scratched its head. It then decided to dangle the big carrot: for forfeiting their right to return home, the coolies were granted land.

Not just granted land, but the land would be made good for settlement. In an ironic progression of history, where the crown had refused to sell to the freed slaves, it now bought out struggling estates for the coolies. Unlike earlier, it also assisted with drainage and irrigation. Every person older than ten was granted an acre and a house lot, those below ten given half that, so the inducement of two or three generations. It was not all that much, but enough to break out of the bondage of indenture and start life anew. And land was land.

The Indians went about using their land and their expertise with the land to raise their lot, coming into wealth mainly through rice farming. Unlike the enslaved, they had been allowed to maintain family, religion, language. They recreated an India, a society of landlords and peasants and cowherds, of Diwali and Phagwah, mandirs and masjids and pujas and even, for a while, panchayats. They became people of the country – agricultural people in an economy of agriculture. And there began to circulate an adage, attributed to a leader who came from India, ominous to the African ear: 'Who owns the land owns the country.'

Of course, the deviousness of divide-and-rulers is accompanied by the pettiness of the divided and ruled. And here was the great friction of planets thrown off their orbits into a new orbit which they must now share. At worst the Africans saw the Indians as illiterate, barefooted, clannish heathens, misers who hoarded coins under their bed, who had strange customs and rituals and wore strange uncivilised costumes, who spread dung on the walls and floors of their homes, stunted, thin-limbed and shifty-eyed. At worst the Indians saw the Africans as the condemned: ugly, black of skin, with wide noses and twisted coir for hair, mimics of the white masters, without a language, culture or religion of their own, frivolous, promiscuous, violent, lazy.

What remained now was a competition of suffering. The bitterest African ideologues even today labelled Indians 'economic migrants' who ought not to be considered Guyanese citizens. The Africans had built the land, built everything on it, and then been oppressed under the immense weight of everything they had built. How differently the Indians looked at it. As later entrants to the colony, they were at a natural disadvantage. The white man ruled them. The black man was hostile from the start. In the beginning they were considered scab labour, and afterwards their admission into the urban society of civil services and the professions was met with resistance. Yet they had worked hard and risen. They had set up businesses.

As the settlements had developed there was an almost striped pattern to the coastal villages. A thin highway ran along them. You whizzed by them, now an Indian village, now, less frequently, an African village. At first I could only see the raw loveliness of these villages and all in between: the coconut groves, the grazing pastures, the blackas, the cemeteries, the broad-hat sky pressing down. Afterwards I could see only the small simmering histories they contained, canals and kokers, Africans who had perished swimming out into the ocean hoping to reach Africa, Indians who had lost their way trying to find India via the interior.

Raw, accidental, those used to be my words. How long it took me to see that everything was brought here. The land which had seemed to me so raw, was created. The crop it was cultivated for, sugarcane, sugar once so precious it was a royal dowry, was transplanted. And the society which had seemed to me so accidental was once made in the most deliberately manufactured way possible.

2

THERE was a particular banna whose passion was attending weddings. Anytime you like, I was told, reach Ramotar Seven Curry, he'll carry you. Guyanese are very good about this: everyone is welcome to a wedding, and it is possible I went to more that year than in my whole life before.

He was an extremely short man, Ramotar Seven Curry, with a belly like a perfectly formed vat. Because of the vat he could not fit into shirts for a man of his height. Consequently he wore sizes where the sleeves tipped past his elbows, and the bottom dangled till his knees where, curiously, it flared like a frock. I found a way of inquiring about this. 'The ole lady had a habit of stretching the base when she clip it on the line,' he said. 'Later I turn it to me own style.' I never ever saw him, even indoors, without a cap. From the back and the sides vines of glistening black hair burst forth with the shine and scent of coconut oil.

'There was one specific weekend when I attended nine weddings,' Ramotar Seven Curry told me. 'Now nine weddings for one day is a big big big number when you consider the size of the population of Guyana. More people would get maar'd in those days. A long time gone now. As a matter of fact, last month I attended one of them same people's children wedding. The fella seek me out. He make cuntact with a certain individual known to the both of us and tell him, "lissun nuh man, you remember that gentleman who does attend everybody wedding? It would be my honour for him to attend me gal's own." That is when, man, you feel, railly an truly, this thing worth it.'

The Hindu wedding fete was held over a weekend. On Friday was the girls' dye night (haldi in India) or dig dutty (dig the earth, mattkor!). Saturday was cooking night at the girl's. Monday night was kangan, which was the greatest feast of all. Sunday was the big day, the morning ceremonies of lawa and sindoor followed by the wedding (at the girl's), and the wedding night lime (at the boy's).

One Sunday Ramotar Seven Curry, though he was from Lovely Lass in West Berbice, lined up a sweep of Canal nos. 1 and 2 on the west bank of the Demerara.

I had been to Canal limes before. The Indians of Canal are the hardest-drinking people in Guyana, by extension the Caribbean, and thus the world. Them don't make joke! They started at noon and rolled on till the next morning. The rum was emphasised with rum chutneys on the sound system, Rum Me Brother Seh (Bring De Firewater), Rum Till I Die, More Rum For Me (Listen Mr Shankar). They had crimson eyes, loose wrinkled faces, hard vaporous breathing. Those in their thirties looked in their fifties.

This Sunday morning Ramotar Seven Curry carried me to the house of a Chinese man in Canal no. 1 who owned a bakery, grew rice, reared pigs, and had an equal love for the Indian political party and Indian women (his wife and his side t'ing were *both*, he said as if to flatter me, Indian). He pumped his fists a lot and, when high, I later learnt, as a gesture of friendly harassment dug his fingers into a secret spot just under the ribs of people. It left behind a sharp pain that kicked in minutes after one had recovered from the surprise of so unexpected a poke. For an hour we lashed rum at the man's house.

At noon, already a little tipsy, a dozen of us proceeded to the bride's. Nobody among us actually knew the bride (and we were from the bride's side). But somebody had spoken to her routinely on the telephone at the work place, someone else used to buy provisions at her mother's shop, so it was all good.

There was a crowd outside the wedding house. The cars were decorated with streamers and flowers. The yard was covered by a large Banks Beer tent. The wedding had finished. People were drinking outside, for there was to be no alcohol inside. The music carried till the gate and some folk, such as the man in a white suit and green velvet jersey, danced in the heat.

Somewhere inside the dulaha and dulahin met guests; for one reason or another we did not see them. This did not perturb anyone. Around the remnants of the ceremonial square, elders sat on chairs with children on their laps. A heart cut out of shiny red paper was pasted on a cloth backdrop. Across the heart the couple's names, Clint and Roseanne, were made with green and pink streamers.

Tassa players arrived and struck up a tremendous beat. A man sweating rum removed his shirt and began to dance around the square in his vest. He was joined by four others. The elders with children on their laps watched sleepily.

We went back to the hot gate and killed Banks. News came in from the backdam that King had badly mutilated his eight-year-old son with a tractor. The boy had gone out to hurry King back for the wedding. 'The man try fuh close aff the tractor and it jook forward pon the bai.' We anxiously made for the backdam to investigate. Instead, and I don't know how this happened, we found ourselves in the backyard, waiting to be served seven curry.

Seven curry was the Hindu ceremony food of Guyana and, as far as I could tell, a purely Guyanese term. Not even Trinidadians used it. The meal was served in a water lily leaf, closed like an enormous funnel, so beautiful mingling was inevitable: boiled rice with spicy achar with sweet pumpkin with fibrous katahar with eddo curry with green bhaji with hot channa with garlicked dhal.

Ramotar Seven Curry and I went at our leaves with intense joy, sweating into them.

'So this is the thing. How you like it? You get it like so in India?'

'Not this exact combination usually.'

'That is surprising . . . That is surprising indeed.'

A seven curry, especially when sealed with parsad, made you want to sleep within moments. The usual way to overcome this sensation was to dunk cups of koolaid and begin dancing. Or else go out and hit shots of rum and begin dancing.

However, Ramotar Seven Curry had mastered the art of pacing himself, and he decided we must leave. It would be in our best interests to move to another house down the road and throw back and gyaff while the sun hot.

'How you leave ahready man, Seven Kori,' somebody asked as we made our way out.

Ramotar Seven Curry rested his hand on the man's shoulder. 'But if we don't leave, brother, how we gon come back?'

Having secured this logical victory, we went on to throw back and gyaff up the road as per plan.

We were now in the house of Mr Jagroop. It was one of Canal's few bungalows, which in Guyana went by the direct term, flathouse. Like all country Guyanese, Mr Jagroop was happy to be hospitable. Inside people drank spirits with coconut water. Ramotar Seven Curry popped open a Banks and I went with Johnnie Walker and coconut water, a magnificent collusion.

From the veranda rose the clacking sound of dominoes. A group of men sat around a table, drinking and picking from bowls of channa and raw mango sprinkled with pepper sauce. I had made forays into dominoes; I could never quite crack it, but I had grown fond of its din. Tickets slapping wood, it was the sound of the Caribbean, as organic to the landscape as rusted zinc. Here was life going on, it said. I liked as well the crooked shapes the tickets made on the table and how they could trail in any direction.

The men played as if in a trance. Their world was contained in that square of tickets, calculations, rum and channa; all ambition, all escape lay therein. Any potential disturbances were dealt with mechanically. Mr Jagroop's little daughter arrived bawling after having been scratched with a pencil by her younger brother. Mrs Jagroop followed her, squealing, 'I ain able with this piece of terror,' and dropped the topless boy on daddy-lap. Nobody paid the situation mind. Once he had played his turn Daddy hung the boy by his underpants and administered three or four cut-arse – *pai! cha-pai! pai!* – the spanks striking a vivid rhythm with the domino tickets. The boy scrambled off bawling towards his sister, who, in a benevolent twist, began to comfort him. Some minutes later Daddy brought closure to the incident by calling out a single word. The word was: 'Com'. The boy came. He rested the boy on his belly, slapped down a ticket, issued a torrent of whispered kisses into the boy's ear, 'I gon buy you the paint set tomorrow, right.' The boy scampered away again to his sister.

Ramotar Seven Curry and I settled in the living room. The television was on. Several ladies, including Mrs Jagroop, and a bunch of children of varying ages reclined before the screen. It was on C.N. Sharma's Channel 6. A Hindi movie was starting, *Zehreela Insaan*.

It began with a young lad running a baby snake through a village. He is stopped by a schoolmaster who marvels that while others raise puppies and kittens this boy is raising the child of a snake. The boy is a terrible menace, throwing stones at the water pots on the heads of ladies and so forth. Masterji takes the boy home where Masterni has made him gaajar ka halwa. '*Gaajar ka halwa – wah!*' exclaims the boy, spreading his hands.

The frame froze here, subtitled, with the boy's hands spread and mouth open, one of many such frozen frames in the title sequence.

Mrs Jagroop wondered about gaajar ka halwa.

Carrot, I told them.

'But what is halwa?'

'Is like sirnee. Muslim does make halwa in Trinidad. Carrot . . . hm . . . sound interesting,' another lady offered.

Mrs Jagroop was more forthright. 'Is how you could put carrot in dah, man. Me would nah ever try such a thing.'

After one of the freeze-frames the picture failed to recover. At first one thought the director was prolonging the pleasure of the effect. But slowly the screen was assaulted by dots and dashes, crackling with beeps and static, the film disappearing behind it like grass under snow. Some minutes later the dialogue – 'You can take the poison out of a snake, but beware my poison,' delivered by a young man – was replaced by the chatter of the network's technical persons. Finally everything went blank. And then they put on some old Sharma programming.

A living legend was Sharma, a smalltime politician with an immensely popular channel featuring mainly himself. Elections were expected in a few months, and Sharma was warming to the task. There he was, beloved hero with his white agitating hair, in a promo set to the ridiculous tune, 'Let Justice Be For One and All'. It was a montage of visuals: Sharma wading through a flood, marching through a field, coursing up a river, thrusting a microphone before the face of a crying girl.

'We wan justice, Mr Sharma,' a black lady said to him, displaying for him the wretchedness of her shingled shack. Sharma yanked the door. It collapsed. He was triumphant. 'See what the goverment doing about aaldis.' He pointed to the choked trench by the house. 'Look at that, Mr President, sheer garbage, sheer nastiness. And that is condom floating pon the trench. I hope Mr President is watching.'

This inflamed Mrs Jagroop. 'Is the president who put condom there?' She turned to me.

'You see how much encouragement blackpeople them get because of jokey mout like Sharma? The man so stupid he don't know how to say the word becaas. He call it becaize. Yes, he say becaize for becaas.'

She flipped the channel with the decisiveness of a vote.

A black man in a black vest and white pants appeared before a fluorescent orange and green wallpaper adorned with bronchi, oesophagi and other tubes. Throughout the wallpaper shook; after several unsuccessful adjustments was removed altogether.

The man demonstrated a sitting position that prevented prostate cancer.

'Cabblers in India sit in this position and 98 per cent of them nah got prostrate cancer. That means, brothers, only 2 per cent cabbler in India got prostrate cancer.'

'Truth?' Mrs Jagroop asked me.

'It is possible. It is possible. Sometimes you cannot trust statistics about cobblers though.'

'Tha'is *exactly* what I'm saying. Especially when it come from blackman. How the hell e could know statistics of India?'

The channel was flipped back to Sharma.

The activism had given way to Guyana's most-watched programme: Death Announcements.

Death Announcements was a mesmerising affair. A mug shot would appear, a suitably oppressed picture of the dead, accompanied by a song, a bhajan, My Heart Will Go On, Suhaani Raat. Text would scroll alongside with the Sunrise and Sunset dates of the individual, with a brief eulogy and a list of relatives and friends categorised, down to, say, 'Uncle-in-law of'.

'Leff it there, leff it there,' urged the other lady. 'I miss de t'ing on Friday. I hear they put out a t'ing for, ahm, wuh e name, Nandlall, Nandlall wife granmudder.'

The scrolls ran slow and sad. People had died in Middlesex, in Vryheid's Lust, in Parfait Harmonie.

All of a sudden Ramotar Seven Curry, benignly sipping his beer so far, announced this is a weddin day, it ain't a day for watching the dead.

116

We took plastic chairs out to the veranda. We put our feet up against the low wall and drank. We talked about wedding things. Ramotar Seven Curry spoke rapturously about groups of women rolling the belna in symphony on cooking night, the beauty, the harmony of it; he spoke of how naughtily the Lucknie (lokani dai!) might be placed between bride and groom on the first night. I'd been reading too, I said, and I loved and admired how they took the ship and crossed the sea and bam! everything overturned! Women, so scarce among the coolies, able to in certain cases, able to *take* dowry! Castes marrying each other! Brahmins conducting weddings for chamars! A historian called the process Chamarisation, and I went on in this manner, when a loud voice—

'The man you been reading is a jackarse.'

We turned towards a bearded gent with formidable eyes and rings, his fingers clasped before his chin.

'A jackarse,' he repeated.

I was taken aback.

'Why do you say that?'

'What you are saying, basically, is that we have forgotten our social organisation, which is the most ancient and scientific organisation the world has seen.'

'What I am saying is that hierarchy matters less here. I can see that without a book. It's a good thing. Like at the wedding, rich and poor people hang out together, drink and chat. India is, you know, paralysed by hierarchy.'

'But what you say is insulting to us as Guyanese and Hindus. You have to understand. They killed our language. They made us bury our dead like them. They made us go to mandir on Sunday like them. Made us get maar'd on Sunday like them. But our culture, our religion, our order, has survived.'

'That is not what I'm—'

Things might have gone anywhere from here; but Ramotar Seven Curry introduced us. The man was a rice-mill owner and a pandit, though not a smalltime performing pandit. He was an important

117

member of the Guyana Hindu Dharmic Sabha. We spoke about rice seasons and the price of rice nowadays.

The drinking continued. No break was permissible. Someone or the other came by and topped you up. I could not keep up with the goliaths. As dusk began to descend over Canal no. 1, and though the sandflies had begun to bite, I fell asleep in the chair.

I opened my eyes to Ramotar Seven Curry's urgings – he had an effortlessly loud delivery, rumbling up from his vat – 'Raise up, raise up, next place got to attend.'

He praised me for sleeping so soundly while sitting.

'This is nothing,' I said. 'My grandmother knew how to sleep standing.'

'Long-time fellas had a lot of skills, you know. Many many skills and techniques that you don't see now. I would like, railly an truly, to reintroduce some of these techniques for the younger generation. The younger fellas must realise it. Say if you granmudder could teach youth them to sleep standing, that is a skill for life. Not just for work or play, but for life.'

People got into vehicles and drove over to Canal no. 2, ten or fifteen minutes away. This was a Muslim wedding, the boy's side lime, the McDooms – from Makhdoom I guessed. I ate beef curry and rice and dhal and baiganee. Ramotar Seven Curry did not eat the beef. We took shots by the gate and proceeded back to Canal no. 1, to the boy's side lime of the wedding we had attended in the morning.

By now things were no longer distinguishable. The scene seemed the same; a canal by a thin mud road, a high wedding house, balloons, streamers, a Banks tent over the yard, dancing in the front yard, food in the backyard. Further the same people appeared to be dancing at both the Canal no. 1 and the Canal no. 2 houses.

People wore striped T-shirts with caps. They wore long shorts and half-buttoned shirts. Some were in glittery suits. Women wore sleeveless tops with long skirts or frocks or dresses with low necks. Some wore loose spaghetti-strap chiffon dresses.

The house rattled with the Bhojpuri orchestration of soca-chutney. To the ear chutney had the quality of a racket, a particular kind of clanging racket. I say this as pure description. Here came the harmonium, tassa and synthesised beats of the new hit Mor Tor. *Lawa milaye, sakhi lawa milaye*, from the old ceremony song: the exchange of rice grains before a wedding, Mor and Tor, mine and yours, mixing together. *Give me yours, I'll give you mine.* Ask a youth what he thinks Mor Tor means, and he will point to his thrusting groin: 'Is like motor, know what I saying?'

The dancing picked up. The main thing about East Indian dancing was to twirl your hands. You could be putting on a heavy winedown, you could be shuffling on your toes, but so long as the wrists were cocked and the hands were twirling and the fingers were making designs it bore the stamp of an Indian dance.

Ramotar Seven Curry was in his element, peaking through long years of experience at the right time of the night. He cracked loud jokes. One minute he was dancing with a stranger's nani, next moment with another's toddler.

He encouraged me to dance with a young girl with long lustrous hair in a red crepe dress and black stilettos, and we did and she asked if there was any chance I could introduce her some day to the actor Arjun Rampal. Of course, I said, I writin a film for him next, would you like a part too? Well, only if it across *him*. Soon she left with her family. It was only weddings she was allowed to attend.

I looked around for Ramotar Seven Curry. I could see his blurring shape in the crowd.

A youthman staggered up to me. He handed me a drink. I took it.

'You know how much Banks I could drink?'

What a riddle! I applied my mind thoroughly.

Searching through my experiences it occurred to me that I had been five months in Guyana. It stunned me. I had arrived in the wet season. A supposedly dry season had gone; another wet season had begun. It was June. My intonations were changing. My hair was cut different. I had gotten accustomed to knocking about doing nothing.

'Like you thinking hard, buddeh.'

I reapplied myself to the task.

I recalled that I had seen three men in Berbice wash down four cases of Banks. That made thirty-two each. To be safe, I added a few to the number.

'Thirty-nine.'

'No.'

'Forty-seven?'

'No.'

'Eighty-one!'

'No.'

'How much then?'

'Hanesly? Countless.'

'Oh.'

He went off and returned with two fresh bottles. He clicked the caps open with his teeth.

'Watch.'

He finished the first in two gulps, flung the bottle by a tulsi plant at the fence, repeated the feat with the next, and began to exchange fist bumps with me.

Another man came over and said, 'Ei, brudder, Seven Kori he tell me you waak from India. Fuh trut?'

'Trut.'

'Trut! Shake me hand, brudder. We's have the same blood you know. *Blood* I taakin bout.'

He pushed aside the youthman, put his arm around me and whisked me off towards the paling.

'Is one favour I ga fuh ask you, buddeh.'

'You ask, man.'

'Me wan a beautiful wife from India.'

'But you got so much beautiful girls right here in Canal.'

'Abidese ah *love* gals from India. Aishwaarya, Raani. Me gat a lil condition, buddeh. Nobody must knock am already. Me ga fuh be the furst to knock am. I thank you, brudder frum India, for this favour. Like Hanuman you gah fuh kerry the message an fetch she.'

Before discussions could proceed further we were distracted by an emotional dispute just outside the gate. We went to see. The quarrel was at a critical juncture. The question was whether one man had chucked the other or not. A chuck was a kind of shove with terribly humiliating implications. Both men, one in a half-unbuttoned shirt and a moustache, and another with dilated almost-crying eyes, knew how pivotal this question was. The pendulum of honour swayed delicately.

'Danny, you know me since when, man, and you chuck me?' said the man with the almost-crying eyes.

'I chuck you? I *chuck* you?'

'You chuck me, Danny. Is chuck you chuck me.'

Suck-teeth. 'If I chucked you, you rass be drownin in the canal behine dey.' Suck-teeth, suck-teeth, suck-teeth.

'I goin bust yo fockin head, Danny, if you chuck me again.'

'Is *chuck* I chucked you? You call that *chuck*!'

Voices rose. The congregation egged on a fight. Suck-teeth rent the air. It appeared that something dramatic might occur when—

'Nuh row, nuh row, nuh row,' Ramotar Seven Curry burst through the gates with arms open.

Even though he was an extremely short man with extremely short arms, he managed to embrace the quarrelling men and jam them up against each other.

He said many things that I could not catch. But the result was that the rowing men shook hands. The gathering dissipated, a little disappointed. Ramotar Seven Curry beamed.

'See what it about?' he told me. 'People in there dancin and fetin. Out here there a little misunderstanding take place. But it's a wedding night, and one of those fellas got to realise that and say, "man, it be so-and-so pickney wedding night, and we must not be going on so." It's a union time. Fellas got to realise that in the family there will be some fighting. But railly an truly, is not how you fall out but how you come together, right, that is what is family.'

Ramotar Seven Curry shone with sweat and coconut oil that streamed down his forehead and on to his thick cheeks. Above us the stars were out in huge numbers. They failed to reflect in the long dark canals. For no apparent reason we began to walk down the muddy road along the canal, passing dark trees and frail houses darkened by the exodus to the wedding house.

A star broke and fell into the canal; it dissolved into the black water.

A little bat slammed against Ramotar Seven Curry's chest and dropped dead.

'Now look how that bat fool heself,' he chuckled. He picked up the creature and laid it by the side of the road, tenderly spreading its wings.

'I could tell you one fact about myself,' he said.

Unusually, he waited to be prompted.

'Go for it, man, Seven Kori.'

'There was a time they would call me Dig Dutty. Ramotar Dig Dutty. Was me alone among sheer gals going for the gal functions. They singing and dancing, you know the long-time wedding songs they got, real sexual. Plenty sugarcake gals.'

He looked embarrassed. I prompted him again.

'What happen then, Seven Kori?'

'You could imagine how much dutty I dig! You understand, right? Eh he. Of course, I was a young fella then. When a fella young, he looks at the world in a very very different way. But the beautiful aspect of a wedding is that the bai grow up. He change. So after my own wedding I request everybody, "hear nuh everyone, it's time you give me a more respectable call name."

'Cause I believe in this institution of marriage, man. Railly an truly, we getting reckless, man, in this society. Even the Indians. Not only that, I will say even the Hindus. That is what concern me. All this thing about reputed wife and thing. In long-time days the white man never accept Indian ceremony. Nobody register and that is how you get the concept of reputed. But, railly an truly, why do we need repute today? That is what I ask people. Is it a good repute or a nasty repute?

'We learning the wrong things, man, we adapting to blackman principles. You find Indian girls now going with blackman too. Is the men too who got to share the blame. Yes! The fellas got to own up for letting she slip away . . . Well, comin back to my story, since that time they change it from Ramotar Dig Dutty to Ramotar Seven Curry.'

We must have walked a mile or more along the canal. Our styrofoam cups had run dry.

In the distance a pair of white lights shot through the heavy muddy dark. We hitched a ride back to the wedding house with a family whose own weddings Ramotar Seven Curry had once graced.

3

LIFE in the country was slow, but upon reflection a fair amount happened in those days. There was a period, for instance, when I returned to the Corentyne, and here to my great regret I missed a grand bank heist by no more than ten minutes.

Very early that morning I had left for the canefields with Moses Moonsee the ratcatcher. Now a name like that breaks open the past straight away. As we hurtled in the truck through the fraying dark, I thought of the forebear of Moses Moonsee, a lettered munshi, a Mughal clerk, who had fled to a distant continent to do manual labour, and whose eventual progeny caught rats. One sees what one wants to see. As Roald Dahl's ratcatcher looked like a rat, so Moses the ratcatcher looked to me pure munshi. I gave him spectacles when he had none. He wore an old pair of jeans, yet those legs appeared to me cross-legged and housed in a dhoti. The object in his hands was a 22-inch, but it was to me a tall register.

Perhaps too it was the hallucinatory hour before dayclean, damp, diffuse, with scattered flares of psychedelia, given to invert thoughts.

As suddenly as dusk turns to night by the equator, so dawn turns to day in a snap. And as we bumped along the trail into the backdam the world had turned yellow-blue, cruel and dazzling.

The cutters and loaders and chainboys and the rest of the cast glistened in the morning. Moonsee set about his task, loading a can of spray on his back and walking through rows of burnt canestalk. It was only once the cane had been burnt for cutting that the rough charred stalks betrayed the harshness beneath the order – why the masters preferred coolies with horns on the base of their fingers. Amid the sweating scything work was the animation that made labour a social place. A drunk worker vomited with practised clarity. 'Watch, you liver faal out,' somebody cautioned. A man came clumping from afar holding up an enormous camoudi. 'The man scarch! The man scarch! But the man nah dead!' The reptile was placed on the ground. It was nine or ten feet long, thick, part burnt, part ash, part golden-green, twitching. Moonsee himself arrived with a set of dead rats, laying them out in incremental sizes. 'Watch, abi get a family heye.' He jabbed each in the chest with his 22-inch. 'Dah daddy, dah mammy, dah pickney, dah nex pickney.'

Afterwards we gyaffed beneath a peepal tree at the estate office. The yard was full. It was Friday: payday. Beyond the gates the Friday market was out in force, competing for the workers' wages before they were spirited away at the rumshop, or deposited pragmatically in the two banks on the main road.

And that is where, in mid-August, a fortnight before elections, which would be won comfortably by the Indian party, the hold-up occurred, an hour to noon. A group of bandits arrived with AK47s, ordered the civilians to the side, shot at the glass facades, entered the banks, cleaned out the vaults and made off with sacks of loot into the backlands. It was a wonder that they hadn't come on horses.

For a week I followed the adventure every morning in the papers, the effect like a serialisation. The bandits hijacked at various stages a pastor's car, a fisherman's motorbike, two tractors, a boat. They had planned to head downriver and escape into the Atlantic. But a series of slapstick blunders – the first tractor bumping into a bike, the second tractor sticking in the mud – had allowed police to catch up. They managed to get away on the boat. But with police in pursuit, they could no longer expose themselves on the bare ocean. They crossed the river, dumped the hijacked boat and hoofed it.

This was a mistake. It was good territory to lay low in, as bandits often did, but exactly the wrong terrain to be on the run. Beyond the elaborate Dutch artifices, the polders and the kokers, the land was the way it had always been: swamp, bush, wet grass, low jungle, inhospitable, empty.

There was water at every step. The bandits were bogged down. There was little, if any, fruit to eat and weak overhead cover. Hungry, exhausted, they were forced to shed ammunition as they went along. Then the heavy AKs. Then sacks of wet cash.

The manhunt continued over long days. Through the accumulation of details in reports, the untravelled, impenetrable landscape opened up vividly to the eye. I wondered how it was that the bandits kept going. Was it an ordeal or an adventure? What questions did they ask themselves? Did they?

It was a good fifty hours before the killings were made. Every day another one or two men were found and executed, because dead men don't tell tales. Their mugshots appeared in the papers, black-and-white squares, expressionless, depthless, defeated. And yet beneath the flatness there bubbled a kind of bravado that said: 'My face flat now, but look, look how confident I was.'

WHEN I thought back these days to my original visit to Guyana, that strange and alluring week in 2002, I no longer saw the flashes and moods that I used to. I only saw how much I did not see.

It had passed me by in 2002 that six weeks before I had arrived, on the carnival of Mashramani, Mash Day, five prisoners had broken out of Georgetown prison. It changed the course of the country forever. Five! It said not so much of the enormity of those prisoners, as of the littleness of the nation, the size of Britain but holding a mere three-quarter million, and the domino trail of how one thing led to another in a small, hot place.

It went back to how the society had been planted, civilisational seeds drawn from here and there and thrown together in a patch to grow. It went back to how the land had been settled, the country and agriculture by Indians, the towns and professions by Africans. From these beginnings emerged the inevitable politics of race, an African party and an Indian party. They were once the same party. Class held it together, workers against masters. And race split it in two, under leaders of charisma and ego, with names like in a movie, Jagan and Burnham.

Cheddi Jagan was Indian, an America-trained dentist, handsome, firebrand, earnest, doggedly Marxist; Forbes Burnham, African, brilliant, suave, a London-educated lawyer, the silkiest of speakers. Together they had formed the party, and in 1953, when they swept to victory in elections, buoyant, America and Britain feared Guyana had gone red. It took just one hundred and thirty-three days for the crown to send in her troops, sack the government, arrest party members and suspend the constitution. The party began to strain; Jagan and Burnham's was a case of 'two man rat cyan live in one hole'; in two years the division was official, the components consolidating in time along race.

Give them five minutes, it was said, and Cheddi could antagonise a friend while Forbes would convert an enemy. And it was Burnham who was helped to the premiership by America and Britain in 1964. In 1966, Guyana became independent, Burnham remained the leader. For twenty-one years, till his death, he ruled as a dictator, running the economy into the ground and alienating the Indians to such an extent that when Jimmy Carter came to assist in Guyana's first free and fair elections in 1992, he declared it the most divided country he'd ever seen.

An aged Jagan won the presidency at last; the Indian party stayed in power thereafter. In the years of its rule, Guyana remained the poorest nation on the continent and the second-poorest in the hemisphere. Eighty per cent of its graduates fled its shores, and of the rest whoever could did, leaving to clean toilets, sweep houses, cut cane, so that it is said with confidence there are more Guyanese living outside Guyana than in it. In a situation of such hopelessness the basest instincts burn; in Guyana it is race.

Everything is linked. Every day you transacted with the world around you, and every day people you met in it knew something you didn't. Looking at smithereens of a bank window on tarmac, they knew things I didn't. It could be debilitating, mystifying, desperate; I wanted to scratch my way in.

Though I came to it late, for me the jailbreak of 2002 was key. It was no more a criminal thing than a political or racial thing. It came in the wake of a disputed election. It was masterminded by extremist African activists. They hid the jailbreakers in a village on the coast. In that village's backlands they set up a camp and tutored in it a posse of youth soldiers, some as young as twelve. Guns were put into their hands, ganja in their mouths, ideology in their minds, and they were let loose.

For months the jailbreakers and their cohorts ravaged the Guyanese coast. Executions, robberies, abductions, arson. Broadly, there were two targets. One was the police. The police, like the army and the bureaucracy, was predominantly black. For this fact it was mistrusted by the Indians; for the same fact it was resented by the Africans. The other target was Indians. They had a special affection for the businessmen.

From time to time the masterminds would circulate handbills as statements of mission. They were signed 'Five Freedom Fighters', or more catchy yet, 'Five for Freedom'. Another name, 'African Taliban', was coined when one of the five captured the public imagination – combining terror and farce, an appealing mix in the Caribbean – by appearing in a video, bin Laden-style, wearing fatigues and holding an AK.

The man in the video was the leader of the five, Andrew Douglas. He was a protégé of the bandit of whom I'd learned up at Kaieteur – Blackie. Such a small place!

Like Blackie, Douglas was a former lawman – a policeman, an ace driver who did the chases. And like Blackie he was given a public funeral when he was killed, some six months after the jailbreak. It was endorsed by the black party, attended by thousands of Africans, his coffin was draped in the national flag, his journey from lawman to outlaw to martyr complete.

The handbill at Douglas's funeral was signed 'One Thousand Black Men'.

It began:

> African-Guyanese built this country over a period of 212 years of brutal unpaid laboured. Today, 164 years after the end of slavery, many of the descendents of these true Guyanese live on pavements, in abandoned buildings and in little square boxes barely large enough to qualify as a prison cell.

It ended:

> The Company of black freedom fighters demand system of Government and distribution of the national wealth that ensure the protection of our human rights and provide equal opportunities for the development of Black business. We demand government expenditure not only in cricket and squash where Indians and Portuguese predominate but also in activities in which African-Guyanese predominate such as athletics, football, boxing, basketball, music and art. Until these basic human rights are equally guaranteed to all African-Guyanese, the builders of Guyana, there will be no peace.

Douglas's death was shrouded in mystery. He had been found in a car, shot in the head. Nobody was sure who made the hit. As time passed more and more bandits, presumed bandits and innocents were taken out in similarly mysterious circumstances. The police claimed to be uninvolved. So did the army. Under pressure for answers, the government finally alluded to 'some kind of phantom body out there'.

And then one day, in late 2002, on the coastal highway, outside the village of Good Hope, an army patrol straying from its zone stumbled upon a bulletproof jeep containing hi-tech weapons and surveillance equipment the likes of which the state did not possess. Outside the vehicle – and on this technicality was release secured – were three men. One of them was of particular interest, a well-known tycoon. Shaheed Khan was his name, better known as Roger Khan.

ROGER KHAN. In the Guyanese enunciation it sounded like Raja Khan: King Khan. I knew his face well – dopey eyes, thick eyebrows, black beard, blank arrogance. Boyo the newspaper vendor told me that its appearance on the front page could hike the day's sales by twenty per cent.

Like every good don, Roger Khan was self-made and his life of crime began early. He went young to the United States, and by the age of twenty-two he notched up a number of offences, including drug- and gun-running. In 1994, while on probation, he fled to Guyana. He was a wanted man in the USA ever since.

Back in Guyana he made a phenomenal rise. He took risks, greased palms. He'd had some training as a civil engineer. He hustled a big contract on the university campus. Coming into some money, his next project was to build low-cost cement houses. His business interests multiplied, lumber, a laundromat. He bought an island in the Essequibo.

But his principal business was cocaine. This was a huge trade in Guyana. Itself Guyana produced no cocaine, but perched on the Atlantic, with its proximity to cocaine nations, it was an ideal transhipment point. The joke on the street was about 'value-added' exports. No item was above cocaine. It was stuffed in fish, timber, fruit, greeting cards, cases of skin cream, intestines of humans, cartons of pepper sauce, drums of molasses, shells of coconuts. Estimates put the trade at anywhere between twenty and sixty per cent of the whole Guyanese economy. And the drug barons were thought to be predominantly Indian businessmen.

All understanding of the Caribbean is available in its music. There is a brilliant satire from fifty years ago, No Crime, No Law, by the calypsonian Commander. It rings open with the striking lines *I want the government of every country / Pay a criminal a big salary.* The logic is established early on. *If somebody don't lick out somebody eye / The magistrate won't have nobody to try.* The fast-powering lines keep rolling out, each funnier, more visual, women parting men's faces with poui, boring out their eyes with saws. Through the humour the essential truths behind the comedy gather a terrific force. The entire rapidfire exposé is done inside three minutes. *So when a man kill, instead of swinging he head,* Commander concludes, *They should make him Governor General instead.*

Roger Khan, basically, was made Governor General. He governed over what came to be known as the Phantom Squad, or simply Phantom. Phantom was abstract. It was a loose association. It did hits and melted into the night. Phantom was a response to the African Taliban. The mercenaries were ex-convicts and ex-lawmen and gunmen imported from neighbouring countries, most of them black. The financiers were believed to be Indian businessmen, some of them druglords, chief among them Roger Khan.

On the street this was suspected a long time, but confirmation came in 2004 when a cattle farmer named Shafeek Bacchus was gunned down in a drive-by shooting. 'Wrong man,' one of the perpetrators was heard shouting as the vehicle drove away. The right man soon came to the fore.

He was the brother, George Bacchus, a chubby balding chap, known about Georgetown as a shady hustler. He claimed to have been the intended target. He confessed to being part of Phantom.

He was an informer. But Phantom had turned ugly and he had cut out. Drug scores were being settled every day, people were killing as part of gang wars; the operation had spun out of control. He made affidavits recounting intimate details of Phantom operations – where the captives were tortured, where the bodies were dumped. The most sensational disclosures were about the involvement of the home minister. He claimed to routinely meet the minister in his office, where, surrounded by weapons, the minister would collaborate on hits.

Two days before George Bacchus was to testify in court, he was found dead in his bed.

There was a limited inquiry into Phantom operations; the minister was cleared. He was moved to India as high commissioner. He had stamped my passport. How much I didn't know!

But now, in 2006, four years after he was found outside his crime-busting vehicle, Roger Khan's luck was out. He had fallen out with the police chief (with whom, everybody in Georgetown gossiped, he shared a mother-daughter pair of mistresses). He was out of favour with the government. He was on the run. He put out desperate advertisements in the papers boasting of his patriotic support to the government in crime-fighting at his own cost. He bragged about the help he'd given the Americans when an embassy employee was kidnapped by the African Taliban.

Yet, the Americans, having no use for him anymore, wanted him for trafficking cocaine. And if the Americans wanted him, the Americans got him. As the June rains fell over Georgetown, he was picked up from Suriname with 213 kilos of cocaine, transferred to Trinidad, and whisked away to the USA. Guyana was circumvented altogether.

The front pages still showed Roger Khan, in a humiliated position, cross-legged on the floor, hands tied, shorn of his beard, in vest and boxers: a fallen don.

Fallen, but in the eyes of much of the Indian population, as Andrew Douglas had been for the Africans, a folkhero, a demigod. When Indians were being butchered and robbed, Roger Khan had stepped up for them. He had changed the very self-image of the community. Our reputation had been for internalising violence, a man told me: slash the wife, chop the neighbour, hang self. But after Roger Khan he could see that the black man was at last afraid of Indians. 'Watch there, man be Phantom,' he heard them whisper.

African Taliban, Phantom; it was an absurd manifestation of the racial confrontation, self-defeating of course. African Taliban had not only attacked Indians, but left in its wake dead black policemen, dead black bandits, made criminals out of able black youth. Phantom had not just attacked Africans, but further criminalised a dubious section of the business class, and cast a pall on the conduct of the Indian party. And between them, African Taliban and Phantom had sprouted scores of new criminals, new gangs, set new standards for violence, a free for all, and driven a vulnerable citizenry, divided by race always, out to the far edges.

CONSIDER the Singhs of La Bonne Intention; a terrible condition of anxiety has choked the Singhs. Their vast property, gated, fenced and electronically secured many times over, is by the main road, but the house has been built deep inside, away from the noise of the vehicles and, crucially, the coveting eyes of passers-by.

Mr Singh lives in borderline paranoia, more so after the minister of agriculture was assassinated in the village some months ago. He is a thin, drooping man with a boomerang for an Adam's apple. He despises the blackman. He is himself going on ebony. The problem in Guyana, he will tell you unprompted – it is the first thing he will tell you – 'Black people don't like work, they like killing people.'

Ask Mr Singh about Roger Khan. He's got a problem with the thing, a serious serious problem. 'The problem is there was only one Roger Khan. You need one hundred.' He likes this numbers game. His solution to kick Guyana into shape is to import fifty thousand Indians. (This is a different figure from the Sindhi trader, who suggests a hundred thousand, or the Chinese pig farmer and bakery owner, who recommends a half million Chinese.)

Mr Singh's routine, you sense, has been developed and perfected over time. 'You ever see a sign sayin Made in Africa? Like you see a sign, Made in India, Made in USA, you ever see any sign which says *Ma-de in Af-ri-ca*? Cause they ain't make nothing in Africa.' He does not wait for a response, instead masterfully segueing the final syllables into a lingering suck-teeth, before adding: 'Actually, is AIDS they made in Africa.'

Every day dawns fresh with prejudice, with a fresh urge to get the juices going. With an early morning breakfast of sada roti and baigan choka, in boxers still, he chances upon the television a black man. Boom! the day comes alive. 'Shut you stinkmouth, nigger! Lock up the man. Arrest he for ugliness.'

Turning to you he asks, 'You know what happen with blackman? God burn them. They skin burn, they hair burn, and with that they brain burn too. They want to talk like whiteman, look like whiteman. Cause they got no culture of they own. They don't like Indians cause Indians got they own culture, right.'

'Well, I feel they have an inferiority complex,' Mrs Singh, up since dawn, monitoring the housework, cooking a variety of food, adds sympathetically.

You begin to think that it is merely Mr Singh's way of talking. For people of various races have appeared on the television, each denounced spectacularly. 'The man so ugly,' he remarks of an Indian presenter, 'he mother push he out after four month.'

And then bam, it's back! 'Blackman is like an alligator. They just done eat from you hand and they want to bite you hand. You got to fight fire with fire. You know how they treat them in South Africa? That was the right thing to do.'

Hatred, disillusionment have permeated the Singh household. It isn't race alone. A young Singh, a soft-spoken, likeable girl, a former volunteer for the big Diwali motorcade on the La Bonne

Intention community grounds, has concluded that Guyana does not deserve to be a country. Nothing is done properly here. No matter what you say about them, white man know how to maintain thing. Best to give it back to the UK, or let USA take it over, as though both countries are actively bidding for the honour. In any event, she is out of here asap, like her sister before her. At present she can express her disgust in minor ways, by, say, supporting not just the Indian team in cricket, but any team against West Indies. What is race is race, what isn't race, that's race too.

Fear and anxiety governs every move of the Singhs. They knew the assassinated minister. They have family who had their business burnt, acquaintances who have been robbed and terrorised, killed. It may very well happen to them. Chores in town are never done by oneself. They are never performed simultaneously, but sequentially, so that nobody is ever alone, even if it means somebody waiting in the car hour upon hour.

The maid at the Singh household is Melissa, a 'thick, red gal' of admirable loyalty, though not above the odd petty filch. In the house she carries the contamination of the low. The Singhs do not let her handle food; though unlike in India, she is permitted to sit on chairs and have a cup of coffee with the missus – indeed, the casualness of the relationship would scandalise people in the geographical India. Melissa has a smiling face, a busy, pleasant air, and altogether not unattractive looks. Mr Singh calls her 'ugly duckling'. She laughs every time he says this. And Melissa, red and not black, will herself find a way to loudly berate 'them stupid black people' at every available opportunity.

Mr Singh runs a prosperous immigration agency (it was he, a friend of a cricket administrator, who had advised me on my visa). He has recently started exporting pepper sauce and curry powder. He is doing better than ever before. The property has too much on it, refrigerators, televisions, SUVs, cash, jewellery. Every new acquisition is a source of greater anxiety. The health problems are piling up for Mr Singh: breathing problems, 'black eye', blood sugar

– 'this bloodsugar something eh, too low and you got a problem, too high and you get a next set of problem.'

And it emerges that this man, proud of proclaiming he is Kshatriya, a warrior, who will refuse to bow down before the blackman, 'Fire with fire. I can show blackman AK, make him smell AK,' is in fact a frighten likkle kitty! He cannot bear being alone, and on those occasions when circumstances have conspired to such an end, he will shut every door and window and fester inside with his fears. He is massaged every day with various lotions to keep his skin soft and fair it up as much as possible. He is contemplating emigrating, to UK, Canada, USA, anywhere, but never to India, no: 'They does treat we like we is blackman.'

CONSIDER too Akingbade, who goes by this single epithet, Yoruba for 'brave one who wears the crown'. As we walk down the line on East Coast Demerara, not many miles from the home of the Singhs, old friends call out to him as Charles. 'Can I help it if certain ignorant specimens insist on calling me by my slave name?'

Mr Singh I had chanced on, but Akingbade I sought out. I tell him so. I had read his letters to the editor. Mr Singh called him a propagandist.

He is a heavyset, slow, tentative man, grey facial hair, in worn-down mocassins, crushed black denim and a bright green dashiki. His hair is in a fro, his spectacles are thick and black, the styles of his hero, Walter Rodney, the great intellectual and activist assassinated during the reign of the dictator. But Akingbade has long departed from Rodney's non-racial agitation. He aligns himself with the party thought responsible for the death of his one-time hero. It is the ultimate indictment of Guyana.

There is much that is inspiring in Akingbade's African pride, the reclaiming of the name, the garment, his interest in old African cultures – the medicinal remedies, the soirées, the drumming sessions. But it has come in this instance with a blindness.

He cannot refer to Five for Freedom as criminals. They are exactly what the name says, freedom fighters. To him the crime spree was not a crime spree but an 'armed African resistance', a just response to police and state repression. The murders, abductions, arson, sexual violations against an ethnic community – it is not revolting, it is revolution. 'A necessary and inevitable corrective.'

He points out that African petty criminals are executed or jailed but the drug barons, architects of the narco economy, are allowed to roam free. 'Twenty-five metric tonnes of cocaine pass through the country every year. They have not made a seizure greater than ten kilos. They are apprehending the mules, the cargos are sailing through. The pickpocket is caught. The dons are safe, building their empires on blood money.'

'Resistance,' he says, making his thick hands into a fist. 'Resistance by any means.'

He considers me not adversarially, but cautiously. He cannot be candid with me as the Indians are (who not only assume I'm on their side but that I have come specifically to bear witness to their persecution). So when talk turns to the black academic who put out the extraordinary thesis that an aim of supplanted Hinduism on these shores was the extermination of the black race, he does not argue in its favour. Yet he cannot bring himself to condemn it. Instead his admonishment is reserved for the ethnic relations commission which had the publication banned. 'It is systemic. It is systemic.'

Anything could be inverted, corrupted.

I thought of something I had seen in one of the Five for Freedom handbills. The escapees, it said, would 'fight for the African-Guyanese nation just as the sea bandits Walter Raleigh, Francis Drake and Henry Morgan had fought for England and been honoured by the queen'.

And I thought, going back to the music, of a Tosh song, Here Comes the Judge. In the special way of reggae it is able to confront tragedy with a mix of rage and humour. Tosh plays the judge, and this judge 'have no mercy'. One by one he calls the names of the mighty explorers and privateers who pillaged the Caribbean, among them Francis Drake and Henry Morgan. Each answers in a splendidly exaggerated English accent, 'yeh-es sir'. They are made to plead guilty to six counts, from robbing and raping Africa to teaching black people to hate themselves. But we were forced, protest the invaders in their accents. *Contempt!*, pronounces the judge, and orders their hanging by the tongue.

What it had come to! Without irony, Africanists looking to Drake and Morgan for inspiration.

Walking down the line from Akingbade's village, Bachelor's Adventure, we reached Buxton. It was an old, proud community, named after an abolitionist, the second of the cooperative villages freedmen had formed a century and a half before. Over the years it had supplied Guyana with some of its most enlightened minds.

It was here the jailbreakers had been sheltered. Following a big bust there would be a lime in the village, food and drinks for all. The perpetrators were kings of the limes. Youthmen saw the flash, the respect in this. Then came the implosion. Petty disputes began to be settled by the gun. The reluctant were dealt with; families, their houses burnt, were forced to flee. The very name Buxton became synonymous with terror. Eventually the army set up a base in the village and remained a presence, a community imprisoned by its madness.

We stopped at a crossroads. The asphalt road ran parallel to the coast, a road which was routinely dug up to slow the entry of police vehicles and halt passenger vehicles to plunder – the road to avoid which Indians who could afford it flew rather than drove, professing the desire to 'piss pon Buxton' as they went over.

Perpendicular to the asphalt a red mud track went deep into the village, till the backlands, where initially the criminals and then the army had set up their camps.

At the crossroads itself was an abandoned rumshop and general store, low and white, its walls covered in half-hearted graffiti, full with youth idling flush in the middle of a weekday, lying on tables barechested, chatting, playing cards, smoking weed.

They would be 'glad fuh work,' they said, 'but nobody going touch we cause we from Buxton.' Among them was a young policeman who had quit the force after the spate of police executions. He was doing nothing much now. Another had a brother who had been shot dead by the armed forces. The friend of one was named recently in a high-profile murder. His mother refused him legal representation. 'He made his choices. He lived his life,' she said. The boy was twenty-one.

And there among the blacklisted youth on an idle corner in Buxton, or in the racial hothouse of the Singhs, things were bared with a bitter simplicity. A section of society was disillusioned with the state so they turned to crime. The state's response was to suppress the movement with more crime. Every act of crime further ruptured the division. Every rupture delivered new folkheroes, demigods, Five for Freedom versus Phantom, Blackie and his heirs versus Roger Khan and his cohorts, each thing seeded from something before, and that from something before, going back to the time the Africans and the Indians were put down brutally on the foreshore of South America.

Beneath the everydayness this was the Guyana I had stepped into. How innocent Baby was in all this! I thought of him, of Menzies Landing, lives blowing in and out, the world turning, up to its tricks.

PART THREE

I

BUTCHER the barber – for he was once the former, an antecedence apparent in his blade work – Butcher was pleased when I told him I'd moved houses to Sheriff Street. 'Nuff fairos on Sheriff Street.'

Butcher liked talking about women arguably more than the next banna, in particular declaring that, 'I doesn't have a race conscience about any gal – as long as she have clear skin.' So when Butcher said fairos he meant hookers not queers. There were some of the latter too on Sheriff Street, like the chubby orange-haired man in the blue flatshop with his painted black eyebrows thick like two fingers. That man was a delight, cussing customers for style, thrilling them as he did. The queen of the Sheriff Street fairos, however, was a queer, a transvestite once Salman and now Misha. She reigned at the other flatshop, below the short-time. She was fine like a reed, tall, with a fabulous sprinkle of glitter over a face that was thin, bony, cruel. Her stubble was green, her voice throaty. Men were served drinks by the two female hookers, an Indian and an African, each of ordinary appeal – but their souls were lost to proud, thin Misha, surrounded already by hungrier men. They stared at her, enchanted. Neutralised by spirit they went upstairs with one of the other girls and got lashed off for three grand or boned for seven.

This was the street, the Georgetown strip: fairos, nightclubs, rumshops, cookshops, taxi companies and restaurants, mostly Chinese, interspersed with regular Guyanese homes. A sad little strip. Its obscenities were small; its excesses were nothing. There were no streetlights. The odd neon glowed as a failed reminder. Herons and egrets visited the lily and styrofoam in the trenches. Donkey carts, dray carts, horse carts, and sometimes horses devoid of carts plied up and down the strip; so too the bling bling; so too big snorting trucks, for Sheriff Street was a thoroughfare between the slim perpendicular highways along the Atlantic and the Demerara. Wild eddo with their wild heart-shaped leaves gushed forth from the margins. And how does anyone explain to anyone, let alone to Mr Bhombal, that you love this place because look, here is eddo growing wild by the trenches on the nightstrip?

THOUGH my move from Kitty came soon after the Joint Services call, that had nothing do with it. They had arrived at 5 a.m., thumping with menace on the wooden wall. I was so certain it was a dream I may have poked the first soldier to check if he was real. He responded with admirable restraint, seeing how he had AK and thing at his disposal. He was very polite – 'Excuse the boots,' he said before entering. Behind him were a dozen armed ranks in camouflage, except for a dainty man in civvies, a specialist searcher. That man stuck his hands up with impeccable courtesy to indicate that he had nothing which could be planted. It was an important gesture. The chief of police himself had been implicated in a sting by Roger Khan, issuing the stitch-up instruction, 'Put drugs pon she.'

They searched every tenement, to a variety of reactions. Uncle Lance denounced them in his gravelly morning voice; Kwesi's mother, frightened her son had been up to something, sat quiet on the bench with dignity; Hassa never woke up – and when they kicked open the door word was he continued sleeping. Conversation about the raid ran hot for days afterwards. Kwesi's mother was not alone in worrying that Kwesi must have made trouble. Some identified a shifty chap from Pike Street as the 'cochore', the informer, who had tried to out Kwesi. Kwesi's alleged crimes ran from ganja trafficking to falling in with the Agricola gang. But the boy was legal.

Nobody ever found out what the raid was for. Or so I thought. Afterwards Uncle Lance told me that 'certain members, and I will not call their names', believed that it was I who was being investigated. For cocaine.

But the raid was a pleasant enough adventure. It was the small things which were accumulating. The noise from downstairs, the quarrels seeping up through the boards, the wailing children and yelping pups over the tin. The bed was breaking, the floor was rotting, the stove had to be tilted in a manner of angles before being lit. Mosquitoes devoured me with an ecstasy that crossed the last boundaries of perversion: once they ate my nipple. It happens suddenly that man loses the forbearance to hold together the small things.

There was more to it, I think. I had in that place begun to feel myself painted into a corner. As I'd started as a watcher and listener, that had become my role. This disturbed me. Lancy could luxuriate in his environment, sitting in his vest, launching broadsides, napping humidly. Kwesi could seek fake jewellery, mend the odd wire, launch daily a bid for a girl, a perfect logic to his days. Rabindranauth Latchman, recently relieved of his wife, could play sugardaddy in the sportsbar. About my own place I had begun to feel depressed.

How sorry to think that here where Africans, Indians, Portuguese and Chinese had arrived and turned themselves into one thing or another, had sired between them entire new racial specimen, a place where a munshi could turn ratcatcher and vice versa, where vulgarity was the lens to life, I had allowed myself to remain myself.

My first instinct was to think of travel. My eyes scanned the large Guyana wall map procured from the Lands and Surveys Commission. Leaf-vein streaks of blue ran through it like electricity. Past the rivers to the west the dotted border gave tantalisingly to the curve of letters, prolonged and syllabic, Venezuela; for now I decided to simply move houses.

It was about halfway through the year. Amid rambles in the countryside, I rifled through the classifieds, newspaper days of Roger Khan.

On my final day in Kitty I rose at the same hour that the ranks had come. It was raining. Through the grille at the back the raining morning looked so wet and beautiful. Things were purplish silver. Two kiskadees tangled yellow on the zinc beneath the whitey tree. The leaves of the welder's breadfruit tree made shapes in the wind. In the other yard fowl-cock went off like a cavalcade of sirens.

Goodbye alyou.

ODDLY I became good friends with Uncle Lance after I moved. I spotted him one day from the balcony, proceeding up Sheriff Street with short bumping steps. He was in trousers, shirt, shoes and a cap. It was the first time I had seen him in anything other than boxers, vest and rubber slippers. Just like that a man is made anew. Till that instance it had never occurred to me that Uncle Lance was a person of the wider world, that he may have a back story, or family, that he might have errands to run, that he could be seen passing on a road. To see Uncle Lance that day was in some way to see him for the first time. I invited him up for a bounce of rum.

How different he was! I had never before considered Uncle Lance's age. It was his temper rather than his age that one absorbed – the flamboyance, wit, wisdom. It had the effect of what people call evergreen. But now he felt distinctly deciduous; dry, but for the sweat on his face. The sweat did not trickle. It lodged in his wrinkles, which were deep rather than many, bringing emphasis to them. His chin, a small, rounded piece, was baggier than I had noticed before, as though a blob of air had leaked into it. When he took off his cap, his hair, wet with sweat and combed back, had formed itself into thin bands through which shone scalp. He was breathing hard. He looked old.

He talked so differently too! I had not heard Uncle speak in a low voice ever. He attracted the ears of anybody in the vicinity; indeed, it was anybody in the vicinity he was addressing. People congregated around him when he made jokes or lambasted the government; they continued a little longer hanging clothes on the fence or draining rice-water in the yard. So it was a shock to hear Uncle Lance say something as prosaic as, 'Nice place you got here.'

It was a nice place. I had got a deal on it because the landlady, who had migrated and operated via a handyman, had that keenest of Guyanese convictions: that Guyanese are not to be trusted. She only let out to foreigners. But the house was neither upscale nor quiet nor large enough for foreigners. It had lain empty a long time. And still, because the previous tenants were foreigners, it was a home furnished down to a toaster.

We stood in the thick balcony breeze, five-year and coconut in hand, watching Sheriff Street. Neither of us said anything.

Below, a tattered man who passed every day at this hour rummaged through the rubbish bin. He found remnants of fried bangamary and plantain chips from the fish shop. He went along his way.

Above, a small plane fluttered in the cloudless sky.

Looking at the aircraft, Uncle Lance said at last, to some degree reverting to his old self, 'I tell you something, bai, if we could grow sugarcane by every airstrip in this country we never got to buy a single barrel of fuel.'

'How so, Uncle?'

'Ethanol, bai. It got nuff ethanol coming from the sugarcane to run them Islander. Like bush rum, you drink bush rum? Bush rum could run a car. So long as you got the converter in the carburettor, right.'

He added with a kind of morose chuckle, 'But we only runnin we own self on rum.'

We watched the plane dip out of sight. He lapsed into his unfamiliar self again.

'Who knows where that plane going, where it coming from.'

'Ogle, I guess.'

'Heh,' he chuckled again. 'You young, bai. You hand soft and you mind clean. Let me tell you, bai, airstrip come up anywhere in the country, and it ain't use to carry people alone.'

I expected him to get into a cocaine riff, at how the government corrupt, but instead he sat slowly on the plastic chair.

'I walking the last half an hour.'

'You mad! Sun hot, Lancy.'

'I coming from a funeral. Beepat.'

I knew what he was talking about. Even by the standards of Guyanese daily crime it was a gruesome affair. The man owned an electronics store. Abducted by bandits one day, his body, decapitated, both feet hacked off, was found weeks later in the D'Urban backlands. A revenge killing, the papers called it.

'You knew the man?'

'Everybody know everybody, bai. It had a time when two or three murder a year was a big big thing. Now we gettin one hundred, one fifty. Now out of three quarter million that does give a rate of twenty. If you look up the statistical recordings, that is a very high number . . .' Momentarily he seemed to find pleasure in numbers.

'Politricks rip apart we country. When I was a bai in Wakenaam,' – he held his hand absurdly low, by his ankle – 'black people kwarril if they see me barefoot. They make me put on something on me foot! Tha'is how much love there was. Then we get the race riot and the same people hold their nose when they pass we house.

148

'It was stupidness at the burial. People talking one set of nonsense. People bawling, people high, calling for phantom to come back. They was a blackman there, just a limer, lookin a lil yardy-yardy. They chase the man away. The wife and she sister bawling, "get that man out of there". I can't take that kind of stupidness. Look, a man dead. People got to understand what that means. I walk away before it speed my head.'

With that Uncle Lance downed the rum and stood up. He rolled the ice cube about his mouth and ejected it in a graceful arc into the yard.

'I gone, bai. Get home and catch five.'

'Alright, Uncle. Take care, right.'

'Maybe I'll pass you sometime.'

'I'll look out for you.'

'Good.'

Placing his cap tight on his head he set out again in the sun, round-headed and wide-hipped, shrinking till he reached Garnett Street, which he crossed, paused, then turned into.

I lingered on the balcony.

The humidest day. Sheriff Street passed. An emaciated Luna. A boy's face pressed against a water jar. The clop of a dray cart. Slow Guyana, its time stretched in the sun.

A red-suited lady in cornrows. She stares at the flaming tips of her shoes. Langour, introspection in downward profile. The suit contours her body. Humidity is falling on her. She tosses back her head, to make air on her sweat. Her nostrils quiver, a face now flagrant, vulgar. I wish I could invite her up. I wish I could drench her.

Her parasol has a rip. A triangle of light flaps on her chest. Her bus has arrived. Her calf tenses as she climbs on.

Not still noon. A day to be negotiated, and another.

2

THE ONE thing I knew about my parents' courtship was that they had met on the train. New to the city, he with his simple side-parting had strayed into the ladies' compartment, where she had ticked him off with a raised umbrella. The following day he made the same error.

On a wet July morning in Georgetown, I was jolted back to the story in a moment of stupidity.

The day began like the others, with the kis-ka-dee of kiskadees, slatted rays, a contemplation of the hunk of hours ahead. Lying in bed, I pencilled in the purchase of a pressure cooker as the main task. I had one already, carried across oceans in the manner of an Indian national – my eldest sister had insisted. I had negotiated on the size. The vessel I accepted was an aluminium knot, good for no more than two fists of rice or six pieces of goat. I hardly ever used it. I preferred an open pot for the company of aromas, for the time slow-cooking consumed. But lately I had begun to feel ghostly tending to dishes in solitude.

In the after-rain morning I walked out to Survival on Vlissengen. There I ran into Mr Bhombal's old flatmate, a reserved, shrivelled accountant from Jaipur with tufts of hair erupting from his ears. 'Namaste, how do you do?' he asked, employing his usual juxtaposition. For the first time our conversation went beyond this. And as he told me of the train bombings in Bombay I was struck by a dumb moment's fright for ma and papa.

The high commission had rung his office to let them know. He was registered with the high commission. Was I not? Why not! It was the duty of every Indian national to register. Why didn't I get registered now? There was an unbecoming forcefulness to him. Didn't I have people in Bombay? Then I had better go to the high commission right away. And get registered. He would not let it go.

Caught between his aggression and the stupidity of my first instinct, I wished to leave. I remember having done this – influenced perhaps by his 'how do you do', or perhaps the magistrates of Georgetown – with the words, 'That will be all.'

Outside the sun had come out. The light dazzled on the dark of the trenches. On the bridge the bearded man of unsound mind, sometimes employed to clean the trenches, peered into the trees, scratching his forehead. Across the road Chin the chinee coconut man sat beneath his umbrella with his radio. 'Kitty Kitty Camville Kitty,' the conductor of the no. 41 shouted as he whooshed by. Nobody had the faintest.

I walked to a phone and internet shop. The lines in Bombay were jammed. I looked at the news online. Things were sketchy: seven or eight coordinated blasts, rush hour, hundreds feared dead, Islamic terror groups.

After a while the first blogs were up, first pictures, helpline numbers. On the line-maps of the tracks the blasts were red flares like a Diwali loom going off. They were my places. Matunga, near where the big family house stood, where I had grown up, where my brother and his wife and child still lived; three flares down, Santacruz, where I had moved into a 1-room-kitchen, to use the Bombay lingo; and though these memories were so recent they felt from such another dependent time.

I stayed a long time in the shop. The more I didn't hear back from people the more I was certain they were safe. In Bombay one learns the probability of anything is negligible.

When I stepped back out of the shop, two or three hours later, it was cloudy once more. I could have gone home, or indeed, to the high commission. Instead I found myself walking towards the hospital.

The doctor had recommended I come in for a platelet count two months after dengue. It had been over four now. I hadn't gone because I did not want to face Roxanne at the reception after the abrupt end of our thing.

'She stop work here,' the guard said.

I now really wanted to see her. I considered ringing her. I liked her laugh, her lips, almost pined for them. But I took it as a sign. Only a fool forces awkwardness upon himself.

There was no reason to check on my platelets, of course. Still I settled in the hospital. The sick white tubes, the antiseptic smell, the listlessness of the afflicted, it was easy to sink into. I seemed to have occupied the section near the obstetrician, for I was among pregnant girls. They flatly considered the bumps of their bellies. One or two were in tears.

The wretchedness of Bombay trains. You teetered on the edge of life's urgencies and futilities, a compressed body in a compressed city. The debasement and energy of slums, pools of sewage, bushes of excreta, the utter fact of India. What dirty ambition was forced out of reasonable persons; abuses flung, shirts tugged, punches thrown, feet trampled, a misery that ceased to be one when you saw a boy without arms or eyes in the same circumstance. People struggling, making do, trying to get home, for a date, a movie, a family function, fighting the good fight – and boom, a mangled limb. What a thing, eh?

I sat in the hospital till I was asked by a nurse, 'You gettin through?' I glanced at my wrist. Though there was no watch on it, I sprang up as if to show I was running late.

It was early evening. With an eggball I walked to the seawall. The tide was out. The shore looked rotten. On the mudflats a dog chased crabs. Elsewhere sweethearts sat in a curl, ladies walked dogs, gamblers gambled with naked-girl cards. Presently the clouds, thick and bulbous, were backlit by the orange sun in a heavenly glow. Before India, Guyana's problems were so fresh and small-scale, and I couldn't tell if more or less hopeless for that.

Walking on the wall, I took a decision to do more journalism than I had been doing. Travel pieces, reportage, cricket articles, preferably for pounds or dollars. The exchange rate being what it was, even one a month would easily sustain me so long as I lived a basic life. I didn't have the heart to eat further into my savings, and frankly, ambling along wasn't a simple business and adventure an expensive one.

Mr Bhombal was right. I could have gone anywhere. But I had come here. To look it in the eye was important.

Returning home, I checked into an internet shop again. Safe. I bought a handsome pressure cooker. It was months before I learnt that explosives in the Bombay bombings had been stuffed into pressure cookers and laid on the tracks.

I LIVED over a studio. El Dorado Recording Studio was the name. It was only slightly older than I to the building but its mood had fixed deep already: the homie sprawl at the gate, the broad-brim NY and $$ caps carefully angled to five degrees, the jerseys, the bling, the low-ass denims, and since some among them were deportees from America, the ghetto talk ringing tring-ta-tring with yo-yo-yo and dawg and ho and shawty. As a matter of fact they'd recorded a song called Ho And Shawty (Ballas Get Notty). *Prick the knife into the apple (ho and shawty)/Twist it round till it shake the chapel (the ballas get notty).*

The composition was by the inhouse trio, El Doriders, comprising 9MM, Midas and Mista Capone. Their sound was American. This was the wheel of music: rap, hiphop born from Jamaican deejays toasting over dub, and American hiphop sent back with new glamour and new context to the Caribbean. They wrote about fucking, cheating, pimping, balling, trafficking. They weren't hardcore bad-ass, I don't think. Their effort was to be badder, harder core than they really were. At any rate, I only once witnessed a bad mofo showdown, and that too had the feel of pantomime.

I was boiling sweet potato or doing something similarly un-hiphop when I heard machine gun exchanges of 'don't fuck with me nigger'. Downstairs Midas and a man I'd never seen around the hood before were shuffling about in boxing stances. They had drawn blood already. 'You wanna play me, nigger? You wanna play *I*?' They leaned on one another at the forehead like battering rams, fucks, niggers, fucking niggers, and don't fuck with me niggers booming about like bullets. Around them people struck casual poses, a finger in the pocket, a smirk, yo-yo-yo, cut that out ya'll. More punches thrown, the crack of knuckle upon jaw. At the peak of the brawl 9MM slunk away into the studio and emerged with a pistol. He struggled with it in a corner; something seemed to have jammed. He worked it out finally, and began circling the fight in a tilt-head, my-hand-in-a-9mm way. For minutes he did this. Nobody took note. He wasn't gangsta enough. Shortly after, a woman appeared and wailed, also in an American inflection, 'Is this how nigger run thing?' She dragged away the bleeding fighter from Midas. 9MM went back inside with the gun, still unnoticed.

I became well-acquainted with the Doriders. The lady at the roti shop had warned me to keep my door locked, but apart from the odd grand bummed off now and then they were very good neighbours, interesting and uninterfering. They'd been deported for small-time peddling. Each knew exactly when he'd got into it; when the mother refused money, when the brother was gunned down, when the girl wanted a diamond stud. They'd cleaned up, made babies, did only ganja to clear their head of negative vibes.

They were young, tall, muscular, wore braids, looked cool, hung loose. They had an exceptional capacity to hang. They came in before noon and returned at night. Almost all the while they hung in the yard, by the gate, on the steps, standing, sitting, watching, waiting, smoking weed, inhaling which 9MM, supposedly Rasta, might remark 'Rome burnin' or something similarly delusional. Their world was getting smaller, from Brooklyn and Queen's to Sheriff and Ruimveldt. They'd signed contracts but had seen no money. It wasn't easy being a recording artiste in Guyana. It wasn't that there was piracy but that there was only piracy. They refused to bow to Babylon and do jobs. Besides, I don't think they minded the hanging too much. 'I do what I want, man,' Mista Capone said. 'Make some music, chill out, fuck some bitches, fuck *a lot* of bitches. You got to keep bitches wanting more, see. You got to tell the bitch, Not today, I ain't fuckin you today, come back Sa'rday, I'm gonna fuck you Sa'rday.'

While the Doriders hung, the studio was abuzz. It was small, two cabins the size of cubicles, a computer and a console. Righteous Man ran it. Lil Miss Hot came by to cut soca and R&B, I-Frikka for reggae and culture, Aggressive Youth for hard dancehall. Then there was hiphop from the Doriders. Between all these Righteous Man amphibiously switched. He played with knobs, generated loops, ran the voices through auto-tune, supplied baritone dubs, and also cut solos. I didn't have a particular taste for the stuff, but I admired its casual Caribbean prolificacy: that there is always more and no matter what it will keep on coming.

The studio was soundproof, of course, but there was music in the air all day. In the mornings the Double D music cart rolled by, hawking anything from Akon to Jim Reeves. In the quiet of the afternoon one might hear Lil Miss Hot practise on the stairs, or I-Frikka rehearsing with touching sincerity into his dictaphone. In the evenings a vehicle pulled up by the gate, a personal sound system for the Doriders, a louvre-rattling two hours while they grooved to their own songs over and over. At night the music from the fish shop was turned up.

On Sunday came the cleansing.

The studio was closed, the traffic was thin, the leftover sound fragments of the Saturday lime at the fish shop were vapourised away by the new sun.

There was music in the air, but mere strains. Across the road in his patched-up balcony, a man transmitted tinny suggestions of oldies or lovers rock reggae from his portable. From the back of the house more strains blew in. These were of gospel. Its feathery notes held a grand and rousing promise, and I liked brewing tea to it. One morning, unable to control the impulse, I put out the stove and went in search of its source.

But in the gospel hall, rather than swell, the notes shrank into something depleted and echoing. It was a small, plain room. There were two dozen people, of all races. Some were in church dress, the majority in everyday wear. They sang reluctantly, seated, with minimal swaying, to a student casio.

I took a seat in the last pew. The preacher, speaking up for evangelists, railed against the mainline churches. An Amerindian brother from the interior told amid quick compressed amens of the spreading of the light among the tribes, and condemned the avaricious businessmen who worked Amerindian staff even on a Sunday so they couldn't pray.

Thereafter people got up one after another and talked of their problems, a teacher refused leave from work, a senior citizen disturbed by a nightspot, a mother employed below minimum wage, yet she knew she had been blessed. There was a strange and lonely semi-confessional intimacy to proceedings. It made me feel, I don't know, like a cheat, an intruder on others' piety.

I stayed till the end.

'I's glad fuh see you here,' I heard someone say as I left.

It was Jackie, the cleaning lady from the studio, and Jackie, no longer in denim three-quarters, had dressed for church.

'I keeping after boys dem fuh come to chu'ch. They en listen.'

'Well.'

'You know what I see Vincent, wah he call heself, Capone or wuhever, you know what I see he doin in the yard the other day? What you suppose to do in the toilet, dah is wah.'

'Sheddin a tear?'

'Eh he! I tell he about it and he go cussin off he mout in the marnin. I axe he if he gon pray that he prattlin off so.'

'Is just how he talk.'

'Well, I's glad you a chu'chman. See you next Sunday, right.'

She sashayed away, carrying her African bearing in her big black dress, humming a hymn we were made to sing at the morning assemblies of my Christian school in Bombay, standing in lines, wearing our ties, Praise, My Soul, The King of Heaven.

'UPSTAIRS, upstairs,' I heard a hoarse voice call out early one Sunday morning. I had returned late the previous night from the bank robberies in the country. I feared it was Jackie hauling my ass to church.

I went out to the balcony. Below Uncle Lance stood in a cuddly, grumbly teapot stance that appeared to suggest that I'd stood him up. I mentioned this.

'You got to be sharp, bai, you got to mean what you say.'

'Mean what, Lancy?'

'You said you going to look out for when I come.'

I invited him up for a cup of tea.

'With lemongrass,' I lied, well aware that the specimen I had planted in a pot had mutated to regular grass.

'Mornin ah wastin,' he growled back.

I splashed water on my face and left in boxers and tee.

He began to walk even as I descended the stairs. We walked a few minutes, over the stink canal to Drury Lane.

'So here you got a little bird-racing going on, right by you,' Uncle Lance said. He had remembered an old conversation from Kitty.

On the grass embankment vendors sold seeds from damply spread sacks. Men stood around by the trench with cages. In them dark shadows of towa-towas and fire-reds flickered and danced. There were parked cars, a clean Sunday vibe. People stood in gyaffin formations, and gyaffin specked the Sunday air.

'Nobody gamblin today,' he said. 'That is good, chap, cause let me tell you, gamblin is worse addiction than sweet woman. I learn it the hard way.'

There was going to be no race, that was clear. It left me mildly puzzled as to why we were here. He climbed on to the boot of a car and gave himself a lethargic morning-stretch against the windscreen.

There was a newspaper beside him. I browsed through it.

Man Shortchanges Prostitute, Gets Severely Beaten

Two Children Were Riding a Pregnant Donkey and Lashing It

Cocaine in Cabbage: Mother of Three Remanded

The short item about a pandit accused of larceny I read out to Uncle Lance.

He gurgled like a child.

'You ever seen pandit in action?' he asked, quivering with laugh.

'I been to weddings.'

'That ain't pandit, bai. That is just like clerk. Me show you what is pandit.'

To my surprise he beckoned me into the car, still quivering, and we sputtered down Sheriff Street, past the back of the botanical gardens, past the rum shop that declared upfront that Malcolm X is a leader not a follower, and the giant lampshade which was the Church of the Transfiguration, through the tall palm of Le Repentir Cemetery and out on to the East Bank Highway.

A short way out of Georgetown, aback a canefield, amid a cluster of jhandis beside a tangle of palmyra, he brought the car to a juddering halt.

The mandir was in a covered yard, lined with waist-high idols. Inside this perimeter of idols a quartet of musicians struck up an uptempo bhajan. A pair of men played the dholak and the harmonium. A young girl went at a dhantal, a tall metal rod clanged with a piece of iron shaped like a horseshoe, an instrument developed in indenture as far as I could tell. *Bhajan sunavo, baidyanath,* a lady in a gaudy salwar kameez sang, *O baba, puja karo baidyanath.*

Pandit was in his chambers. A group of people stood at the door, watching him at work. And from the door one got a close view of Pandit, a man with a harelip, white hair, broken teeth and fleshy breasts peeking through a Hawaiian shirt. He sat at a desk and considered the matter before him.

The case was of a young boy dying of asthma. It was presented by three generations of ladies, possibly a grandma, ma and sister. Pandit began by making inquiries about the family and the property – a process in which he frequently closed his eyes, feigned anger and on occasion looked downright violated. The matter of the property he pursued further, its dimensions, its division, the strain on the family over the division, how the boundaries were aligned, which tree on which boundary. As he received the answers, his earthen face turned scarlet, his eyes shuttered tight, his breasts trembled and one cowered at the prospect of the final eruption. But he kept sustaining the build-up, going often to the terrifying brink but not beyond. One time he blew out two candles in a huff. Another time with an unexpected shout he summoned fresh cloves via a woman with bright lipstick and enormous cleavage, all the while keeping his eyes shut. Opening them at last, he created something on a notepad with abandon. It was the property.

'Piece ah land they fightin fah. It causin all this destruction, this scatteration.'

'Do sumthin nuh, Pandit,' the sister pleaded, with the liberty of the young.

'The thing gone too deep,' Pandit replied.

'Come nuh, Pandit,' the mother joined in.

The grandmother looked on with stoic fatalism.

Pandit raised his voice.

'The evil spirit going round-round round-round and it settle right here' – he stabbed the pencil into the pad – 'right here pun the eastern boundary, pun the noni tree.'

He fixed his gaze, one by one, on each of the ladies.

'The spirit weigh pun the bai. It press down pun he till he cyan breathe—' he put his hands around his own neck and made large asphyxiating sounds, 'and the same spirit going to kill alyou.'

Silence.

'Is true,' the grandmother said at last. 'He granfadder go dah way too.'

Pandit adjusted his harelip into a pout; then, leaning forward, he delivered the blow.

'The bai not goin fuh live. Me nah do it.'

More silence, followed by the twinkle of tears. The situation deteriorated rapidly thereafter. I couldn't tell exactly what was going on, but it felt fatal. Minutes later, when all seemed lost and it felt like the boy was already dead and the mother had let her forehead drop against the wooden table – that is when Pandit administered the turnaround.

He would consider assisting. If the boy was still alive they were to return with barley, turmeric, and fifteen thousand in cash the next day.

'Wha I like bout Pandit is he honest deh,' the relieved mother said as they exited the chamber.

'When pandit seh it he mean it,' the sister concurred.

'Trut. He not a man fuh give false hope. Da'is a thing to respeck in today daynage.'

It was so massively Naipaulian that for long afterwards I suspected it was an elaborate wind-up, and the joke deh pon me.

That afternoon, dispensing a slow rub to his dhal-belly, Uncle Lance not so much said as dictated the aphorism, 'Bai, in Guyana it have pandit and it have bandit and sometimes it hard to tell the two apart.'

Ever since, Uncle Lance and I called each other Pandit and Bandit, each using either name for the other.

I LEARNT of Uncle Lance that he once had a wife who fled with a lover to the United States, that he had a son who worked there 'programming computer', and that he himself once ran a plastic-wares shop in Kitty Market and thereafter a three-car taxi service – 'such a roaring success that I could enjoy me a early retirement'. The last of these facts had a practical bearing on us.

For there came a period that we devoted our Sundays to cookery. These days began with Uncle Lance appearing in a shaky white Toyota AT 192, one of his old taxis hired out to a friend through the week. With three short blows he'd announce his arrival at half past five. Off we'd go in the drizzling dayclean. He would lean suspiciously on the steering wheel as he drove, squinting at the windshield as if alarmed to find a world beyond it. He never ever pushed the needle beyond a hair's breadth of 30 mph, an aspect I called attention to frequently.

'You ain't see me drive, Pandit. I could reach GT to Kwakwani in one hundred minutes. You know Kwakwani? You cyan know is where! You only bin here a couple of days! Is sheer bush. One hundred minutes, Georgetown to Kwakwani. O my foot heavy, O it made from lead. But you ga think for the fool on the road, right. That is what an upstart like you don't un'stand.'

'Nobody on the road, Lancelot.'

'There was a time we had nice zebra crossing, right. They would paint am steady. Could see them stripes from a mile, eh, shining pon the road. The stripes now vanish, the zebra done exstink.'

'Nobody on the road!'

'Jackarses them does take an *angle* into the crossing. You not allowed that. You got to start one side of the crossing and walk *over* it till you reach other side. Now people cuttin in from any part of the road, causin one bundle of confusion and jumpin on the stripes, "look I's pon the zebra."' Suck-teeth.

By six a.m. the wharf at Meadow Bank was already crowded. Riches were everywhere, smell of river, stink of fish, blood in the morning. Alive in the drizzle, filthy-footed, we'd hustle with zeal. It was serious fare, no jokey trench fish, no hassar and hourie and patwa. Here were shark and trout, ten kilo gilbakas and their pricey heads, whiskery catfish and highwata fish, mounds of shrimp and bangamary and packoos, their tails twitching behind stupidy flat heads like the fronts of woebegone school shoes. One watched the skinning of the packoo with sorrow. It was so honest and foolish. When a cutlass was introduced into its mouth, it would bite and not let go. The skinners were vicious. They stood at wooden platforms and let rip at the creatures, splotching customers with scales and entrails. It was an unfathomable violence, such a contrast to India, where men with moustaches sat tranquil on their *hasiyas* making meditative incisions as if in penance.

On the way back we would stop at the Sunday market in La Penitence. Here, shopping, chomping on a pink guava or a cassava ball, Lancy might break into a calypso, and it had to be said he did well for a voice like his. He knew all the folk songs, the shantos and calypsos, the Bill Rogers and Dave Martins.

At Sheriff the session would begin. We might make a herb and pepper batter for the shark or the banga and lash her with tennis rolls and Hot West Indian sauce. The catfish we might curry with raw mango. I might impress him with my breakthrough invention of pumpkin with karaila and butterfish (in the same pot). Lancy was an expert chopper, saying a chinee gal taught him, and he could do two onions in the time I did one. His stance at the stove was a hand on hip, a heavy lean back, eyebrows arched, a man bemused.

Over cooking and eating we encountered the connections and disconnections with India. Every now and then Uncle Lance would pull out a remembered term from his youth, for instance, *bartan manjey*, to wash dishes, a verb morphed into a noun. There were words he knew which meant nothing to me. Like *sanay*, to mix and eat with the fingers. This bewildered him. No less than the fact that I had never eaten a dhalpuri before Guyana.

There was good reason for this. I had never lived, only travelled in the Gangetic plains from where the coolies were drawn. My contact with its peasantry was so limited, I knew so little about them, and Bombay Hindi was so different from the dialects of the eastern plains. It took me a while to work out that the Guyanese verb, 'chunkay the dhal' – dhal to rhyme with shawl – derived from *chaunk*, for *tadka*. Equally it amazed Uncle Lance that we didn't use curry powder in India, without which no curry in Guyana qualified as one.

One day, a good three months before Christmas, we thought to make the putagee Christmas dish of garlic pork.

We drove out to Mon Repos on the coast looking for fresh pig. The capped ladies giggled with Caribbean punning, 'Me ain't givin out me pork. Hear nuh, Anusha, the bai does wan pork, you givin out you pork?' Anusha giggled, we all giggled, and she supplied us two fatty pounds.

At home we washed and lowered the pig into a transparent bowl. We threw in bruised cloves of garlic. We deleafed the fine leaves of thyme from its stalks and sprinkled them in with holy abandon. We halved the firebomb peppers and threw those in with final fingerfuls of salt. We covered the pig with vinegar and fastened a cellophane over the top. It was to be left like this for three weeks. Our pig, she would breathe in every last rumour of flavour.

The bowl we placed on a doily – such a furnished house! – on the central table. No matter what, I could not stop staring at it. Lancelot too eyed it heavily. Every other sentence contained the words, 'gyalic poke, Bandit, gyalic poke'. After two hours we decided to fry one piece 'jus fuh see'. An hour later a quarter of the bowl was done. Three weeks on, two pieces remained. Damn fine pieces though.

In this manner, in between rambles, assignments and long days in the country, I became Sunday friends with Uncle Lance, and through him I met many people in this easy, informal world.

From the vantage of the Sheriff balcony, standing red rum on ice, we watched people. He would divide passing citizens into two categories.

The first type were 'Western Union people. Them does live pon remittance like leech. You hear that biggest industry in Guyana sugar. I say no! Is Western Union!'

The second type were 'visa queue people. Them just come from cuttin a round of the embassy or they going fuh cut a round. Is in their eyes, Pandit, focus pon the eyes!'

He held each in equal contempt. He could never be a Western Union man, a blasted parasite. As for the second, he thought of himself as a modern man, and 'the Caribbean man is a madern man, right, a mix of culture'. And so this was the reason that he'd never leave here, never cut a round of the embassy: he did not want to leave modernness to go to backwardness.

Often he would point out someone and start a story about them.

'That man there, he got the longest dong in Guyana.'

'How you can be sure, Pandit?'

'Every single lady of the night refuse the man. The moment he pull down he pant, they frighten.'

Another time he identified a chickenfucker.

'Chickenfucker?'

'Eh he.'

Once he regaled me with stories of a man who had more girl problems than anyone. He lived in the Kitty house that I'd lived in. He liked country gals because he could feel like a bossman around them. One such girl he reduced to tears once by asking for a blowjob. 'Is wah job me got to do now? Wash job meh done

164

finish, cook job meh done finish, clean job meh done finish, wha'is this blow job?' Another girlfriend would bite him and beat him and threaten to take her own life. Often Uncle Lance was awoken at night to shouts of 'ketch she, Lancy, ketch she,' as the girl took position at the window.

It was possible, of course, that Uncle Lance was spinning yarns. But when we saw Kevin pass again an hour later, he confirmed the stories. He supplied one from the previous evening. A girlfriend found a condom in his bed. 'Hear what I tell she. I tell she I was tryin it on. Oh boy.'

Like Kevin, people frequently came upstairs for a bounce, sometimes with friends and cousins, taking a call from somebody, inviting them over too. As a result our limes grew manifold; and it triggered in me at sudden moments the strange but satisfying sensation that I was now living here.

As Guyanese of all ages and genders cooked and enjoyed it, the open kitchen raged with activity. A number of pots were sparked at once, here a corn soup with dumpling, there a fish stew with okra. The range had an oven, and a trout might bake in it, heaped with eschalot and thyme and fresh juice from La Penitence, the starburst of five finger or the sour of passionfruit. A chicken might go in massaged with jerk and washed with pristine coconut milk. Sticks of cassava might be roasted on the flame and smothered with butter, people, foremost among them Lance Banarsee, fighting over the 'bun-bun', the charred bits. The wind blew through all the open half-doors but the flames never outed.

Afternoons ran on to evenings and nights, cackling and narrating, arriving and departing, old stalwarts, sporty lads, vibrant university girls and all in between, finishing eventually in a great drunken fornicating winedown somewhere – or else at Big Market Big Mamma's. She was a colossal loving lady, Big Market Big Mamma, shining black in a loose T-shirt, a head wrap and a long flowing skirt, a face that wanted to feed the world and make it a happier place. She was Mama Creole. All the movements of the new world met in her. Chowmein from the Chinese; metemgee from the Africans; pepperpot from the Amerindians; roti and curry from the Indians; baked chicken from the Europeans; the menu dripping off her tongue like honey when you asked, 'Wah you gat fuh me tonight, Big Mamma?'

Sometimes there were trips to somebody's cousin's friend's plot of land by the black-water creeks off the highway, trips that killed me with nostalgia even while I lived them, driving aback a pickup, silvery rain pelting bare backs, leaves dancing on the mud trail, branches snapping back onto faces, puddles like lakes forded in the sinking vehicle, bushcook and red rum and drenched cricket, jamoon splattered purple upon the wet soil – the remarkable freedom of a forgotten and irrelevant place on earth.

But Uncle Lance himself retreated. Said he'd been up those highways too many times.

3

WHEN the lull came around again I turned to de Jesus. I had met him at one of the limes. He was a Brazilian and a Guyanese, and like most such people he had bright red skin, green-brown cat eyes and enormous red calves shaped like frozen whole chicken. He came from a family of old money and influence, though he himself, incongruous to his physical giantitude, was but a thin limb of the tree. Yet it was a branch still connected, and de Jesus had people everywhere, on the coast, on the border, both the Guyanese side and the Brazilian side, as well as in several cities of that immense country. His business was to transport goods between Georgetown and the border. It was a long, rough journey, but de Jesus's Bedford went up and down every month and de Jesus himself on it every now and then.

'Any time you want to walk shout me,' he had told me, and when I shouted him he was leaving the following evening. This implied certain logistical challenges. For one, I would have to travel without a visa. I therefore became determined to obtain the other mandatory document, a yellow-fever certificate.

I went down to the ministry of health to get one. There I learnt that the certificate was issued ten days after the shot. I asked the nurse if she would back-date it.

'You going to make problem for me?'

'No.'

She blinked slowly.

'You does go to church?'

'No, not really.'

'What kind of church you doesn't go to?'

'Any, I guess. Why?'

'I just like to ask.'

She pulled a face of suppressed frustration, of what is the world coming to, wrote a bribed date on the certificate, and injected me.

I gave her a raise and left.

Soon after, I was struck by a doubt. Who knew what she had injected me with? What did she care? Perhaps she was out to punish, to set right. Idly I entertained the possibility that I might collapse on the embankment and pass away. I might roll into the trench, and some days later be located by a stench. Years on I might make it to the Murder and Mystery section of the Sunday paper, where unsolved crimes were reprised over a thousand chilling words.

It was hot. Everywhere were listless people and everything felt wretchedly hot and uninteresting. It was the third week of November. Where had the last two months gone? Limes, trips, reading and writing, elaborate cooking. The year was about to clasp shut, an unforeseen situation.

As I walked in the heat, I was taken back to the hot walks in the early days. Everything, in fact, the ministry, the paperwork, was reminiscent of the early days. I considered going down to the street by the big market where Baby hung out. I discarded the thought. What would be the point?

I walked instead till German's at the top of New Market Street and there I ate raisin rice with bora pork.

Afterwards, when I returned home, having walked foolishly once

168

more, and switched on the standing fan and lay down in the safety of my mosquito net, I felt choked by circles – that I had gone in circles, was still going in circles, and this was not supposed to be part of the plan.

WE left after dark. The Bedford was a magnificent clunking lump of metal with 15,000 pounds in its tray, primarily vats of petrol. De Jesus looked large, red and freshly bathed. Topless Anand Moonsammy, sporting a green beret, drove the truck. 'How yuh do, Panjabi?' he said to me by way of curious greeting. He had mammoth Steve Buscemi eyes that did well to stay on his face.

'Is sheer Panjabi building the cricket stadium, you know. I meet them one time. They open up they head wrap and long out they hair and listen to they jump-up music.'

'Bhangra?'

'Eh he. Sheer Panjabi. Me a Madras, though.'

And for a while thereafter he told me about being a Madras, how they were going strong with worship of Kali, how blackpeople and them were close-close for they themselves were black and had kinky hair and ate beef and pork. We discussed the genesis of Moonsammy, probably derived from Munuswamy, and talked of Sonny Moonsammy, a tremendously dashing batsman I'd heard about from many an old-timer on the Corentyne. And from there we spoke of cricket, and thereafter numerous other topics, such as the Bedford, and automobiles in general – until I wrecked his mood by mentioning Uncle Lance's theory of running cars on bush rum.

'You hear that, Jesus,' he snapped, 'you see why Guyanese get reputation for chupidness? Is because some people *determined* to be chupid. Bush rum *evaporate* too quickly. A chupid man tell this man that it use for fuel. If me nah know that bush rum evaporate too quickly, me would tell a next man. Just so all Guyanese come out looking chupid.'

As Moonsammy spoke no more, sucking his teeth hard and shifting gears with a previously absent harshness, it was de Jesus all the way till Linden.

And de Jesus told tales of the supernatural. There was a man everyone knew had Kaneima. De Jesus once saw him go to a pond where nobody had ever caught a single fish and return with a string of lukanani. Another time the same man went into some bushes and came back as an anteater. Whenever I laughed during these stories, de Jesus pointed out my absurdity – 'the man laughing!' – to Moonsammy, who stared furiously ahead with his basketball pupils. De Jesus kept em coming. Of Ole Higue – that is, aged supernatural ladies who shed their skin and become balls of fire – he narrated the incident when a ball of fire accompanied the truck for thirty miles one night. Another time a girl in the family told people she'd seen Ole Higue outside the window and guess what – the next day her thigh was covered with blue marks. At Linden he told of the time when, outside this same stall where we were now stopped for a snack, he'd come face to face with a very black man, a very ugly man. Rain had fallen hard; de Jesus had made for the shed but the man had disappeared, no trace of him, and there was nowhere he could have gone. The man was a jumbie.

Soon after we hit the laterite trail de Jesus began snoring. I stared at the headlit mud, the red so bright in the lights, the trail so cratered, but not wet as it was the last time. I thought more of that time, of Baby and the birdman and the candidate, who'd put up a respectable show in elections after all, and splinters of spoken words and lived scenes carouselled by; and the feeling of being on a carousel, the circularity, it returned to me as we rumbled down the chilly, herby forest. We hurtled past the intersection where we had once turned towards Mahdia, where soldiers had been told I'd come for butterfly, where there had once been such a burst of rain. We pressed down towards the sensation of Brazil.

THE first blots of morning were in the night sky when we arrived at Kurupukari on the Essequibo. De Jesus looked beatific with fulfilled slumber, Moonsammy looked deranged from his eye-popping concentration.

We waited on the wood benches of a shack. The trees were frilled with wisps of grey cloud that melted softly, discernibly into dayclean. Behind the shack, three Amerindians roasted a tatou – armadillo. A tiny tawny kitten fought off three rowdy dogs and held her own. A monkey in a cage watched with interest, letting out sharp cries. We drank tumblers of milkpowdery coffee.

At six o'clock the pontoon opened for business. The Bedford clanged slowly on to the iron, joined by a ruined red sedan, a 4×4 and a dozen pedestrians. The pontoon motored off, drifting across the river. The water was an olive green, a shade I had not seen in Guyanese water before. There was a great and hungry tranquillity in the air. Though people chatted, and the 4×4 blasted Natural Black's Nice It Nice, the river swallowed everything.

Over on the other side the red sedan, peopled by two youngsters and a girl with a tattooed dagger plunging towards her anus, failed to get going. As de Jesus was a good man we hitched it to the labouring Bedford. We ploughed through the high forest till the ranger's cabin at the head of the reserve. People did things to spark the vehicle but it was dead as scrap. While they played with it, I read the boards on the ranger's lodge, telling of the four main timbers of the reserve, the greenheart, wallaba, mora and kabakali. I fell asleep.

IT was only the first sighting of the savannah, hours later, that aroused me to the special ecstasy of a journey. So fucking sudden! There we were in the trapped heat of the conserved rainforest and its trapped bird twitters, Moonsammy mate-calling the greenheart bird, de Jesus sleeping at high volume, when sheer as cliff the forest finished and there was savannah. It was the Rupununi and I don't know what that meant but it said everything.

We paused at the forest's abrupt edge. The mud trail snaked through naked grassland in a dry, killing run. Things were hot, flat and infinite. The only undulations were ant hills or sandpaper trees. In the distance noncommittal shapes of mountains fluctuated in a haze. Otherwise the lines of sky and earth spread towards perpetuity.

We chugged through the dryness, though there were occasional swampy bits. In the mind's eye there were buzzards and rancheros. The sky was a brilliant blue, the air was yellow. The trail was red, the savannah was straw-brown rather than green, and the first sight of any other colour came hours later at an unexpected restaurant in Annai, where on the back of a parked pick-up a fresh head of cow glistened in a pool of fluorescent crimson.

Beside it the hillock, meant to be dotted with flowers, was bare. I suggested to de Jesus we run up it, but on account of the flowers' absence as much as the heat, the proposal was rejected. Instead he lay down and honked hard in a benab while Moonsammy went into the village to bone a lil wife he'd made there.

It was twenty hours on the road when we pulled into Lethem. Lethem was pure sand paths and people cycling about. Moonsammy was pleased: in the old days, whose treachery grew with every narration, it could take five days in the wet season. You had to fell trees and make bridges. We were in another continent – for it was now the continent proper and the coast was a frill that floated in confusion. The houses were flat and brick. We went to one such, de Jesus's people, with a large yard of flambouyant trees currently out of flower, laden avocado trees, tangerine bushes beneath which were such surprises as minute turtles and a bottle of Johnnie Walker. The bottle had a few pegs left. We squeezed tangerine into it and sipped it while Clarence and Suzette, who lived in this fine yard and ran a fine little shop in the front, talked of Lethem. People of Lethem were people of the Rupununi, a mix of Amerindians, Portuguese and white settlers. Being people of the Rupununi was the only thing that meant anything to them, and Guyana and Brazil were simply ideas on either side. There were plans for the town. A library was being constructed; the first bank had just opened. Crime had arrived, three break-ins in the last two months, and though this was mentioned with regret, it hinted at progress.

Sundown and the tingle of Brazil was getting closer. Clarence dropped us to the speedboat on the bank of the Takutu, a slim brown river one could swim across had one the leisure.

The sun was dying . . . and we going Brazil!

We cruised along the river for five minutes before the crossing was made, by a massive bridge that Brazil was constructing.

We stepped off . . . into Brazil!

I saw the lemon yellow painted on a low, round flagstone.

Brasil.

We drank Nova Schin, Brazilian beer, watery after Banks, but sold by a Brazilian woman under a Brazilian mango tree, and it felt pretty swell.

De Jesus pointed to the Policia Federal station up the slope. It was a formidable edifice of white concrete and glass. Guyana had not even a watchie and a shack. Guyanese were allowed to stamp in at the checkpost, but my passport was Indian. Hence, my only option was to pass for a Brazilian. But things were tight at the checkpost. There had been an incident a few days ago. The head of a water company had been abducted; afterwards his body was found in a culvert. They suspected that the killers had escaped into Guyana.

Knocking back a second tin, de Jesus considered the vehicles making the crossing. There was a minivan, filled with fake Nikes and the like. Sometimes they were busted but mostly they were allowed in because Georgetown was so much closer than any of Brazil's ports. The other vehicle, a jeep, was Ricardo's. De Jesus knew the federals but not as well as Ricardo. The plan was to get into Ricardo's car, I in the back, and they wouldn't think to ask for documentation.

At the checkpost the conversation was long and in Portuguese and made me a trifle insecure. It was dark when we pulled out of the station, on to: beautifully paved tarmac! Manicured bush in the median! Streetlights!

We glided twenty minutes to the village of Bonfim. I was dropped off at a yellow posada on the outskirts. De Jesus said he'd come back for me.

My room was a 12x12 furnace with a chair, a standing fan and nothing else. The bed was a mattress mounted on a concrete plinth, slowly releasing the heat of the day. The toilet paper was thin and fell apart at touch.

I sat in the doorway looking into the open prairie night. A woman in a Brasil vest and big orange hair appeared from down the corridor and said something I didn't understand. I wanted to make love to her at once. However, a bald man drove in and they began speaking and thereafter the bald man left. Then two youths came in and they all drove off together laughing.

I read the book I'd borrowed from Clarence and Suzette, an old imperialist travel account of these parts by Evelyn Waugh. An hour later de Jesus arrived on a bicycle, left it in the room, and we walked towards the village. There was a white horse on a dark patch of grass. Men without shirts sat with ease on benches under the wonderful streetlights. Young children of all colours cycled oblivious of night.

We ate pizza at a brightly painted brick wall. Across, children were doing: dodge 'em cars! Young girls were playing football versus young boys on an indoor pitch with lights. In the socialist way it was free. It was going on ten. 'Watch,' said de Jesus, 'watch how the youth spending out their energy. They gon go home and sleep now instead of doing crime.'

We ate soursop ice cream, we kicked pebbles. We walked the long way home and de Jesus made off on his bicycle into the free streetlit village of Bonfim, looking very much like a ball on a pin, and I slept my first night in Brazil.

My concrete box faced east. Soon after dawn hellish tongues darted in through the curtainless windows and licked the flesh. There was nobody at the reception, no scope for ice, coffee, water. At seven sharp de Jesus arrived on his bicycle to fetch me for breakfast.

In the morning Bonfim had the feel of a mad empty prairie town. The revelations of the evening had run their course. On this open road, in the malevolent sun, with smouldering grass and that suspicious unmoving white horse, it was a place of the mind. There was incest in those brick and concrete homes, stick-ups in the closed cafes, tatous waiting for the dust to die.

We walked a long time in the savannah heat, strolling the cycle, till we reached a flathouse of gentle blue on a street of brutal red sand. We ate a stellar breakfast of fried eggs and calabresa, seasoned sausages, a single one of which, as I found when I took a frozen pack back to Sheriff Street, when fried with onion and married-man pork constituted a whole meal. In the background a Portuguese soap opera played, watched by members of a family whose relationships to one another I couldn't quite work out. They spoke both Portuguese and creolese, the latter with a whole different accent so that it was really not creolese any more. As I too had picked up some creolese I reflected I too must sound as ridiculous.

We settled in the veranda with Brazilian coffee which was strong and real. At the faintest sigh of air the sand blew and people spent their days sweeping it out. Our benefactor, elderly Aunty Mimi, spoke lovely, measured English with immaculate pauses and cadences. She talked softly and wisely and watching her sit there, considering the sand from behind her spectacles, I felt she knew everything. She did not have to say much to capture big themes. Bonfim, and even the city of Boa Vista a couple of hours away, they used to be nothing, and she summed up the contrast in development by invoking a mere four words: 'When Georgetown was Georgetown . . .'

I went off to discover the backyard, which yielded the excellent psidium, a fruit not wholly unlike guava I suppose, and hinting at an even greater jam. I was joined in these pursuits by a golden-brown child with long dark curls, nude but for an underwear of Brasil yellow. We had lengthy stream of consciousness conversations where he spoke in Portuguese and I responded with an assortment of sounds and faces. He dragged a baby palm frond from across the yard and slapped me with it. He jumped into my lap and whispered and shouted in my ears. There was no more beautiful and vibrant child in the world, and we were happy for at least an hour.

At last de Jesus emerged from the house. Resting his tree-trunk calves on a stump, he looked at me with his green eyes and said in the manner of an emperor:

'So you step into Brazil as you did wish.'

'Yes. Thanks, bro.'

'The truck not going for a couple of days. You wan go back Lethem or check out Boa Vista?'

'Check out Boa Vista!'

'Licks gonna share if they catch we.'

'What could happen?'

'They could put you in jail.'

'Leh we go.'

At the bus terminal de Jesus spotted a federal. We hurried out of there and headed for a shared taxi. The road was smooth, straight, wide and without challenge of any sort. Every ten minutes we might pass a bus. A woman beside me did sudoku without once needing to look up. The driver appeared to be asleep. He had the reddest face I ever saw; beside him de Jesus looked positively bleached. The land remained flat, but the vegetation thickened with manicole and ité and every now and then we saw big black and white birds which de Jesus said were called niggercups.

Alighting at Boa Vista, de Jesus gave me a fist bump and said:

'Boa Vista!', to which I said: 'Boa Vista!' We took a lotacao into the city and walked to a hotel.

A clean governmental vibe had the hotel. There was socialism in the flask of coffee at the reception from which any passer-by could help himself to a plastic cup. At the rear was a pool, where we lounged with Nova Schins to Portuguese pop driven by accordion. When we headed out, plucking fruit from low-hanging berry trees, it was to the meat that awaited at the churrascaria.

Every part of cow and pig was barbecued and racked upon iron rods, and waiters swished them through the large hall with the martial splendour of samurais. Now came a man with ribs, now with tongue, now with the rump, now with pure fat. Brazilians pointed with humid elegance to a portion of the rod and with equal elegance the waiter sliced a piece on to a separate meat plate. People had poetic noses, troubled brown eyes. There were black people and white people and mostly all the in-between shades. De Jesus said 'it have no Indo-Guyanese and Afro-Guyanese and that kind of thinking here,' and I said, of course, for it would have to be Indo-Brazilian and Afro-Brazilian even if it came to it. He grunted placidly, which he did when amused. The eaters were graceful and their gluttony casual. They drank a litre of soda with their meal. De Jesus himself threw down two and a half litres of Brazilian Fanta which had real chunks of orange in it, and boasted that when he was a young man he needed five litres of liquid with each meal and another five in between meals. No wonder you move to the land of many waters, I said, eliciting another placid grunt. He heaped his plate with crystals of farine without which no meal for him was a meal. I stayed clear of it. It wore out my enamel.

We took a lotacao and beat about what appeared to be the city centre. There were snackettes with high barstools upon which men sat and read newspapers in serenity. Others sat in the tree-shaded squares playing chess and dominoes, the latter without the Caribbean noise and, de Jesus said, with different rules too. Women had flaming yellow perms, braids made up in buns, oval bellybuttons.

Golden arms. The shops were numerous and first-world. There were enormous watermelons in huge supermarkets, hip gaming cafes into which mohawks entered. The scale of the city was large, its avenues broad, its conception European, and afterwards I found out it had been modelled on Paris.

In the evening we walked along a main promenade, and here, enclosed in worthy fences and under floodlights were: a concrete football pitch, a sand football pitch, a handball pitch, a basketball court, a tennis court. And a go-kart circuit. And mud-bike tracks! Everything except the last two was free, and indeed socialism was carried to such lengths that the medals podium was built to not three but five places.

At the completion of this series, the promenade opened out into an Arc de Triomphe-like gate. Here, on a stage was a man in bicycle shorts and before him hundreds of all-encompassing hotties. Free aerobics class! The hotties moved on to be replaced by a new set, and on the stage one bicycle-shorts conductor swapped with another. Free dance class. Somewhere were also children bouncing on free trampolines.

Coming from India it was such a marvel to me. And later at night, as de Jesus pulled punts and I read of a two-bit missionary flea-stop called Boa Vista whose inhabitants looked ill, discontented and fleshless, my mind went to bespectacled Aunty Mimi saying 'When Georgetown was Georgetown . . .' and to the minivan of smuggled fake Nikes hurtling down the bruck-up trail of startling red mud through the Cooperative Republic of Guyana.

WE returned the next day via the dust and grassland of Bonfim. We crossed the ever thinning Takutu, leaving Brazil to our backs, and soon we were in Clarence and Suzette's yard, lying on hammocks between trees and strumming a guitar.

I felt I'd come out of a dream. The spool had unspooled slow. The senses had detected every change, yet they were unprepared –

as there was rainforest and then there was savannah so there was Guyana and then there was Brazil. I walked about Lethem. Walking about, a little tangerine whisky in my head, I felt easy possibility. Boa Vista becoming Boa Vista, Brazzos dancing with fluid harmony under the Arc. The world was out there, to be partaken of, without observation, hindsight.

What an innocent little thing was Lethem. Mountains and grasslands and a football field dropped in between them. O to be a child kicking a ball in that exact field, at this exact hour of low sun! I liked how the warm sand felt between my toes as I let my slippers sink in. I liked how people cycled in holidaying ways.

I walked further along and came to a little store which sold slippers.

And there, as it happens that men are bedazzled by a fleeting glimpse, so I was. The precise glimpse was a thin bra strap of shocking pink against smooth burntsugar skin. I responded with the involuntary utterance of something stupid, namely: 'Nice colours.'

She whirls around. Her hair is full going to big, and streaked a long time ago so that only the copper tips glow on the whiplash curls as she turns.

'What colours?'

Front on, there is the quality of a mane to that wild frizz, a brown that stops short of black. Beneath it her forehead is large, high rather than broad, moistened in the heat. Her eyes burn brown and bright, a touch intimidating.

'The pink, uh . . . slippers you got there.'

She glances at the pair in her hands.

'Is blue slippers.'

'It's nothing.'

'You bin starin.'

'I was just thinking it looked nice on your skin.'

'So you *bin* starin.'

A mole on her collar bone, moles on her shoulders. Sweat on her chest. Breathing pores.

'Not starin really. It just caught my eye. I mean, I might be starin now.'

Her face relaxed a little. The blaze in the eyes switched off. On cue, the cheekbones softened, the lips loosened. Their parting suggested warmth. On their edges the intimation of a smile.

'People only stare in the zoo, that is what Aunty Horretta did tell me.'

'Aunty who?'

'Horretta.'

'That's a mighty name.'

'Well, she nobody to you. So I look like anybody in the zoo?'

She was playing.

'Like the macaws. They're pretty.'

'Them birds is a real festival . . .'

Re-al fes-ti-val. It was beautiful how she said it, slow, saturated, round-mouth.

'. . . I wonder if you would say tapir or agouti or one of them funny kind of thing.'

'When I went by the zoo the tapir, it had a hard-on. Was like a fifth leg, it almost touch the ground.'

'I seen donkey like that.'

'But think how funny a tapir would look that way.'

She laughed. Some girls with their laughs can make you feel so close to them.

'So I look like a macaw? Like I got a beak and feather to you?'

'No. It's just that someone took joy in making it.'

She threw back her head in complicit exasperation. Cleft between her nostrils.

'Is the yellow-and-blue macaw I look like, or the red-and-green?'

'Uh. Let me close my eyes and think.'

'You must remember to open them again or I won't be here.'

180

'Shh . . . Yellow and . . . not blue . . . green. Yellow and green.'

'It ain't have any like that. Funny you say that though. Was green and yellow slippers I was looking for.'

'Me too!'

'You look like you full of lie.'

'What's your name?'

'I don't tell strangers.'

'We still strangers?'

'Well, you *is* kyna strange. I thought it was your eyes. But when you close them I find you was still strange.'

'I should be in the zoo?'

'Yes. Zoo a nice place for you.'

'I'd like to be a manatee. They get so much respect. They got they own pond, and everyone come to feed them and stroke them. You live in Lethem?'

'O lord, you ask plenty question.'

'I was thinking how nice it must be to live in Lethem.'

'Be nicer to live over so.'

She pointed towards Brazil.

'What about over so?' I pointed the other way.

'Is nothing there. Sheer savannah.'

'I thought the coast up that way.'

'The coast up over *so*.'

When she pointed, it looked pointed. Her arm stretched out long and taut. Her palm arched and her fingers curled. The tip of her acrylic nail cut through the air like a spear.

'What design you got on the nail?'

'O meh mamma! There you go again with question.'

'If you get it done you must be happy people notice.'

'You noticin too much.'

'I hear it's painful.'

'You must get it done and see.'

She giggled.

'I'm staying by Suzette's shop. The green room by the avocado tree.'

'Uh huh.'

She giggled again. The giggles were unnerving and encouraging.

'I got to go now,' she said, returning the slippers to the rack. It came as a rude surprise.

'Of course. Bye.'

'Layta.'

'You coming to the Frontier tonight?'

'Maybe.'

'You must come.'

'Why?' she asked with deliberate blankness.

I hesitated. 'You can show me the acrylic design in the moonlight.'

'Well,' she said coolly, 'maybe I'll see you there.'

She went off up the broad, darkening path in the finishing day, puffs of red sand rising as she walked. I watched her exquisitely balanced silhouette, slim, swaying, bouncing mane, Caribbean derriere, electrified.

WE ate tough beef and farine at dinner, waited, got dressed and waited again for the hour to grow sufficiently late – a routine which seemed to spoof the scale of this savannah outpost.

But down at the Frontier I understood. This was a Saturday night crowd. SUVs screeched up in the sand, their sound systems competing with the Frontier's – Mavado on the Frontier's, Evanescence from an SUV, the overlap a phantasma, a hideous dream. There was an unlikeliest hipness to the spot. There were aid workers from Britain, Brazilian youth from Bonfim, four bank employees from Georgetown, several Rupununi sons and daughters.

Moonsammy was there as well, talking hard with toxic eyes, following the batty of every girl who passed him. He'd had a productive couple of days in Lethem. He'd stood third in the lolo competition at the Chineeman shop.

'When it small it called a peepee,' he leant against a car and explained to a set of youthmen. 'When it big it call a lolo. When it extra large it called a dunlop. Some man got a lazy dunlop, though.'

I looked into the crowd outside, stepped inside the premises and let my eyes casually scan the garden.

No, not yet.

I got a rum and went back out.

'A buckman win fust, blackman win second.'

'Buckman win blackman?'

'Eh he. Blackman chupidness compare to buckman. Blackman *saaf* in the middle, bai. Lazy dunlop.'

Over on the other side of the sandy road de Jesus exchanged hugs with enormous people. Their necks were thick, contained by big gold chains. Looking at de Jesus's neck I concluded it was bigger than my head. I tried to put across the observation, but the music was too loud, and few things can make a man feel as immeasurably foolish as yelling 'your neck is bigger than my head' in the savannah and not even being heard.

I took a walk up and down the lane.

No.

Everywhere individuals were looking interested in each other, all kinds of individuals, with pincered eyebrows, with chipped teeth, with heavy flanks, with tattooed forearms or swollen biceps, people with the honest desire to play the game.

I tried to look like I was liming easy. Inside, I was beginning to wilt.

I got another five-year.

I chatted with the British girls. They had blunt bobs, pert noses, open eyes. Conversation was terribly deflating for an odd reason. They only spoke in pairs.

'The fishing was bloody brilliant, wasn't it?'

'You've really got to experience this once, don't you?'

A second person always reaffirmed these statements. Every single time. 'Could you please not do that,' I almost told them. 'We could, couldn't we?' I heard them say back, 'Yes, we could.' It had a disastrous effect on me. With every reaffirmation my soul sank, and after about twenty minutes there wasn't much of it left.

I lost appetite for all conversation. I drifted away.

The moon was high and shining, eating up the stars around it. I switched to Banks. I thought of the lad in Canal who could drink a countless Banks. Under a tree I drank one to him.

Looked around. Took a few rounds of the garden.

I returned to Moonsammy, who was now reduced to holding court for a single youthman. Despite the dwindled attendance there was no slacking on his part. 'Face and waist, cooliegal win the race,' he recited, 'bubby and arse, blackgal kick she rass.'

The youthman nodded.

'Coolieman got to learn from blackman how to take care of a gal. That is why cooliegal going to blackman. He bring she a lil chinee food, get she a lil earrings, take she out fuh a lil dancin. That is when she do everything for you. Me neighba a blackman get a coolie wife. He say the lady roti like the pages of the Bible.'

I went to de Jesus. He held a Nova Schin in one hand and a Banks in another and told extravagant accounts of our Boa Vista sneak-in. It was an unrecognisable excursion which included naked women in the hotel pool and federals giving us chase through the goldwasher's park. He tried to involve me in the telling; but my anti-participation in what I'd ordinarily have jumped into with relish was brutal.

I looked everywhere, in the bushes where people had begun to make out, at the deejay's table, in the cars.

'F.B.I.' I heard Moonsammy say somewhere, 'Flat Butt Indian. That is wah we did call them. But now you find even coolie growin big beattie.'

I left suddenly. I returned to my room beside the avocado tree by the gate, and there I lay in sweat for several hours, feeling inadequate, dull and charmless, acutely aware of my lack of confidence, of the fragility I tried always to keep hidden.

4

RETURNING to the room after breakfast I noticed folded paper under the door. In light swishing crayon lines of yellow and green was drawn a bird, curving beak, long trailing tail. A macaw. There were no more than a dozen strokes. It was eloquence.

Below, in neat blocks an address was provided. At the bottom, in the petite running hand of a whispered note: *Get me a fone. Jan.*

I stared at it for a whole minute. And then, drained in the porous night, I treated it with deliberate nonchalance: that is, I stared at it no further.

It was a day of dry wind. Sand blew and settled on the skin. You could draw on your forearms. I spent most of the day in the hammock slung between coconut trees trying to read. I could not concentrate. *Janelle. January.*

The Bedford had a car to transport to town. From time to time I went to assist in the loading and strapping, an act which accrued no discernible benefit to the process. It was a precarious affair. The vehicle, a white Seventies kind of hatchback, was as long as the tray of the truck and so permanently on the edge of catastrophe. It took till evening to secure it properly, and even then the straps required tightening every hour.

At the fuel-seller's Moonsammy sucked a pipe and siphoned a vat into the truck. De Jesus and I took the cabin. A Wapishana youth lounged with furniture inside the strapped vehicle.

We left Lethem as we'd come, in the hour approaching sundown. Soon the light died on the Rupununi. There was a hatch above my head. I climbed up through it and sat on the roof to watch.

The whole round sun glowed red on the flat expanse, bold as a bloodprick on a finger. Swiftly the colour broke around the edges into a plum post-dusk. Within fifteen minutes the big black night fell on the earth that had burned all day with a hiss. Thereafter only blackness remained except for dotted orange flares of savannah fires.

We stopped for the night at the restaurant in Annai we'd stopped at on the way in. We ate sandwiches, sausage, drank coffee. We slung up hammocks between pillars in the open corridor.

Sleep was impossible, first because of the coffee, then the cold. The wind howled down the savannah. I was still with my thin camouflage hammock from the Baby days, and I had no other sheet to cover with. De Jesus was housed in his heavy Amerindian hammock, so large that even a man of his size could fold over the sides to make a blanket.

I shivered. The wind kept blasting across the plain. It gathered a tunnelled intensity in the corridor. I put on a second shirt, a pair of socks, and finally shoes, but the wind pierced everything.

In the middle of the night a bus of music screeched in and expelled squealers. Venezuelans, de Jesus said. He'd been snoring till then and was not happy to be disturbed. Two couples, frolicking upon the wooden tables, created such a racket that he stunned them and the entire endless savannah by yelling in Spanish. Afterwards he told me he'd threatened to pulp them with a stool. A stool! Of all the things de Jesus liked recounting, he took most pleasure in narrating how he, a calm man, a reasonable man, was provoked to such a degree by somebody that he threatened them and scared the shit out of them.

The Venezuelan couples piped down after the threat. They lay atop tables, giggling, being lovesome in the cold. The night blew bitter and teary.

When the cold got into my bones I went to the Bedford. I was hoping for room in the hatchback, but the Wapishana youth and the furniture had filled it up.

I climbed into the cabin. Here dangled Moonsammy. His trick was to tie the hammock around the roof, suspending himself in an arc above the seat. The chill was here too but it was windless. There was the smell of stale sweat. I slithered on to the seat, under his hammock, twisting, one leg splayed on the floor so my groin did not make contact with his sagging posterior.

I closed my eyes. I could not sleep. The proximity was killing me. Imagine how her ass would have dipped low into the hammock, how imperceptibly narrow and hot would be the space between her curve and my groin.

Janet. Janine. I could feel her hair roll over and tickle my arms. I could see her in very tight focus, between brow and lower lip, the cleft on her nose. I sensed her heavy breath in my ear.

I fell into a fever. In cold awake sweats I dreamt it was her, and till the time the Bedford ejected me on Sheriff Street, a round twenty-four hours on the road, I lived in a delirious wet daze, not a single flicker of thought if not sexual, sensual, worth the price of admission.

5

WE are on the road west from Georgetown, over the pontoon bridge on the Demerara. We are skirting along the pastoral ocean, timorous goats, absolute sky, the paddy between sow and reap. We are on the mouth of the Essequibo, twenty-two miles wide, brown waves cleaving open the continental head of dull mangrove. We are crossing by boat, faces sheeted with polin against the spray, breaks at river islands big as Caribbean republics, and beyond a sawmill on the water the lazy shady stelling at Supenaam.

The Essequibo coast, thirty-five miles along rice fields and awara palm, their orange fruit glowing like lozenges in the dark fronds, until the stelling at Charity – which stelling is the stink of river commerce, of comings and goings, booze on the waterfront, sacks of fruit and drying trulli leaves – which stelling has once, in inimitable Guyanese fashion, untethered itself and sailed down the Pomeroon whole like a raft.

We are on the Pomeroon, downriver, past Nauth's floating fuel station, past the perfect pleasure of the riverine villages, shooting out between mounds into the Atlantic. We are bumping parallel to the shore, the spray now saline, singeing the hot skin. The continent is re-entered from the slender slit that is the Moruka.

The boat wends through forest. The high trees drop off to walls of mokamoka bush, wild and arrowshaped. The mokamoka recede to savannah of bisibisi, thick, reedish, bright green there, burnt yellow elsewhere, exposed till the big water rains down to reclaim its space. Warraus, Arawaks, Christian Missions, whitewood churches, ité, clear, gleaming air. The river the only road. The untoothed aged to children pink of cheek jumping into woodskins natural as hopping on to a bicycle and skimming over glassy trails of water.

We are in a house on stilts amid profusion. In its immediate circumference seven type of palm, stray coffee bush, cocoa, fruits called Fat Pork, called Civil Orange, called Big Mummy, grapefruit devastated by swarms of Acoushi ants. Barbeque chicken and cassava bread, drunken midnight rowing, singing. In a pre-dawn mist I pay accidental obeisance. High on vodka and Fly, I make a false step and sink into swamp. I try to climb out but my slippers come off. Afraid that the mud will close over them, I go armpit deep with my hands, fetching a slipper at a time, hauling up a leg after another, batty high in the mist, face kissing swamp.

The sun rises over this blessed patch of world, mud washed off gold. The leaves are waking, the first fruits are falling. We are gone in Sparrow the boatman's boat, laughing into dayclean, the mokamoka, the forest, the filthy unbound Atlantic.

BUT I've gone two rivers too far. In the daydreaming heat, the giant estuary gentle, winking with sun, I thought back to an old travel article, conceived spiritedly at Big Market Big Mamma's. For now, I had no further to go than the Essequibo coast.

The stelling at Supenaam hustled to life with hitherto card-playing taximen, four passengers per share-car. We zipped down the thin road, silver with glare. I was dropped off outside a shop on the public road. The car beat on.

Inside the shop a man reclined in a chair, palms resting on his belly. He had a pleasant face and a tilted mouth, altogether approachable. Behind him hung an enormous photograph of the Kaaba, the clock beside it ticking to three.

I asked for help with the address.

'This same place the address.'

It threw me.

'You know Jan?'

'The red gal?'

'Yeah.'

'She does come by the phone shop sometime' – he made a hooked finger towards the adjacent door.

'You know what time?'

He sized me up, wary.

'Me don't really watch that, you know.'

'Thanks.'

'No mention.'

I went next door to the phone shop. There was a sole woman in the room. 'He want to suck cane and blow whistle too,' she bellowed into the line, with such passion that I withdrew at once.

Beside the shops was a two-step wooden bleachers under a tamarind tree. I took a seat.

A static white day. Not even birds were to be seen. Run-over crappos were pasted flat on the road. Something like smoke rose from their dead skins.

Fone. Cheaply titillating. Like a flirt's laugh, or popped bubblegum.

I waited.

Time passed, and people. A grandmother on a stick walked by, crumpled as forgotten silk. A boy sat down, twelve or thirteen years old, a butcher he said. He shared star apples with me. He bounded into the fields. Cyclers, walkers, limers in the heat. The house across, ravaged by ocean and apathy, its bright red and yellow jhandis astonishing against the blanched day, the blanched wood. Who lived in it? Man and reputed wife? A fisherman and his mammy?

Extended family – step siblings, chachis, nanis? It didn't feel like a nuclear kind of house. This felt somehow exciting. These lives.

Guyana was revealed in the country. Not because the city was so different, but so much like it. A large rurality, a social experiment, a time warp. Everybody was from the country. Hadn't Rabindranauth Latchman sprung from one of these villages here? It was one of the generic ones. Adventure? Perseverance? With trembling self-regard he had told of his rise – 'blood sweatin tears.' Rabindranauth Latchman. Just the other night I'd seen him again in his print shirt, hosting a piece of ass on his lap permitting him access with a stirring mix of power and vulnerability.

Waiting, it occurred to me that I had waited a great deal since I left India. It was so different from Indian waiting. Indian waiting was the waiting of competitiveness, of crowds. Here I'd idled. To idle now would be to fail. But what was to be done? The mechanism was delicate. To be exposed to her was one thing, to the village quite another. It would be like walking in underwear. As it was I was drawing long looks, attempts at conversation.

The sun was going canary to marigold. The pressure-cooker day was building to a release, the air heavier by the minute. In the hot shade, wet jeans pasted to the wood, the mind dwindling to nothingness, I fell fast asleep.

When I woke I couldn't place where I was. This kind of thing had begun to happen to me. It wasn't a failure of memory, just that it felt surreal that I should be asleep on bleachers between the rivers of Essequibo and Pomeroon, or on a concrete plinth in the Brazilian savannah, mixed up deep but in nothing. While recovering my balance I'd be assailed by a variety of Indian flashbacks. A lover that was or wasn't. Breaking a window in the building compound. The tension in the house when I abandoned my caste thread. It would take fifteen or twenty minutes to shake this mood. Sometimes there would be a mild headache.

It was turning to dark when I awoke and it disoriented me

further. The sun had lost shape. Hours had been consumed. The ideas in my head had been foiled.

Unsure of the next step, I did as usual. I walked. Along the straight open highway unsuited for walks. To the right were the village houses, beyond them the courida and blacksage bush on the South American foreshore. To the left were the paddy fields. Above, sunset was a mauve smear over man and his preoccupations. There was mud in the air. Here and there one could hear stray voices, beating with phrases like 'shying seeds' and 'pulling shrimp'. From the fields came the trombone of cows. *Godhuli* was the beautiful Hindi word for sunset: the dust raised by cows returning home. *Godhuli*, so right with dayclean.

With the slightest intimation, a rustle of leaves, a flutter of hidden birds into trees, the pressure was released. I was stunned by the intensity. Rain blew in lilac gusts over the rice fields. The palm at the margins were bending. Mud exploded onto my dust-encrusted feet, into the crevices between my toes. On the nape and the forearms the new air felt like new skin. It was like waterbombs. I ran for a shed in the distance. It was a small lumberyard. I stood inside the curtain of corrugated rivulets. The zinc took a pounding, rising and falling in waves over the rafters, flapping. In utter din twilight was obliterated.

Darkness was ecstatic. Scents seeped from the earth, the bushes. The world was raw and desperate, all contrition washed off. It was ten minutes, till the wind abated and the zinc settled, that I caught the folkish Bhojpuri rhythms jangling through the rain. Sounds affect me in the most visceral way. I felt a little drunk and perverted. The mood of silver anklets, licked navels, sex in a haystack. I walked around the drenched perimeter. The sound grew closer. *Lotay la, khub lotay la*. I knew it from so many wedding limes. It was a red-hot drunken chutney. The dholaks beat relentless over cymbals and harmonium. It made you feel to dunk your head in a bucket of rum, spin in circles. It was an old Indian theme, wife and brother-in-law, rolling, soaping, bathing, and it ended in an Indian way, with wife-beating.

Three men were inside the lumberyard, surrounded by logs of timber, ghostly around a flambeaux. Their faces were full of rum. A portable stereo, a tiffin with phulouries, the smell of mango sour. There was a fourth man; he raindanced in wide arcs, his small dark body lost against the logs.

'Who that jumbie there?'

I introduced myself. I was an Indiaman. They fussed over me, they plied me with their alcohol. The sharp ferment of bush rum. Two shots to begin with, one for blood, one for rain.

They were the lumberyard watchie, small-scale rice farmers, a postman. They could be thirty, they could be fifty, I couldn't tell. They'd curried iguana in the backdam. They'd traded rifle cartridges with Amerindians for the iguana. They'd traded cases of smuggled Venezuelan beers with GT people for the cartridges. The meat was white and soft, soaked in curry powder.

We talked about flims, about Dharmendra, about Veeru of *Sholay* and Veeru Sehwag of cricket. 'Man bat like he sleeping with one eye open and give one *bap* to mosquito.'

Bush rum has a stabbing, localised high. One can press the points of intoxication. Evasions dissolved in drink and rain, I let slip it had to do with a girl.

'Ei man, the man want to ketch a t'ing. Abi take the man backdam, buckgirl sisters start t'ing there. Pink, bai! Sweet, bai! Abi take you in tonight.'

'Tomorrow.'

The floor was smoothened concrete. Crappos leapt on it. Earthworms crept in and back out. The dry logs absorbed the smell of rain and the vibrations of the chutney. And the chutney clanged on. *Phulorie bina chutney kaise banee?* I had thought of chutney as a music without pain, but I had begun to see I was wrong. Reggae was the music of slavery. Its impulse was resistance, confrontation, a homeland severed so absolutely, seized back by the force of

194

imagination or ideology. Chutney was the music of indenture. Its impulse was preservation, then assimilation. There was a pain in this act of attempted preservation – a homeland part remembered and protected, part lost and lingering.

'Ei brother, I's make chutney good, you know. Is only one thing keeping me back.'

'Contacts?'

'Genetics, man. Me nah get the voice.'

They spoke of Bachchan, of Bachchan having come one time to Blairmont. After a while I couldn't follow. The wind had risen again, playing with the zinc. Their intonations were too fast, drunk. Still the situation was effortless. I couldn't have been in it in India. No chance. And standing at the open back of the lumberyard, the sleeper logs in proximity, looking out into the fields, was the feeling of travelling Indian Railways, the great Gangetic sweep, a country palpable, unknowable.

It was hours. When the rain tapered to a drizzle we left. We were going to Bunny's. The night was fresh and silhouetted. Crappos were singing tenor. The wind lifted the smell of wet paddy from the fields, faintly like asafoetida. We passed the house across the bleachers.

'Who live in there?'

'*Churile* live in there. She ah *churile*.'

At Bunny's the night was ending. The room was thick with alcohol and chat. Bush rum yielded to five-year. Fairy lights were wound around the safety grille, I couldn't tell if left over from Diwali or in anticipation of Christmas. Against the dim lighting they made the mood of a finished occasion. The sound system issued old Hindi film music, of longing, of suppression, the idea of what it is to love, what it is to lose, Indian fatalism.

I looked around me: middle-aged Guyanese men in caps, T-shirts and short straightforward moustaches. They'd shied rice in the morning, brewed bush rum, sold timber, worked the post office, or who knows, done nothing or picked fights, and now they were happy and they were sad and the world was loaded with a thing you could not touch.

'Ei, Bunny, jam the mike, we get an Indiaman heye,' someone said, and there was singing. *Suhaani raat dhal chuki*, obscure among Hindi film classics, forty, fifty years old, maybe more. A man called Chabilall sang. He was joined by a few others from their spots.

I watched mesmerised. To sing in a language one didn't know, it seemed to me an act of devotion. The half-baked, heartfelt, creolised delivery, I felt it in my bones.

'Hear wha'happen, brother,' Chabilall said to me after. 'Rafi you ain got to unstand words. Rafi in we blood.'

'Kishore?'

'A great man. But hear wha'happen. When Rafi sing a dance song, you dance. When he sing a sad song, you cry. When he sing a love song, woman get fever. Rafi get inside of you, he become you an you become him.'

He went to a line from Suhaani Raat.

Tarap rahe hain hum yahaan, tumhare intezaar mein.

'Hear how he play with the syllable. He make ten from one. Now that is feeling.'

'You know what it means?'

'Part part. But I feel it, my brother, I feel it. Let me tell you one story, my brother. When I was in school, I get suspended one time. Because why? Because in the patriotic song I replace "Guyana" with "India".'

I would spend the night at Chabilall's. The mile to his house we walked and sang, Kishore upon my insistence, Yeh Dil Na Hota Bechara and the oeuvre, under the wettened stars, the floating drizzle. These songs, these fields, in one of these houses her body in a damp bed.

HER mane was pushed back by an alice band. It drew attention to the shape of her face, cut like a rough heart. She squinted in the sun. The sleeves of her pink tee were rolled up. Her white shorts were folded up to half her long brown thigh, a line of muscle on its side. I had built her to absurd heights in my awake dreams. She was not a miracle, no. Rather, simply very attractive in a teasing, swaying way. Her face hadn't finesse. It had energy. Her knees were grey. It came as a relief. She was within grasp.

'Good morning,' she said, walking up from the shop.

At once there was such a distance between us. The intimacy of dreams is a deceit. We did not know each other.

'Marnin,' I said, rising from the bleachers.

'I was sure I wasn't going to see you back,' she said.

It was a curious comment, for it appeared to shift the initiative of pursuit on to her.

'I love your hair but it's nice how your face shows this way.'

She twinkled me a look.

'So you get me the phone?' she asked, playing with the bracelets on her wrist, slender.

'The phone, no— I wasn't sure what you meant.'

She pulled a mock cross face.

'How we could be in touch otherwise?'

'Oh.'

'Motorola bring out a nice one. The pebble.'

'I was thinking maybe if we together a lot we don't need the phone.'

'So how you get here?'

'No. 32 from Parika, speedboat to Supenaam, share car till here. I thought it's the only way, unless you fly.'

'They allow vehicle on the big ferry. You got a vehicle?'

Phoneless, vehicleless: within minutes our electric cocoon had been demolished. I was a letdown.

She leaned against the bleachers. Her legs glistened with perspiration.

I changed the subject.

'How come you give me the address of the shop?'

'How I could trust you, man? You could be who. You could be bandit.'

'I could be pandit.'

She laughed.

'How long you been here?'

'Maybe an hour.'

'That ain't much at all.'

'And all of yesterday too.'

'You lie!'

'Ask the shopman.'

'Where you spend the night?'

'Right here, on the bleachers. How it rained, how I shivered.'

'So what part you from?'

'India.'

'Tell me for truth.'

'Truth. You couldn't tell?'

'But you talk good! You talk like a Guyanese. I mean you talk a lil strange, but I thought is just because you *is* strange. You know how some people go foreign a couple of days and they come back and talk funny till the time they lie in coffin.'

'I pick up a couple of things.'

'You doing good! When you come here?'

'A good while. Since the start of the year.'

'What you come for?'

'Look who asking so much questions now!'

'I don't believe you from India! You got to prove it.'

'Even the federals didn't ask for my ID, you know.'

'I know you lie. You look full of lie.'

I showed her my driver's licence.

'Oh lord, is true. How old you was in this photo, seven? Nice name – is a starbai name! Say something. Let me hear whether you sound like a starbai.'

'Is what you want me to say?'

'That is up to you.'

'I could say anything, how you would know it's right?'

'I ain't stupid.'

And the words which came to mind were not, 'How are you?' or the 'The sky is blue' – no, the only thing that came to mind was a song Chabilall and I sung last night, the song Bollywood had nicked from Shorty, Shanti Om.

'*Maine kisi ko dil deke kar li, raatein kharaab dekho.*'

She wasn't sure, I think, whether I had sung or spoken, and then she wasn't clear if it was over or not. She tried to work out how to respond.

'What does it mean?'

'Well, that I've given my heart to somebody, and now my nights are, basically, ruined, destroyed. Like sleeping on the bleachers in the rain.'

'Uh huh.'

'I still don't know your name, you know.'

'Jan. I wrote it for you.'

'The full name I meant.'

'Janaki. Don't call me that, I hate it.'

Janaki! I hadn't expected it. Not at all. She had some Indian in her, that had been certain. It was in her features, her skin. But I hadn't expected the epic name.

'How you spell it!'

'J.a.n.k.e.y. But is Jan – just Jan. Is only the country gals who got names like Jankey and Parbatti.'

'But you *is* a country gal.'

'I ain't! I only been here a lil while.'

'You know what it means?'

'Is like Sita, not so? My grandfather tell me so. He knew Hindi part part. *Pagalee*. That is what he would call me.'

'Look at you – you a full-blooded cooliegal!'

She laughed.

'Not all the way. My father got a lil Brazzo in him. But I ain't seen much of him.'

Jankey.

We stood in the flush shade, surprised by one another's Indianness.

'You live here?'

'Part time. Part time in GT. Part time Lethem. I grow up in GT, you know.'

She sat down on the bench, and I sat beside her. 'I just trying to cut out of Guyana now. Is got nothing.'

'Where would you go?'

'North. I got peeps there. Life there good, you know. People got options. They get ahead. My friends send me pictures and tell me about all what it got there. Brazil I'd like to live too. I love Brazil. I been till Boa Vista one time. Barbados, they developed up there. Anywhere but here.'

'It's not so bad,' I said, somewhat offended on Guyana's behalf.

'You only think that cause you been here a lil while. So why you come here?'

'I wanted to get away. Like you do.'

'You want to get away so you come to *Guyana*? I thought you was full of lie. But is not the case. You just mad.'

'It's a good place for madmen, you must agree.'

'It got to be *something* that make you choose Guyana,' she persisted. She rested her fingers on my forearm:

'Tell me.'

'I came here a few years ago. I felt something that time. Sometimes you want to follow it . . .'

I congratulated myself on the directness.

'What you come for the first time?'

'For the cricket. I used to report on cricket.'

'For truth? I love cricket! But West Indies gone to the dogs. You see how Gayle and Sarwan liming in the mound after they lose— Cha! I don't buy it.'

'What?'

200

'I don't buy it at all. You didn't come here just so.'

'You want to go away just so.'

'That make sense though. I trying to go to some place develop. You didn't like it in India?'

'I was thinking of something while waiting for you. A little before I decide to come out to Guyana I was at the airport, getting off the plane. To take you to the terminal they got the bus, right. So I'm trying to get on the bus. But Indians just not moving from the door! There's empty space in the middle of the bus, but everyone jammed up against the door. They want to be the first to rush out of the bus when it stop. I ask people to move inside. Everybody refuse. They want you to fight your way through them and get to the centre. I get so pissed off that I walk away.'

'So then?'

'Is not like at Timehri where you can get off the plane and walk to the terminal. You not allowed to. I start to walk towards the terminal. The security guys come after me.'

'Then what happen?'

'They arrest me!'

She giggled.

'They put you in the prison?'

'They keep me in a room for two hours.'

'So then what happen?'

'I give the man a raise. He said they could book me under anti-terrorism laws.'

'How much you pay?'

'Five hundred. Rupees. Say twenty-five hundred Guyanese.'

'Cha! No wonder you leave, man. You could get off with fifteen hundred dollar here.'

'There you go. So you better stay in Guyana.'

'I still not buyin it.'

She pressed her finger to my forearm again.

'You didn't come to Guyana because they arrest you in the airport. I think it got to do with a girl. You chase up a girl?'

'Maybe.'

'I *knew* it. You find her?'

'I think so.'

I let our hands touch, almost clasp. She was unsure.

We talked a little longer.

'I got to go now,' she said eventually.

I had felt it coming.

'Well,' I said casually, 'if you come to town, I'm on Sheriff, just past the fish shop. Is the house over the studio.'

'Every time you must leave me an address?'

'You left me one too.'

She got off the bleachers, smiling.

She kissed me, a cruel flashing kiss. Her breasts flecked my rib. She pulled away with a smile.

'If you coming back, get me the phone, right.'

And she turned and left. I watched her easy sway. Her great frizz fell till the tip of her shoulder blades. My eyes followed her ass. I could watch myself staring. *You got to tell the big man you enjai you life*, Baby's words.

I ran up after her.

'Listen, I wanted to ask you something.'

She stopped, delicate, her hand to her eyes.

'I have to return to India soon. I want to travel. Maybe I'll never get to come back ever.'

'So you want to carry me?'

'Yeah.'

'Is where you wan carry me?'

'I was thinking Venezuela.'

'Uh huh, we going to make house there?'

'I'm serious.'

She blurted a high laugh, taunting, taunted, I could not discern.

'What do I get?' she said.

'What do *I* get?'

'You getting me.'
'You getting Old Year's holidays.'
We stood under the burning white country roof. I waited.
'Is joke you making.'
'No, promise.'
'You gon treat me good?'
'Like a prize bird.'
'You stupid, you know.'
'So?'
She looked at me quietly, pores breathing.

6

THERE came a moment after the packing, after the dash for tickets and visas and amid the great shine and rain of romance to come, when I could have sold my soul to cancel. There wasn't anything especially dramatic about it. It was the confluence of a number of small things. The man with the music cart rolled by with Eric Donaldson's reggae version of Come A Little Bit Closer. A bright blue butterfly floated in from the balcony and spread itself on the ceiling. A truck passed on Sheriff and rumbled foundations so that the Guyana map blew off the wooden wall and fell softly to the floor. At that instant it felt utterly wrong to be leaving in my last days, and I was seized with the panic of having discovered an enormous mistake.

Thankfully it was only a moment. The cravings for sweet sinnery on the move, for her crumpled mane blown into my eyes, for vast broad-brush motion, the anticipatory thrill of roads to be taken, borders to be crossed, faces to be seen, bars of music to be absorbed, they reinstated themselves. It was December in Georgetown. You could feel in the humid air a search for renewal. Pork was doused in vinegar, ginger roots were left to ferment, fruit was forgotten in rum. Houses of every religious persuasion were made over. There were jingles on the radio, sales in the newspapers and limes in the yards.

These were the days between rendezvous and departure. They were busy days, wrought with logistics of travel – no direct flights to Venezuela – of commissions sought in view of forthcoming expenses and completed in a haze. We hardly saw each other. Once for paperwork, followed by the seawall. One date, surprisingly traditional, to the cinema, if either *Rainbow Raani* or the Strand qualified for the term. Another time she came to Sheriff and investigated it with jumpy energy for signs of another woman, the hooks behind the bathroom door, the toiletries by the basin. Satisfied, she teased, gave nothing. I wished the most vivid shamelessness upon us.

On the holy morning she arrived bearing a hunk of black cake and ginger beer. Her hair was wild from the breeze, her face intensified by the wildness. Her ribbed top was sequinned, jeans with studs at the pockets.

'Merry Christmas.'

There was something absurdly picnic-like about the cake and ginger beer. They seemed to open a new dimension, a companionship. Each was so high that we were a little tipsy on the way to the airport. Any awkwardness was overcome by it. It heightened her electric touch. Her hand sometimes grazed my crotch. We stayed in the moment, talked of the things before our eyes. Sometimes she called me hon.

At the airport she and a boy, a questionnaire-wielding surveyor from the statistics bureau, spoke for an hour of their itch to leave the country. He'd been at the airport for two months, and he saw how it worked, with gals in particular. 'Is like a movie. They goin out poor. They comin back rich.' While the discussion proceeded, her hand resting lightly on my thigh throughout, I took note of a tiny little scam: the free government pamphlets stacked on the racks, I remembered Baby had been trying to sell those along with cherries by the big market.

We flew from the timbers of the continent. Below, the Demerara purged its phenomenal mud into the Atlantic, which gave unto pristine Caribbean waters – it happened abruptly, not in a straight line but in lurid undulations, like crayon hills against a crayon sky. We watched the window, bit lobes, clung together and watched everything. A part of me marvelled that this had been made to happen, the calculated recklessness, the majestic confidence.

Trinidad, with its memories from my cricket tour. Petite Trinidad, its gingerbread cottages and winding hill roads, pee trickles they called rivers, fields they called savannahs, oil-dollars Trinidad and its mean seascape of pointed cranes and its sad sweeping bright malls, Trinidad where beneath the revels of mas and headlines of crime people were secretly serious and cradled first- or at least second-world concerns in their bosoms.

She'd been brought here once when she was six. As we drove to the city, she observed, 'I like here.' She added decisively, 'If I had to choose I would prefer Barbados.'

At last we were in Woodbrook.

What I can remember of the lovenest is that it was how a lovenest ought to be, with real memories buried in its paint and nails. A garage room with a door to the driveway where cars would have pulled in so many times, so many times with squirreled lovers in a rush or in quarrel. Here they must have lain in chrysalis. The window opened to a lawn. Through it they must have watched rain fall, fireflies die, heard frogs sing.

The floor was carpeted. There was a ceiling fan. On the bed a mosquito net was already pulled down.

It was the first time we were in a bedroom together. That, the creak of the fan, the net like a meshed boudoir, it brought on a magnetic formality.

'Want some rum?'

'That could work.'

I opened the ten-year from duty free. From the proprietor's

kitchen I brought lime and ice. In the warm room with the hot rum the ice felt like a cold silver spoon on the neck.

'More ice?'

'More rum.'

We were the nervous flirts of a date. Our talks were like rabbits in gentle pursuit. We spoke with faces close enough to feel breath, resistance a hot tickle.

The room felt small with the bags on the floor. She decided to settle them in the wardrobe. She opened it, scanning the mess of pillows and sheets inside. I looked over her shoulder, pressed towards her. She held her position in acquiescence. My nose and lips were inside the blown curls of her hair. She put her hands up against the frames of the door, backing her bottom into me. I held her at the love handles. We contoured tighter into one another, rubbing, now kissing. Her lips were heavier than they looked, she liked to linger and pull with them.

We stood there kissing a long time.

'Mosquito bitin,' she whispered finally.

'Let's go into the net.'

She gave me a slap on my chest. 'You bad.'

'It'll be more comfortable there. Or we could spray Shoo and smell like Shoo.'

'You bad,' she said again, smiling.

She lifted the net and led me inside by the finger.

The mattress was foam. We stood on our knees, chests pressed. Our kisses, slow and feathery so far, grew deep and desperate. She had a frank sexual smell. Her skin was moist, breathing. We kissed till our mouths were numb. I felt her crawling nails. My hands ran down her arched back, her stupendous bottom. At some point she entered my boxers – and emitted a startled yelp.

'Oh lord! It must have crablouse in here!'

She clutched in her hand a shock of pubes. She looked petrified.

I studied the growth as she released it.

'You hear of the kamasutra?' I asked after a moment's consideration.

'Yes.'

'It say there that the pubes suppose to tickle the lips.'

'Cha! You think you a Gooroo?'

'I'm telling you.'

'Man, look at it.'

She made to clutch them again, then withdrew her fingers with a fright.

'How long since you had a girl, man.'

The moment was beyond coyness.

'It heightens the pleasure. Make you stretch to de ceiling.'

'I ain't goin nowhere near that nest.' She sat back on her heels.

'So how do you like it?'

'Clean.'

'How clean?'

'Clean clean. To the bone.'

'Alright, clean it.'

She stared at me with a defiant smile.

I said nothing.

'Alright.'

She left me for her bag.

Over the white lace she drew the drapes, shutting the floating dust beams of the sun, the dark splash of almond leaves. It was black. She switched on the reading lamp. She was down to her chocolate underwear.

'Lie back, right,' she said, touching my shoulders. 'Close your eyes, and no sudden movement.'

I lay back, afraid. I could not keep my eyes fully closed. She was bent over, cleavage brown and beautiful in the bulb haze. Her gaze was fixed in concentration. Her hair was tied in a bun. I saw her magnified as though in a collage, the shape of her curling nostrils, the shadow of her chin, the cavern of her armpit, the big beads on her neck.

I was throbbing.

'I'm scared,' I started to say.

'Shh . . . Close you eyes.'

It was excruciating. I received her smell and her fingers. She massaged with her free hand as she trimmed, sometimes stopping one or the other, sometimes letting go a little laugh. Infinite submission. I felt on drugs, not a narcotic, a medical drug, like the intense psychedelia of an anaesthetic before it kicks in. In the creaking swirl of slow clip-clops I was spent full on a rubble of soaked shavings. In those half-hallucinations we stayed, ten minutes, thirty, an hour, I couldn't tell.

The texture of that time, the clopping, the creaking, and the embarrassment of the growth, it would return to me often, sometimes with killing self-consciousness, other times with the pure energy of a vine bursting through brick.

BUT it was, actually, an evening of emptiness. Port of Spain was closed. In the evening the proprietors had us over for their get-together. They were an elderly light-skinned couple, a French name on the man and Chinese eyes on the lady, who spoke in severe Trinidad singsong – you could oscillate like a pendulum on their sentences. It was a sombre gathering, though, seven or eight people. Other than the kittens, we were the only ones below fifty-five. There was rum punch, mincemeat pastilles, Christmas cake and baked ham from the previous night's feast. I learnt here that she didn't eat wrenk. Wrenk was a flexible term covering a gamut of impurities. In her case wrenk was pork, beef, shellfish and wildmeat.

Conversation was local and middle-aged, who'd bought Christmas linen and blinds from where. I was languid. We were quiet. We had little conversation of our own, or a way of being with each other in company. In the course of the bourgeois talk, always one person speaking at a time, sentences flanked by ellipses, a retired bureaucrat remarked, 'Boy, the servant class has gotten so Guyanese, I find children using Guyanese as a cussword.' He added jovially, 'Guyanese have a real fowl-thief mentality, boy!' Charming, boy.

Afterwards we walked about downtown on strung-out hamstrings, hoping against local judgement to find a lime. The desertion was absolute. Our footsteps echoed on tar. On a corner we came upon two prostitutes in Santa caps. They soored us. At the Queen's Park Savannah there was a lone drunk coconut man in an orange truck. There we bought two medium jelly, and sat on a bench, more or less quiet.

That was the last thing we ate.

Now, past three o'clock on Boxing Day, on a much delayed ferry, crossing the steely Gulf of Paria, we were starving. We had been up since four, the dawn hours given to the mechanisms of getting accustomed to swollen faces, ridiculous hair, the newness of habits, words uttered in minor stress, a mystery gone.

The comfort of familiarity came much after, with hunger and deprivation. On the ferry with hands clasped we thought of the wrenkest things we could eat. Crappo, camoudi, the tatou they were roasting at Kurupukari when I was on the way down to Lethem to see her. Manatee, she said. I sucked my teeth. Macaw, I said. She bit my arm.

A Trini man helped kill time by making constant ethnographic incisions. He observed that 'them working-class black people drown real easy, eh'. When someone drank from a bottle without it touching their mouths he berated them for 'drinking like a Hindoo'. He boasted that his little girl could 'sing like an American – while smiling'. He put her up for display, and she indeed sang while smiling Rohini the lady prisoner's song she'd picked up at the Prisoners Calypso contest.

But how can there be a message without a mess?
And how can there be a testimony without a test?
Next time I'm on a plane
I'm on vacation, not trafficking cocaine

At last Venezuela appeared in the form of distant mountains, as I imagined all new land must do from the sea. As we drew closer Venezuela was hundreds of grey pelicans on a pier of identical colour.

Stepping out on to the cement of Venezuela it was apparent: we were alone now. The red-bereted soldiers who searched our bags didn't speak a word of English. Neither did the Pam Grierish mulatta immigration officers. Fellow passengers had made off quickly. Her Spanish was limited to a dozen words, including *Si* and *Da me mas gasolina!*, and still a greater range than mine.

We were on the edge of a very small, second-rate town called Guiria. Struggling, trying to appear confident, I surrendered us to a stammering stranger who offered to help. The opportunity of alien circumstances is that the first inkling of a breakthrough can send the spirit soaring. The stammerer was an angel. He spoke English. For nothing but fleeting friendship he helped us change money (at a pharmacy, naturally), guided us to a restaurant to rescue our dying bodies, through the meal himself refusing to eat, and thereafter saw us into a shared taxi.

These Venezuelan automobiles. Stripped to metal, devoid of handles, cavities for dashboard compartments, semi-exposed spring for seats, imparting a final effect not bruck-up but the opposite, shells conceived so far ahead of their time that they had degenerated to this while mankind developed something commensurate to their potential. In one such fabulous contraption we made off into Venezuela. I wished to have her nuzzling me but she was in the backseat with Carolina. 'I love communication,' Carolina had declared early on. She was mother to a geerl she sent to Trinidad

211

to study English. English was everything in the world today. Jan and she fell into involved discussions and I, in the front seat, gave my neck a rest and the driver, a black man in a cap sighed, the resigned sigh of a man who knows that women will now chat.

Outside was rolling savannah. We thrummed through the vibe of Latin America. Breastfeeding mothers sat in coloured doorways, walls of bright running colour, no relation between one and the next. Villages in pastel orange and lemon, men in coloured vests sitting on low, coloured walls. There was such a sophistication to every colour, the subtle aestheticism refined over centuries. It was evening, and the rightness of the moment and our actions was indisputable.

We reached Carupano after dark. The driver took us from hotel to hotel, they were full or unaffordable or characterless – I had ambition in those early days. At last he snapped out of his resignation with a series of baritone gesticulations and left us on the waterfront.

We walked with our bags and guidebook. Anabel was full. Some doors away the peeled and shredded Anabel Karol was giving out cheap rooms. Took it, on account of our weariness, the location and especially the yellow walls. In fact, took three rooms in succession. The first two were stale to the point of nausea, the third marginally superior. The sheets were filthy, the floor filmed with grime, the air-conditioner given to emit nuts, screws, bits of plastic and coils of wire. The windows opened into a covered courtyard, with no prospect of natural air or light in the morning. A slobbish man in a yellow vest seemed not to see the room we did. Jan gestured to him for a broom: he brought it and slobbered off.

A frail lady on a walker appeared. She had no teeth and luminous white hair. Her veins were thick as her thin arms. She was undoubtedly a centurion. When she saw Jan with the broom she began to cry. It shamed her to see it. She spoke gently in Spanish and walked away.

She herself was Anabel Karol. She once ran the place with love and devotion, the kindest guest house in the continent. The yellow-vested son and his fat wife had ruined the great lady's work. How did I know? Of course I did. In a foreign land you can know everything, don't even have to ask. I attempted to entertain my partner with these interpretations as I dusted out the pillow covers.

But an air of squalor had descended on our first Venezuelan night. The smell, the suffocation persisted. It was a mood that could not be defeated, only allowed to pass. The last two days were feeling coldly factual: a non-Christmas, a day of hunger, now a rancid hole. Mopping the bathroom, her hair tied, her jeans rolled up to the shin, her wet tee clinging to her skin, her brown nipples showing through two layers, she said, 'I thought you were going to care me like a prize bird.' She said the words without the tenderness of a grouse. It was pure ice, and only a tenth of the iceberg does show. What could I do? Conjure up a hotel?

We went to bed in utter exhaustion, straight on our backs, not touching any, and it was just short of morning before our bodies entwined.

IN the relief of the morning we ate stuffed empanadas and arepas at a corner stall and learnt essential words from the guidebook, *comida* for food, *frio* for cold, *no entiendo Espanol* for don't understand Spanish. For a hundred thousand bolivars, we bought her a pair of ice-blue jeans.

'All the ones I got getting nasty,' she said.

In fact, the pair she had on looked fresh.

'I putting them on for you.'

They rounded her bum beautifully, creased nowhere along her slender legs. They imparted a lustre to her sunkissed face.

On a stone bench in the shade of a cathedral we kissed without reserve in the manner of the newly coupled in a new land. We ate cold custard on ice. At the terminal, looking at the map and bus times, the seaside town of Puerto La Cruz four hours away seemed an appropriate choice.

With pinkies tied we boarded the bus. The vegetation, full and tropical in snatches, for the most part was scrub, thorny plants with sudden blooms of bougainvillea. We climbed. It was dry. Villages were perched on rocky outcrops. The heat was metallic and the sea shone with metallic hostility. At resorts people swam. That colour of heat on that colour of water, I knew it well from somewhere. It came to me at last, the colours of Algerian heat and water that Meursault saw, the unbearable glare. She was asleep on my shoulder.

There was effortless success with accommodation in Puerto La Cruz. The room overlooked the sea, a humble happy room with a large spring bed. The room type was classified as 'matrimoniale'. The presentation of this unexpected intimacy led to the tender and luxurious making of love.

It was the first time I saw her entire nudity in clear and prolonged light of day. Her shoulders were narrower than they seemed, narrower than her hips. Her breasts were at different angles, adding depth to her cleavage, mystique. Stretchmarks on her rear, their merest hints on her lower belly. Her breath was raw from travel.

Her pussy was cleaner than her armpits. She was warm as a lamp. She was consummate and reaching.

We lay a long time after, bouncing softly on the springs, watching sunset creep through the wreath of holly tied on the balcony grille.

'You know in Urdu the word for beloved is *jaan*,' I said.

'What is Urdu?'

'It's a language, a lil like Hindi.'

'You could call me that. Jaan. I like it. Though it sound like you making fun of we accent. Jaan. Yeah, I like it.'

We stood in the balcony half-dressed, I in boxers, she in my T-shirt. Those long torn sedans cranked by. The boulevard was sparking to nightlife. The neons were coming on. Couples exchanged Venezuelan hugs, lengthy and meaningful.

But later at close quarters the boulevard revealed itself trite with lacklustre craft and trinkets. It did not prevent us getting her shell bracelets and coral anklets. The line of neon curling around the water was another deception. Not one swinging spot among them. There were Arabian restaurants, ice cream parlours, the word for which, *heladeria*, had the ring of extra-terrestrial significance, and here in the land of Chavez, McDonald's and Dominos.

We ate mediocre food. The evening carried the weight of the sea. We walked back with ice lollies from the heladeria. After so long, a companion at all moments, a comfort as well as pressure.

In the room I lay on the bed and read. She washed in the bathroom and settled herself before the mirror.

'What you readin?' she asked, fiddling with the curls of her hair.

'In a free state.'

'Is a love story?'

'No, no love.'

'What is it about?' she asked a minute later.

'Displacement, kind of, colonialism, people in different places.'

She went into the bathroom and returned with her toilet pouch.

'Who write it?'

'Naipaul.'

'He from India?' she asked after another minute.

The interruptions of idle questions irritated me.

'Trini.'

'They bright, you know. It carry information on Trinidad?'

'Africa mainly.'

It seemed to have satisfied her. She got absorbed with some spots on her forehead.

'You ever had a black girl, hon?'

'Why?'

'You never say nothing, you know, never answer with answer.'

215

'How do I know where you going with this.'

'Well, I just sayin that they put so much chemical in they hair, is always smelling chemical chemical. I had a friend and I tell she this and she stop talking to me.'

'What did you expect!'

'I ain't making racial. I just tell her she don't *need* to do this. God make everybody a certain way. You got to accept that. But she take it the wrong way.'

I returned to the book.

'You got black people in India?'

It was no use: I put it away.

'Not really.'

'Wha! Is sheer East Indian living there?'

'I guess you could say that.'

She stretched her dark legs on the bed and worked crabwood oil into them. It was produced by a branch of the family. She carried it around in a Viva flavoured-water bottle.

'Hon, you hear how the country-country cooliegals speak?'

'Yeah.'

Her toes touched mine. She was in shorts. The line of muscle on her thigh had now a rich brown shine.

'And them young blackgirls in town?'

'Yeah.'

'You find I speak better than them?'

'Like more standard English? Yeah, I notice that.'

'Is because I make the effort. I find if you got to go away, you got to speak right English. I watch the American shows. Is not so difficult, you know.'

'Well, meh taak hard creolese, gal.'

She looked at me attractively.

'Nah vex meh, man, is blows you settin up fuh.'

'Nah eye pass me, gal. You mout getting plenty talks these days.'

'Me cane you rass till it tun purple like jamoon.'

216

'Me go fetch me cutlass jus now.'

'Now you getting too coolie for me.'

Sitting on the edge of the bed, she applied oil to her nails. She rose to the mirror.

I contemplated reaching for the book.

'I study up till CSEC. You?'

'How old do you sit CSEC at?'

'Like sixteen or so.'

'I do a bachelor's degree. But it's not much use.'

'You know, my mother, she always make it a point to talk good English when I was young. So that is why I appreciate what Carolina was saying yesterday. Making sure she "geerl" learn good English. She remind me of my mother. I going to learn my boy good.'

'How you know he going to be a boy?'

'I would know, man. He going to turn four next year.'

'What you mean?'

'He going to turn four. What that must mean?'

'Who going to turn four?'

'The baby.'

'Which baby?'

'My baby.'

'You got a baby?'

She spun around.

'Yeah.'

'What you mean! Where is he!'

'He by mummy, I tell you so.'

'You never said anything about your baby.'

She walked to the edge of the bed, staring intently.

'I told you. I told you nuff time.'

'Like when!'

'Like at Shanta's after we get the visa.'

She was burning with a fierce kind of integrity.

I turned my gaze. I had a very imprecise sense of her family. The cousins, the aunts and uncles, the many locations. It wasn't perhaps her family. I had always been inattentive to families. Growing up, I was the only one not well-versed with the extensive nomenclature for Indian relatives, the only one ignorant of a particular relative's connection with another. It was part of my isolation. I thought back to the afternoon at Shanta's. Sour dripping off dhalpuris, footsie . . . it seemed vaguely familiar, like something one might have been told in school.

'What did you tell me?'

'I told you the baby by mummy.'

'I thought you meant you mummy baby, not you own.'

'Well, you never ask anything after. At first you got all these questions jumpin out of you.'

'How am I to think to ask that? Like, let me check, does she have a baby?'

'Why? What the arse so strange about that? Besides, I ask you about you family so many times and you never say nothing about them.'

She returned to the mirror. It wasn't an intemperate withdrawal. There was something casually triumphant in it.

There was silence.

'But you only twenty-one.'

She looked at me in the mirror.

'And you said I looked twenty-five.'

'I meant it in a good way.'

'Uh huh.'

'So you had him when you were seventeen?'

'Like you study maths good.'

'Where the father?'

'He deh.'

'Where?'

'All over the place, fockin skunt.'

'Where's he live?'

'More in town now.'

'What does he do?'

'Me en know really. Some kind of exporting business. He never tell me details. He turn big.'

'He look after you?'

'He give me a little house there on the coast, near to mummy. But he fist get tight, man. Anytime I ask him he give me a lil t'ing and say he done give me the house already. If I row with him, he tell me something like, "When you got hand in tiger mout, girl, you gat fuh pat the head."'

'What's his name?'

'Goldy Persaud. Well, his right name Devkumar but everybody's call him Goldy.'

'And the boy?'

'Brian.'

'And—'

'And stop! Questions!'

It broke the tension.

'We call him Awara,' she said, coming over, resting her hands on my folded knees. 'He like awara bad.'

'You know, *awara* in Hindi means vagabond.'

'Vagabond, cha! That is a lot of words you learn me today. My Hindi going to get better than you creolese.'

She reached for her purse, handed me two pictures.

Three months old in the first, cradled in the arms of his mother – so delicate, so teenage! – with long wispy hair, a tight pout, big brown puppy eyes looking with longing at the one who held him. Three years old in the second, in vest and sneakers, a football by his feet, the eyes no longer a child's eyes, hair falling on the forehead in the Guyanese fringe.

'He growing up quick. He look smart.'

'Yeah. He the best. He love playing.'

I handed her the photographs.

'Guess what,' she said. 'I still got your perfume on my neck. I like it. Is sexy.'

She slipped in beside me, crumpling on her side. I put out the light. The broken sedans rattled and hummed.

Soon her eyes were serenely closed. Her lips were still orange from the helado. Her mouth, never fully closed at sleep, afterglowed like spent coal. A mother. But I saw her now like a child as I had never before. Outside our matrimoniale balcony the moon was low and yellow. I stared at it. Idly I urged it to fall further, into the round of the holly wreath on the grille, but it never sunk so low.

7

THE BLISS of the city is when it awakens – not the dawn hours haunted by the middle-aged shedding fat or burnt out adolescents returning home, but a little after, when the cleaning machines have brushed away yesterday's evidence and the fresh day is falling crisp as golden wafers, when reasonable people with reasonable habits are coming out of their holes to dot the world with their strange faces, their gestures, costumes, voices, until bit by bit, by living magic, the grand tapestry is made.

In the backstreets shutters went up, rattling with commerce to be transacted or frittered away. Nude silver mannequins were carried into store windows. A woman pulled a rack of dresses onto the washed pavement. The angled sun hit the concrete roads and Latin American walls, extracting their carefully calibrated flavours, making a mesh of contrasts. Empanadas sizzled deep in renewed sin. Coloured pillars of *jugo* revved in unison, fruits with names as gorgeous as their colours, *parchita, durazno, lechosa, manzana*.

An hour or two in this ambience is enough. You've got the nourishment you need. You've been doused in a particular mood, felt a particular brightness not felt before, been reassured that there are small wonders in the world, and further familiarity is liable to ruin things.

In short, it was time for terminal. Where to go? Caraca-Caraca-Caraca, we heard a tout call. Of course, Caracas!

The bus was a cold luxury operation, overseen by a militant hostess in uniform. She forbade the slightest parting of curtains with wags of the finger. The cabin was white with the air-conditioned breathing of luxury travellers, people who'd organised their sleeps to perfection.

We reclined into the cold seats. Every minute the bond between beings is on the mend or on the fray. Were we closer or further since last night? Every time I looked at her she was a little changed. Our lives were mixing, encroaching. We hardly spoke. It seemed we'd been together a long time.

The wheels moved smooth and straight beneath us. I made a crack in the curtain and pressed my eye against it. A whole country out there. Sceneries were tearing by. On the run, that was the thought that came to me – I hated it. On the run – the momentum, the weight of it. It was an adult dream and nightmare. It is a thought that came to me often in my life. Each time it left me haunted.

Running and seeking, they were sides of the same coin. I had run from a serious education, then from cricket reporting. From the expectation to 'settle down' I had run. And eventually I had run from India. Had I? Running or seeking? What were my duties, to whom? It stayed on me like dampness.

Beside me she was creating a pattern of holes on paper with a toothpick. She was so immersed in it. She was raging with concentration. 'Cha,' she exclaimed softly whenever the automobile thwarted her piercings. She must have made a hundred pricks. Was she running? Away from something or into something?

I was feeling brittle. The part of me that had marvelled at the perpetration of this affair suffered under my own unhelpful scrutiny.

I had broken in a proper way the auto-restrictions of Indian life, but I was not sure if I had shrugged off its reflexive guilt.

I went to take a leak. For a while I sat motionless on the WC in the phonebooth toilet. It was warm here. Alone, I felt stronger. From the window the day was parched and flat, blank with scope. Two mighty and distinct anthems sang in my head, Dekker's Israelites (. . . *like Bonnie and Clyde*), and Thunder Road from the Boss. Back in the seat I pulled them up on the pod, heard them over and over. They soothed me, deceived me into mild heroism. As in sport so in art, so in life – heroism, trite or tragic, to the rescue. Everything which can be glorious is worthwhile.

Thunder Road led to the first fight, the more sinister because it was required to be conducted in whispers. I told her lyrics, including the one about ain't a beauty. It was, of course, ill-advised. She could not fathom why I'd tell her that she ain't a beauty and is just alright. I wasn't really saying that, I said, it was just that the song reminded me of us on the road. She countered by saying that I had specifically told her the lines in my head, which were ain't no beauty. Don't take it so, I said, it's just that it comes at a crucial point of the song, gathering till this moment and busting open after, and in the live versions the crowd sang these lines and it was about the exciting thought of escaping with her and *that* was what I was focusing on. But why would I think of the song if I didn't think she ain't no beauty, that don't make sense. I kept dripping fraudulent rose and syrup on the incandescent yet charred romanticism of that gigantic creation. She was running hot now. 'Yuh skunt cyan wait two minute before breaking every night in you Miss No Beauty.'

I laughed. I took it to be a mock heckle like last evening; but really I laughed from pure gratitude, from the relief of being pulled back into an everyday thing. I laughed because I was grateful for the fact of her. Mistake. We spoke no more for hours.

Not till we changed buses at the highway terminal for a local into Caracas and over the valley the first stunning accumulation of shanties appeared on a mountain. The scale of the *barrios*, their utter verticality, colour dots toppling towards the sky, it supercharged our retro bus with anticipation. A country boy, aiming to capture the terrific thrill of the journey on his cellphone, finding himself on the wrong side of the aisle recorded instead the meaningless red rock face. A lady pulled out her hand mirror and applied bright pink lipstick. The city was coming.

We disembarked at Avenue de Mexico and made a long inspirational walk towards a recommended budget hotel in the guidebook. There were refrigerators and printers and electric saws being sold bare on the jumping metropolitan road. The girls of Caracas were thick, to use the Guyanese. 'Look you get all you Miss Universe here,' she said, still smarting, 'an you stuck with you Miss No Beauty.' Men could be fair with dark eyes. Some looked like pimps. A city of bursting boobs and frightened shot-at pigeons who fluttered through the hilly tall buildings carrying echoes of the shot with them. Epical, vivid, a city of slopes and angles, vicious little cigarettes, umbrellaed stalls of mobile payphones hanging from chains.

We hauled our bags uphill through the brilliant evening market streets. Latin horns were spilling out of shops and tascas that smelled of fish broth. Around small grassy squares Caraquenos bought grocery and newspapers. People were everywhere: to be in a city of millions again!

I had been almost offended by her semi-passivity towards the miracles of travel. But now I felt her genuine participation.

'It got this much people in India?' she asked, pressing my arm.

'More. But the cities are ugly. There are wires everywhere, unpainted buildings, garbage on the streets.'

'I can't imagine more people. Is like this when everyone go down to the tarmac at the national stadium for concert. But here they just movin about streets like so.'

The hotel was on a sloping corner. It was a high matchbox

room. The small window opened to a Bombay view: pigeons, grilles, sliding windows, shredded noise. We went downstairs straight away. We sat at a tiny sidewalk corner cafe and drank sharp café marrón from plastic thimbles, inhaling Caracas. Outside a licoreria a woman in a long dress roasted what looked like kababs. A posse of upstarts threw handbombs, giving off illusions of a student riot. A black maga dog attacked a battered taxi that groaned uphill. Men reeking castaway regret turned corners, putting things behind them once and for all. Down the slope and far away on hills was the glimmer of lights.

We were in synchronicity. I was so grateful for her presence, I wanted to hold her and kiss her all the time. The night was primed to unfurl before us like a silver ribbon. Even so, I could never have bargained for the forthcoming stroke of fortune.

We went out to a terrace pizzeria in Altimira. There we drank numerous Solera Lights from blue bottles so pretty you could stand them in display cases, and she cleaned the chicken wings to the white of the bone, claiming it to be the mark of a Guyanese – even the president did it so, she'd seen. Skipping down the steps a little high, walking the hip circles of Altimira, we came upon a posh jazz bar. It was dim and rich, reeking of cologne, cigar, petrodollars. A band played fusion cosmopolitan. Large oil barons danced with small aristocratic movements, spreading their thick fingers on barebacked ladies. They would return to their seats after every song, only to get right back up when the next started. Everybody in that velveteen room moved like smoke. She did too, but I knew not how to salsa. We wined down without shame. 'Bravo,' shouted the oil tycoons. We drank from long crushed-ice glasses Black Label and Baileys, the best thing she ever tasted she said, and in the gentleman's she whispered to me, 'leh we stay here, we could learn Spanish, we could live here'.

We wandered drunkenly again, speaking marginal sense. She made assertions. 'Goat more stupid than sheep,' she said. Sometimes she let slip a 'fuck, bai, cole breeze, bai'. Her cheap blunt heel stuck in a gutter grating. About then, pausing to pull it out – that is when we struck divine luck.

Its first intimation, as with many good things, was the molecular thump of bass, and tracing it we arrived at a plaza. It was a West Indian music extravaganza, planted on earth just for us.

We talked again amid people who spoke English. The freedom of that! What exertions and isolations language had brought on. We'd been fluttering fish. The difficulty of every transaction, the handsigns, the stupidity of making as if to shiver while saying frio to a bus hostess, the exaggerated presence of one another.

We swigged rum and ate dukanu. The burlesque Caribbean was out in force making vulgar harmony. The Bahamians played the greatest music of all. They blew away jump-n-wave Trinis and slack raw Jamaicans. Full-blooded black Bahamians played rake-n-scrape; they played saws and accordion, they meshed cottonfield blues and carnival jump-up and zydeco stomps. They told everyday truths. A black man in a suit and hat and beautiful crepe skin sang, *Don't tell on me, and I won't tell on you.* Those were the only words. There and then he kept summing up life. They marched to the junkanoo, the terrific noise of drum and brass and whistles making exuberant madmen out of everyone, sweeping up people in its path like a tornado, a whole infantry of masqueraded music makers led and trailed by feathered, costumed Bahamian girls getting up on their toes and letting their heads drop and their pelvis round over in free perfection.

It was the vitality of the Caribbean, waiting for deflation. Jamaicans dropped their 'h's and put them in where there were none. Bajans wore Christian moustaches and slapped their thighs in great old laughters. They spoke of cricket at Pickwick in slurry Scousey tongues and said 'shite'. Saint Lucians said awrie and drank sweet beer from green bottles of Piton they'd brought with them. Guyanese weren't there. Jan, she wound and unwound her waist around mine, and not a bitter word was spoke.

CARACAS days of morning baths, wet towels and unmade beds. Burgundy negligee. Eyeliner, her brown eyes energised to ferocity. Days sunk in quicksands and intimacies. The ooze of sex and obstacles, friction and revelation. Resentments burnt up in furtive fucks. Misunderstandings plucked from the air.

Afterwards I thought the ain't a beauty fight was crucial. It loosened our behaviour. It was the first time the frontier of brinksmanship was breached. It permitted sulks, gesticulations, the odd cussword. There were no standards thereafter. Soon our tongues moved past the early stage of clearest dictions. She could groove into something too fast for me, I could mumble. Her eye-rolls infuriated me.

And the city offered so many chances for disagreement. Where to go, what to do? Walk or take the bus? Get an empanada at the cafe or hold back for a big meal afterwards? The matter of food was loaded. She was fussy about what to eat and I when.

The tension that gnawed and grew was that she always wanted and asked. The bolivars flew by. We bought brassieres, dresses, perfumes, tees and toys for the child. Her own attention to money was keen, when she talked about tomatoes at 240-dollar a pound or the speedboat fare to Parika. But she thought nothing of asking.

Anything was liable to catch her fancy. Passing a salon, she wanted highlights. This meant not only money but time, and I pointed it out. 'But I want to look good for you.' A sexy directness like that: and man's pre- and post-orgasm wisdoms are very different beasts.

The treatment ran to hours. I went out for a wander and a bite. When I returned she had, on the advice of the stylist, got her hair ironed as well. Her nails had been redone, to French. Further he had encouraged her into cherry lipstick to bring out the highlights, which were blonde rather than copper. It gave her a certain Latina appeal, but the full effect – the ironing, the wet lipstick, the white nails – it was plain mollish.

My reaction to these expenditures grew progressively worse. Sometimes I withdrew or became deliberately inattentive.

Disarmingly, she appeared to carry no weight. It occurred to me that it is how she saw things. She'd always expected indulgence of this sort, and I had set us up for it. Guyanese men had a term for it. 'Fat fowling.' I could tell she had experience. She wasn't a fowl, she was a cat.

I learnt about her life, felt it on the landscape like a memory, the line down from the cowbelt of north India. She was born in Georgetown Hospital on a night of November, early enough for Scorpio. She loved Scorpio and town. She liked liming, shopping, lived often with her wild friend Aaliyah. She did have a few boyfriends, 'nothing you got to worry about'. Her mother, named Savitri, no less, had turned Anglican. She was a crochet and embroidery expert. They moved to Essequibo for an assignment some years ago, and ended up staying. The mother lived with the man who converted her. Jan hated him. He looked for excuses to hug her up, wanted to know where she was going, when she was coming back, and she didn't like staying with them. She stopped working eight months ago, it was sheer exploitation. She'd been a salesgirl. Brian's cousins were in Lethem. Goldy Persaud, his father, she hardly saw. He chased up all kinds of girls, girls she felt were just like garbage.

Caraca days of altitude and sunshine at twenty-two degrees. The central districts cool and lime, the streets selling mounds of yellow panties, *Bush Assassino* scrawled on walls, music stalls sampling Alphaville and a-ha, wheelchair queues awaiting state concessions for the handicapped. And the plazas, plazas upon plazas, the mandatory Plaza Bolivar with the statue of the besworded liberator, plazas with stone fountains, with tribal flautists, Latin Americans. The plaza where we first lost each other.

We were on steps, I between her legs. She sketched. I drifted into sleep on her sunny thigh.

She prodded me to show the sketch: the pillared cafe on the far side, the edge of the fountain, a boy with a dinky car. It obliterated movement and crowd, yet it caught the essentials so that when I gazed up I could not for a moment see what she'd omitted. I asked her if I could have it.

'I'll keep it with the bird,' I told her. 'You know, I always thought about the crayons. Was because of the baby.'

She smiled.

'He draw nice too. He got to learn to loose up he fingers. Mummy workin with him.'

I visualised the homely scene. I could see a bottomhouse in the country, sun outside, a clothesline, a bench of old 2×4s, a drawing child, an observing mother, a teaching grandmother.

I asked something that had been on my mind.

'What happens if the big man find out about me?'

'He gon take a gun and bust a hole in your head.'

'Oooh. Exciting.'

I laughed. She didn't. She ran her pencil on the back of my neck.

'Why does he care?'

''Cause he a fockup. He want me always to be there for him.'

'Why don't you ask him to fuck off? Give him back his house and ask him to fuck off.'

'Is easy to say. Who going to look after the maintenance?'

'You still love him?'

She thought about it for a while.

'I don't know. I give up on all that now. I just want to leave Guyana.'

'And the baby?'

'Is for he I want to get away.'

She played with my hair, looking into it as if for something.

I became consumed by her predicament, the tug of her strands – her youth, her dependence, her independence, her responsibility.

'You ever wish you had waited a while for the baby?'

Her fingers froze on my head.

'What you mean?'

I didn't answer. I could feel her posture stiffen.

'You mean I shoulda throw away the baby?'

'That's not what I'm saying.'

'Is what you meant.'

'No, it's not. I just wondered what—'

'What. Be a sweetman when time right and then ask for kill the—'

'It's not killing.'

'It is fockin killing.'

'I'm not even saying that.'

'You are.'

'I'm not, and I didn't.'

'You are.'

'I'm *not*. I just wanted to know, you were so young then, I just thought if you ever feel it happened too early—'

'The baby ain't a piece of toy, you know. He got a fockin right to live, you know.'

It was far too sharp.

'He does. But you not there for him right now, are you. And you don't know where the fucking big man is.'

She tossed the pad off her lap. She was on her feet.

'You a real fock-up, you know. A real fockin fock-up.'

She stood there a few moments. I looked away. What a misrepresentation. She began to walk off. I determinedly faced away, fixing my gaze at a far end of the square; children with paper masks ran after one another. I could sense her getting further away. I did not want to have anything to do with it. When I turned she'd covered a good distance. She was walking past the central fountain. She had a moment of hesitation. She looked to see if I was coming. I wasn't. I was wishing for her to come back, I was challenging her to go on.

She turned and quickened. The sun caught her brilliant highlights. She was a blur of skin and clothes. She was merging with other blurs. She was a point. And then indiscernible. I stayed rooted to the spot, blandly looking at the sketch in my hand.

CORO, the thirty-first of December. Not a soul trod the streets, not even a dog. These were streets of the like I had never seen before. Narrow, bare streets tunnelled by high looming walls of peeling paints, once bright oranges and greens worn down to suggestions of their former selves. The doors were enormous and forbidden. The windows were of coloured glass, set behind baroque grilles. Underfoot were cobblestones and overhead a fading sky.

We had travelled all day to reach Coro, taken three buses. I had found her sucking on an orange ice lolly on a bench in Plaza Bolivar. I apologised; she conceded she could have handled it better. We kissed fingertips. It felt like the most intimate thing we had done. I suggested we'd been here long enough, perhaps too long so let us, jaan, go away somewhere nice for the new year. She agreed quietly it was a good idea.

Part of the reason I wanted to leave was to find more romantic accommodation. Our small, sun-starved room in Caracas had been much too harsh. Everything about it said: it's a jungle out there, man must hustle. We'd made inquiries in the city centre, but the inns were full.

But here in Coro the posadas were abandoned. Their doors opened after minutes of knocking. Their walls were mustard and dim-lit, their furniture was old and rich, their open courtyards filled with sad pots. We walked on in simple wonderment and settled in the third such. It too felt like a place where ghosts rested with roses in their teeth, but with the crucial difference they were well-intentioned.

Our room had a fifteen-foot ceiling and a television. We watched jaunty salsa, and she tried to take me jauntily through the bits she knew. In retaliation I taught her the bits of yoga I knew. In the nude we did the tree pose, facing each other on single right legs, left legs bent into our thighs, palms stretched above our heads in a namaste. She stood tall on her toes. My nipples were lodged over hers, her breasts were smashed against my ribs. I was hard, pressing against her navel. 'I ain't feel like a tree at all, bai,' she said through suppressed laughter. We collapsed into tangled limbs.

We had begun to go bareback. It happened first in a stairwell at the National Gallery in Caracas, and repeatedly thereafter. There was no thought to disease. I knew her now. I knew her like a quick addiction. I knew the bittersour smell of her armpits and her vagina, the mingle of our fluids. I knew my nerve endings against hers. Did she feel it so? Was it true that a woman's pleasure cannot be approached by a man? We were kissing big. Her breath was all over me. She was pressing my nipples till they hurt. She was bearing down, wining down.

We were wasted on the floor. Her hair was spread across my torso. It occurred to me that the one true intimacy we had was sexual. She would tell me about dicks and how they felt, about watching 'blues' with boys. She asked me things I had never been asked and I, surprising myself, answered.

With climax behind us, the dim energy of the posada was nibbling at our mood. In my miscalculating head in this courtyard here would have been violins, accordions, champagne, hands around dancing waists. But it was weak lights, large flower pots and the sound of the simpleton caretaker watching television in a dark corner. There was no food or drink. I was hungry.

She wore a new red and white top from Caracas that showed bellybutton and we made into those haunted streets again. Walking past the white cathedral, blinding as noonday snow even by night, we entered the Plaza Bolivar. Here were empty benches and closed shops bleached in sickly halogen. At the next cathedral, grand and lemon yellow, there was a service on. She said a prayer from outside, standing on the cobblestone with head bowed and hands clasped. She said her mother would like it. How vulnerable she felt at that moment.

We walked on. A ragged wind blew. The restaurants and cafes remained closed, the doors remained inscrutable. It occurred to me that perhaps when they said this was the capital in the sixteenth century, there was something to be gleaned from that. Maybe we were just a little late.

We met a broad boulevard heralded by two drunks on inverted crates as though they'd grown out of them. There was a lit cornershop. Its front shutter was down, but they were making the final transactions of the year through a side grille, a pa and son, with every movement you could see the son turning into the pa. There was something eerie about them, as if they knew our gravest secrets. We bought a bottle of apple wine. Comida, I said to them, gesturing to my stomach. They pointed in a direction and we obediently set out towards there. The suggestions were worthless. I looked up the guidebook again. Closed. Closed. Closed. It was the land of the dead.

We drank the *manzana vino*, which tasted like wine and cider both. We wandered off the broad avenues and into the streets. Neither sound nor light emerged from the homes we passed. They felt like they had been built as haunted houses. Sometimes we tried to push our faces through window grilles like robbers. Once or twice a car with loud music passed us. Somewhere behind a crimson wall a confidential orgy must be soaked in a pit of grapes.

Older and older streets appeared, pale and cracked. An hour into our futility a great wind began to blow, pulling dead leaves and bits of paper off the ground into our eyes. Her mane, having long shrugged off the effects of ironing, conflagrated into an electric storm, streaks like lightning. She looked sassy. We were back on a boulevard, and in a hotel doorway an Arab-looking man in bright white sneakers pointed down the road. He held up his fingers one by one. 'Five blocks. You go five blocks. Enjoy.'

We walked fifteen. The wind blinded us with debris. We made turns. Lured into the chase again – I found there was something addictive to this futility.

We strayed into the oldest ancient streets. These were affluent now. Here and there black cars gleamed like polished hearses. Otherwise the same deserted howl rang through them. Yet we walked, curving along, crazy in the blowing night, until we chanced upon a vision: a sliver of miraculous light streaming out of a door left ajar. At the threshold one could hear the sound of people, maybe even the tinkle of glass. The sound of the chatter was refined. I could not tell if it was a restaurant or a home. What was indisputable was there were humans inside.

As the prettier one, it was decided she would go in to see. I could see bits of the courtyard as she entered, the edge of an ice sculpture, canapés, backs of suits, strapless shoulders. She returned in a few seconds with word that 'place fancy'. It wasn't clear if it was a restaurant or a home.

But the sortie had alerted the Coro gentry to our presence. A bearer arrived, followed by a large man in a black tuxedo and shining waxed hair. His face was fair, fleshy, full of folds. He had beady, diverging eyes. I knew the type, the fleshy tycoon: it was universal. He studied us with the particular self-confidence and self-indulgence of a man who'd made his fortune on the strength of sizing things up quickly. He had such distracting eyes, not quite 'looking London, going Tokyo', but just a little obtuse, so that he seemed to be addressing your ears. He spoke in an American accent. He was amazed to find us here. I conceded our own amazement.

How I wished the magnate, the possessor of this fabulous colonial house and many others, this baron of petroleum, would say, come on in compadres, come on in and partake of my banquet. And precisely such a wish appeared to be in the fulfilment when he announced in a loud voice, as though for an audience: 'Since this is your first time in Venezuela . . .' – I began to smile and blush, I thought of asparagus and prawn, of lovely pig, of champagne, strawberry dessert, almost started to say, *that's so nice of you* – '. . . I would like to offer you a drink.'

He went inside and returned with two plastic cups. Rum and coke. 'The finest rum in Venezuela.' Yuh mudderskunt, yuh jackarse, yuh pattabrain, I wanted to tell him, yuh ever taste a Guyanese rum, the greatest fockin honey in this universe that you coming out here with this piece of lil plastic fuckery, get the fuck outta here yuh piece of shit.

We accepted it and thanked him several times and departed, rum in one hand, manzana vino in the other.

After two hours of walking like this, through slim streets and bigger avenues, past minor unpeopled plazas lit with harrowing fairylights, we were on the outskirts of town. A black road and a closed gas station. We'd walked Coro over. Our legs were aching, our hunger was debilitating. The world never felt so large as in little Coro and we were on the perimeter of the earth poised to walk off the edge.

We touched hands, but there was a static dissonance between us. At the start of the hunt we had been chatting. The last thirty minutes were completely silent. She was negotiating the space between disappointment, anger and helplessness, each kept in check by the other. And I, for the first time in our entanglement, I felt I'd bitten off more than I could chew.

We turned around. After twenty minutes a long collapsing taxi passed us. He could not help with comida.

He dropped us to the posada.

The simpleton was watching television, satisfied in his small dim world. He was oblivious to our pleas for food. 'Comida?' 'Pan?' I put fingers to my mouth and made a miserable face. He looked at me without motive.

We seemed to be on to something when our entry into the kitchen jolted him out of his seat. We waited for him to settle again before the television. A few minutes later we sneaked into the kitchen.

In the fridge there was a hunk of bread, a small bowl of red beans, another of beef bones in gravy.

We took them to the room. We ate it cold. It occurred to me we could be eating the simpleton's dinner. Also, that she was eating wrenk.

In moments the food was done. The room, site of passion a few hours ago, was dry as husk. She looked stonily resentful. Her face was naturally expressive; when she turned like this, it was deliberate.

I felt responsible for our plight. Yet, we'd both together browsed the guidebook and found Coro. It was a World Heritage Site. The pictures of those walls, the gay cafes on cobblestone! I was struggling as much as her. I felt hunger more acutely than she did. Besides, there was something about the situation, the stolen food and the ghost town, at least mildly amusing.

'Is twice already I make you starve,' I said, recalling the day on the ferry. 'I am sorry.' It was a tactical sorry, aimed at getting something out of her, a return consolation, a lightening up, anything.

Her response was to turn wistful.

'We would sport so hard on Ole Year's. Everywhere you look people sportin. I remember one time we go to like seven limes. Start from Sandy Babb Street, Kitty, to the seawall, up the coast at Mon Repos, come back down to Lamaha Street . . .'

'You missing Guyana,' I said. Though I really meant: 'You missing him.'

'Nah. Those times gone, man.

'I must call Brian tomorrow,' she added after a few minutes.

We talked a little.

Her answers came in one or two words.

From hunger I took sips of the apple wine. She refused any.

'I changing,' she said at last, and got off the bed.

The bathroom was large. Her elaborate nightly ritual I think she performed inside, for she was gone a very long time – I can't be sure because, waiting, sipping from the apple wine, I fell asleep. It wasn't still midnight.

8

SHE bit my ear early in the morning with the words, 'Leh we eat.' In truth, we had long passed the critical points of hunger. Like survivors of a storm we savoured the morning. In the crossed rays and shades of the bathroom she took a cleaner's satisfaction in ridding my hair of Coro debris. With less diligence but more pleasure, I polished her soles, her toes. She was slippery in soap. A new year, new promise, its brand new loving.

The streets were sick with light, the colours were burning off the walls. The leaves blew dry in the plazas. At the terminal, a woman grilled submarines, layering tomato and lettuce with three kinds of cheese. 'I could have eaten four, you know,' she said, munching on her second, 'if we ate last night.'

What a funny, brutal place was Coro. From nowhere people had arrived for the lone bus of the morning. Where were you last night, I wanted to shake each one and ask. With their bags and children they ran from one bay to another and another, attempting to predict which one the bus would dock in. They were Indian scenes; and it was an Indian squeeze in the bus, a too-full bus, standers and splayed legs and luggage in the aisle like spilled geometry boxes.

We passed palm, scrub, hicktowns, possible oilfields of what felt like a Soviet scale. Apparently we were going to Valencia. From there I didn't know. I only knew we were far out west and Guyana was east. Through the half-tints which turned the mad day into something autumnal and viscous, it was possible to imagine rosy futures. We could go to Merida in the Andes, from there cut through the animaled savannah towards Guyana. Or hit Caracas for one last fling. We could make for the beaches, skinnydip at night and wake on sand wrapped in a single sarong, or head to the far colonial riverport of Ciudad Bolivar. And six hours later, at Valencia, the decision was made for us. It was still holiday season. Buses were barely plying. There was one to Puerto La Cruz. From there, the tout said with a double thumbs up, 'Ciudad Bolivar.'

The bus was hours away. We waited. On the tarmac we ate barbeque pinchos. Cats skittered for crumbs under empty Venezuelan skies. Our tenuous grip on the new year was slipping. Soon it was dark.

Thankfully the next service was high-luxury. We took the upper deck, right up by the windscreen. The continental highway opened out before us, smudged with dreamy flashes of headlight. The air conditioning, the comfort of the seats, it encouraged tenderness. 'You hands cold!' she whispered, pulling my hands under her sweatshirt. We blurred in and out of sleep.

At a silly hour of the night the bus pulled into Puerto La Cruz. People must have got off along the way, for we were the only ones to disembark.

We settled on a dark bench. We bought café marróns from a man with a worrying TB cough. We waited again.

In hushed voices we spoke of Guyanese politics. 'Is only the barons who keep shopping cheap in their stores,' she argued. 'Nobody could afford toaster or washing machine if cocaine don't keep thing cheap.'

The night grew colder and colder. We hugged up tight, hanging on for morning. We made giggles about little things, the worst bits of *Rainbow Raani*. She told stories, of her neighbour Girlie who used to hurryfuck Larry the sand-n-polishman through the palings at nights till one day a dog mashed his ass. I told her of Uncle Lance, and the people he told me about. I even told her of Baby, the whole affair, the first person with whom I'd shared it. Immediately I regretted it.

'You stupid bad, you know.' That was her conclusion. 'You get mix up in this kind of thing and you get nothing out of it.'

I get everything from it, I wanted to tell her, all understanding, all motivation, but I said nothing.

Presently we fell asleep, sitting, shivering mildly into one another, prongs of a tuning fork.

THE sounds – buses pulling in and pulling out, the grunt of touts, the shuffle of travellers – the sounds came before the light, and the sun rose from a strange place and recalled the fresh morning on these same streets here, when we were going westward.

An early bus, full of agrarians with ruddy flesh, wearing hats and moustaches, the men too. They were in a farmer's convention. The hostess conducted a quiz for them with trinkets as prizes. At a makeshift clinic they all climbed off the bus and received injections.

We fell asleep again, in a terrible exhaustion.

WE lost each other a second time. On the steep blazing inclines of Ciudad Bolivar, we were knocking about from posada to posada, rejected by each, directed finally towards one with a possible vacancy, when she flung her bag to the ground.

'I ain't walking.'

We'd been on the road two hours short of twenty-four, four buses including the local. It was not a time for cajoling.

'It ain't walking to us.'

'Is the blasted bag,' she said, landing a kick on it.

Her eyes were shot. There was a rash on her legs, from a spider she said.

'Just a few minutes more. We'll have our own bed and room again.'

'We got to take a taxi.'

'You seen one?'

'I ain't walking.'

'Wait, then. I'll go see if they got room or not.'

'And leave me alone with the bags? You ain't feel no shame at all?'

Now that was a provocation.

'I gon carry *all* three bags with me.'

I did. It was an act of dumb pride. She sat on the abandoned steps of a corner and left me to my foolishness.

I struggled with the bags, grunting. There was room at the posada. I went back to fetch her. And I got lost in that slopey maze. I passed places that I knew I had passed already. The colours on the walls swirled before my eyes. The strawberry corner of our estrangement was elusive. When I did find it she was no longer there. What the *fuck*.

It was forty-five minutes before we saw each other, she walking downhill, eyes still shot, I uphill, a hopeless moment.

THE truth about travel and relationships is much the same. To ride the highs one must hate the lows, or at any rate feel some form of passion for them. Else what is the point? Frustration rationed is frustration wasted.

So it was that gratification followed. It was the stillness, the stillness after the motion. Our room was a simple rectangle. It had a window of amber glass, filtering sunlight to the texture of honey. A door opened to the roof-terrace, all to us. From here one could look at the bright clay tiles down the slope, the wrought iron grilles, the changing colours on the walls, jade, opal, corn, crimson.

In the room and on the roof we luxuriated for two days. We slept like babies. We fucked with long intuitive pacing. We got Alizé Gold Passion and pizza and had them on a sheet under the waning moon.

Still, heavy Angosturan days. Alizé on fresh fruit and ice. An absence of strain, which was loaded. I could not tell if our understanding was secure or non-existent.

Outside, the city had resonances. It was old like Coro, the same lyrical air blowed through it. It was a lookout point, this hill. Somewhere there was a fort. The slopes went down to the riverfront. Orinoco, in the very name you could feel the proximity of the looted Caribbean, ruthless doomed conquistadors and their hunt for El Dorado, Raleigh and his stupendous hallucinations. You could feel the proximity of Guyana, a river that was large and dirty, though this was the narrows of the Orinoco.

Despite the proximity Guyana meant nothing, not even the word. In the morning, while she readied herself for the day, I went out searching for a way back over the border. Nobody had a clue. Travel agents stared at their computers and offered tickets to Georgetown, USA. The guidebook said nothing. The only good tip came from a Trinidadian waiter at a pastelleria, a phone number for Gomattie, a Guyanese vendor in the city of San Felix.

When I returned home she'd soaked all the clothes. She glistened naked among them. 'Look how nasty they get.' We washed them, spread them on the roof to dry in the Indian way. The domesticity: from afar someone might have thought us man and reputed wife. Time together is so frightening. One is running out of points to make. One is unravelling all the while, stripped to basics.

I learnt her suspicion extended to detergent. She held that it coloured water grey to fool people about how much it cleaned. Her suspicions were not to be misunderstood. I was realising that she believed in things. She believed in top-loading detergents vs front-loading detergents vs hand-washing detergents, in garbage liners as opposed to plastic bags. Arguably no escapery in her. Her quitting the job, that wasn't to be misconstrued. Her ambition was different from mine, not the flimsy ambition of journeys but of destinations. In five years I wasn't sure if I would be anywhere, but she probably would. She was formidable. She knew childbirth. If we were in battle I suspected I would lose.

She was prepared to tackle the world because the world to her was not absurd. To think the world absurd is a privilege. Those who do so consider themselves enlightened. In fact, it only means their struggles are shallow. Sooner or later the real world will rain down upon them. That, or we shall go slowly mad, or seek recourse in meditation, narcotics, writing.

Laundry, amber light, silent streets: stillness which was mounting. And then, on a drunken second night, the bottom fell out.

A lavish meal in a posh courtyard, Bailey's and whiskeys in a bar of Europeans. We were staggering through the slopes, laughing with liquor, the ochres so pale in the moonlight, washed out like shells. She squealed as I almost fell into a dry gutter, scratching my arm. Staggering and squealing, we tumbled arm in arm into our room on the roof. I sang a folk song Uncle Lance used to sing.

Ah Nora darling, don't you wake me fore day morning. She turned me towards her.

Me go give you polish furniture, me go give you pressure cooker. 'My grandfather would sing that,' she said softly. She looked at me with a look I shall never forget, deep affection, in that instant like adoration, and I was consumed for a long moment by the thought of what really was going on between us, when she caught me offguard.

'You carryin me back to India, right?'

'Of course, jaan.'

'Be serious, man.'

'It's not a nice place. I don't think you'll like there.'

'I could decide that for myself.'

242

'Well, leh we get to Guyana first nuh.'

'I knew it! I knew it! All you is the focking same.'

'What do you mean!'

She pulled away.

Me go give you cement bed gal, me go give you miniskirt gal, I sang but the mood had changed. I tried to look at her, but she averted her bitter brown eyes. The Alizé had swigs left in it. The sour was tingling on a corroded tongue. I tried to offer her some, went around to her from the other side of the bed. *Ah Nora darling, don't you wake me fore day morning*, I sang again, but there was no response at all.

SHE didn't wake me fore day morning, she didn't wake me at all. She was already dressed when I stirred out of sleep. She'd taken the chair to the window, her wet hair pulled over to one side. She must have known when I woke: I rustled about with deliberate noise. She continued gazing into the shine of the terrace. The sun caught her in parts. Her burnished, braceleted forearm, her French nails, her crossed knees in the icy jeans from Carupano.

'Marnin!'

It was a gamble.

She looked at me as one does an annoying child.

There was no further communication. In any case, another lady was on my mind, and she worried me. It was Gomattie, the Guyanese vendor in San Felix.

Gomattie was our only way back home. It occurred to me that in the languor of the previous days I had reposed too much faith not just in Gomattie but things she had no control over. She was to have checked if the backtrack boat to Guyana was around. I had spoken to her on her home number. She didn't have a cellphone. I was to meet her in the market at San Felix. For the first time I considered the possibility that it might not have worked out. My ticket to India and my Guyanese visa both expired in a few days, one year after I'd arrived.

We left for San Felix. Ninety minutes on the bus we sat like cardboard cutouts. She made sure she didn't stray on to the armrest even. What was there to say? There was nothing to say.

At San Felix the taxi drivers refused us. They didn't know where to take us. Market? Mercado? Covered market, Gomattie had said. Covered mercado? Half a dozen rejections from the taxi queue. By chance a passing taxi honked for us. Fortunately, he drove off as we entered.

Conversation began minutes later. Mercado? Covered mercado? He was driving in circles. I looked through the guidebook. Nothing for covered. Indoor: *cubierto*. Mercado cubierto? No recognition.

He pulled up and gestured for us to get out. The facts hit me: looking for a person one didn't know in a city one didn't know in a language one didn't know. It was crusts of diamond in a pool of filth. She was beside me, looking precious, burdensome. *Mercado?* I said it to him like a prayer. Please, *cubierto* mercado? Gracias. *Mercado cubierto?* He was an unassuming sort of man. He drove again.

After a long and anxious ride he deposited us at what was blatantly a market. Too much so. It was defeatingly large. Worse, its scope kept growing. Every few metres there appeared a side street, and those with further branches, each a slap in the face. There was a clamorous market air. People had no time for queries. To offer the words 'cubierto' or 'Guyana' was to be blinked at and dismissed.

I considered examining the side streets one by one, but that way lay madness. We kept walking along the central road. Perhaps we'd already gone past Gomattie. Then the central road itself forked. Took the one which sloped down. There in the distance the most beautiful sight: the vast dull spread of tin roofs. *Cubierto!*

The moment was ruined soon enough, for nearness brought bewilderment. The place was humongous, eight or ten times the

244

size of Stabroek. And so dense. There was no way of standing back and taking stock. In fact, there was not place to stand. If you stood women pulled you by the arm towards their foodstalls.

'Guyana?' 'Gomattie?' For half an hour we sagged about among vegetables, clothes, plastic wares. 'Guyana? Gomattie?' She was tiring. She'd begun to shift her bag from shoulder to shoulder. She usually carried mine, the lighter, but not today. She was ready to say something in irritation, I could tell. She didn't. It was wicked. What to do? I couldn't let it show. Panic at this stage would be pathetic.

I switched to 'Gooyana', as Carolina of Carupano had called it. To Gooyana a lady vendor responded with a nod. She led us inside to the very innards of the market, to a man with a smashed face, and he nodded and led us further inside to another man, who was – a prapa coolieman! And he led us to a section at the very end, where like magic there appeared a set of cooliepeople, some tending to stalls, some milling about just so. From a tower of speakers the song played loud and proud: *Yaad aa rahi hai, teri yaad aa rahi hai*. Love Story. It was Lata singing all right, but big Caribbean beats had been added in.

An unexpected thing happened here. A tear welled in my eye. I don't know. There was something in the scenes. The Venezuelan shed, the song from *Love Story*, the beats. Cooliepeople milling about in coolie ways. The shabby, sparkless dressing, the uninspiring hairstyles, the flat resignation in those eyes that I knew from India to Guyana. The packets of Guyanese curry powder and Guyanese chowmein and bottles of brandless coconut oil, the stacks of Hindi discs. Twice-removed diaspora, twice-removed attachments, perhaps twice-strong, the absurdity and obviousness of so many journeys, so many displacements.

And there in the far corner, I could tell without asking, was our Gomattie, named for the river Gomti. From the banks of that river her great great grandfather came across the world to cut cane, and at the immigration depot he would have humbly answered what was asked of him, his birth, an approximate year, his caste and village and tehsil, the spelling of his name and those of his progeny mangled forever by the white officer, and he would have put his thumb on the paper, put his time in, and now, generations down the line, in the covered market of San Felix, Venezuela, selling curry powder and masala and Hindi movies, was Gomattie.

Gomattie, wall-eyed and maternal in a flowery dress. She'd checked for the boat. It had gone. No, she didn't know details of the overland route. One could fly from Eteringbang but she wasn't sure how to get there. She only used the boat. Everybody here only used the boat. It was much cheaper, didn't need papers. I asked others nevertheless. No, they all went backtrack.

Jan was no longer with me. She'd turned away at the mouth of the Guyanese section. I found her at a cosmetics stall outside.

'We stranded,' I told her.

'Good,' she said, examining a hair clip.

THERE was only one thing to do in the circumstances, which was follow urban man's primal instincts and make phone calls. I took directions to a phoneshop. It was on the riverfront. We walked in silence towards it. My panic had receded. In its place there was contemplation of a serious fear. In a few days I would miss my flight back to India. It wouldn't even come to that. My Guyanese visa would have expired. They wouldn't let me into the country. Was there any other way? We couldn't return as we had come, because the ferry to Trinidad had left for the week. Flying via Caracas and Port of Spain would cost 1,500 dollars each, out of the question.

I called and waited, called and waited, a sweating iteration performed for an hour. She was outside. She was under a canopy. She was sitting on her bag, drinking a juice.

Information trickled in. I had called de Jesus – I had a recollection from a lime of his pardner saying his childmother was Venezeulan.

De Jesus rang his friend. His friend rang his childmother. His childmother rang her friend. And that friend had a number for Admiral Rambo.

I rang Admiral Rambo.

'Is that Admiral Rambo?'

'Ai.'

I explained the situation. He asked for my exact location.

'Don't move. I comin there jus now.'

In twenty minutes Admiral Rambo arrived, stepping out of a grey jeep, a fluffy gent in an old green T-shirt and fawn trousers, with big tits, a split-legged walk, a thick smile under a bushy-tail moustache and thick black hair heaped in a bouffant.

'Ai, Sharook Khan' – I had told him I was from India – 'wahpun there!' He took my hand to shake, and did not leave it, swinging it gently side to side with constantly shifting grips for two or three minutes.

'Is wildlife you got in India – me foreparents from India, you know, me right name Rambarran – so we got jaguar right, but in India you got tiger. Tiger. Yeh, that's my cat, bai, dah is the cat for me. Yes, Admiral, well I tell you why, you see I used to run a boat – eh he, Essequibo – sweet guess, man! I like how you make the guess there, Sharook! – so there is where I pick up the name of Admiral. Nah, nah, nah, Captain is too . . . too . . . *common* you know. Any banna playing cricket pun the tarmac could turn captain. Now Admiral got a lil style, a lil power, somebody you could *admire*. That is a man which can take on tiger. Eh he, 120,000 bolivar each passenger till San Martin. Eteringbang . . . yeh yeh yeh, is the same thing, you see is San Martin on this side, Guyana side is Eteringbang. The plane to Georgetown, that is next cost of 125 dollar, so that is 250 for you and the mistress. Yeh, US dollar not Guyanese. Ha ha, Sharook, is joke you jokin, bai! Yes, man, pay in any currency, so long is in cash not kind, I ain't know what is the kind of kind people givin nowdays! Eh he, day after marnin we leffin, say about twelve o'clock time.'

By the time he had completed the handshake – slap to clasp to swings to jousty push-pulls to squeeze-and-release, the thing was done fix.

We got into his jeep. He gave us a ride across the river to San Felix's twin city of Puerto Ordaz.

'YOU got a wife in India, right?' she said, changing out of her jeans. The white hotpants revealed the final suggestions of the streaky stretch marks under her cheeks.

'She deh waiting pon you, a nice fat wife. I know it. Man, I know it. Is easy for you. Go away after you lil adventure. And look at the shit you get me into. I stuck in the same place. Worse. Worse than before.'

Her voice, thin anyway, assumed a trembling quality in the echoing room, not the tremble of rage or emotion but of suppressed bitterness leaking out.

'My mother vex with me. And the dog going to give me licks – if he even realise that I gone. Sometimes he could go two month without checking on me. But somebody must have told him. People wicked, man.'

She began to perform unnecessary tasks around the room, shifting a bag from one corner to another, which in that degenerate cement square, devoid of furniture, would make no difference this way or that.

'You ain't done me nothing good, you know. Nothing nothing nothing. You ain't even anything to look at. If I show you picher to my friends they will say, gal, he must rich or you get a raw deal. I thought you were different. I thought you were genuwine.'

'What do you mean!' I interjected. 'You never said anything. We never discussed anything.'

She ceased her activity and leant for a moment against the wall. She flashed me a serrated, cheated look:

'You didn't even gimme the phone. Not even the *phone*! I ask you it when!'

Upon this utterance, she slid down slowly to the floor, as if to demonstrate the effort it had taken to withhold it all this time.

'Tell me what happened to yours. Tell me really.'

'He take it back, the skunt. He try to call me one time at night, and he get it busy busy busy. He come over, smellin like a distillery, create a stink scene, the baby start to bawl, the neighbours come out to see, and he snatch the phone from me hand and drive off. Good thing I done erase all the records before he come in.'

'He hit you?'

'No. He never done me that. He try one time. But I tell he I would report he skunt. I know what happen to mummy. I ain't one for keep quiet.'

I felt the situation was improving. Right then she charged me with trying to sidetrack the discussion. She may have been right. She called it tactics. I disagreed. Perhaps it was a mechanism, but it wasn't a tactic. Regardless, she spoke with twice the earlier bitterness, sometimes with venom, with touching frailty. I lay on the bed, not hearing her as much as watching her.

Her eyebrows were knotted. Her eyes held a blaze of defiance. Her wide mouth, her brown lips, were pursed even as they moved. Her arms, a sprout of hair on them now, were crossed tight on her shins. Her toes were curled in. Every bit of her was in resistance.

I felt it was not right to be lying down at this time. It felt dissolute. I considered standing up. She rose before me, and began to pace about, moving the bags again, letting the physical momentum raise the pitch of her voice. I didn't think two people pacing about that stifled space would help the situation. The room made me feel claustrophobic. I felt to get away for a walk. But where? It was one of those modern planned towns of exalted dreariness. Nothing was walking distance. The holidays were still on. In the city centre a few hours ago the shutters on restaurants and cafes had shone like metallic barbs. The roads (there were no streets) were devoid of people. When would Santa stop waving from a rooftop to nobody? When would the felize navidad lights go out? At any rate, walking out would have been too escalatory a gesture.

So, I didn't throw myself into combat, and I didn't escape it through the door. I remained on the bed, propping myself against the wall.

THE rest of our stay was a sequence of implosions. Inevitably the echo of one carried into the next. Of course, we were not fighting about things we actually fought about. The things we actually fought about were petty. Food, we had one fight about food. She rejected an empanada stall, because she felt sick to be eating stuffed cornflour all the time. She wanted fried chicken. Out of spite I refused to eat anything but fried chicken. Thus we reprised earlier starvations, of Guiria and Coro, starvations which had acquired a retrospective glow, descending to deeper hells than they had been.

Another fight around money. I had given her a hundred dollar bill. I needed to change it. She said she didn't have it. 'But I gave it to you,' I said. She shrugged. I looked through my wallet again. 'You got to have it,' I insisted.

'Are you saying I thiefed it?' she said with her eye-roll.

'No, I'm not fucking saying that. Why must you twist what I'm saying?'

'Don't fockin be cussing off you skunt on me.'

'I ain't cussin *you*. I just cussin.'

Afterwards I found it in an envelope of souvenirs: bus tickets, beer labels, the perforated paper from the journey to Caracas, a scrap of her burgundy negligee that had caught on a bathroom nail.

Till some time ago these incidents might have prompted passionate reconciliation. We seemed to have run that spirit dry. What we were really fighting about hung before us all the time like accusations. It no longer took much for me or her to say something irretrievably mean, and elicit a worse response. She liked a crystal figurine of Simon Bolivar on a horse. She wanted it. 'For memories.' It was four hundred thousand bolivars: a hundred and fifty US. I couldn't afford it, I told her so.

'Why the hell you ask me to come with you?' she asked, she spat it.

'Why the hell did you agree?'

'I should never have. I thought you knew how to care for a woman. Even that dog better than you. At least he give me something. You ain't going to leave me one red cent.'

'I pick up all the expense for the trip!'

She looked at me aghast.

'You the man, you suppose to.' She sucked her teeth. 'I really shoulda never come.'

It inflamed me to the point of disgust.

'You'd go away with any fool if he gave you a couple of things.'

Having pierced one another with these arrows, we left one another to bleed separately. We were at an enormous supermarket. And there, in the neutering maze of products, diapers and repellents and onions, we lost each other again.

9

SHE looked like a fairy in the morning. A feather had blown in from the ventilator and fallen on her brow. She slept on, innocent, and unbeknownst to her I pecked her lightly on the forehead.

By noon we were gone. We left with Andre, the leather-gloved son of Admiral Rambarran. I took the front of the jeep. It was a crush at the back. There were elder, greying Mildred and her three grandchildren. There was another child with her large Indian mother.

The two ladies were in conversation. Grandma Mildred was speaking of her daughter's death. 'In her prime.' When she got the call she thought it was a prank. Then her daughter's husband called. 'That's when I knew. I knew.' She'd moved to Venezuela and been raising the grandchildren since. Long-time it used to be so hard to cross over, she reminisced. You could wait up to three months before someone undertook the trip.

It was a hot day. The air was thick with the stifled sounds of heating, struggling children and their minders. We left the conurbation of Puerto Ordaz. We were in tropical country. We were slowly leaving Venezuela behind, Venezuela properly settled over centuries, given a chance, and we were going towards the rudimentary construct of Guyana.

I turned to steal a glance at her. She was lost in the clutter. She was staring out the window. She was flushed and sweating. Her hair was tied. The danglers on her ears were like onion rings.

As the journey grew, the rush of autobiography matured to comfortable silence. Before long the children were knocked out in the heat. One of them, a mulatto boy with brown curls, had climbed into her lap. He must have been the same age as Brian.

'The bai gettin lawless!' she had squealed after speaking to him from Ciudad Bolivar. 'He learning words to Dutty Wine! I tell mummy to clean out he mouth with Foam.' He had been playing football, fishing with his cousins, hardly sleeping.

She herself was falling asleep against the metal. It would have been hot on her temple.

It must have been in Caracas that I had thought of the final days. Caracas, or Coro, roughly then. Last year. The thought came to me at ordinary moments, in the boredom of weak conversation, in the lethargy of nudity, playing with her spots. I thought of it and postponed the thought. I could not sense it. Nothing which is made is without wound.

But what was the problem? There was no problem, that is what I was trying to tell myself. These ought to be hours of triumph. Despite troubles the trip was fab. The girl was sexy. We were bold and true.

We were going through landscapes. High tropical, palm, plantain, clumps of jackfruit and their clumps of dark leaves. Then we were on the hills. From the hills we were lowering into green savannah – Venezuelan landscapes receding to a far point in the forest, never to be tramped again. I tried to yield to the liberty of the road, its idea of everlasting impermanence; to music, What a Botheration and Tenement Yard, floating in the jokey lightness of their despair. Life was attitude to circumstance, no more no less. The plains were flashing by with emptiness and occasional baseball. Soon it would be the border. Soon thereafter India. It must have changed. I had. I could approach it differently. I went to U-Roy. No more sighing, I told myself.

It was evening before we reached the dust and cheap bars of Tumeremo. We stopped here a while. The ladies and children stayed in the vehicle. She went to check out some stalls. In the failing light I sat in the doorway of a bar and tried to read. Dusk thinned. We hit the road again. We met a highway where trailers roared past us. 'High-high vehicle,' Andre called them. The highway would have taken us to the glorious moment where Venezuela, Brazil and Guyana trisected on the tepui of Roraima. Instead we turned off into a mud trail. It was rank dark now. At once the sensations of the interior came flooding back to me – scent of herb, give of mud, intuition of water, feeble stream of moonlight swallowed by great tangles of vegetation. And it was an interior shack that we suddenly turned into, in a little clearing by the trail, surrounded by high trees, the smell of rotting soursop.

By the looks of it Admiral Rambo and his jeep had arrived a good while back. In a tin yard people were arranged around a bare table under a bulb pulled from the jeep battery, dangled over a beam. They were all men, Indian. Beside them was an enormous ice case, stuffed silly with both Guyanese beer and Venezuelan cerveza. Chutney on the car stereo: I Ain't Touch De Dulahin (But She Belly Start To Swell).

She tried to busy herself with the women and children, washing up, relieving themselves in the bush, settling down in the other arm of the tin yard, but her separation was as clear as mine from the men.

'He's here.'

'Okay.'

Those were the only words we'd spoken all day.

I talked with a man of trimmed moustache like a line of ants. He, like me, didn't participate in the games. 'I ain't a cardsman, I'm a draughtsman,' he said often, as though I might be judging him. 'Is good to mark time.' He played it quite a lot at work.

Security work. Decades ago he'd started out at Blairmont Estate as a chain-boy (in crop season) and a punt-tarrer (in the off season). The islands paid ten times the wages. He left Guyana. In the islands he was a victim of discrimination. He backtracked into Venezuela, and in Puerto Ordaz he was working in security. I guessed he was a watchie. He was pleased to be returning home for holidays. 'Is the greatest country in the world. When me die, it got to be in Guyana.' And live? 'Nah, man, not live, die.'

I sought lightness in Admiral Rambo. He was sweating effortlessly, sparking a serious bushcook. He had those wonderful bushman skills, of peeling potatoes in unbroken peels without ever looking at them, of chopping directly over the pot, perpetually nourishing it. It was a red peas and beef cookup he was concocting, with a bit of dhal too – a beef khichdi, in other words. Beef khichdi, what a tremendous corruption! How you like that, eh, Pandit, I said to Uncle Lance in my mind. It had been so long since I saw him. I yearned for his reassuring presence at this moment. The nearest substitute was Admiral Rambo, and I stood by him and his bouffant, chopping herb for him.

The cookup was brilliant. The mothers arrived and filled plates for their children. She took a light helping. She didn't meet my eye as she served herself. She ate alone, sitting on a bench under a tree at the edge of the clearing. I could see her in the dark, fastidiously sifting wrenk from rice with her plastic spoon.

I became acutely conscious of what everybody must think of us. Our alienation felt absurd. In games of the heart, rectifying absurdity feels like the most heinous capitulation. We had thrown ourselves into sustained, wilful hurtsmanship. I wished I could rise above the situation, in one way or another. I was falling between stools. I was still stung. I was more than stung. I thought she was grossly wrong, mean, to portray things as she did. On the other hand I had nothing to offer but an attempt at passing the last hours happy. I couldn't tell what plane she was on. With some people you know – or else you don't. The trouble is with those with whom one treads the in-between spaces. Every fact can be assumption, every assumption fact.

'Eat, bai, Sharook, I en't charge by the plate, you know,' Admiral Rambo kept urging me. 'Throw a nex one to Sharook,' he kept instructing the man beside the icebox. I performed my learnt Guyanese trick of leaking streams from the bottle as I walked about.

It was getting late. The women and children had settled inside one of the concrete cabin rooms: Jan as well. So decisively she went in, didn't come out again.

The watchie fell asleep on a chair. The men arranged a wreath of thyme stalks around his head. They dangled wiri peppers from his ears.

Admiral Rambo too called it a night. He'd put up a whole blooming tent inside the other room. It just about fit. In this shelter within a shelter, he and Junior crept in one behind the other to rest their weary bones.

The remaining men continued playing, sometimes arguing, routinely slapping the mosquitoes on their chubby arms.

On the wooden framework of the tin yard I slung up one of the hammocks Admiral Rambo had passed around.

Soon the music died. The bulb went out. And then there was only the high pitch of the forest. I lay awake a while. The chill was seeping into me. I thought of the last time it was like this, when the cold wind had howled down the savannah, when I had sought refuge beneath dangling Moonsammy, consumed to a fever.

THE awakening was vicious. Admiral Rambo pried open a single eye and shone a torch in it with a belly laugh. We drove through a wet, fog-drenched forest dream and reached San Martin shy of dayclean.

I only awoke from the shock of hearing Mildred, the textbook grandma, emit the words 'Oh shit.' It was the first sighting of the river. She'd never seen the water so low. Here we were, driving on the red mud where there was meant to be river. I remembered just how disorienting had been the appearance of the submerged stelling at Menzies Landing that strange morning.

I saw more lovely sights from those days gone. I saw a pair of yellow longboots drying inverted on a pair of sticks. I saw beside them two plastic barrels covered with mesh. I saw a dripping palm, a long dark jackfruit tree. It was the Cuyuni, where the man said he had chopped his pardner nine times.

It was a long wait on the riverbank. People got off, stretched, brushed teeth. I slept again in the jeep.

When I awoke again, there were a surprising number of travellers. They were liming by a small shop that had opened. Some were dragging their bags through the mud towards the river. They had the bright excitement of the returnee. The act of dragging or hauling bags through mud contributed to the brightness. It was the familiarity of the bruck-up, an allegiance. I know, I felt it too.

Looking around at the crowd I was rudely interrupted by the sight of her chatting amiably with a man. He was a well put-together chap, an Indian. There was something burnt and shameless about his face. His hair was shaved down. He wore a crisp bush-shirt and light pleated trousers. On his face he wore the mark, running around like a strap from ear to ear. On his wrist hung the bracelet of Guyanese gold that West Indian cricketers sometimes wore. They were smiling and chatting, now walking and chatting, and he was carrying her bag, looking for all the world that it was them together on vacation.

I wished there was a girl equivalent of the man I could walk with, slower and closer than they, laugh sweeter than they.

I looked for Admiral Rambo. He was in hectic negotiations with the boatman. He came out on top, securing for his passengers the first ride across the river. I got on. She didn't come.

We motored with clunking sounds through inert clouds. The river was calm and brown. The trees were long and solemn. There were many small islands, perhaps newly made by the low water. The boats weaved in and out of channels. Grandma Mildred giggled as the light spray leapt up at the sides of the boat. She held the polin to the side of her laughing, weathered face. The mulatto grandchild kept yanking it down, delighting her.

Ten minutes and we were on the other side: Guyana; Guyanese mud; short trail through forest; citizens struggling with bags; a clearing; Eteringbang police station.

THERE was makeshiftness in the air, remote Guyanese makeshiftness, and the station itself was a freshly painted wooden home, like a proud wife's dwelling, bright white and powder blue, standing upon white concrete pillars. On the signboard pitched into the ground somebody had failed to account for the length of the name. Realisation had struck halfway in: the bang after Etering was less than a whimper. On the stump in vertical letters came Welcome, oddly inviting for a police station.

People gathered with their bags around the station. I had underestimated it: this was also the airport.

In the bottomhouse Admiral Rambo arranged a ramshackle seat behind a ramshackle desk. This was the check-in counter. A second agent, a squirrelly man named Simon, began to tear bits of paper from a pad, scribbling numbers on them. He passed them around to passengers, encouraging them into a queue. Admiral Rambo then called out a number at a time, holding both his hands in the air as he did so, as though receiving applause. The called number stepped up to the peculiar Guyanese challenge of balancing herself on bathroom scales with all her bags while clearly spelling out her full name by the alphabet. Those with lengthy names were at an obvious disadvantage. Poor Chandrawattie Bisoondyal!

Progress was blundering. People were resigned. Somebody suggested that passengers and their bags be weighed separately, but

Admiral Rambo cussed it down saying it was sheer stupidness to do in two turn what you can do in one.

Simon the squirrelly agent began to come under severe pressure from the station chief. Things were running behind schedule. There was a big group today. Five planes were due to come in. There was plenty to be done. Accordingly, every few minutes a thundering 'Simon' rang out from above, and off he would go scurrying and scurry back faster, cussing under his breath.

I didn't join the queue. I sat on a rock beside the station. Some way away, people were liming under a large mango tree, as people would at Menzies Landing. An Amerindian lady had set up a stall. The waiting room.

I walked about, tried to look purposeful. I chatted a while with a Rasta, who'd just chided somebody for photographing him from behind. 'Rasta nah believe in backside business.' He added after a few seconds, 'Whatever done in darkness soon come to light.' As a fee for having chatted with me, I think, for having let me hear the proverb, he asked for a raise. I gave him some useless bolivars.

I joined the queue, coming around to believe that mechanical activity was the most sensible option. And indeed, never had a queue felt so therapeutic. All I had to do was look at the shapes of the heads and necks before me, occasionally watch Simon skitter about, hear Admiral Rambo call out numbers, followed by the slow recitation of a Guyanese name.

Half an hour passed this way.

'Weh the mistress deh?' Admiral Rambo asked as I ascended to the bathroom scales.

'She coming.'

Security was next. People threw open their bags on the grass as the chief, the man who'd been chewing Simon's ass, beat his fist against his palm and let his eyes run over the contents. Occasionally he directed a constable to hand him something which he examined with a variety of pokes, thumps and sniffs. He was a big black man, with laughing red eyes and a thick, loud voice. He looked like a fun man who enjoyed playing the part of a menacing cop. My stuff was searched.

I proceeded to the next queue, at the bottom of the stairs. It led up to an accounts register in the station. Immigration. I filled in the columns. That too finished.

I stepped back out into the light. And down the stairs, under the mango tree in the distance, bronzed and superior with her man in tow, Jankey Ramsaywack, 21.

Secretly I was hoping I'd emerge from these procedures haloed with a golden new clarity. I would know precisely what to say, how to seize back, if not the girl, then at least some great lasting beauty from our thing. No such dawn.

GRADUALLY the people who'd been liming beneath the mango tree began to queue up, and those who'd been processed took their place. I resolved not to look at her. The sky was blue, the blue of a flame. Beneath it the police station dazzled white.

Eventually two little Islanders pecked through the sky like a pair of storks. This cued more classic Guyana scenes. One plane began dipping towards the turf, then curved back up, drawing murmurs of interest from the mango tree. The two planes made long, wide circles; the first descended again, before swooping back up. Heckles and suck-teeth rose from the assembled. Shortly after, a bunch of sleepy soldiers emerged from the bush in half-buttoned fatigues, rubbing their eyes with exclamations of 'o skunt, bai!' They sprinted out, buttoning up as they ran. They cleared a set of barrels from the turf and lined them up along the sides. The airstrip. The planes circled one more time, low over the Guyanese forest, and landed.

As soon as the second aircraft hit the earth people rushed towards them, to the great alarm of Simon the agent. 'Is not the buspark, ya'al hear, that is *plane* there, not minibus, this ain't big market.'

Fifteen minutes later three more Islanders arrived. They pulled up beside their companions. In the distance they looked like toy planes. It felt that at any moment the pilots, wearing dark glasses, leaning casually against their crafts, might pull out a remote control from their pockets and send them soaring up.

The planes formed a large triangle with the mango tree and the station, where the procedures were continuing. Simon, under dreadful pressure to dispatch the first flight, made frantic dashes between the three points.

The entire drastic possibility only struck me now. It occurred to me that I could be ushered on to one of these planes by Simon the agent at any moment, and we might be forever cleaved as though by a knife. In lovers' hurtsmanship one precludes such possibilities, assuming always that the other party will come to their senses before it is too late. Simon's frenzied scuttling was eroding my confidence in this matter. She could not tell, how could she, she was in the middle of procedure. To her the point of ultimate reckoning was far. Out here beneath the mango tree it was getting precarious.

I considered going up to her and asking courteously, directly, 'Are you coming?' On deliberation it didn't seem like anything at all. All it did was lob the ball in her court. Perhaps it was what I wanted, to not be saddled with the act of abandonment.

Nevertheless I tried to rouse myself into making the approach. I would be firm, look straight into her lovely, fearsome eyes, disdaining the male beside her. Perhaps it would be attractive.

About then a young constable sought my attention.

'Me?' I asked.

'Yeah, you.'

He confirmed with the chief, some fifty yards away, who pointed at me with his baton, holding it like a sten gun.

We walked over to the chief.

The constable took guard beside him with a smirk. 'The man make innocent face, though.'

The chief too was grinning. He had a scar on one cheek; it turned into a crater when he grinned.

'Whoa, boy, is the Indian national,' he remarked.

He lingered on the statement. Addressing the constable, he added:

'You right, the man pull innocent face for true.'

'What going on, chief?' I asked, myself grinning.

'Who permitted you to ask a question?' he shot back in a raised voice.

It startled me.

He turned to the constable.

'You hear me grant permission?'

'Negative, bossman. I ain't hear that at all.'

The chief grinned once more; then took it off as if it were a sticker.

'It is *I* conducting the investigation, do you understand?'

'What investigation?'

'Sir,' he said very deliberately, 'I don't think you heard me. *I* ask the questions. *You* give me answers.'

He returned his baton to his waist. I noticed he had no eyebrows.

'You know the girl?' he asked, with sudden belligerence.

He pointed to the side of the station, beyond the stairs, another fifty yards away. She stood with the man, both appearing to be in conversation with a constable.

'Yes,' I said.

'How so?'

'She was my— I was with her.'

'How do you mean you were with her? You fuck she?'

The constable blurted out a short, snorting laugh. The chief glanced at her.

'She look like she give sweet pum-pum, though. You ketch the meat fresh? Like it getting stale already.'

The constable gurgled. 'Go easy, bossman. Man be from India.' The chief fixed me with an eyebrowless stare.

'Explain to me, sir, how you know the lady.'

'We travelled together through Venezuela.'

'What for?'

'Just so,' I shrugged. 'We were travelling.'

'*Just so?* What kind of jackarse travels through Venezuela *just so?*' He left his mouth open. I could see his tongue, white, thick, rising up to wet his palate.

'Sir, I strongly suggest you submit a reasonable answer.'

'It's the truth, chief. It was just . . . tourism.'

'Tourism!' He involved the constable.

'Look where the man tourism take he. Eteringbang! How much tourist you see here?' The depth of his boom, the deliberated certainty of his delivery, they had a mesmerising quality.

'Let me start from the start,' he said, rolling the thick syllables out slowly. 'What were you doing in Guyana?'

'I came just' – I was about to say 'just so' and reconsidered – 'for a holiday.'

He looked at me with a mix of incredulity and contempt.

'It's a very interesting place. I came to look at the culture.'

He sighed. He looked at the constable.

'Dis bai deh pun serious skunt, bai.'

Turning to me he said as if handing back a term paper: 'You are not doing well, Mr India. Not well at all.'

He paused for a response. I didn't give him any; I felt I was going to snap. I stared at his cratered face in silence.

'Let me ask you again: what are your exact relations with the lady?'

I tried to catch a glimpse of her. But he stood like a wall between us. I tried to subtly peer around him. He shifted to block my sight.

'She is, she was my girlfriend, I guess.'

'How long you know her?'

'A couple of months.'

'And in that time, you go with her to travel around Venezuela.'

'Yes.'

263

'And come back from Eteringbang.'

'Yes.'

'Where you enter from?'

'Enter where?'

'Not she. Me en wan know dah.'

The constable giggled.

'Venezuela,' the chief clarified.

'From Guiria.'

'Where is that?'

'The ferry from Trinidad. It runs to—'

'So you enter by boat from Trinidad, and you exit overland from Eteringbang?'

'Yes.'

'For tourism? With your new girlfriend?'

'Yes.'

He looked at the constable. 'I seen a lot of joke, boy, but I ain't seen such a joke in a long long time.'

'You know the man?'

He pointed with his baton.

'No.'

'If you say the girl is your girlfriend what the arse she doing with him?'

'I told you she *was* my girl—'

'Don't tell me what you already told me.'

'We split up. I think she met him only this morning. I don't know, maybe they know each other. I'm not sure. Why don't you ask them?'

He shouted so loud the forest shook.

'WHAT MAKES YOU THINK YOU CAN TELL ME WHAT I SHOULD DO?'

I could feel every pair of eyes in the clearing searing into me. Out of sheer embarrassment I kept quiet.

'Why you split up with her?' the chief asked, his tone acquiring a momentum of aggression now.

'I'm not sure.'

'What the arse does that mean?'

'You know how it is, chief. We start to fight. Deliberately . . .'
I paused.

'What the arse the man talking!' He shouted: 'Tell that skunt
Simon to release the flight before I rearrange he goolies. And bring
back this gentleman's bags.

'Sir,' he turned to me and said, 'you are being detained.'

'What do you mean?'

His laughing red eyes were merely red now, devoid of
expression.

'You tell me one set of stupidness. Girlfriend, tourism, culture.
O *rass*, boy. The things a man must hear on this job. Every day
a next kunumunu must come along.'

As the constable went to retrieve my bags, I felt a genuine
nervousness, and with that a genuine anger.

'You can't bloody detain me,' I said.

The chief stopped pounding his fist into his hand. He raised his
non-eyebrows, to make deep crevices in his glistening forehead.

'You want to repeat that?'

I remained silent.

'Would you like to utter that sentence once more?'

'I said you can't detain me, it's simple.'

'Are you sure about that?' he said, his voice deep. 'You want me
to check the book? Is going to make it worse for you.

'So I ask again, would you like to repeat that sentence one
more time?'

I looked away, into the trees.

'Good,' he said at last. 'You should be glad you get that right.'

'Look, chief. I don't mean to tell you what to do. It's just that
I have a flight to India day after. It's the last day on my ticket
and my visa. I'm anxious about that.'

He appeared interested in this piece of information.

'You plan to carry the stuff up to India?' He began convulsing with laughter. The constable returned with my bag.

'The man want to carry the shit till India,' he told the constable amid booming laughs.

The constable began to laugh too, little squirting laughs, and those too built up to something like a convulsion.

'The man should glad you ketch him out here, bossman. The man would land in Gwantanamo.'

'Please tell me what's going on,' I said in the calmest, firmest manner I could.

The chief and the constable were in a proper gyaff.

'. . . Smalltime fool like that,' he said, flicking his thumb over his shoulder, referring, I assumed, to the man with Jan. 'He can get past *me*?'

He turned to me.

'Cooliepeople got big business, you know. Massive.' He spread his hands before his ample face and shook them. 'You hear the name Roger Khan?'

'Yes.'

'You work for he?'

'No.'

'Of course I know that!' he laughed. 'Cause you smalltime. All you smalltime.' He flicked his thumb over his shoulder again. 'Coolieman tryin fuh squeeze through a lil thing like blackman. Show how much the competition strong.'

He addressed the constable mentorishly.

'Watch, I know how them mind work. Them think that the beauty queen get ketch with makeup, so is too stupid for anyone to use makeup again. So they think makeup the safest place. The girl thinkin this is not Timehri, is just Eteringbang, easy pickings.'

He paused.

'There is a term for this behaviour. Ya'al hear it?'

He looked at the constable, then at me. Neither said anything.

'Reverse psychology.'

The constable said, 'Yeah.'

I nodded.

'I ain't turn chief just so. Y'understand? They thinking, Miss Guyana get ketch with the powder in she cosmetics, so cosmetics *done*, nobody would think to use it again. Reverse psychology, boy, reverse psychology.'

He considered this for a few seconds. Then he began to beat his baton against his palm, sizing me up top to tail.

'Sir, how many kilos would you like to declare?'

I smiled, suspecting this might be a wind-up after all.

He ignored the smile.

He looked at his watch. He assessed the action around him, and almost involuntarily I did it with him.

On the airstrip two planes had already departed, and a third was taxiing. At the station, the last of the passengers were getting processed, waiting in the queue for immigration.

I now saw Jan and the man being led up the stairs by a pair of officers. Her face was obscured by her hair. I could see the sun glint off her silver bracelet as her hand slid along the banister.

No, it did not actually feel like a wind-up.

My mind burned. How to extricate myself? She swivelled before me in such a variety of ways, in a variety of emotions, the phone and the vehicle, the hundred bill two days ago, now in a careless burgundy negligee, now with ice lolly marks on her mouth, now in stilettos with a flare in her eyes, that I felt I was hurtling punchdrunk through a masquerade. I had a strange flashback: the putagee lawyer from the earliest days. I saw his face vividly before me, ruddy and cussed with fleshy cheeks, grey hair peeping out of his nostrils, a strong face, equipped, chapped lips to which he raised whisky and coconut. *I'm not concerned with innocence or guilt. Anyone can kill their baby.*

'Yes, sir, so how many kilos will that be?'

It took me a few seconds to return to the situation.

'You checked my bags yourself, chief. You can check them again. I got nothing.'

'You could be a body packer. You hear the word? You belly, you arse, all kind of funny place, lined up thick thick thick with snow.'

'What did they tell you, chief?' I asked with utmost humility. 'Why don't you let me speak to her?'

'Why don't you shut up and let *me* decide how to proceed?'

He turned to the constable.

'Next thing the man tell me let they siddung, give praise to the Lord, eat a meal an discuss they strategy.'

'Chief, I told you the whole story.'

'That sure was a story, boy. A bundle of pu-re, un-dil-uted, un-adul-ter-ated *skunt*.'

'It's true,' I continued. 'I haven't spoken to the girl for a day now. I never seen that man in my life. I have no idea what is going on.'

'She call your name. That is enough for us to investigate you in the manner we see fit.'

'But you checked my bags. You can check them again. I told you what happen—'

'We get handcuff for the man?' he asked the constable.

The constable chuckled.

'What you skinnin you teeth for, chap? We got handcuffs for the man or not?'

'Not sure, chief.'

'Well, haul you ass up and check nuh, man. The fella getting fidgety here.'

'Yeah, chief.'

He left.

I drew a little closer to the chief. I thought to put my arm on his shoulder, but thought the better of it.

'Listen, chief. Let me see the girl, please. I can help you with this.'

'You going to see her. The man coming with handcuffs for you just now.'

'This is the situation. Everything will crash. I will lose my ticket to India. I'm out of money. It costs more than two thousand dollars. US. I will have overstayed my visa. That will mean my presence in Guyana will be illegal. Please let me see her.'

'You think that is *my* concern? Your blasted ticket and visa?'

'Just think, chief. If you hold me wrongly, it could become a big thing. I am an Indian national, the high commission will get involved, they know me well – I'm registered with them. And the high commissioner knows the president well. They will ask why you held me without proof. It will make trouble for everyone. Me. You. Everybody.'

He laughed. Then he fixed me with a red-eye stare for an entire minute. I could not tell whether he was working something out or trying to intimidate me. At any rate, I was a little intimidated. In the background I could hear an Islander fluttering away into the sky.

I could not match his stare. I looked at the station beyond him.

'Trouble . . . Trouble,' he said finally. 'Trouble trouble trouble.' He laughed again.

'We in the profession of trouble, pardner. You follow me?'

'Yes.'

'It ain't hard to make trouble. You follow me?'

'Yes.'

'Ain't hard at all. You got no idea how much trouble I could make for you if I want. Do you?'

'I do.'

'What is hard is to *cir-cum-vent* trouble. You know is which word? *Cir-cum-vent*.'

'Yes.'

'That take a little, eh, *in-vest-ment*. You with me?'

'Yes.'

Instinctively I began to reach for my wallet.

He slapped my wrist with a rapid flick of the baton.

It stunned me. I felt stupid. And then a sharp pain kicked in.

'We going to search you bags again,' he said. 'Search them good, rip em up, crack open the wheels, mash up everything. The constable going to strip-search you. If we find something you going fry, boy, you going bun, you understand?'

'He won't fin—'

'Sir, may I suggest that you shut your hole.

'If he find something you bun. Follow?'

'Yes.'

'When we finish taking apart your bags, when he done with you strip-search, when all of that done, *then* you go for your passport, right.'

'Right.'

'You got US?'

'Yes.'

'Fold the bill and put it in there. Do it with your hands inside your handbag, right.'

'Right.'

'Come over to me and hand over the passport for examination, right.'

'Right.'

'Make it a big bill, good?'

'I got a fifty.'

'Is all you got?'

'Maybe a twenty too.'

'Good.'

With that he turned around, towards the station. I watched the folds of his neck, and beyond that the louvres in the station windows and the door leading in. I tried to discern any movement. Soon a figure emerged from the door, momentarily exciting me.

It was the constable.

He walked jauntily towards us, handcuffless.

'Negative, chief.'

'We going to bust the man just now,' the chief replied, firing up the constable with a sense of mission. 'Send Crappo over a.s.a.p. for the bag. And you take the man and strip him down, good. Report me in three minutes.'

Things happened quickly.

The constable led me behind the station to a little enclosure in the bottom house. Pasted on the wall here was the faded liner of *Guyanese Girls Gone Wild*, a porn film that had taken the country by storm. Beside it a marijuana leaf was painted in blood red.

'Please strip for me, sir,' he requested politely.

I did, down to my underwear.

He examined, one by one, my T-shirt, my jeans, my shoes and socks.

All the while he kept softly singing Tick Tack, a big Guyanese soca. *Tick tack, on she bumper* . . . The words came in and out as he bent down and stood up with a garment, *tick tack* . . . He leant towards me and snapped the elastic of my underwear and peered inside casually. He walked around to the back and snapped the elastic again.

'Alright, sir. You may get dressed.'

We walked back, from the other side this time. Admiral Rambarran shot me a perplexed look as we passed. I half caught it, looked away.

Out on the grass the chief and Crappo stood over the remains of my bags.

'Legal,' the strip-searcher declared. Chief dismissed them.

I began to gather my things into the ravaged bags. I did as per instruction with the passport. I handed it over. How much did 14,000 dollars mean to him. A half-month salary? Less? More? Would he share it around?

He flicked through my back pages, releasing baritone hmms. I didn't notice when he, to use the newspaper term, relieved the passport of its cash.

He handed it back to me.

'Don't do nothing bad now, straight home right, no unlawful behaviour, no whores, no drugs, nothing, you hear? G'lang quick, the last flight leaving.'

The end was so abrupt, I felt lost, clueless.

The chief looked relaxed.

'What about her?' I asked.

'We going to take care of that,' he said amiably.

'Please tell me what they told you, chief.'

He surveyed things around him with his hands clasped at the back, talking as he did, as if instructing a minion.

'She say the man fix she up. Put drugs pun she. She called your name. She say you would know that she ain't done nothing wrong.'

'Oh.'

He said nothing.

I felt by turns flushed, drained, limp. I was shot through with shame and heroism. My heart beat hard. I tried to reach for the grand gesture.

'Maybe she's telling the truth, chief.'

'*Put drugs pun she!* Is what every blasted mule does say. You say she only just meet him. Why the arse she give him she bag?'

'It could be innocent.'

'She does need money?'

'That doesn't—'

'Trust me, chap, I seen things. Is always wha they say.'

There was a long silence. He was stretching his neck, making big shining sausages every time he rolled back his head.

'Chief. If I stay, can I find a way to get back by tomorrow?'

'Boy. You testing me now. You testing me bad. O fuck, boy. You best beat out of here before I change my mind.'

'It's not so simple.'

'What is not simple? You either part of it or you are not.'

His loud voice ascended almost to a shout.

'I—'

'ARE YOU A PART OF THIS OR NOT?'

'No.'

'Then you best beat out this moment or go in there and grab onto she bubby like a kunumunu.'

'Can I go up and see her for a minute?'

He stared at me.

'Sure. You can go see her. But you ain't stepping back out.'

I considered the words the best I could. I thought of them first as a threat. But they were not a threat, not at all. They were an offer. The choice is yours, that is what he was telling me.

The blood rushed to my head as I bent to lift my bags. The rest was spots. Some were perfectly formed and of immaculate clarity. Some were pulsing blurs. I trod them all, sometimes floated over them. I remember the constable waving me off with a pleasant 'watch it, right'. I'm sure he said it once, but it rang in my head five, six times.

I tripped on the way to the plane. There was a buzz of curiosity as I climbed aboard. People, sweating shapeless people, tried to ask, I could hear their silent voices, but as we taxied and climbed the noise defeated their curiosity. I sat behind the pilot in a broken seat. It was like a punishment chair. Everything inside was in soft focus. In a bid for sharpness I concentrated on two dials. One was altitude, one was speed. I stared tight at them till their needles loomed close to my eyes like fine silver daggers, beautifully defined and gleaming. There were red markers on each dial, at 9000 ft and 175 knots. The needles climbed towards the markers. Neither got there. They came to rest at 7500 ft and 150 knots and thereafter there was no movement in them. The sun poured in very strong. The rays kept getting trapped in our aerial box, amplified. Soon people fainted to sleep. And I myself was not there.

I was on another plane, in another flight. I was returning from the miracle of Kaieteur to GT, that strange creation, transplanted people on a fake coast. The guide was clutching his short hair.

'Pure, man, pure.' The ill American groaned, sickening groans. It was a hotbox up here in the sky. I heard the horns and words of Maga Dog, sweet and vicious, turning cycles, stabbing truths, a proverb in reverb, *turn around bite you*, with the American's sick groans, with the hair-clutching guide saying 'pure, man, pure' and the drone of the engine.

My passport was still in my hand, stuck to my palm like wet cloth. I shook it off. I reached for my bag to return it to its envelope. Her two sketches were inside, facing each other in a kiss. I shrank from the sight. My head pained. I wanted to vomit. I tried to pull out of the old flight and the new flight. I looked through the porthole.

Outside was bright burning space. Just above were the clouds, I could see their bottoms. Below they made shadows on the brown waters etched into the great green forest, aglimmer at parts, essential Guyana. It rolled on, eternal as the sea, broken once or twice by red dots of timber works. To the forest you could surrender yourself. Its eternity comforted me; the world didn't cease; we were small. Minutes passed, tens of minutes. Soon came the isles on the mud-red Essequibo, where the Dutch built their first forts. Beyond them the Guyana which was captured, conceptualised and executed. The enormously long straight canals ran through strips of estate like lines of molasses, dizzying in their sly symmetry. We were dropping altitude. The paraphernalia became visible, the creases of mud dams, kokers erect like little guillotines on the bloody water.

Now came the dull flame of the Demerara, its city snout poking into the old ocean. We dipped towards the rust spread of Stabroek, real as burnt earth. Then over the scrap iron roofs of Georgetown prison in the old plantation of Work and Rest. We were low. The seats were shaking. We rattled over the grids of GT, a melange of mix-up destinies fermenting over the humid dots of the equator. It was Sunday. Somewhere below Kwesi's mother passed around black pudding in Kitty. An Amerindian brother walked after preaching off Sheriff Street. We made a broad swerve, tipping over the coast to the ocean and coming in again. Somewhere below in Pradoville the rich played dominoes under an umbrella by the pool. We began to descend on the former plantation of Ogle. In a patch of grass between trenches a pair of matchstick boys kicked a football to each other, acquiring size, length, a third dimension, and as they vanished altogether I was frozen to a fright by the image of little Brian Persaud, eyes like hers, the ball at his feet in the savannah, wondering if in a moment of miscalculation, calculations that till now seemed so impregnable, wondering if I had left him a sibling.

10

IN the morning there was a chase across the road. I had always wanted to see a pursuit like this in Georgetown, and how odd that it should happen now, on the last day, outside my own home. It was the man's luck that there was a patrol vehicle around the corner. They went after him. He darted up a street.

'Why they don't shoot he in the foot?' Jackie the cleaning lady said from below. She had barely acknowledged me after I'd failed to return to church. 'Yo, listen,' Midas told her, at his post earlier than usual. 'You're not allowed to shoot a man without a weapon. Though out here, out here anything goes. In *New York* . . .'

The thief was hunted, dumped in the back of a pick-up. He was bare-chested. His hands were cuffed.

'Chop off the man hand in public,' Wazir the water-jar delivery man said. 'Chop off ten body hand the problem done solve.'

Everybody retreated. I stood staring at the chase long after it was finished. It was still early.

I learnt a day can be the sum of the parts of a year, and so acutely lengthier, heavier, too heavy for a single day to bear. In the place where guilt and accusation collide there was no room to breathe. Night was a slow fire, daylight disfiguring, its pinpricks leaving nothing to conceal.

I would go to Uncle Lance. I would tell him everything. I would purge my soul before him. He would make the correct pronouncement. He would know who is who, what is what. I hadn't the courage to think anymore – someone else must judge.

It was the finest kind of Georgetown day, with low grey clouds and the lush suggestion of wetness that would at some point yield to rain.

What a rambling route I took to Kitty, walking north and east, into Section K Campbellville, and what a different world were the Camville backstreets, community folk liming at corners, Rasta snackettes, some abandoned, high green vegetation, crooked signs of broad confidence, 'fixing done here'. At Redeemer Primary School I played cricket with schoolboys. I wanted someone to like me. I wanted to feel healthy and young. I could barely look at my own shadow. I made one direct hit, didn't bat or bowl. They didn't notice when I was gone.

I drifted on to Prashad Nagar and then to Sophia, and such a fine line between Prashad Nagar and Sophia, such different sides of the tracks. A cloudy radio day in Sophia. Women hollered to one another, each asking the other to speak harder. Parrots and toucans in small leaning houses, buffaloes and cows in proper shit-smelling stables, goats stagnating on bridges, a minor sawmill, fumes in the air, rows of posts. I came back through Prashad Nagar where India lived on in Chandranagar Street, in Premniranjan Place, in the Dharmic Sabha Kendra, in concrete houses and in paranoia.

Back out on Sheriff I walked till the embankment road, wishing away slow time with every step. At the intersection of the breadfruit tree I turned west towards Kitty. I walked, and the houses, the palings, the girls on stairs, the trees, the smell of distemper, the trenches, they all kept bringing back a sad freshness, an old excitement. I went into Alexander and stepped along. In the distance appeared Kitty Market with its icicle clock tower and rusted roof.

How remarkable it had felt, the roof, the tower, the community beneath it, the very name, the low skies and the running wires on wood poles – how remarkable it had all felt, murmurings of a new world.

My old home looked abandoned. There was nobody in the passageway, not even on the bench outside Uncle Lance's door, where there ought to be at least Uncle Lance in his vest.

I knocked on his door. There was no reply. 'Pandit, is me,' I called out, and kept knocking. Still no answer.

I peeped through his louvres. The house looked bare and dark.

His silly cuckoo clock loomed large on the wall over the table. I could go to the magistrate's court, as I used to in the early days. It seemed the only reasonable place to go. I could sit there and watch, pretend to be sentenced or pardoned – at any rate, there was a promise of a judgement.

. . . Even so, I tried to tell myself again as I walked, even assuming it were indeed the case, that she was innocent – and it may not be at all – she could have at least held her own damn bag . . .

The court was full. People were spilling out. I stood at the door.

The case was of a collision, a boy in a car with a lady on a scooter. The boy was wealthy and Indian, the lady was working class and African. She had lost an arm and a leg. She was riding without a fitness certificate, a permanent licence, a helmet and insurance – 'bareface and boldface in a naked bram,' as the boy's lawyer kept exclaiming. He was a big black man of many quips, an orator, an entertainer, a provocateur. Petty criminals tittered at his jokes. One felt sorry for the limbless lady. In this atmosphere, under these provocations, she was unable to answer the simplest questions. She stared blankly out of the window, and I blankly at her. She wouldn't get her limbs back.

By the door the mood was running hot. 'The only blackman

278

you can trust is a dead blackman,' the boy's supporters said. 'It have some honest coolieman – the dead ones,' the lady's supporters said. A barracker, a regular, he kept saying, 'A collision, sah, there be a collision, there has been a mighteh likkle collision.'

On my own case there was no judgement. Court was dismissed.

Town was busy. I could not bear to confront it. I walked up Hadfield, up all the way till the D'Urban backlands, where people dumped dead bodies. Again I turned towards Kitty. There was nowhere else to go. Through Bel Air Park and Newtown, back past the corrugated tin wall to Uncle Lance's door.

'Open up, Bandit,' I pleaded. There was no answer. I sat slumped on the bench for a while.

I looked for Bibi Rashida Rawlins, the dougla coconut lady. I saw her there, fat, dimpled, cloth-hatted, and I wished to sink into her loving matronly bosom.

'Cyan hear from you, bai,' she said brightly as I approached her. 'Me think you gone back India. You miss out on me Qurbani too.'

'Gone tomorrow morning, Aunty Bibi,' I told her, casually as I could. 'Where the Uncle deh?'

'You en hear?'

'What?'

'Uncle gone.'

'Gone where?'

'Gone outside. US.'

'For what?'

'Is *gone* he gone. He pack he bags an give up the house an gone.'

'What happened?'

'He get rob after he take out money from Western Union—'

'Uncle did Western Union?'

'Yes! How you think he retire so soon. He son does send he t'ing steady. They try fuh choke n rob he and he get vex an decide fuh leff. You know how he does know everybody. He cut a round at the embassy, in like three week time he get visa.'

'He get hurt?'

'Nah, he nah harm. They get he money, but he only pick up couple ah fine scratch. He just turn, ahm, emotional. Me tell he, watch Uncle, me go fallo you . . . You alright, bai? Look how weak you get so.'

'Yes, Aunty Bibi, alright.'

I felt tears coming. To disguise it I reached forward to hug her goodbye. And the tears, they kept returning at intervals, involuntary, undramatic.

I left her.

School had broken for the day, and the air was full of it. I walked among the children, craving for their easy camaraderie, their hope. It was elusive.

I plodded on, looking desperately for somebody but there was nobody. Uncle Lance, he was gone. I walked to the old haunt of Baby, searched hard in the clamour, but Baby was nowhere. And she. I could feel her walking beside me, her great frizz tickling my face . . . She must have, I tried to tell myself again, what else could it have been?

Afternoon was finishing. I walked and walked, I walked out of fear of stopping. I went out as far as Lombard Street. There a grand madman upon a plastic chair invited me to take the chair beside him. I am the great Flood, he said, clutching my hand, and remember, don't cork the bottle. He was in a headband, crisp trousers, an old bowtie. 'The negritude of your corruptions,' he jabbed a finger in the air, 'the crablouse in your *aarti*.'

The sun began to lower on Georgetown on the Atlantic. I walked in slow curlicues, unearthing new corners, new windows, new bruck-up moods and, with a start, like a cat leaping at my head, there appeared an old scene, that place there the site of a great washdown one time, this one here of a legendary winedown, and now the erstwhile residence of Mr Bhombal, the wet prints of his green longboots on the stairs.

In the evening it rained. Georgetown was so gorgeous when it rained. Its green shone and its white was washed, and the old woods, the greys and the blacks, they kind of gave off that fragrance of greying and blackening wet wood. Soon the streets were deserted. Light crept like a thief out of the fragile wet houses. Somewhere in the drip drop dark a maga dog whined. And my tears, they kept returning at intervals, and I tried to purse them to no avail.

Dayclean.

Gone.

The sly company of people who care

ACKNOWLEDGEMENTS

I want to thank, firstly and mostly, for generosity that I will never forget, the great ladies Vaneisa and Aunty Marlene, and ole ho Brian P.

For kindnesses, Amy, Erika, Sherry, Anil Beharry, Marc, Maga, Warren, Uncle Lloyd, Ann Savory, Mikey and Harold and Jackie, Grajo and King and John, Mr Adams, Uncle Bill, Honey, Anjie, Ameena Gafoor and Andaiye and Nigel Westmaas, Dale Andrews, Naresh Fernandes, Pragya Sinha, Rajdeep Mukherjee, Kim Johnson, Michael Atherton, Doreen and the late David de Caires, the Gobins, the Persauds.

For permission to quote from her calypso, Rohini Jones; and for clarifying the successor membership situation for Alan Daniel aka Lord Commander, Mr Camejo of the Copyright Organisation of Trinidad and Tobago.

For insight, Eusi Kwayana, Dale Bisnauth, Roy Heath, Jamaican musicians.

For their attention, Leslie and Pallavi; for that, and much much more too, Anand Persaud and Eric Chinski.

For allowing me to take them for granted, my mother and sister.

And, lastly, more than mostly, magnificent Shruti DB.

picador.com

blog
videos
interviews
extracts